# CTHULHU UNBOUND

## EDITED BY
## THOMAS BRANNAN
## AND JOHN SUNSERI

**Permuted Press**
The formula has been changed...
Shifted... Altered... *Twisted.*™
www.permutedpress.com

A Permuted Press book
published by arrangement with the authors

Cthulhu Unbound
edited by Thomas Brannon and John Sunseri

ISBN-10: 1-934861-13-8
ISBN-13: 978-1-934861-13-4

# Table of Contents

# NOIR⊨LATHOTEP

Linda L. Donahue

hrieking pain intrubeb on the barkness of my slumbering soul. It woke me from infinite, disjointed dreams that only made sense while sleeping.

A sharp pain punctured my consciousness, ripping out a piece of my collective whole, leaving behind a cold absence. One of my thousand aspects was gone. As the primary, I—Nyarlathotep, men call me—felt a sudden severing that my others would likely shrug off as an inexplicable shudder.

The loss forced upon me a tangible state, as if by possessing a physical body I could somehow replace the missing part. Without conscious thought, I found myself in a small, dark office. Moonlight shining through the glass door illuminated a body on the floor. It was murder.

I flipped on the light. The harsh glare of a bare bulb lit the blackish liquid spreading beneath the corpse. I staggered into a credenza. Poor Number 71. He'd been one of my favorite aspects, a likeable sort. A good Joe. Who would snuff out an upright guy like 71?

A blood stain oozed from beneath the empty, mortal husk, surrounding 71's body like an arcane symbol, the sort found in the oldest books, those recorded by the Great Race and stored in hidden libraries.

71 would have liked that about his murder scene. It would've intrigued him. Omens and portents had been his hobby. Ironically, of all my aspects, only he might have recognized the symbol. He could've designed it, having created many famous ones still used by secret cults on a dozen worlds, including this one, Earth.

Too bad I couldn't hire him to solve his murder. Considering we were part of a whole, maybe I was solving my own murder—in a sense.

Why 71? Sure, 71, aka the Brown Man, was superfluous, a paler version of Number 30, the Black Man.

Paler was right. Having bled out, 71 wasn't brown, but greyish-white. A funny feeling crept over me and I wasn't in a funny mood. I was staring at the answer but not seeing it.

Then it hit me square in the face. 71 wasn't *brown*. Neither was the wooden credenza. Everything was black and white. Something weird was going on, even from my perspective. I felt it all the way to my hooves. Even the voice in my head sounded different. I reached up. Nope. Still the same old bald scalp.

Of course, I was used to hearing voices—most of them insane. It was part of the job. But this was different, this voice came from a bygone era.

The credenza was a liquor cabinet, containing every kind of booze imaginable. Funny, but I didn't recall 71 being an alcoholic. I guess dealing with humans all the time finally led him to the bottle. That was the trouble with Earthers, a half-predictable, semi-chaotic race. Sooner or later they always let you down.

Looking at 71's corpse, I needed a drink. So I poured a glass of vodka, straight up. It burned the back of my throat like I was drinking gasoline. Figuring it was an acquired taste, I chased it down with a shot of whiskey.

About then two black-and-whites pulled up. Headlights shone through the glass door, casting a shadow of 71's logo and Earth name on the stark, white wall. *Arkham Investigations* curved around a bloodshot eyeball—the eye of Azathoth. Beneath it was 71's alias, *Jonah Pariah, Private Eye.*

Two uniformed flatfoots entered, brandishing hardware. Then *she* walked in—one of those lanky, beautiful dames in a grey trench coat, her hat perched askew, shading half her face. The half that showed could stop a man's heart. Luckily, I wasn't a man. I stared at her full, pouty lips, wondering what shade of lipstick she wore.

I couldn't remember the last time a doll had made me go all googly-eyed. Figuring my jaw-dropped stare probably made me look guilty, I said, moving my lips in sync with my projected voice, "Forgive my surprise, toots. But I didn't figure on a dame detective."

"Why's that?" Her sultry voice commanded my attention. "You still living in the 1930's?"

Considering everything was black and white, it seemed a distinct possibility.

Or maybe it was my dark mood, unable to reconcile my loss, that painted the world in grey. Even the light drizzle outside made Arkham a duller, drearier place than usual.

The dame in the trench coat spoke while the boys kept their heaters pointed at me. "Who are you? And what are you doing here?"

"I could ask you the same, Detective Harris, but the corpse on the floor is a dead giveaway. I didn't kill him, if that's what you're after."

Usually a simple trick like knowing a person's name rattled him, or her in this case, to a stammer. But Harris didn't bat an eyelash.

"I didn't expect to walk in on the killer and get a confession," she said. "You still haven't answered my questions."

"Let's just say, Num"—I'd almost slipped and used 71's numerical reference—"Jonah was a close relative."

"He's not our man, boys," she said to the badges. "Go around back and find the point of entry . . . and try not to step in any evidence, okay?"

The office door hadn't been jimmied and the windows hadn't been touched. It all pointed to the supernatural, but humans had a funny way of fabricating a mundane explanation for the most abnormal situation.

"Now that we're alone," Harris said, "will you tell me who you are and what you're doing here?"

Curious to see her reaction, to see if my name registered, I said, "People call me Nyarlathotep. I'm gonna solve Jonah Pariah's murder." What was I saying? Solving things was against my nature. I created puzzles; I didn't put the pieces back in order.

"Nyarlathotep?" She whipped out a pad and pen. "The real thing? The first aspect?"

She was cool. Nothing phased her. A real ice queen. Made me wonder what it'd take to melt her—but a dame like her would never go for a bald-headed man with cloven hooves.

"Mind if I call you Crawling Chaos instead?"

Once more, the broad took me aback. Seeing as nothing surprised her, I dropped the pretense of moving my lips. "Crawling Chaos is Number 12. If you're thinking of interrogating him, doll-face, plan a week around it. He's not called *crawling* for nothing. No one talks slower or wanders farther off track. But if Nyarlathotep is too hard to say, call me Number 1."

"You go by numbers? What was Jonah's?"

"71. But he was more than a number. He hung around this backwater planet so often he was practically half-human."

She brushed back a wavy lock of hair and her eyes twinkled. Was she a blue-eyed blonde, a green-eyed redhead, or a dark-eyed brunette? This loss of color was maddening, even more so than what I was used to.

"What troubles me, Number 1, is you didn't sense the murder coming and prevent it. You are omniscient."

"Sure, I know a lot about the universe. Sometimes I catch glimpses into the stream of time. But I don't know everything."

"But you and Jonah were connected. Don't tell me you didn't feel something."

Just like an Earth dame to talk about feelings.

"You gotta understand, toots, I'm connected to about 999—or maybe now it's 998—other aspects. The thousand faces of Nyarlathotep is just an estimate. Even I don't know the actual count. I can't pay attention to the doings of every one of them every minute of the day. Half the time I don't even recognize myself. A faker could claim he was Aspect Number 301. How would I know any different?"

Harris scribbled a few notes. "I suspected as much."

Apparently this dame had my number. But what would it take to get hers? Having a sudden suspicion, I studied her face, noting her well-defined cheekbones and luscious lips. Was it possible she was another aspect? Did that mean my growing infatuation was incestuous, or vanity?

"Where were you when the murder occurred?"

That was exactly the sort of pedantic question I expected from a badge.

"In my usual place, the twilight ether engulfing Azathoth."

"The Idiot God. That's not much of an alibi. You won't find a jury between here and the outer worlds that'll listen to a word he says."

"I listen." I was His messenger. Yet right now, only the dame's words resonated in my thoughts. "You're not from around here." Moreover, I realized, she wasn't another version of me.

A whitish shimmer glistened around her trench coat cinched tightly at her tiny waist. A holographic image of a ten foot cone-shaped being ghosted around her. Numerous, thick cords sprouted from its apex. A head and various organs dangled from the snaking cords. She was less human than I was.

She—or rather her mind—was one of the Great Race of time travelers from the planet Yith. Creatures who'd long ago discarded their bodies to hijack others for joy rides.

"I thought you Yith left Earth," I said.

"I like it here. I've been transferring my mind from body to body for centuries. Good thing, too, because there's something unnatural going on. For the past few months, I've been searching for *one thing*—and I'm betting you know what it is." Her gaze wandered over the desktop.

I didn't, but she wouldn't believe me. And I didn't need to tap into the swirling knowledge of chaos to know she was looking for answers, not more questions. Nevertheless, sensing a personal connection between her and 71, I pried, "You knew 71, didn't you?"

As I flicked my gaze at 71's body, I was again transfixed by the strange blood pattern. Surely it was more than a random smear. Perhaps in death, 71 had left a clue by controlling the flow of his blood. Too bad he hadn't spelled it out in words.

"He was afraid of you," Harris finally said.

"That doesn't sound like 71. But he'd hardly be my first aspect to develop delusional paranoia." Perhaps some residual depression hung in the air; perhaps it was affecting me, sapping my perceptions of color.

"Delusional?" The sarcasm in her tone was as thick as honey and somehow still as sweet. Again, she looked at the desk.

"Given what I know, I suppose there really isn't any such thing as delusional paranoia." The sane liked to believe that paranoids were deluded, but the truth was paranoid individuals knew more about what was going on than the sane could handle.

"Delusional, paranoid or just depressed, either way, that makes you my number 1 suspect." Harris tapped her notebook against my chest; if I didn't know better, I might've thought she was flirting with me. "Don't leave town and make me chase you through the dimensions."

"Do you want to solve his murder or fill out paperwork?"

Harris quirked one finely shaped brow. "What are you suggesting?"

"That we collaborate. We'd make a great team." Besides, having a hot dame around improved any situation. Although with her nearby, I might not be so eager to solve the case.

Harris cocked her head. It gave her a sassy look. At the same time, it let me know she'd be in command. I was fine with that.

She agreed with a nod. "It'll make it easier keeping an eye on you."

Watching me seemed the farthest thing from her mind, considering she barely looked at me. I tried not to take it personal. More likely, it was her detective nature, studying the crime scene.

"Wanna drink to celebrate our partnership?" I asked.

"A drink," she murmured. Harris knelt before the liquor cabinet. "Jonah didn't used to drink. Not when we first met."

Suddenly, I had a picture in a nutshell. Bombshell broads like Harris never looked twice at ordinary Joes like 71. Maybe that had driven him to drink. Maybe this was her fault. Beauty and danger had a way of going together.

"He started drinking about three months ago," Harris said, digging through 71's extensive booze collection. "About the same time weird stuff started happening. Don't get me wrong—there's usually weirdness in Arkham—but this was strange, even for this place."

"Looking for something particular?"

She held out a black lacquered box inlaid with white pearl. "Yeah. This. But it's not *the thing*, if that's what you meant. At least I don't think so. It was just something Jonah always kept on his desk. It seemed important to him, like maybe it had sentimental value."

The box was valuable all right, but its worth wasn't measured in sentiment. At least now I knew what had happened to it. I'd just figured I'd lost it, or it was buried somewhere in my collection of bizarre, arcane, and catastrophic devices. If I wasn't chaotic by nature, I'd have long ago organized my collection.

Before I could caution Harris not to open the box, she'd already removed the lid. Dames couldn't help themselves, especially pretty ones. I learned that lesson with Pandora, bless her curious little heart.

The box was empty, a rather surprising revelation.

Harris stared so hard at me, I swore I saw Yith eyes behind mortal pupils. "Looks like I found the motive," she said.

"Is that your real interest, toots? Or were you hoping to lay your pretty paws on what used to be inside? If that's the case, doll, I suggest you reconsider your scavenger hunt."

"What was inside?"

"Something mankind doesn't handle too well."

"If you haven't noticed, I'm not a man."

"I noticed that right off. You're a special kind of woman, no argument there. But unless you've something against humanity, that ain't what you're looking for."

"We won't get anywhere dancing around the truth. So to prove my intentions are honest, I'll go first. I'm searching for something to close the holes opening Arkham up to some pretty nasty dimensions."

Her candid response startled me almost as much as the fact transdimensional tunnels were appearing on Earth. "Guess that makes it my turn to share. The box holds the Shining Trapezohedron. It doesn't open gateways or tunnels. It summons the Haunter of the Dark. Believe me, doll, that's one shadow creature you don't want to meet."

"So what's it mean, the box being empty?"

"The Haunter is on the prowl." I thought I'd made that clear.

She looked at 71's body. "Could it have killed—"

"Nice and tidy theory, but no. The Haunter serves me in all my forms. Given the bizarre blood pattern, I'd say sorcery was involved. If you'll trust me to leave, I'll commune with Azathoth. Perhaps He'll give me access to His book."

"You mean Azathoth's little Black Book of names?"

"It's not so little. Listen, sweetheart, if sorcery killed 71, it'll have the sorcerer's name on its pages in blood. In the meanwhile, if you'll teleport to wherever your people built the Great Libraries, you could save us some time by looking up the answer." The Great Race, having traveled forward and backward, recorded all that has ever been and all that will ever be.

But the Yith didn't hand just anyone a library card.

"You're kidding, right? I could spend eternity searching for something as insignificant as the murder of one man on one planet in one universe. As much as I liked Jonah, Number 71, he wasn't even a man—but one thousandth of one. It'd be faster to comb every bar in every dimension and question the usual suspects—twice."

I had to take her word on that. At the same time, I felt a twinge of envy. To have all the universe's knowledge and be unable to access it was one of the most original chaotic systems I'd encountered.

Harris handed me the empty box. "If that doesn't prove I trust you, I don't know what will."

"It'll do."

We agreed to meet outside 71's office at first light. How Detective Harris would explain my sudden disappearance to the coppers investigating around back, I had no idea. I imagined she'd do just fine. Yith were pretty clever—and this one was pretty enough she didn't need to be clever.

# # # # #

The Earth's sun lit a pale, grey sky. Metallic grey cars drove on grey-black asphalt and pasty mortals in shades of grey walked along the grey-white sidewalks. Grey brick buildings stretched upward. And black and white birds perched in grey trees.

Last night I'd blamed the lack of color on residual depression—not just 71's, but my own mood, considering part of me had been murdered. Now, I had to accept the fact something more than murder and a stolen artifact was afoot. Unless Earth *was* black and white and I'd never noticed before.

I cursed. I should've thought of this before

Another meteorite containing a Colour must've struck Earth. The globular creature then escaped and feasted. With luck, it had retreated—its appetite for color temporarily sated— into a state of semi-hibernation. Not that it could be ignored forever. In time, it would awaken and absorb so much color that life itself would crumble into dust.

I'd hate for that to happen. Earth was Azathoth's favorite play-toy. Even I admitted a fondness for the planet and its people. I tuned in weekly, hooked on it like a really good soap opera.

When Detective Harris showed up, I asked, "How long has the world been in black and white?"

"I don't know what you're talking about."

I dropped the subject, trying to remember if creatures affected by the Colour noticed the change. As a victim, she might accept this as normal—or her mind might think it saw in color. Cursing my chaotic memory, I hoped there wasn't really a blob of color-sucking goo attacking the Earth, that only I suffered from severe and sudden color blindness.

"Follow me." Harris headed to the alleyway behind the office strip. She knelt beside a pool of slime. "Protoplasm. A Shoggoth's been here. And someone—or something—injured it."

Though most mortals would walk past this narrow back alley, noting nothing out of the ordinary, I—and I suspect the Yith Harris—saw the faint, oval distortion hovering above the slime. "A tunnel." Eying the Yith's currently occupied, shapely human body, I added, "it might lead underwater." Shoggoths were marine creatures.

"Although I'd hate to discard this body, I could transfer my consciousness if I have to."

Looking her over appreciatively, I added, "I'd hate for you lose that body too. It be a *real* crime."

"Looks aren't everything."

Trying to pretend that wasn't what I meant, I said, "I was referring to killing your host. Doesn't that bother you in the least?"

"I claimed this body after it took a fatal gunshot wound. Harris's unexpected survival is considered a medical miracle."

A Yith with a conscience. The day was filled with surprises.

Harris touched the slime and rubbed the ooze between her thumb and finger. "I've got what I need. Let's go."

The tunnel dumped us on a grey beach. Again no color, supporting my budding theory that this phenomena had supernatural causes affecting only me. Ergo, it had to be related to 71's death. Anything beat dealing with another Colour.

Ragged mountains edged the horizon. A stretch of Cold Wastes led to familiar ruins on the desolate, icy steppes.

"I know this place. The Plateau of Leng. And there's the City." We were still on Earth, or rather within the Earth's bowels. *Great.* I hated this place with its gigantic albino penguins. They creeped me out. Worse, it meant I couldn't absolutely discard the potential presence of another Colour.

We entered a partially submerged cavern, a favorite place of Shoggoths. The water rose to our chests, but never deeper. I sensed great relief from Harris, whom I guessed was more fond of her curvaceous body than she'd admit.

Being fond of her human form myself, I wondered if more than my eyesight was affected. Maybe the Yith was doing something to me. Yith were strange—even from chaos's perspective.

The cavern ended at a crude altar carved into frozen rock. A Shoggoth's shapeless body of protoplasmic, luminous bubbles oozed like a glop of fizzy ice cream. Ocular pustules swelled and popped, each emitting hazy light by which the creature saw. It made a shrill sound, mixed with clacks and clicks, the closest to language these semi-intelligent creatures could manage.

So they were ugly. No one ever said the Old Ones possessed aesthetic sensibilities. At least I was saved the additional visual-pain of seeing the Shoggoth in color.

Harris made a gagging sound, the way mortals usually described these creatures.

"They were designed to be functional," I said.

She hacked like a cat with a hairball.

I arched my thin, almost hairless brows. "Funny you suddenly becoming appearance fixated." Though I'd never been accused of being diplomatic, I actually refrained from mentioning some of the Yith's earlier and stylistically hideous forms.

"I have a mold allergy." She coughed up phlegm. "That's better."

The Shoggoth squished around, turning, revealing a gash in its bubbling hide.

"Looks like we found the right one."

"I want to be sure." Harris touched the slime dribbling from the Shoggoth's wound. She rubbed her finger and thumb thoughtfully. "Same DNA."

My expression must've exposed my amazement for Harris added, "Human tactile senses are exceptional. If they exploited their senses to their full potential, they'd have no need for analytical instruments."

I grimaced, being rather fond of instruments.

Like a dame, she kept talking. "Did you know, dogs can smell cancer cells?"

Though interesting, I didn't see her point. Yeah, ironic coming from the originator of pointless, random acts. Unless her babble was more than just air passing across her bow-shaped lips. "What do you smell?" I asked.

Harris tapped her dainty nose. "I smell a rat."

"Figuratively or literally?"

"Literally."

"You sure it's not another allergy?"

"See what the Shoggoth knows." From the flash of her eyes and her commanding, used-to-getting-her-way tone, I figured she was a redhead. Damn, but I had a thing for hot, fiery redheads.

I approached the Shoggoth, squinting against the weird lights flashing off him. He'd be perfect working in a goth-disco. "How'd you get hurt?"

Screeches and gurgling noises issued from the wounded, bubbling blob. <<It scratch and bite. Steal shiny thing.>>

"I think we're getting somewhere, doll," I said. "Whoever injured it stole the Shining Trapezohedron." And I had an idea of who, based on something Harris had said. To verify my theory, I asked the Shoggoth, "Who attacked you and stole the 'shiny thing'?"

There wasn't any point in using the actual name. Shoggoths were simple-minded with even less loyalty to their masters than brains—fortunately for us. It meant the Shoggoth wasn't likely to protect anyone.

<<Evil, nasty rat-creature attack.>> The Shoggoth oozed sideways and a part of its gelatinous body glooped—for lack of a better term—up the wall. When the slug-like limb retreated, it left behind an acid-etched image in the frozen rock. <<It steal shiny thing Outer God give me.>>

So 71 had given it away—he, we—I was an Outer God. Of greater interest, the Shoggoth had drawn the pointy, beady-eyed face of Brown Jenkin. Harris was right; she had smelled a rat—specifically the mutated familiar who'd once served the witch Keziah Mason.

"We're looking for Brown Jenkin," I said. "There's a hitch: the rat fink is dead." Tiny rat bones found in the ruins of the Witch-House had been identified as his.

"Apparently he's been resurrected. Did the Shoggoth confess to killing 71?"

Though a distinct possibility, given their history of rebellion, I rather doubted it. If the Shoggoth had turned on 71, its master, it would have eaten 71's head. It was their usual MO.

"Who killed your master?"

<<Not I. I only take shiny thing. Master say keep it safe in cavern.>>

"We've gotten about all we're likely to get here. Shoggoths do what they're told and don't care why."

"But why do you think 71 gave away the Shining Trapezohedron in the first place? And why to a Shoggoth?"

"Why ask me?"

Harris gave me a you-should-know look.

"Like I said, toots, I don't keep up with the day to day details of my other aspects' lives. They're grown-ups. They can fend for themselves."

We returned through the transdimensional tunnel. If Brown Jenkin was back, we figured the best place to look was where the Witch-House had originally stood.

Harris parked the car at the base of the hill. For a moment, we stared agog. Atop the hill, a dilapidated structure leaned precariously. The Witch-House. Its existence was entirely unexpected, improbable... interesting.

If Brown Jenkin *and* the house were back, maybe even Keziah Mason had escaped the reaper's hold.

As we crossed the overgrown lawn, a sudden tingle rippled across my flesh. We'd entered a time-distortion. We were no longer in Earth's present, but sometime in the 1920's.

Even back then, the dilapidated house looked ready to collapse, in part due to the strange angles where walls met the floor, all part of its design to manipulate and warp space. Riddled with rot and decay, the house would naturally appear black and grey. But in traveling backward through time, the world should have reverted to color—*if* a voracious Colour was feeding in the present. Seeing grey skies, grey grass, and a grey Harris proved beyond doubt that only I suffered from color blindness.

I was really starting to miss blue and green.

Harris sniffed like a hound. "We've traveled through time."

"Looks like more than tunnels are riddling Earth. Time dilations and, who knows, maybe space portals and wormholes have opened." Should these phenomena reach critical mass, the entire planet could be ripped apart and turned back into the space debris from which it originated. I had a sudden urge to step back and wait for the fireworks.

Then 71's murderer would go unpunished. And that I couldn't allow. Yeah . . . something was definitely wrong with me.

The uneven wooden stairs and sloped floorboards creaked with every step, threatening to splinter underfoot. Having cloven hooves, I walked sure-footed on the most difficult terrain, but that wouldn't stop me from plunging into whatever fissure cracked open, if the floor gave away.

Fond memories of witch Sabbaths and human sacrifices flooded my mind. Naturally, the recollections weren't my own, but those of the Black Man, Number 30, who had dealt with Keziah.

A scissoring, tittering came from the wall. Brown Jenkin's beady eyes peered through a hole gnawed in the paneling. "That you devil?"

"You've long known me"—or rather an aspect of me—"as devil," I said. "I have a message for your master." Familiars never thought for themselves. Ergo, if the opossum-sized rat wasn't in Keziah's service, then he served someone else.

Brown Jenkin crawled from a shadowy fissure, his pointy nose twitching. He scratched the scraggly beard on his humanoid face. Hunched over his haunches, he rubbed his tiny, human hands and squeaked in an ear-stabbing pitch. "You too late, devil. Master dead. But you know that. So you have other purpose. Maybe have something to do with object."

"The Shining Trapezohedron?"

"Yes, yes," Brown Jenkin tittered. He chased his tail. "Yes, yes. Take object. Haunter want to eat Brown Jenkin. Haunter already eat master."

"I thought you said the Haunter wouldn't harm 71?"

"It wouldn't," I reassured Harris. "The rat serves another, don't you, Brown Jenkin? Why did you steal the object from the Shoggoth?"

"You see Shoggoth monster? Brown Jenkin bite monster, take shiny toy. Master tell me to. But Haunter follow. Now Brown Jenkin hide. Master not control Haunter. Haunter kill master. Now Haunter free. Roam house."

Harris's gaze darted nervously around the seven cornered room. "Are we safe?"

"I am. Don't worry, doll, I won't let anything happen to you."

"Don't be offended, but coming from chaos incarnate, that's not very reassuring." Then she smiled like a siren.

Brown Jenkin was gone. He could be anywhere in a hundred holes riddling the old house.

"Looks like we have to search the premises ourselves," I said. "Stay close."

A melancholy howl echoed through the house, causing shredded wallpaper to flap.

"My thoughts exactly," Harris said.

Deep within the hallway's darkness, a shape lumbered toward us, stopping on the edge of pale light filtering through holes in the roof. Its glowing three-lobed, hellish eye and razor teeth showed clearly from the shadows. Saliva dripped from its gaping maw of death, its jaws able to crush an elephant's bones. Poor thing; he was just scared and misunderstood.

I strode toward the Haunter and patted its head. "Go find the Trapezohedron," I said, as if asking it to fetch.

Harris clutched the back of my robes. If only I was a mortal man and she an ordinary woman and this an entirely different set of circumstances, then something else might have happened. Instead, we followed the Haunter's baleful cries up to the garret loft.

What remained of Keziah Mason's partly-devoured, charred body lay on the floor. Paw tracks of yellow residue, the Haunter's tell-tale sign, covered the warping and sloping wooden deck. Even before the creature of the black gulfs of chaos had torn the old crone Keziah to pieces, she'd been mostly bone. Maybe to the Haunter, she'd looked more like a chew toy than a master. In Keziah's current condition, there'd be no questioning her without a necromancer's help. Unfortunately good ones were hard to find—especially on this world of snake-oil charlatans.

"Is that it?" Harris asked, stooped beside a severed arm.

Clutched tight in the witch's palm was the Shining Trapezohedron. "Good eye." When Harris reached for the hand, I stopped her, saying, "In a human body, I suspect even your Yith mind can't protect you from the madness."

Being a carrier, I was immune. I placed the artifact back in its rightful box and my pet howled gratefully, extended its leathery wings, and vanished into the dark, quiet voids where it rested.

From a hole in the floor, Brown Jenkin poked out his head and tittered. "Haunter gone. Brown Jenkin safe. Thank you, devil. Glad you no longer mad."

"What do you mean?" I asked.

"First devil bring back Witch-House. Then bring back master. Master call me. But master say devil crazy. Say devil will destroy world. Then devil summon Shoggoth monster. That when master tell me take object. Say must stop devil."

"Then Keziah Mason killed Jonah?" Harris picked up one of Keziah's severed hands and snapped off a finger. "For DNA evidence. Now that I know what I'm looking for, let's go back to Jonah's office."

"Master no kill devil. Devil know that. Devil know who did." The human-faced rat scurried into a hole and scuttled through the walls.

Harris eyed me suspiciously. "There something you're not telling me?"

"I'm thinking there's something *I'm* not telling me. Forget the rat. He's as crazy as the old hag. If we have to, we can come back and run the rat downtown for questioning."

"Maybe in another dimension. But I get what you're saying."

We returned to 71's office, slipping beneath the crime scene tape. A chalk outline replaced 71's body. With the corpse gone, the bloody symbol was revealed in its entirety.

Harris circled the symbol, swearing softly. "I'll be damned. I was looking at the glyph upside down. 71 was casting a blood spell."

"Can you read it?"

"Sure. Can't you?"

I didn't want to answer that.

"I was an idiot not to have recognized it sooner," she continued. "I must have been distracted."

I liked to think I was that distraction. Rather than ask and end my delusion, I gave her an easy out. "With 71's body covering the middle, I hadn't seen it either." In truth, I still didn't see what she saw. Symbols were 71's thing, not mine. I was more of a hands-on kind of chaos.

"Remember when you asked me when the world had changed to black and white? Well, this particular spell glyph affects the first person"— she eyed me then shrugged—"who sees it."

"I'm not the murderer."

"Didn't say you were. As I figure it, Jonah, 71, wove the spell as he died." She frowned. "Having seen the body after the autopsy, I would've thought he'd died instantly. The back of his head was torn open and his brain ripped out."

"What's your point?"

"That he couldn't have woven the spell, not *after* he was dead."

Apparently Yith didn't know everything. Feeling a bit superior, I explained, "That's not how chaos works. Chaos is an all encompassing state. It exists throughout our bodies, making us distinct, yet still pieces of a whole. 71's physical brain merely controlled physical activity. Chaos controlled his will, his mind. Chaos shaped his blood, creating the spell glyph, even after his body was dead."

Harris regarded me with her limpid eyes. "Dead and without a brain, 71 created a blood glyph. Impressive."

"What's the point of the spell, besides turning me color blind?"

"I think you've been hanging out with the Idiot God too long. The answer is simple. It's like putting a dye-marker on ransom money. Under a special light, the dye shows up—on the money and on the kidnapper's hands. In this case, the dye is color. To your eyes, the murderer will appear in color."

"Surrounded by black and white, he'd be unable to hide." That sounded exactly like something 71 would have designed. Damn, had I realized he was so talented, I'd have given him more to do. Just imagine the chaotic devices he might have designed. "If you're right, doll, then I haven't seen the killer."

"And you won't standing around here." Harris leaned against the wall, looking out the window. "Don't know why, but there's a lot of off-world gateways in and around Arkham."

"No big surprise. Arkham is popular with Azathoth and Cthulhu, among any number of Old Ones and Outer Gods. Even the Elder Race liked this place—geographically speaking." Arkham hadn't existed when the Elder Race had plagued the planet.

Harris shuddered. "Don't remind me of *them*." The Yith and Elder Race had a history—an unpleasant one.

"Sorry. Didn't mean to dredge up bad memories."

"It's forgotten." She stared at the liquor cabinet. "Boozers don't drink alone," she said. "I say we tour the local bars, here and off-world, and let you have a look around."

"Hoping I see someone in color?" I shook my head. "That's a lot of bars." And a lot of walking on my old hooves. "I say we lay a trap here." *And maybe spend some time getting to know each other better.*

But I couldn't say that last part aloud. I'd never been a smooth talker with dames. Though I could convince sane men to commit the most insane atrocities, a hot babe left my mind a blank. Women had always been a mystery to me.

"Criminals don't return to the scene of the crime, except in the movies."

"Even when we have what the murderer wants?" I held up the box. "I figure 71 was killed for this. Why else would he have passed it on to a Shoggoth then hidden an empty box?"

"I'm still working on why he took the object out."

"Maybe when we catch the killer, toots, we'll figure that out. Or maybe we won't. Either way, whoever wants the Shining Trapezohedron will return here looking for it."

"You seem pretty sure of that."

"Let's say I plan to stack the odds in our favor." I opened the box. From a dark corner in the office, a very unhappy Haunter let out a mournful howl. "Sit. There's a good boy. When we get home, I'll give you a treat."

I sat at the desk while Detective Harris perched on it. She crossed her shapely legs. Wearing stilettos, her calf muscles were taut and sexy. I imagined walking on those heels was similar to walking on my own, hoofed feet. Except, of course, hooves didn't do a thing for my calves. Maybe I was just too thin and bony. I should work out more. It wasn't as if I was busy.

While we waited, I asked, "Why are you sticking with the case? You're too smart to think a human is behind this." Meaning she couldn't prosecute the criminal in a human court of law.

"Because I liked Jonah. I want to see his killer caught. Jonah was too nice a guy to end up murdered and forgotten. At least he used to be nice . . . before. . . ."

"Before he started drinking?"

"Yeah. Something had gotten to him. It ate him up on the inside." She grabbed a bottle from the liquor credenza. The label read *Absinthe* "He was drinking this like water."

"No wonder he was going bonkers." That's what wormwood booze did—it ate away at brain tissue. "Wait . . . did you mean something was eating him from the inside literally?"

Before she could answer, Number 942 walked out of nothingness, wearing yellow robes, his face flushed red. Having gone so long—at least it felt like an eternity—without seeing color, 942 appeared in Technicolor.

At that moment, the blood stain symbol vanished and my vision returned to normal.

"It's him." Then I made a mistake and glanced at Harris. Damn, but she was even more gorgeous in color and twice as distracting. Chocolate brown waves of hair cascaded around her shoulders. Her luminous blue eyes reminded me of the coldest oceanic waters. She wore scarlet lipstick, a fitting color for a bold, commanding broad. Shaking off her mesmerizing effect, which surely drove mere mortals wild, I finished, "Number 942, aka the Voice of Madness."

"Another aspect killed Jonah?" Harris asked.

"Yeah. Go figure. I should have known I was the killer." I hate it when I disappointed myself. "Why did you do it, 942?" 943, sure, him I would have understood. 942 had always been stable, a good worker. His whisperings into the minds of men created serial killers, madmen, despots and CEOs. He was good. It was a shame he'd turned on his own. But the quiet ones usually snapped the hardest.

"If you were around more," 942 said, "you've have known 71 was deteriorating. He needed help and not from AA. He knew it, too, up until the end."

"For that, you killed him?" Harris asked.

"I ended his misery," 942 said. "It wasn't murder. More like euthanasia."

"Yeah? I've got a newsflash for you. That's not legal here either," Harris said.

"Like I care."

"Maybe you'll care when you're trapped in the Screaming Abyss." I hated punishing an aspect, as it was really a self-flagellating experience.

"So that's it?" 942 asked. "You're going to condemn me without a trial?"

"Chaotic, isn't it?" I smiled at the sad irony. I hadn't lost one aspect, but two.

"If you don't mind," Harris said, "I'd like to hear 942's story."

"You're all right, dame," 942 said. "71 really liked you. He wanted you to know how much he enjoyed those morning cups of coffee together."

Harris smiled fondly.

"All right, 942, enough with the greeting-card moments," I said. "Spill it, and don't leave anything out."

"You're giving me a fair hearing?"

"Don't push your luck," I said.

Shrugging, 942 sat in the client's chair and began, "A few months back, 71 stumbled across an interdimensional traveler infested with an unknown parasite. By the time 71 figured that out, he was infected and the creature had taken root. 71 thought he could control it—but said if it ever completely took him over, I was to kill him."

"What kind of parasite?" I pressed.

"The kind that devours worlds, sucking out emotions, turning the inhabitants into mindless automatons. Then it eats life, leaving behind husks. After which, it takes its host to another world."

*Damn.* It sounded worse than a Colour.

"If it arrived here in a host, why transfer to Jonah, I mean 71?" Harris asked. Coming from a Yith, that seemed an odd question.

"The original host couldn't survive here and died in the alley where 71 found it. The parasite, however, can survive anywhere, even in outer space. It latched onto the first host it encountered. After oozing into 71, it bonded with his brain like a fibrous tumor."

"Meaning you're infected now," I said.

"I knew what to expect. I came prepared."

"Say I buy that, for the moment. How does the Shining Trapezohedron fit in?"

"In his madness, 71 thought that by killing the Earth's inhabitants, he was saving them from the parasite. He planned to unleash the Haunter for good, but that's getting ahead of the story."

The Haunter, still lurking in the shadows, howled.

"Sorry, boy," I said, remembering then to close the box. "Do continue, 942."

"Before 71 realized what was happening, the parasite took advantage of 71's chaotic abilities. It used him to open endless tunnels and wormholes, turning Earth into its home base."

Again it struck me just how skilled 71 had been. It was a damned waste of promising talent.

"Then I've been looking for 71," Harris mused. "He was the 'thing' causing the rifts."

"Don't blame 71," 942 said. "He was just the parasite's hand puppet. That I found out was just dumb luck. Or maybe it was the Hand of Chaos giving me a nudge."

That sounded like something 333 would do.

"But more likely," I said, "it's because you're the Voice of Madness. You probably heard the parasite taking over 71's mind and responded to its call." As the Primary aspect, I understood my multiple aspects better than they did—I just didn't keep up the way I should. I planned to remedy that in the future, but chaos being what it was, the odds of sticking to a plan were slim.

"71's created quite a mess here," Harris said.

"So wrap it up, 942," I said.

"When 71 was drunk, he gained back a shred of his own lucidity. Alcohol temporarily dulled the parasite's faculties. During a drunken rant, 71 told me everything. That's when he asked me to kill him, if need be. At the time, I believed 71 could defeat the parasite's will. I was wrong. On my last visit, I saw that chaos no longer reigned in his eyes. Insatiable hunger filled him. So I ripped out the parasite, killing 71. Knowing the creature couldn't be destroyed, I stranded it in the Outer Reaches." 942 sighed. "I returned for the Shining Trapezohedron, but it was gone. In hindsight, perhaps I should have taken it along with the parasite—but it took all my concentration to hold the parasite at bay."

"The box was empty when we found it," I said. "And I'm guessing it was already empty before you killed 71."

"He must've realized I'd take it."

"He'd given it to a Shoggoth." Images of what might have happened flashed through my mind, one of those chaotic insights along the various paths a world, universe, or individual might take. "With the Shining Trapezohedron concealed in the bowels of the Earth, no human could have found it. The Haunter would've been forever unleashed, roaming the world in misery." And more than company, misery likes to eat.

"And Keziah?" Harris asked.

I answered. "I suspect she realized 71 wasn't himself and sent her familiar to keep watch. Lucky for us, Brown Jenkin knew that letting the Shoggoth get away with the Shining Trapezohedron would be bad."

"Or maybe," 942 said, "the filthy rat wanted it because it was shiny."

That seemed an equally probable motive.

"What now, boss?" 942 asked. "Still going to exile me to the abyss?"

Harris pleaded his case with her doe-like eyes. "I could use some help cleaning up the mess. But I don't suppose you'll hang around, Number 1." Deep within her hypnotic gaze, I could almost see her Yith mind peering through mortal pupils.

"You know I would if I could." I nodded at 942. "He's not busy. There's nothing on his schedule for at least fifty years."

"You're exiling me here?" 942 asked.

"To close up the tunnels, wormholes and time distortions. See if you can't get things back to normal."

942 laughed. "Normal? Hardly seems the chaotic thing to do."

"Depends on your vantage point. The parasite's handiwork had a purpose. Undoing plans, whether of mice or men or alien parasites, is what we do."

"I'll forge some paperwork," Harris said, "declaring you 71's—Jonah's—brother and heir."

I felt a twinge of jealousy that 942 would spend the next few years, or longer, with Harris. Remembering 942 was another part of me, I decided it was time to pay more attention to my multiple selves—or just to 942.

"You'll be taking over the business," Harris explained. "Which means you'll need a human name."

"I've always been fond of Bogie," 942 said.

Harris grinned. "Bogie Pariah it is."

My own murder solved, I slipped back into the black ether surrounding Azathoth, taking with me the colorful image of the Yith Harris. Her blue eyes would keep me company in my bizarre, endless dreams.

# THE INVASION OUT OF TIME

Trent Roman

ai Quosan was out of his bunk and running towards the fighter hangar before he was even awake. The strident sound of the scramble chimes echoed through the corridors of Watches-Without-Rest. He was jolted out of sleep only when he half-ran and stumbled into Xian Feng, who righted him without comment and kept running. Blinking away the last vestiges of sleep, dreams of disturbing shapes and shades, Bai followed his colleague into the hanger. It was the work of a moment to recognize his Dragon's Fang from among the row of similar fighters. True, all the fighters were manufactured to the same standards, and pilots were not permitted decorations that would distinguish one craft from another, other than the squadron's identifying I Ching hexagrams (in Bai's case: ¦¦¦¦¦¦, Sheng, the Ascendant). But Bai and the others had spent so much time in their hearts, had relied on them for survival so often, that a bond stronger than any alloy had been forged between man and machine.

Taking the steps two at a time, Bai clambered up the ladder to the top of his fighter, whom he had mentally christened *Lady of Thunder* despite the interdiction on individuating the planes. He flipped open the access hatch at the rear of the craft and dove in, sliding down the soft, membranous tunnel to the centre of the craft. His motion was arrested by the high-friction panel at its heart, which would also secure him from any sudden jolts and shocks to which the *Lady* might be subject to.

Lying on his stomach in the familiar pose of fighter pilots, he wrapped his hands around the inset piloting sticks, activating the virtual Head-Up Display. Instantly the warm mechanical guts of the *Lady* vanished, replaced with the linear representations of the hangar and his fellow fighters, transparent script appearing over the latter to indicate their speed, vector and repair condition. The fighters' conditions were all at 'excellent', of course; Bai would have tolerated no less from the indentured maintenance crew. It occurred to Bai that he didn't know how much time had actually elapsed since they had last flown, since he had gone right to his bunk after landing and debriefing, refusing even a massage from his concubine; but he dismissed the issue as irrelevant. Pilots who did not live in the present were pilots who soon would not be living at all.

The ever-calm voice of Control was already counting down to takeoff when the *Lady*, detecting his thermals, activated her engines. As the number-two ranked pilot in Sheng squadron, Bai would be one of the first to launch. He kept his sights fixed on the red wire-frame outline of his squadron leader, Do Kaij; when he began to accelerate, Bai punched his throttle in turn. Soon the hangar was behind them, replaced with the solid-coloured plane that represented the ground, and the vast expanse of colourless sky above. Bai's display flashed a heading, and the squadron wheeled that way. It was only a matter of minutes before the heading indicator vanished, replaced with three of the black wire-frames representing their elongated, tubular foes: the flying, polypoid invaders from eras past.

Bai watched their avatars as the flying polyps became aware of the squadron's presence and changed their course to meet them. This in itself was a victory, though one Bai did not take much comfort in. When the invaders had first emerged from the subterranean hollows where they had subsisted for the last several hundred million years, they had not paid any attention to human craft, whether of True People origin or from the Barbarous Nations. The otherworldly creatures had simply flitted about the globe in their unexplainable way, causing hurricanes, typhoons and tornadoes to ravage the land without rhyme or reason. Here as well they had not bothered with humanity, destroying inhabited and uninhabited tracts alike, pursuing a campaign of destruction which, if it had any cause or pattern, continued to defy the minds of their best strategists. That the flying polyps now turned away from their inscrutable goal to face Sheng squadron was a testament to the long years and many lives spent in research and exploratory attacks to uncover a way to harm the Polypous Race, to finally make humanity a threat worth paying attention to.

Onscreen, the wire-frame avatars of the flying polyps shifted as they turned, their dimensions contracting or expanding without any regard for the integrity of matter and space. Bai knew from scientific briefings that the polyps existed only partially in this reality, extending into higher dimensions which the human brain could not conceive of. According to those reports, to actually see the polyps with the naked eye—to see pieces of their bodies become translucent, vanish, and then become opaque again even as some other portion phased out—strained the mind of the viewers as they glimpsed incomprehensible planes of existence, usually breaking their sanity. This was why the Dragon's Fang class of jet fighters had no windows, but used virtual displays to guide their pilots. Bai was glad for it: just watching the impossible contortions of the polyps by virtual proxy was enough to give him a headache.

At the centre of his display, lines of text from Leader Kaij scrolled down and vanished: attack instructions. The eight-fighter squadron, already divided into two wings of four, would further divide itself: the first three fighters of each wing would go in close on strafing runs against the elder beings to sap their strength and weaken their concentration, while the last two planes would hang back and prepare to launch the displacement missiles when the rest of Sheng squadron was out of the blast radius. It was the standard tactic developed by Great General Tsan Chan to combat the polyps years ago, but the alien creatures, perhaps due to their impossible age, were slow to adapt. And even this tried and tested method was not without danger. It took a steady hand and impeccable timing to make sure that no fighters were lost.

The six attacking fighters merged and then split once more, this time into pairs, each targeting one of the polyps. As they got close, red indicators flashed across Bai's display: a sudden, gale-force wind was bearing down on the *Lady* from above and to his right, trying to drive him into his wingman. Bai decreased his speed and angled the Lady into the gale, seeking to use the sleek, conical shape of his Dragon's Fang to present as slim a profile as possible against which the winds could beat.

This was the polyps' primary weapon. Although the monstrous creatures could seize a plane with their five star-patterned tentacles and crush it into their maws, the principle danger the polyps posed was their elemental mastery over the winds. They could make the currents of the air obey their will and wield seemingly empty space like a massive club against the engines of man. The best philosopher-scientists of the Empire of the True People could not determine why this was so, although they theorized the polyps' alien minds exhibited a low-grade telekinesis to which the light particles of air were particularly susceptible. This was also theorized to account for their ability to fly despite lacking any clear means of propulsion, even so basic as wings.

Counteracting the sudden gales, Bai and his wingman slipped in towards their designated target. When in range, Bai pressed the buttons that enabled automatic fire of the nose-mounted TEDs. Each Dragon's Fang had eight Targeted Electrical Dischargers, arranged concentrically around the narrow front of the fighter, each of which spat in sequence a purple-white lance of engineered lightning. Bai knew from demonstrations that the sky would be vibrating from a barrage of thunder crashes, like a monstrous storm in blackest sky, though he heard nothing ensconced as he was within the depths of the *Lady of Thunder*. The thorough soundproofing was another precaution against the polyps: strange whistling was reputed to accompany their movements of air. While supposedly not as dangerous as viewing the polyps, prolonged exposure to this sound could unhinge the mind.

Bai and his wingman were on target, naturally; the virtual display showed the majority of the lightning lances striking the semi-material surface of the polyps, each bolt stripping away matter and leaving a hollow, tubular indentation in the wire-frame of the polyp. So far as anybody had discovered, concentrated blasts of electricity seemed to be the only things capable of injuring the ancient creatures. But it was only an injury; even as Bai and his wingman blew past their target, their damage done, the scrolling text on his display indicated that the polyp was shifting its form, re-orienting the wounded parts of their bodies along angles no human science could imitate. The polyp's mass was slowly increasing, being funnelled from realms out of mind, in defiance of the allegedly inviolate physical laws of the universe.

As Sheng squadron flew through the polyps' formation, if such it could be called, the polyps took their revenge, summoning more powerful blasts of wind to drive the planes into each other, or catch the fighters at such a slant as to shear through the tough alloys. Bai kept his grip firmly on his control stick as the *Lady* shuddered under the assault, his eye locked on his display, keeping track not only of his own course through the chaotic air streams, but also watching his squadron in case any of them should lose control of their craft.

Indeed, it looked like the newest addition to the squadron, a nervous man whose name Bai had not bothered to remember, was overcompensating against a downwards blast, pulling his nose up too hard. The polyps, either sensing this or just getting lucky (it was a matter of ongoing debate if the polyps understood any more about humanity than humanity did them), switched to a lateral angle. The exposed nose, catching the brunt of the blast, made the plane drift to starboard—right into the fighter of Do Kaij, the squadron leader, who, as tradition dictated, took all rookies as his wingman until they were ready to fly with less supervision.

On Bai's display, the statistics for the hull integrity of both fighter craft suddenly plummeted, and although the virtual render did not show it, Bai could imagine alloy shredding and the conical forms of the two Dragon's Fangs being ripped apart by internal explosions as the planes collided. In short order the wire-frame avatars of the fighters vanished, replaced with chaotically shaped diamonds and wedges representing large chunks of debris. There was no shape corresponding to a human's, of course; the Dragon's Tail atmospheric fighter did not come with ejector seats. The pilot's central location within the plane made it impractical, and Great General Tsan Chan's philosophy of war made surviving a failure a shameful condition. The bodies, assuming they had not been ripped to shreds, would simply plummet for a thousand kilometres to an unnoticed watery grave in the South China Sea.

Bai felt the urge to turn around and try to exact vengeance on the polyps, but he kept his course fast and steady away from the creatures. Vengeance, he reminded himself, was already on the way in the form of the quantum displacement missiles that had been launched in the wake of the squadron. Turning back now would only get him caught in the blast. The bombs flashed on his display, an ever-shrinking number indicating the estimated time until they reached their targets.

Detonation—and the stylized blast radius on his screen rippled to engulf all three of the flying polyps. Unlike the lightning lances, the missiles had no impact on the overall form of the polyps, and their structural integrity (insofar as entities only partly material and in constant dimensional flux could be considered to have a structure) remained unchanged. But their mass was reduced to zero faster that the computer could calculate: one moment the three tubular invaders hovered menacingly in the skies, the next they were gone.

The quantum displacement missiles used the polyps' own hyper-dimensional geometry against them. According to the principles of quantum indeterminacy, there was always an unknown quantity in all measurements, and the closer one came to the absolute definition of one variable—momentum, for instance—the more indeterminate the related variable became—location, in this case. The wisest scientific-philosophers of the Empire of True People had, under Great General Tsan Chan's guidance, devised a method to weaponize this principle. For a fraction of a nanosecond after the missiles detonated, the momentum of everything in the blast radius was arrested at the quantum level, approaching absolute zero. And as momentum became more determinate, easily measured, location inversely became less probable, more diffuse. The net effect was that the polyps' being was pushed out from this reality along the same mind-bending angles from which they came, like creatures of folklore who must stay in the shadows or vanish when light is shone upon them.

The displacement did not kill the polyps; at least, in theory, since it was impossible to distinguish one of the elder creatures from another. But it did force them to reconstitute themselves somewhere far away from their original location, although more likely than not still within the solar system proper and thus only a few weeks away from Earth at the maximum velocity which had been recorded for the flying polyps. Still, every polyp banished in such a fashion meant lives and resources saved; every attack averted gave the philosopher-scientists more time to discover a better method of eliminating their foes.

Bai frowned at his display: all three polyps had vanished, technically a clean sweep. But they had also lost two fighters in the operation, a disgraceful waste of resources for a supposedly elite squadron like Sheng. If Do Kaij hadn't been killed, he would have faced severe consequences once the squadron returned to Watches-Without-Rest. Now, as second in command, Bai called on the surviving planes to turn around and return to base, assuming leadership of the squadron—though he well knew, returning with reduced numbers, that it might prove a very brief-lived responsibility.

# # # # #

Bai received the summons to his first Walking Meeting as he had any other order in the past: crisp, unvarnished ideograms that made no mention of his new status. When he showed up at the central command post where such meetings frequently began (several minutes early to avoid any appearance of tardiness), none of the other high-ranking personnel of Watches-Without-Rest acknowledged that there was a new face among their number. It was, after all, not the individual that mattered, but the authority he was vested with, the skills and knowledge he was expected to bring to bear; though in the case of a squadron leader, that mostly meant quietly keeping pace and being ready to take his orders when they came.

Acknowledging the change would also have meant acknowledging Do Kaij's absence, which would violate the edict on shame under which he had been posthumously placed for his failure. Bai had overheard lesser personnel of the outpost say that Kaij's family back on the mainland had been stripped of their status as True People and conscripted into the imperial slave markets less than three hours after the returning pilots of Sheng squadron had been debriefed. The cost of personal failure was high, Bai knew, but it was nothing against the cost of collective failure: extinction at the 'hands' of the polyps.

The base commander was a tall, thin man named Tsoren Dan, a protégé of the Great General himself. He eschewed the more traditional, sit-down type meetings, preferring to combine his briefings with a walking inspection tour of Watches-Without-Rest. The effectiveness of the inspections were somewhat lessened by being scheduled in advance, but spot checks ensured constant vigilance, and it was good for even the lowest of labourers to see their commander every so often. He greeted the gathered section heads with a perfunctory nod, not slowing at all as they fell into step behind him. As they walked, Dan would call out names, and those persons would accelerate until they were abreast with the commander, so he could receive their reports or give them orders. They all spoke loud enough so that the rest of the train could hear, take note of what was being said and anticipate how the commander's orders might impact their own departments.

For his part, Bai paid particular attention to the briefings of the Detection Officer and the Flight Captain. The first was in charge of the outpost's vast array of sensors, both on-site and distributed across the islands of Southeast Asia leading to Australia; the second was, despite not being a pilot himself, in charge of all fighter wings and their small army of support personnel. They argued over potential cover flights for further installations of sensor emplacements, the Detection Officer suggesting it would improve his teams' odds of returning alive, the Flight Captain countering that it would sacrifice stealth, certainly a ground team's best defence against the polyps' conjurations of dangerous winds. Bai agreed with his superior, though of course it was not his place to say so. That deep into enemy airspace, the number of polyps would easily overwhelm two lone fighters, or even an entire squadron.

The Walking Meeting eventually finished where it began, Commander Dan finally turning to face his personnel in order to dismiss them. The command staff saluted sharply, and Bai made an about-face to leave, but he stopped when he heard Dan call out his name. Spinning back around, Bai stood at attention as the rest of the staff left to attend their various duties, leaving only Dan, Bai and the base's chief philosopher-scientist, Sien Wonjin.

"Leader Quosan, come with us," Dan said.

Bai fell into step behind the two men as they walked once again, this time into an elevator. Commander Dan, catching Bai's attention to make sure he was watching, pressed three specific points on the elevator's control panel, around the actual buttons. The bottom of the inset intercom fell open, revealing a single toggle switch, which Dan flipped. The elevator started moving downwards.

Bai had an inkling of where they were going. He often listened in on the gossip of the maintenance crew and other indentured personnel when they thought he was involved in checking his fighter or running simulations. Their rumour-mongering had betrayed the existence of a hidden level to Watches-Without-Rest… and hinted at what was allegedly kept there.

"You have taken the time to familiarize yourself with the intelligence available to an officer of your grade, Leader?" It was not really a question—or rather, it was a question to which only one answer was acceptable.

"I have," Bai confirmed.

"Consider this, then, an extension of that education," Dan said as the elevator doors opened onto a darkened corridor.

Bai had been up late several nights that week, in fact, reading through the new information. There was a great deal of new insights contained within the classified data packets, including reports on a nuclear bombing campaign which is what actually transformed Australia into the wasteland it is today, rather than the polyps alone, although it failed to have any effect the ancient creatures; spy data identifying to other major entrances/exits to the Polypous Race's underground warrens beyond the known aperture in Australia's Great Sandy Desert, located in northern Africa and in the southwest of North America; any number of contingency scenarios devised by the Great General and his advisors, including the use of the anti-polyp technologies they had recently developed to invade neighbouring territory belonging to the Lesser Peoples, with the intent of using the land and population of the Barbarous Nations as shields against the polyps. Bai thought he had spotted in those last stratagems means that would allow for more permanent occupations; it seemed the Great General was planning for every eventuality in this war, including victory.

Dan led them past a number of unmarked intersections to a large area staffed by grim-looking men who monitored feeds originating from the other side of a large glass window that ran the length of the room. Beyond it were a number of small padded cells, in which people had been lashed to the walls. They were of both genders, and there were members of both True and Lesser People. A network of IV tubes streaming from the cell walls into their bodies made them look as though they were caught in a spider's web. Bai presumed this was how they were being fed: their naked bodies looked emaciated, the muscles atrophied, the skin deflated. The expression on their faces, when they looked up, was gaunt and crazed.

These, then, were the Screamers.

"As you well know, the Empire's traditional insistence on manned fighter craft rather than planes controlled via remote telepathy like the Barbarous Nations utilize is one of the foremost factors in the Empire's rapid ascendancy as the primary defender of humanity in our conflict with the polyps." This was philosopher-scientist Wonjin, evidently speaking for Bai's benefit but his gaze firmly locked on the chambers beyond. "What you don't know is the reason. Propaganda has suggested this edge is due to the experience of our pilots, but in fact remote fighters fail because the polyps have demonstrated an ability to broadcast on, and interfere with or outright hijack, telepathic frequencies. When the polyps finally began to pay attention to us, the pilots of remote craft soon descended into gibbering madness, the polyps apparently intruding into their minds and projecting thoughts or images which our psyche cannot accommodate."

Wonjin waved to encompass the Screamers. "But the polyps' mental attacks are not directed, they are broadband. And so anybody receptive enough is also affected, whether it is merely disturbing dreams, or full-blown psychosis as you see here."

Bai nodded, remembering that his career as a pilot had almost been scuttled a few years previous, not long after the emergence of the polyps, when the Empire introduced new guidelines requiring pilots to be below a certain threshold of psychic potential. Bai had only just scraped under the threshold, despite never having had a glimmer of abnormal mental abilities. He was also thankful that he had not, despite guidelines requiring him to do so, reported the dark and unpleasant dreams that had haunted him of late.

"However, because they receive the thoughts of the polyps, they are also one of our best, if unorthodox, sources of intelligence. These specimens have been injected with compounds designed to increase their receptivity, that we might try to glean something from their ramblings as the polyps' mental waveforms ebb and flow. Right now, the mental blanket is weak: the specimens are speaking their original languages once more, which usually only occurs at the very beginning of their descent into madness, to be replaced with whatever shrieking, trilling and whistling passes for language between the polyps. They are also not thrashing or screaming, as you can see, which is something they used to do quite often."

Bai took a step closer to the glass. The woman in the cell in front of him chose that moment to look up, and her eyes managed to look both glazed over and abysmally deep at the same time. She was True People, although her current condition robbed her of all the dignity inherent to their great race. She might once have been beautiful, but shaved of all hair, skeletal, and entangled in tubes, she could elicit only horror. Her eyes darted about madly for several moments, then stopped, seemingly locked on his, and she began to laugh histrionically. Bai felt ice water trickling down his spine.

"Can they see us?" he asked, momentarily forgetting his place.

The commander did not rebuke him, however; he motioned at Wonjin to answer the question.

"No. Even if they were aware of their surroundings—and they are too far gone for that—this glass is overlaid with a virtual projection of a wall from their side."

The Screamer woman kept laughing, interrupting herself only to cry out: "Learning! Soon they will know it all!"

As the technicians and analysts leaned towards each other to comment on this utterance, Dan gestured that they should step away.

"We are showing you this, Leader, because we believe that the slump in the intensity of the polyps' mental projections might be symptomatic of greater weakness. As such, now is the perfect time to strike a decisive blow, to try a new approach that will tip the war against the invaders in our favour." Dan paused. "Tell me, do you know how it was discovered that they could be harmed with electricity?"

Bai shook his head in a negative.

"The answer came not from our researchers, but from our librarians. It was discovered that an ancient text known as the Pnakotic Fragments, long believed to simply be a hoax claiming ancient extraterrestrial origin, actually had a very exact description of the Polypous Race. The manuscript is, as the name implies, only fragmentary, but we were able to deduce that the polyps are a foreign species that came to this world before vertebrate life even appeared on Earth. Some time later, they fought against another species, known only as the Great Race, who claimed credit for driving them underground with electrical weaponry."

The origin of the TEDs, Bai concluded.

"But electricity, as you know, only harms them temporarily. It might be that they developed limited immunity to it, or it might be that our technology simply can't harness the magnitude of electrical weaponry the Great Race had available. Most of our researchers lean towards the former, since the same manuscripts record—oddly, in a future tense— the polyps rising up again millennia after their initial defeat and chasing the Great Race away. But our philosopher-scientists have been working on a more powerful electrical discharger just in case, and it is finally ready to be deployed. The size of it, however, means that it can only be affixed to this installation, not made mobile. To test it, then, we will need the polyps to come to us."

Dan smiled tightly.

"We will continue to monitor the psychic specimens. When they are at their most comprehensible, and thus the polyps at their weakest, will we dispatch three squadrons under your command to penetrate enemy territory, engage briefly, and then lure them back here. Then we will see to whom this world belongs."

# # # # #

The notice to launch came eight days later, after an unusual lull in polyp activity that Bai assumed was related to the apparent low ebb of their mental projections. His nightmares had persisted throughout the week, but since the Screamers were quiescent, Bai believed such dreams stemmed from the stress of the upcoming mission rather than residual shades of the polyps' psyche which he was sensitive enough to detect. It would be a very dangerous undertaking. Not only were they flying into enemy territory where they would encounter many more of the elder beings than they were used to fighting against, but if the TED cannon the philosopher-scientists had devised failed, they would need to banish the polyps at close proximity to Watches-Without-Rest itself. And the consequence of a quantum displacement missile detonating in an inhabited area was too gruesome to contemplate.

Bai had his squadron—as well as the other two participating in this mission, ¦ | | | ¦ ¦, Heng, the Persevering, and ¦ ¦ ¦ | ¦ |, Jin, the Prospering—train relentlessly for large-scale dogfights and precision missile strikes. When the order finally did come down, he could only hope the training would prove sufficient. Calmly, in notable contrast to the usual controlled chaos of a scramble, twenty-four Dragon's Fangs launched from Watches-Without-Rest's hangar, their vector taking them directly for the interdiction zone around Australia.

As Bai tried to keep himself from fidgeting on their flight into danger, he noticed that a number of the other fighters in the squadrons, including his newly appointed second, Xian Feng, were drifting away at a slight angle. It wasn't much now, but over a long flight it could split their force. Using the communications window of his virtual display, he tapped out orders to the others to fall in line and keep to course.

Xian Feng answered: Negative drift, instruments indicate correctly on course.

Bai bit back a curse. Now was not the time to be having computer problems. He considered the situation, and then ordered all planes to slave their readouts to his, so that they would see the same telemetry he did. Since he was the only one aware of all the mission goals, it was critical that the rest of the squadrons be able to follow him. And if it was *his* display that was in error, they would know soon enough, when they engaged the polyps and failed to score shots. In that case, he would slave all their controls to Feng's display, and hope not too much damage had been taken in the meantime as a result. Either way, Bai was determined that for this, there would be executions amongst the maintenance staff when they returned.

It took almost a half-hour before they made first contact, a lone polyp hovering above what used to be Jakarta. They couldn't have it following them and mucking up their formation with its gales, so Bai reluctantly had one wing pair engage it while another fighter expended his displacement missiles, temporarily exiling it to higher dimensions. At least he was able to confirm that his virtual display was, in fact, reading accurately. After that, however, the polyps seemed to become aware of the intrusion of humans into their nominal territory, and the virtual displays began to light up with contacts.

Bai quickly punched in orders: break by wing pair, engage targets at will for one or two passes, then regroup along the vector back to Watches-Without-Rest. None of the fighters were to launch displacement missiles, since they wanted the polyps intact. It was doubtful the missiles would work at the moment, anyway. The polyps were known to resist the displacement at times, shifting in and out of the higher planes so quickly that they re-emerged exactly where they had been before. This, however, required that they be at full strength and that whatever passed as their minds was focused on such a task, which was why the missiles were never used without the polyps first being weakened by TED strafing.

Following his own commands, Bai broke for an approaching polyp, keeping a close eye on his rookie wingman (Do Kaij's fate was still fresh in his mind). The number of polyps present and the various directions from which they were being attacked created a confusing hurricane of conflicting winds that battered the planes from all sides. Bai had to continually adjust his course, his grip on the control sticks white-knuckled, as the *Lady of Thunder* dipped, drifted and popped up at random. A flashing square of ideograms off to the side of his display alerted him to the fact that two fighters from Jin squadron had just lost all structural integrity, probably as a result of a collision. It was a regrettable loss, but not of too great concern for Bai: this mission had a much higher threshold of acceptable casualties than most.

Bai dipped his nose in towards his target as they passed by, firing all cylinders. Only half of them actually hit their target given the way he was weaving through the hostile winds, but that didn't matter. The strafing runs were just to ensure that the polyps would follow them. Bai broke high as soon as he was past, angling the *Lady* around in a wide, overhead arc that would take him above the polyp he'd attacked. The elder thing tried to follow, but Bai outpaced it and was soon past, maintaining a comfortable lead. Soon enough twenty-two other fighters aligned themselves to his left and his right, above and below, all of them pointed at the direction from which they'd came. Bai was pleased to note that they hadn't lost anybody else when they had broken off the abortive dogfight.

The polyps launched themselves in pursuit, but the Dragon's Fangs managed to keep ahead of the vile creatures: if the polyps summoned a tail wind to propel themselves, the fighters went faster as well; if they created a counter-wind, the polyps were likewise slowed and could not catch up. The polyps alternated these conditions, trying to get the fighters to overcompensate in one direction or another; indeed, halfway back to Watches-Without-Rest they succeeded and latched onto a fighter from Heng squadron that had slowed down too precipitously to avoid a shearing wind from the front. The wire-frame representation of his plane vanished as polyps clustered around it, tearing into the Dragon's Fang with their tentacles.

The rest of the attack force was able to keep ahead until they came within sensor range of Watches-Without-Rest. Bai was pleased that the mission had been relatively easy thus far, but here there would be some tricky maneuvering. They couldn't allow the polyps to get too close to Watches-Without-Rest, for the same reason that any defence against the polyps had to be entirely aerial: the creatures could use their winds to crush any terrestrial object against the ground, like a twister pulverizing a bamboo hut. At the same time, however, they had to make sure the polyps followed them into the path and range of the TED cannon, which meant the fighters themselves had to be in the weapon's projected cone of destruction until the last possible moment.

Bai glanced at his display, where a timer had appeared once he'd entered communications range of Watches-Without-Rest. He waited as the numbers crumbled, and only when the TED cannon timer was at time minus ten seconds did he give the order to break formation. The fighter craft dispersed in a starburst pattern, each along their own unique path arrayed regularly along an imaginary circle, so that the polyps would have no clear vector to follow and would hopefully be momentarily confused.

Then, when the timer still read time minus five, the cannon crackled and fired. Bai pulled back sharply on his stick, yanking the *Lady* up and out of the path of the electrical storm heading in his direction. The plane trembled as the bolt passed beneath him, and Bai thought (though it may just have been his imagination) that he felt a charge in the air. The virtual display fizzled and lost cohesion, momentarily leaving him blind in the air, nothing but the darkened mechanical entrails of the *Lady* about him.

What had happened? What made Watches-Without-Rest fire early? Could Tsoren Dan have decided to shoot in advance rather than risk the polyps scattering in the wake of the fighters? Bai knew that Great General Tsan Chan and his protégés like Dan had a perhaps not underserved reputation for callous efficiency, but nothing he'd observed of commander Dan suggested he was the type to deviate from a judiciously planned and carefully timed strategy.

With a hum, his virtual display returned. Bai made a quick scan of the readouts, trying to assess the impact of the TED cannon on both the polyps and his own men. With a sigh of relief he saw that there were still twenty wire-frame representations of Dragon's Fangs on the screen, though many seemed to be flying erratically—perhaps their displays had been fried as well. Even better, the pursuing polyps had been noticeably reduced in numbers to just over a dozen. The cannon had evidently not been successful in annihilating them all, but just demonstrating that they could be destroyed rather than displaced was a notable victory. It would now be up to the fighters of the Empire of the True People to finish the job, since the polyps were dispersing and moving evasively in a fashion that would make it impossible for the ponderous cannon to target them once more.

Bai transmitted orders to engage, although few acknowledged, no doubt still having problems with their computers. Even his wingman was flying off on his own, following a seemingly directionless course. He picked one of the remaining polyps and chased after it, quickly overcoming its feeble attempts at evasion. When it was in his sights, he fired his TEDs at the ancient creature in the hope of keeping it weak enough to give the others time to arrange a displacement barrage. But, to his surprise, its structural integrity plummeted and reached zero, disintegrating into a cloud of debris.

Bai grinned viciously. It would seem that even those polyps that had survived the cannon blast were so weakened that even standard

TEDs could destroy them. After relaying the information to his squadrons, Bai looked for another polyp nearby with which to repeat the process. For the next ten minutes, in this fashion, Bai hunted the polyps down— almost single-handedly, in fact, although a few other virtual fighters managed to make the wire-frame polyps vanish. Bai knew he should probably be disappointed in such poor performances, even on the cusp of victory, but at the same time it would garner him even more glory and attention from his superiors.

One by one, the polyps dropped from the sky, until there were only five left. These seemed to have tried to disengage from the battle, and were hovering in a group below his immediate horizon, just a few metres above sea level. They were directly opposite Watches-Without-Rest but too far, Bai thought, to use their wind weapon, although Bai couldn't fathom what their intentions were. Deciding not to take any risks, Bai switched his weapons over to activate the two quantum displacement missiles the *Lady* carried. It may or may not kill them in their weakened state, but Bai was suspicious of this new behaviour and didn't want to expend the time to hunt them all down individually with his TEDs. He probably oughtn't have worried, however: the polyps remained immobile as the missiles sought them out, detonating just shy of the group and propelling them all into dimensions beyond.

Bai smiled as his virtual display showed no enemies in range. He considered whether to break protocol and send a congratulatory message to his pilots, when he noticed that they were behaving in a rather odd fashion. Instead of angling themselves to land at Watches-Without-Rest, they were clustering together, and were pointed once more towards the distant Australian interdiction zone. As Bai puzzled over this, something— either his eyes or the display, he couldn't tell—shimmered and lost focus, and when the image returned it showed a much different picture than before.

Gone were the wire-frame avatars of his Dragon's Fangs. In their stead, angling towards the southeast, was a cluster of irregular, tubular shapes—the flying polyps. Where before there had been no foes in the sky, suddenly there were no friendlies. And Bai realized that his own position had shifted: instead of the relatively flat expanse of sea he was looking at before, the bottom plane of his display swelled and fell in the distinct fashion of a coastline and land beyond. What was worse is that he recognized this particular stretch of coast, even from its featureless virtual representation: it was the promontory on which Watches-Without-Rest had been built. Right along the vector where he had fired his missiles.

"No. Oh, no."

Ignoring the cluster of apparent polyps as they were ignoring him—he had no useful weapons left to engage them anyway—Bai brought the *Lady* closer towards the promontory. As he neared land, the plane's sensors began to make out the outlines of objects to aid his navigating, but Bai did not recognize the confused jumble of structures which burst from the ground like the frozen waves of some icy ocean. If his memory served him well, he was on approach to where Watches-Without-Rest's hangar had been, though now there was only a chaotic mass of objects whose constituents the sensors could not recognize.

Finding a clear spot amongst the anarchic landscape, Bai brought his Dragon's Fang in for a difficult horizontal landing. Even with the landing struts, the craft settled at a rakish angle, nose pointing downwards as though eternally moments away from crashing. Bai popped the hatch and—without any pneumatics to assist him—crawled backwards and up through the pilot's access, choking slightly at the warm and rank tropical air that seeped into the short tunnel as though it were the sour breath of some colossal cannibal. His feet dangled out first, kicking at the air to find a purchase on the sleek exterior of the *Lady of Thunder*, and finally he pulled himself out. He looked around.

It was a nightmare. Colours, materials and textures blended and overlapped all about him, surfaces refusing to slot themselves into even simple categorizations like 'ground' and 'building'. Although mounds of unidentifiable mass jutted at upsetting angles, there were no corners, no sharp planes; everything in his immediate vicinity segued into itself, a flash-frozen ooze made up of thousands of no longer disparate parts.

Bai felt dizzy and tumbled off the *Lady*, hitting a hard patch of 'ground' and wrenching his shoulder out of its socket. Concentrating on the pain to give him focus, Bai pulled himself to his knees. Doing so, however, gave him a clearer view of just what he was resting on. There was regular, brownish earth, and something that looked like turf which became inlaid with leaves and ferns. Spotting this was chunks of basalt, a lighter color than the bars of metal streaking the soil. Pieces of bamboo changed the texture again here, and the colour of the plant melted almost artistically into a patch that combined flesh and muscle, wiry black hair poking out at random. The expanse of skin seemed to have come from someone's face, judging from the crescent of a lip lying there like a dead fish and a single unblinking eye staring up into the unclouded sky, the running jelly still retaining an expression of surprise that graded into accusation as Bai met its fixed stare and began to scream.

# # # # #

Bai lasted longer than he would have thought. How long, it was impossible to tell, because time was a rational concept and Bai could not fathom reason when the very environment about him had gone mad. Often, particularly when his gaze drifted towards the omelette of the eye, Bai thought it would be best to just nod, agree with the rest of the world and go mad in turn. Histrionic laughter would bubble from some dark recess of his body and come bursting out, injuring the air with a shrill sound that reminded Bai of the Screamers. At those times, a hidden part of his mind that still recalled notions like 'duty' would cautiously risk itself to take control of his right arm and shove at the opposite shoulder, the pain of bone grinding on bone momentarily quelling the laughter.

He'd decided the eye belonged to Commander Dan. There was no reason it couldn't be the eye of Sien Wonjin, or Bai's concubine, or one of the legions of anonymous menials who had worked at Watches-Without-Rest. But Bai had decided it was Dan's, and that made it so, giving context to the accusation of failure he read there.

Seconds or epochs later, another craft—larger, broader—landed nearby. Bai turned to watch as a ramp lowered and three men walked down. One of them was the Great General Tsan Chan himself, the concealed sliver of sanity noted, though it was not strong enough to summon fear or respect in the wake of the fact. Chan looked around slowly, carefully, his mien never changing, and then nodded at his two visibly disturbed aides, who quickly unfolded a table and two chairs. Chan sat in one, and the automaton sanity, aware its time had come, moved Bai's body into the other.

For another irrelevant interval of time, the Great General asked questions, and Bai answered mechanically. He outlined their plan, though Chan was naturally familiar with its broad strokes, having authorized it himself. Bai spoke of his belief that the Screamers had begun speaking in their native tongues once more not because the polyps had weakened but because, as one woman had tried to say, they had learnt the languages of humanity. In doing so, they learned of the trap planned for them, and began scheming to reverse it. He told of the moment when he first noticed the discrepancy between his display and the others', and of the retrospective realization that the error had come about after he had made a number of changes to the *Lady*'s computer settings—actions he had instantly forgotten about—resulting in so many of their fighters being lost when the TED cannon fired on schedule, but with the squadron's slaved readouts showing the wrong numbers.

That cannon had not worked against the polyps; the polyps must truly have developed substantial immunity to electricity, because as many of the elder things left the ruins of Watches-Without-Rest as had arrived. Bai then recounted how the polyps' mental projections had made him see his own surviving fighters as the foe while he hunted them down, easily pulverizing their planes with his TEDs. Of how he'd been made to believe that the Dragon's Fangs in the outpost's hangar was a cluster of polyps, and how he'd fired his missiles straight at Watches-Without-Rest. How, with no accessible higher dimensions for matter to flee to, the quantum displacement field had the effect of randomly redistributing all atoms within its sphere of influence, culminating in the visual cacophony in which this debriefing was taking place.

Through it all, the General never spoke apart from asking questions. The sole exception came when Bai, his narrative finally finished, recommended that the bar for officers with psychic potential be lowered even further, since obviously the current standards were insufficient; he had passed, but still he'd been fatally compromised.

"We will take it under consideration. I believe we are finished here."

Chan pushed away from the table.

Bai took that as his cue to finally let go, to allow the cold, rational icicle of reason to melt in the mad heat of his overstrained mind. In the time it took for one of the general's aides to walk around the table and put a gun to his temple, Bai was already far away, buffeted by winds and whistling sounds as he fell down a deep, dark crevice not unlike the well of an eye.

# JAMES AND THE DARK GRIMOIRE

Kevin Lauderdale

"James, hand me the periwinkle tie! Top drawer, left side!"

Caesar with his troops could not have been more commanding.

James, my valet, handled the periwinkle as if it were a drowned mouse he had just removed from a bowl of lobster bisque.

That these sartorial battles should continue to rage, even after James has been in my employ for so many years, vexes me. Nevertheless, I will not have it be whispered in butcher shops and wine merchants that Reginald Brubaker is irresolute.

"I know you don't approve of the periwinkle, James. But it's the very latest. Seen it on at least three fellows on Oxford Street this week."

James, the very embodiment of discretion as assuredly as the Bank of England is to pecuniary matters, issued only the most muffled of coughs.

"Yes, sir."

"What would *you* recommend, James?" I asked merely for curiosity's sake.

"Perhaps the old school colors, sir. Seeing that a number of your fellow Old Etonians will be attending."

Point to James. Dicky Byrd-Norfolk's wedding was likely to produce a sea of light-blue-on-black neckwear as a flood of our former classmates turned up. Dicky had been notorious for handing in his school assignments not only late, but frequently incomplete. Most of the Old Etonians were coming just to see if Dicky would manage to make it to the altar at all, let alone on time, let alone if he would actually go through with it. When the *Times* had announced his engagement to Miss Ursula Herne, the members of my club had started a pool re: how long it would take before said engagement was called off. I had said six weeks and had lost a guinea. Now the wedding was only a day away, and it looked like nothing could stop it. I was to serve as best man. Wonders, as they say, never cease.

The telephone rang, and James went to answer it. I continued with my four-in-hand.

"Mrs. Kendall, sir."

Stepping into the living room, I took the receiver.

"Hullo, Aunt Agnes," I said.

"Reggie?" I did not deny it was I, and she continued. "I understand you're coming down to Bootchester Grange this afternoon."

Her particular grammatical construction of 'coming down', as opposed to 'going down', suggested that she was already there. This did not escape me. And it made me worry.

"Are you attending the nuptials as well, Aunt Agnes?"

"You know very well that I'm the godmother of the bride."

I knew nothing of the sort, but said nothing of the sort. James does not have the market cornered on discretion. And discretion is by way of being the better part of . . . thingy.

"Ah," I said.

That seemed to satisfy her, for she pushed on. "Lord Bootchester is putting a number of us up. When you arrive, you must see me first thing."

"First thing?"

"I have a task for you."

"A task?"

"Are you hard of hearing?"

"Hard of—?"

"Never mind! I won't discuss it over the wires. I'll see you there."

She rang off.

"James, what on earth could Aunt Agnes want?"

"I could not say, sir."

"She always comes to me when there's something unpleasant that needs doing."

"So I have noticed, sir."

"You will recall that only last month she had me pretend to be a French painter so that her gardening club wouldn't know the real one she had invited was passed out drunk in the hydrangeas."

"With vivid clarity, sir."

"I don't suppose this task is for me to make full use of her apartment in Monte Carlo for a month in order to keep the staff from getting rusty?"

"Most improbable, sir."

"James?"

"Sir?"

"You will note that I am firmly ensconced in the periwinkle."

"Yes, sir."

"But you may pack the old school."

"Very good, sir."

It takes so little to make him happy. *Noblesse oblige.*

# # # # #

While I enjoy the amenities of the Grange, I don't like the fact that I have to pass through the hamlet of Bootchester-on-Trivet to get there. I've been a little skittish of the place ever since the time I came up before His Honour Judge Halfrick on the charge of pinching half a dozen hamsters. That I was merely doing a favor for a chap who'd passed by and asked me to hold them while he popped into the chemist's was completely ignored by H.H. I was fined five bob and informed that should I ever come before him again, I would suffer the most dire of consequences.

"Watch my pen, Mr. Brubaker!" he had bellowed as his quill hovered over some piece of paper—most likely the order for me to be transported for life. If not to Australia, then to some even more remote location unfriendly to the sophisticated tastes of us Brubakers. Iceland, perhaps. Or Tea Neck, New Jersey. The eventual revelation that H.H. was president of the Southern Counties League for Hamster Protection and Preservation came as no surprise.

The Grange is one of those huge country houses that were built by yeomen of centuries past solely for the purpose of impressing visiting monarchs. Alas, none ever did, and legend has it that the ghost of the first Lord Bootchester still haunts the place, unable to rest because he never got to hang his "King Henry VIII Slept Here" sign.

James and I were just pulling up to the end of the manor's gravel path in my two-seater when Aunt Agnes leapt upon me with the over-enthusiastic ferocity of a spaniel.

"Reggie!"

"What-ho, Aunt Agnes." I climbed out of my car and handed my driving gloves to James.

"This way. Quickly, quickly!"

"I—"

"Later. Into the library."

Leaving James to perform his duties (viz. our luggage, the lugging thereof), I allowed myself to be hauled past the back gardens and through the double glass doors of the library.

A huge room, that library. It was filled not only with maps and marble busts of grim-looking chaps, but also with a fair number of books.

"I need you to get me a book," said Aunt Agnes.

I looked around. "Plenty to choose from."

"No, a *particular* book."

"Ahh. Something naughty from a high shelf? An illustrated Chaucer, perhaps?" The aged ancestress had unexpected depths.

"No, this is called the . . . oh, dear. I've forgotten. The *Nickel Norman Chrome*, I think. Some such nonsense. It was all the chatter at my Ladies Auxiliary meeting."

Her Ladies Auxiliary . . . Aunt Agnes had mentioned it before. Thirteen old biddies who met on full moons to trade recipes and wear odd hats.

She continued: "Apparently all of the other members are antique book enthusiasts. And at last night's meeting Mrs. Phelps-Hampton told me that Bootsy had purchased a copy. Given our connection, I was assigned to obtain it."

"Bootsy?" I asked.

"Well, that's what we used to call him back when he wore knickers. Lord Bootchester."

"Dicky's father?"

"Yes."

"As a sort of scavenger hunt?"

I was glad Aunt Agnes was keeping busy, but if her coffee klatch ever ran afoul of my club on one of our hunts—if our troops ever met face-to-face over a stuffed polar bear to be liberated from the lobby of the Explorer's Society, for instance—my lads and I would take no prisoners.

I said, "I don't suppose you could ask Boo—Lord Bootchester to let you borrow it."

"No, the Ladies Auxiliary must possess it."

"Why do I have to be the one who gets it? I'm always running these errands for you. I have not forgotten The Affair of the Victorian Butter Churn. And now you have me sacking Lord B's library like I'm a barbarian at Alexandria."

"Because" she said, fixing me with two very beady eyes, "if you do not, I will see to it that several hamsters disappear from the Bootchester Loveable Pets Boutique under questionable circumstances. Your presence in town, even with the excuse of a wedding, should prove quite damning."

The specter of His Honour Judge Halfrick's pen hovered about my mind like Marley's ghost.

"Where is this tome?" I asked, looking about.

"Most likely not in here. Bootsy may have it locked in a safe somewhere."

"Somewhere?"

"You really should have them looked at by a specialist."

"Specialist?"

"Your ears! Honestly, Reggie!"

"Well, what does the dashed thing look like?"

"Oh, what did Mrs. Phelps-Hampton say? Big, thick volume. Bound in tan leather. Kind of a five-sided star thing embossed on the cover."

"If it's not here—and especially if it's locked up somewhere—how can I possibly—"

"Why don't you get James to help you? As I recall he was of considerable use last year when you formed a syndicate to bet on the Bootchester Grammar School Latin recitation contest."

"James! I don't need James. Are you casting aspersions upon my gray matter, Aunt Agnes? Because I'll have you know—"

"Just have the Book for me by tomorrow. Before the wedding." She turned to leave through the double glass doors. "See you at the cocktail party in a couple of hours."

"Yes, Aunt Agnes."

"One last thing, Reggie."

"Yes, Aunt Agnes?"

"Change your tie."

# # # # #

"I believe that Mrs. Kendall was referring to the *Necronomicon*, sir."

I sat in the bathtub with two rubber ducks and a bar of Pears' soap, reenacting the routing of the Spanish Armada. I had regaled James with the details of my encounter with Aunt Agnes, and he was now laying out an appropriate suit, and, of course, the old school tie.

"The what, James?"

"It is a dark grimoire, sir"

"Grim or what?"

"A book of magic, sir."

"Making rabbits pop out of hats?"

"No, sir. The Dark Arts: the secret history of the Elder Gods, profane methods for summoning He Who Is Not To Be Named, maps leading to the astral gates guarding the Netherworld—"

"Oh, no, that can't be it, James. Aunts do not dabble in the Dark Arts. Aunt Agnes doesn't even like lemon in her tea."

James produced a towel, and I began to dry off.

"No," I said, "it's probably some sort of history of British architecture: *The Wreck of Norman Domes*. Or a whodunit about stolen topiary: *The Hedgerow Llama's Gone*. Though why the Ladies' Auxiliary would care about either of those is beyond my ken."

"I still believe my estimate to be most likely, sir."

Honestly! While James may have memorized *Burke's Peerage*, and is, admittedly, unassailable on the topic of vintage port, he knows dashed all about llamas.

"My shoes, James."

"Very good, sir."

# # # # #

The party held on the Grange's grand veranda was, as James had predicted, well-stocked with my fellow Old Etonians. I was barely into my first G and T and already I had caught up with Cloudy Foggston, who had made a pile investing in Canadian maple syrup futures, and Bongo Dorset, who promised he could get me in on the ground floor of a company working on wireless electricity transmission.

"No grass grows under the feet of us Old Ones, eh?" I had just said to Bongo when I felt a hand lock upon my right shoulder much like what I imagine a badger trap would feel like.

"*Old Ones?*" said a voice much like what I imagine a badger would sound like.

I turned and faced a man who, not to make too fine a point of it, rather resembled a badger: broadly-built, white hair, dark circles around his eyes, jowls, and not wearing an Eton tie. It was Lord Bootchester himself.

"Did you say, 'Old Ones,' young man?"

He clamped his other hand on my left shoulder, nearly dislocating it. I would not be in top form if called upon to play croquet at any time during the next week.

"I—" I began.

"This way. Quickly, quickly!"

"I—"

"Later. Into the library."

It took only three or four hard shoves from Lord B, and we were in the library.

He looked me up and down.

"I know you. Been here before. Friend of my idiot son. Brewmaster, isn't it?

"Brubaker, sir."

"Well, look here, Brickbaker, what do you know of the Old Ones?

"Um . . . Bongo once swallowed fifty-two Spanish olives—"

"No, I speak of Those From Out of Time and Out of Space. Monstrosities whose very appearance is enough to drive a man insane. Tentacles and gaping maws and lidless eyes."

"I don't think there was anyone like that at Eton when I was at school. Mind you, some of the chaps from Harrow that we rowed against—"

"You pretend to be an imbecile, but I suspect you know much more."

"Do I?"

His lordship grunted.

"If," he said, "you are here for the Book—"

"Ah, yes, the Book. You see, now if I could just—"

"No matter how much you think you know, you do not know enough. I have spent most of my life studying fragments and chasing rumors. Afghanistan, New England, Shanghai. I've been around the world three times. I know more than anyone else on this island of the Book's power and mystery. And now that I finally have it I shall tap its ancient knowledge . . ." He examined me, from toes to forehead again.

"You are not prepared for the True Horrors of the universe. You should flee from the Book."

"Ah, well, I'm Dicky's best man and all that."

"That reminds me," His Lordship grunted. "I need to go meet my prospective daughter-in-law."

"Meet?"

"Yes, meet. Something wrong with your hearing? First time my son's brought her home. Never seen her before. Can't imagine why not."

He started to leave the way we had come in. But without the shoving.

"Remember," he said. "The True Horrors of the universe."

# # # # #

After dinner, during which many toasts were drunk to the happy couple, and Dicky and Ursula positively beamed like lighthouses, I returned to my room where I took up with James, somewhat reluctantly, the matter of the Book.

"Apparently you were correct, James. Aunt Agnes'—and Lord Bootchester's—book is, indeed, a . . . What was it that fellow called that book he was pondering?"

"If you are thinking of Mr. Edgar Allen Poe, sir, it was 'A quaint and curious volume of forgotten lore.'"

"Yes. Well, apparently that's what this *Nickel Llama* jiggery-pokery is. I got word from Lord Bootchester himself."

"Indeed, sir."

There was a knock at the door. James answered it, and in ran Dicky, looking agitated.

"What-ho, Dicky," I said. "Come for a nightcap? Pre-wedding jitters and all that?"

"No, Reggie, it's my blasted father. He won't let me marry Ursula!"

Dicky plopped into a nearby chair.

"What?" I asked. "Why not?"

"Her hair."

"What?"

"Strawberry-blonde. It's a long-standing prejudice of his. Dates back to a chorus girl he once knew, I think. I had hoped he was over it. Or that meeting Ursula would disabuse him of it. But no."

"But he only met her this afternoon."

"And after dinner he informed me of his displeasure. He said that upon meeting her on the veranda, he had hoped it was the afternoon light playing tricks, but upon seeing her by electricity at dinner, the truth was unavoidable."

"All because of her hair color?"

Dicky sighed with the air of a man about to listen for the fifth time to Colonel Tracy at my club recount his adventures among the natives of the Marquesas Isles.

"My father has threatened to cut me off without a penny if we go through with it. *And* to have my beastly cousin Gerald inherit instead of me. We've never really been that close, but . . . really!"

"But the wedding's tomorrow," I said. "Tents have been put up on the south lawn."

"Yes. That is why I propose to blackmail my father."

"Dicky!"

"I know it's an ugly word, Reggie, but if I can just get my hands on that book of his—"

"Book?!"

"Yes, he's just added a very special book to his collection. Spent a packet on it, too. If I could get that, I could hold it hostage until Ursula and I are well and truly hitched. He won't stop us if I threaten to destroy it."

"The . . . uh?" I turned to James for the necessary elucidation.

James asked, "Would that be the *Necronomicon*, Mr. Byrd-Norfolk?"

"Yes. Gosh, James, you know about it as well? So much for the fabled discretion of Dwolly and Dwolly, Purveyors of Rare Editions, Cecil Road." Dicky leaned forward. "You have to help me get it, Reggie."

"What? Steal the Book?"

"Yes. We get the Book, see? And I say to the guv'ner, 'If you interfere with the happiest day of my life, I shall consign this volume to the nearest blaze.' He wouldn't dare."

"*We* get the Book?"

"You know what a fumbler I was at school, Reggie. I can't do it without you."

Well, there you had it. Never turn down a chum in need. That's The Rule of the Brubakers. Absolutely inviolable. Besides, I was sure that Dicky would happily pass the Book on to the Ladies Auxiliary at a moment's notice. To him it was merely a pawn.

I asked, "Do you know where it's kept?"

"No."

"Ah."

He settled back into his chair and I settled back into mine. After half a minute, a muffled cough, like the flutter of cherub's wings, broke the silence.

"Yes, James?"

"In this morning's *Times*, their correspondent from Greenwich reported that the Grand Harmonic Convergence will occur tonight. I understand that this alignment of planets is felt to be propitious in matters of the Dark Arts."

"So?"

"As such, it is likely that Lord Bootchester will have the volume in question out of its hiding place in order to utilize it."

"To do what?"

"I could not say with any precision, sir."

"You think Lord Bootchester is going to use it to conjure demons and ask for their pots of gold?"

Dicky bolted upright from his chair.

"I say!" he said. "All we'll have to do is follow my father. Conk him on the head, grab the Book, and then hold it until after the wedding. Simplicity itself."

"But what about *after*?" I asked. "He threatens to cut you off and you threaten to burn the Book, but once you are actually married, he could still cut you off."

"Then I'll burn the Book."

Mrs. Phelps-Hampton and Co. might have something to say about that, but that wasn't the point of my inquiry.

"But, Dicky, you'd still be cut off and disinherited. You will have inconvenienced him, but he will have inconvenienced you quite a bit more."

Dicky rose and slowly paced the room.

"Look here, Reggie . . . it's a collection of spells and such, right? So—follow me here—maybe there's magic in it about changing a bloke's mind. Bending him to your will and such."

"James?" I asked.

"Possibly, sir. I have not perused the folio in question, but it may be quite likely."

"Excellent," said Dicky. "James agrees with the course of action. No better seal of approval. What time do you reckon?"

James said, "Midnight is traditional time for such activities, sir."

We arranged that Dicky would wake me at around 11:30, said our au revoirs, and I excused James to go below stairs and do whatever it is valets do between ten at night and nine in the morning.

# # # # #

Dicky and I crept down the marble staircase into the main hall. Dicky had his electric torch.

"Dicky," I whispered, "if we don't know where the Book is, how will we even start to follow your father when he goes to get it? If we're in the solarium, for instance, we'll never see him go past the dining room."

"We'll just lie in wait here in the shadows. His bedroom's in the south wing, so he'll have to come down this way just like we did."

"What if the Book is in his room?"

"Then he still has to come this way with it en route to wherever it is he's planning to do his magic. You've never seen my father's bedroom. Chocked full of Queen Anne furniture. No space at all."

We left the stairs and turned to our left to hide beneath them.

"Good evening, gentlemen," said James, holding a mahogany tray with two drinks on it. "Would either of you care for a whisky?" He had turned on a small table lamp, which cast just enough light for us to see by.

"I say, James!" declared Dicky, reaching out and grabbing a tumbler.

"What are you doing down here?" I asked.

"In conversation with Milly, one of the under-house maids, I learned that Lord Bootchester had requested that this room"—he pointed to a closed door to his left—"have its furniture rearranged earlier this evening."

"The Chinese drawing room," said Dicky. "Of course. It's got scads of space."

I said, "Fine, then we're all set. We'll just freeze like statues right here until we see your father come by, toting the ol' quaint and curious."

"Actually, sir," said James, "Lord Bootchester entered the room approximate five minutes ago."

I stepped up and listened closely at the door. Odd noises and faint chants I could hear from within.

"Sounds like your father is not alone," I said to Dicky.

James said, "Indeed, he may be in the presence of an Old One."

"Bongo? What would he doing up at this hour?"

"No, sir, an *Old One*."

"Oh, yes, of course. Tentacles, etc."

Reaching for the second tumbler, Dicky said, "So much for conking him on the head. How's this, Reggie? You hold him and I'll wrestle the Book from his hands."

"That may not be so easy if he's got a . . . friend in there."

There was the all-too-familiar sound of a muffled cough.

"Yes, James?" I asked.

"Might I suggest a course of action, sir?"

"By all means."

James put down the tray and handed me a small piece of paper and a silver salt cellar in the shape of a porcupine.

"Simply enter the room," said James, "quickly pour a circle of salt around yourself—make sure it is continuous, sir, with no breaks—and then recite what is written on this paper."

"What is it?"

"A banishing spell, sir."

While I am not ready to admit that James knows absolutely everything, that he possessed much more than a casual knowledge of diabolism did not surprise me. His ability to torch a *crème brulée* to perfection *every time* suggested no less.

"Why me, James? Why not you?" We Brubaker men are cast of pure iron and do not shirk our duties, but James was clearly already intimately familiar with the proper procedure.

"I do not qualify, sir. While anyone may conjure, the ancient ways demand that if someone else is to banish, that banisher must be a personage of . . . immaculate state."

I detected neither egg nor jam upon his lapels, and he had clearly shaved within the past hour. Nonetheless, he knew the turf better than I . . .

"What about you, Dicky? He's *your* father."

Dicky looked at his feet and muttered something about a French maid.

For whatever obscure reasons, it was clearly up to me. Thus, true to the Rule of the Brubakers, I took the proffered porcupine and paper, turned, and soldiered on just like that Brubaker who rode into the Valley of Death with those other 599 chaps.

I entered and the door slammed behind me, pulled shut as if by some magnetic force.

A good two dozen candles provided light for me to see that all of the room's furniture had been moved against the walls, making space in its center.

In that center was a writhing mass as big as two gaming tables. It had the same general shape and bumpiness of a toad, but with huge, crab-like claws for legs and tentacles emerging from its back. They were rubbery things that dripped gelatinous foam.

Vile it was. And impure. Not to mention repulsive. All in all, it was enough to put anyone off calamari for a whole month—even one with an R in it.

Lord B was sprawled out on the floor, dead as a gross of doornails. There was a circle of salt about four feet in diameter, and, based on how his body now lay, face up, he must have been standing in it when he had gone the way of all flesh. His dressing gown and nightshirt had been torn open and huge sucker marks covered his chest. His face wore an expression of abject terror and agony. The visage was the color of a cod's underbelly three hours after it has been landed.

A tentacle approached me slowly.

I quickly poured my salt into a circle within which any two cricket teams comprised of ants would have been proud to play. I then glanced at the paper for the first time. The words made no sense whatsoever. They appeared to be the lyrics to a Cab Calloway song.

"*Heilo k'mgl k'mgl goh, Heilo k'mgl k'mgl goh,*" I intoned in an— if I may be allowed to flatter myself—not indifferent baritone.

The abomination shrieked. Its tentacles recoiled, and it began to twist in upon itself. But one tentacle shot forward, a spiky tip piercing what could only be the Book, and lifting it from the small Persian rug it had lain upon.

Terrible, wet gurgling sounds not unlike those made by the drains in low-cost bachelor flats in Kensington were heard as the beast collapsed inwardly and spiraled away into a miasma of unhealthy green light.

It and the Book were gone.

After a moment, there was a tentative knock on the door.

"Reggie?" called Dicky.

"You may enter," I said. Dicky and James did so, and I gestured towards center of the room where the brown hardwood floor was slick with slime. "The beast has descended forthwith to the Netherlands."

"Nether*world*, sir," said James.

"Hmm? Oh, yes. Of course."

Dicky asked, "So there was something in here?"

"Yes."

"And you vanquished it. Remarkable."

"Oh, all in a day's work, you know." Humility: just another part of The Rule of the Brubakers. I turned to James and asked, "What was that bit with the salt?"

"It formed a protective circle around you, sir. Nothing Dark could touch you, nor magic assault you."

"Wait," said Dicky. "Where's—I say!" He noticed the body of his father and walked towards it. "What happened to the guv'ner?" Dicky crouched down on his knees and, after a moment, looked up at me. His eyes were, I think, consistent with shock. Dicky swallowed hard. "He's snuffed it."

I nodded. "James, Lord Bootchester had a salt circle as well. Why didn't it protect him?"

"I believe, sir, his circle of protection was not all it should have been."

"Looks continuous enough," said Dicky, still crouching. "That's odd. It doesn't . . ." He filled his nostrils vigorously, like a connoisseur tackling a snifter of Napoleon brandy. "That's not salt." He licked the tip of a finger and dabbed at the white circle.

James said, "Operating on the assumption that your father would use the salt that was most readily at hand, I took the liberty of replacing the salt at the front of the larder with sugar, your Lordship."

"Your Lord—?" began Dicky. Rapidly his eyes returned to normal and a smile spread across his face, bright (as the poet says) as the dawn. Dicky was the new Lord Bootchester. Now he was free to marry Ursula. And he had just inherited.

"What about . . . um." I gestured toward the former Bootchester pater.

James said, "Given the deceased's age, his demise would hardly appear suspicious. I doubt any questions will be raised. Nonetheless, I suggest a dark shirt to cover matters, as well as a tightly-knotted tie to further deter any investigation by enquiring hands. A Double Windsor knot."

Dicky nodded. "No one wants to have to undo a Double Windsor. Good thinking, James."

"Your Lordship is too kind. Also, cremation—the sooner the better—might be advised. A spring-weight suit will burn most readily."

Dicky said, "I think I'd better see to that personally," and started to leave the room.

I said to Dicky, "I'm afraid the Book's disappeared. The thing took it with it. Sorry about that."

"Doesn't matter now, old bean" said Dicky. "No need for it." And out he went. For a moment it almost looked like he was skipping.

"Won't the discovery of a dead body," I asked James, "turn loose the dogs of woe on Dicky's wedding?"

"I believe that any sorrows will be tempered by the celebration of the former Mr. Byrd-Norfolk's elevation, sir."

"A sort of 'winter made summer by this Son of Bootchester', eh?"

"As you say, sir."

"Lord Bootchester is dead, long live Lord Bootchester!"

"Yes, sir."

I could tell James was not getting into the spirit. I did not press matters.

"This squared everything for Dicky, but Aunt Agnes won't be pleased."

"If I might suggest, sir?"

"Please do, James."

"The Grange's library contains several other arcane volumes, complete with similarly-decorated bindings. It is most unlikely that any of Mrs. Kendall's associates are familiar the exact contents of the vanished edition. I would be happy to select a volume for you to present."

"Select away, James."

After a few minutes, which I spent studying a splendid silken tapestry in the room (mountains, meadows, dragon), Dicky came back in, carrying a suit and one of his father's shirts: a forest green, spread collar job that I thought looked just the ticket. James, however, coughed with marked disapproval.

"Look," said Dicky, pointing to a grandfather clock by the door. "It's just past midnight. My wedding day has arrived."

A particularly ripping witticism about what might constitute True Horror crossed my mind, but I said nothing. Discretion: the watchword of the Brubakers.

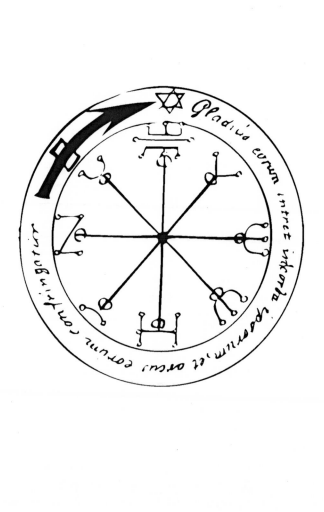

# HELLSTONE
# AND BRIMFIRE

*Doug Goodman*

he town sat on the edge of a scintillating river. The paint was still wet, the main street unspoiled by the weight of horses and stagecoaches. The forests that had been culled for the church and the general store had not yet been turned into farm fields; tree stumps ringed the town like the crenellations in a series of connect-the-dots bulwarks. Unfinished homes stood out like skeletons half-exhumed from a graveyard, bones jutting from the landscape. Most townsfolk lived in tents or rented rooms in the hotel.

From the hillside, a swarm of bats streamed out of the trees and fluttered over the Ranger, who looked down upon the town, a newborn so young it had not yet been named and was only referred to as "baby" by the parents. He shook his head. Those canvas tents would be as useless as paper shields. The houses still being birthed were no better. His eyes followed the contours of the church. The place most likely to avoid complete carnage. Not much better than the rest, but at least it was something to stake a wager on.

He glanced back at the young woman behind him. She was of marrying age, and anywhere else she would probably be doted on by every man in town, even some of the ones who were spoken for. She wore a crimson bodice and a long, black dress. Her black gloves were tied by a thin rope to his horse. She would not look him in the eye as she tested her fetters.

He would have cut out her heart if he could, but he was no murderer and she was tough like duranta bushes, like barrel cactus. He liked tough.

Church had just let out when the Ranger rode in on his Appaloosa, the young woman in the crimson bodice tied to the saddle horn. She stumbled through town, and just as the Ranger passed the church with all the congregation in front, she jerked back on the reins and plopped down on the ground. The minister and all the townspeople watched the stranger in the black wide-brim jump off his horse and slap her hard across the face. Several women gasped. One of the men started down the steps, a righteous glower on his face, but the minister stopped him.

"Next time I won't be so nice," the Ranger warned her. He had a hard voice, like hammers on iron. He went inside the hotel and waited for the clerk to return from services, then bought a room for the night.

"You know, we're a good, God-fearing people here," the wiry hotelkeep said as he handed the guest book and a quill to the Ranger.

The Ranger scowled at the keeper and slashed a big, fat X in the guest book for his name. The hotelkeeper seemed to consider the gravity of that scowl and came to a decision, saying, "If you'll give me a moment, I'll tidy up your room for you."

The clerk walked up the staircase, and the Ranger sauntered back outside to where he had hitched the woman and the horse to the post. There was not yet a horizontal beam for hitching several horses, so she and the horse were tied to the same post. His horse had the lower, more comfortable knot. The Ranger stared at the throng of people still watching him from the shade of the church's facade. Sat down in a porch chair and lowered his wide-brimmed hat. Within seconds, he was snoring. Within minutes, three big men had surrounded him. They tipped their hats to the woman with the bruised face, then tapped his boot. He didn't move.

# # # # #

"Look at this guy, Jesse. Not worth a pound of potatoes," said the shortest one. "Maybe he's dead."

Jesse leaned into the Ranger. "He's got no guns." Took a whiff. "Stinks, too. I think he needs a bath." Jesse reached into the man's breast pocket and pulled out a rock and a dead twig. "Ha! Big Nasty's carrying around rocks and twigs."

As Jesse removed the stone and stick, he brushed aside the Ranger's jacket. On his dusty lapel a badge shined. The badge registered like an earthquake through the town.

"Oh, hell. He's a Ranger."

"No he ain't," the woman said. "Check out that star. It's upside-down. He called himself a Dead Ranger, whatever that is. You should shoot him."

The shortest man tapped the Ranger's boot again. "Hey, buddy. You alive?"

"No," Jesse laughed. "He's a Dead Ranger." The other two laughed with him.

"What kind of man walks around with this crap?" the shortest one laughed.

The true giant of the group, who was rummaging the Dead Ranger's saddlebags, stopped laughing all of a sudden, like the air in his lungs had vanished. The others looked back. They watched in fear as hand-over-hand he pulled out a string, the kind that is attached to dynamite. Thankfully there was no dynamite connected to the end. Just more rocks. Not a stick of TNT anywhere on the horse.

"What kind of cowboy carries dynamite string, but no dynamite?" They all got another good laugh.

The click of a hammer pulling back grabbed their attention. Jesse reached for his guns and realized they were gone.

The Dead Ranger aimed Jesse's guns at them. "The kind who doesn't need dynamite or guns to stop the likes of you three."

"We're here on the preacher's business, stranger," Jesse said. We all saw you strike this lady."

"She ain't no lady."

"Maybe so, but we don't like that sort of thing in these parts. We're good Christian folk."

"So I hear. Maybe you should turn the other cheek and mind your own damn business."

A voice came from the side, "Jesse, Wayland, Albie, leave this rattlesnake alone. We don't want needless violence." The Dead Ranger didn't have to look to know it was the preacher. The preacher had his hands up.

"I'm here tonight, gone tomorrow, preacher," the Dead Ranger said. "But if anybody tries to separate me from her, they're a dead man."

"You'll get no trouble from us," the preacher said.

"That's all I wanted to hear. My things." He motioned to the rock and stick. Jesse placed it on the porch in front of him. In return, the Dead Ranger unloaded the pistols and tossed them into the dusty street. The men collected their guns and retreated.

"You can't treat her like that," the preacher said, his long finger pointed at the young woman. He had a dry voice. A gaunt face. "We all have sisters here. Mothers, daughters, and wives. We won't suffer it." The preacher said no more, but clasped his hands together and crossed the street back to the white-walled church as people started walking back to their tents or getting into their wagons.

# # # # #

Him, with the saddlebags over his shoulder and the shotgun in one hand, the rope in the other. Her, sun-dried, lips cracked, her lustrous black hair ravaged by the heat. Despite the heat and her pain, she smirked and refused him.

"What do you mean, no? You been complaining about the heat since Orion came up in the east. I'm offering you a chance to get out of the sun."

"Go ahead," she said. "Force me. These people won't tolerate it, Dead Ranger."

To show her defiance, she stuck her uninjured cheek out for him to slap.

He looked at her, obstinate, then to the long coil of thin rope on the ground. "I think you should be more concerned with what I can tolerate." He untied her knot from the post and dragged the rope inside behind him. She looked out across the street. A few people were watching, but most had started on home.

Inside, the Dead Ranger stopped by the desk. "Apparently I need a bath," he said, and flipped him a dime. "Draw one for me."

The hotelkeep nodded, looked at the shiny coin in his fingers, the seated Lady Liberty struck in the center. His eyes followed the rope drawing up the stairs behind the Ranger. Suddenly the rope went taut and he heard something slam against his door. A sucking sound, of somebody being punched in the gut and losing their breath, then a wild scream as the young woman was dragged down the hallway, kicking.

She hit her head on the first step, and tried to stand. But the Ranger jerked hard on the rope, practically lifting her up on her feet. The hotelkeeper watched the bizarre sequence of events, then gazed at the dime.

# # # # #

His clothes and saddlebag on the post behind him, the Dead Ranger sat down in the metal tub back behind the kitchen as the hotelkeep poured another bucket of hot water. The Ranger relaxed in the calescent bath. While the hotelkeep walked behind him to fetch another bucket from the fire, he noticed the giant gashes up and down the Ranger's back, like ragged tears or jets of acid had sluiced across his body.

"I've seen a lot of strange scars, mister, but I ain't never seen a scar like that. They boil you as a kid?"

"Something like that."

He wanted to ask more, but the preacher appeared at the door, Bible in hand. To the Ranger he demanded, "Can you read?"

"Very well," the Dead Ranger said.

"Good. I want you to read this. You might learn something." He placed the Good Book in the Ranger's dry hand. The Dead Ranger sneered at it and plopped it on the ground. Reached into his saddlebag and pulled out an ugly book with a rippled leather cover and another turned star. "Since you're such an advocate of learning, preacher, you'll probably enjoy this. Read it. As you said, might learn something."

The preacher dropped the book as if it had bitten him. "I know the mark of the beast when I see it."

"Yeah, I bet you do," the Dead Ranger said as the preacher left.

# # # # #

He took his time. The bath felt good, rejuvenating. He hadn't had one in weeks. Was too busy ranging across the hill country, assisting priests with exorcisms in Cuellar, and tracking down chthonic gods in Sterling. The past thirty years or so of war and Manifest Destiny had planted a lot of bloodshed and anger in soils better left unharvested.

When he heard the door to the hotel opening and steps creaking up the stairway, he had a good idea what was going on. He casually redressed. Tossed the saddlebags over his shoulder and took out the dynamite string. Said good-day to the hotelkeep, who had returned to his desk, and walked upstairs.

The hotelkeep watched his ceiling intently. Listened to the stranger's boots cross the threshold. The door to his room opening. A scuffle. Punches, and a body thumping on the floor. He put down his ledger and guest book with the big X on the bottom line and walked away from his hotel.

Upstairs, the woman, tied to the window, nursed a black eye. So did the preacher, who was roped to the bed perpendicular to its length, his pants pulled down so his pale buttocks showed. The Dead Ranger sat down on the floor so that he was head-to-head with the preacher.

"We ain't seeing eye-to-eye, preacher," the Dead Ranger said. He pulled out the shiny black rock from his shirt pocket. "So I think we need to have a come-to-Jesus meeting. I am a Dead Ranger. Instead of hunting Comanche and horse thieves like the other Rangers you are familiar with, I hunt the things that go bump in the night. Ghosts, demons, brujos, that sort of thing."

"Superstitions. False idols," the preacher said.

"You keep interrupting me, and I'm gonna have to do something to shut you up. Now listen. I want to make this clear. I am here on state business, so anything you do to compromise me is a state offense, and I don't think you, or any of your people, want something like that on them. I need to hear you tell me you are going to leave us alone."

"I *am* my brother's keeper, and you are my brother and she is my sister."

"You have good intentions, preacher. I thought you'd say something like that." He held out the rock. "This is hellstone. The stick is brimfire. They are two pieces of the natural landscape of hell, pieces the Dead Rangers have acquired."

"Don't you mean hellfire and—?"

But then the Dead Ranger mashed his thumb up against the rock and flicked it. The woman and the preacher watched as the rock ignited. The bright flame burned on its side. "Hellstone is highly incendiary, and the flame can burn forever." He cupped his hand over the rock, then pulled back. "But it can be controlled."

He thumbed off a small flake from the rock and hurled it at the dresser. The flake struck the boards under it, followed by a large CRACK that lifted the dresser off the floor and scarred the wood.

He cut off a chunk of the rock, much bigger than the flake he tossed at the dresser. Plugged it with the dynamite string, which curled down over the preacher's head and coiled on the floor. He shoved the rock between the man's cheeks.

"What are you doing?"

"I'm making sure nobody messes with my affairs." He lit the dynamite string with the original piece of hellstone.

"Don't do this!"

The Dead Ranger watched the sparkling flame follow the coils of the string and rise up towards the preacher's face.

"You're going to have to trust me on the woman, preacher. I know it seems odd and makes no sense, but not a lot of sense is being made out here lately. You and me are here on the same mission, preacher. We're both here to make sense out of the chaos, to control it somehow. Course, the alternative is I put a hole in your caboose as wide as West Texas. Choice is yours, preacher."

The preacher watched the spark race past his sweating face, his crying eyes, and out of sight.

"Gettin' close to gone, preacher."

"Stop! Stop!" the preacher said, squirming on the bed. "You walk your way, we'll walk ours!"

"That's all I wanted to hear, preacher." He licked his fingers and dampened out the spark somewhere over the middle of the preacher's back. Untied the preacher, who rolled over and pulled up his pants.

"You can keep the rock if you like—I got more—but I wouldn't walk too fast. Might ignite." He grinned, and while he wasn't looking the woman decked him. Then she kicked him between his legs. He doubled over, and she made a hideous face. Such fury in those eyes. Slowly, because the pain coursed like overtures through his every nerve ending, the Dead Ranger reached into his jacket and pulled out a brass relic, a large bar with smaller bars sprouting from the sides. The woman backed off; her face became something less demonic. She set her jaw and scowled at him while the preacher looked on with amazement.

"What is that?"

"Elder Sign."

"What have you brought into my town?"

After catching his breath, he said, "Tell your people to stay inside tonight. I want nobody on the streets, not even you preacher, understand? Keep them in the church. That'll be the safest place."

# # # # #

All the doors were closed, all the tents tied down. The townsfolk had gathered in the church; the Dead Ranger heard them singing. She stood to the side of the road, once again tied to the hitching post.

The Dead Ranger dropped his saddlebags in the middle of the street and searched the night sky. He turned around twice before finding what he was looking for. He drew a few lines in the sand. Then he used his rifle barrel to outline another circle around the woman and crossed it with several lines.

He took a big step into the circle so as not to disturb his drawing. Removed the rope that bound the woman. "Hairs donated from maiden girls at a Catholic school from when I was working an exorcism in Cuellar. That makes them virgins, and that's powerful mojo." Another large step, and he was outside the circle.

"You're crazy, you know that?" she said. "Those hypocrites may be too scared to stand up to a bully like you, but you wait and see. Somebody is going to knock you off your pedestal."

He ignored her and pulled out the thick book so hated by the preacher.

"You're not fooling anyone. Just sit back and relax. This'll all be over soon."

Out of the north sky a bright light flashed from out of the darkness. The flashes struck the hills beyond town, the same ones he had used to survey the town earlier that morning.

The Dead Ranger took no notice. Opened the book, flipped to a specific page, and held his hand out, his first two fingers crossed. He said a few words in a subterranean language that was inhuman at best. Then he looked to the church. The preacher had appeared on the front steps and was studying them. Said nothing.

The Dead Ranger asked him, "Did you know this place was a Spanish mining colony around about two hundred years ago? The Spanish thought they'd found El Dorado, but all they mined were these strange, black rocks that they couldn't make use of. There were incidents—unexplainable deaths and strange explosions—and then the Spanish left." His voice echoed off the flatboard walls in the empty town. Then he said, "You should really go back inside, preacher. Death is on its way."

The preacher stared fearfully in his direction. Not at him though, but to the thing beside him. "Told you she weren't no lady," the Dead Ranger said. He looked back at the disfigured head, the tentacles dangling from where the mouth should have been. There was no woman left, neither dress nor bodice. Only the nightmarish urine-colored creature with bulbous legs and four slits for eyes. The creature paced in the circle, but could not break the spell.

"Been a while, Haestrum. The Unnamed Hunter. You should have known you can't hide from a Ranger."

The ensnared abomination roared at him. It sounded like horses screaming, like rabbits dying. Almost human, but sinister and alien. The kind of sound that makes women miscarry and men cry. The Dead Ranger held up the Elder Sign. The creature backed off.

"Lucky you, we've found your immortal enemy, straight from the furthest reaches of Yugguth to the hill country of Texas. The Mi-Go. Now, here's the deal. You get to hunt the Mi-Go, but you have to spare the town. And I need the girl back."

The creature lifted its tail, fat and bloated like a scorpion. Instead of a stinger, though, Haestrum had an emollient pouch that flexed and contracted like a breathing organ. Burning pus dripped from the pouch and sizzled on the ground. The Ranger winced; a phantom sear of pain ran down his back.

The Dead Ranger placed the brimfire stick on top of his hellstone and flicked the black rock. A crystalline shield with a fiery refulgence surrounded him. "Fool me twice, shame on me. Now make your decision, quick. They're coming."

The Dead Ranger could hear the Mi-Go in the sage outside of town. They were drawn to the strange black rocks of the surrounding country, and to get to them the Mi-Go had to go through the new town. Nobody told the townspeople when they settled here, and it wasn't their fault they built their town in this otherwise idyllic locale, but that didn't change what was about to happen. The Mi-Go would raze the town to get to those black rocks.

Haestrum nodded assent. The Dead Ranger drew two lines to break the circle, and the creature jumped out and roared like a bonfire at the Dead Ranger. At the same moment, the first of the Mi-Go entered the town. The Dead Ranger heard the congregation singing. Didn't recognize the tune, but it was a loud and powerful hymn. The perfect soundtrack to the hunter's battle.

The Unnamed Hunter left behind in the circle a young girl in a crimson bodice and with long flowing black hair. Her face unblemished, but confused. The Dead Ranger entered the circle and helped her up.

"We need to get out of sight."

Confusion bloomed on her dewdrop face. "Where am I? Who are you?"

"Don't matter. All hell's about to break loose and we need to get inside."

# # # # #

He offered to let her watch the slaughter from the bedroom window, but she didn't want to. She was still trying to put together what the Ranger had told her about demons and possession. She tucked herself by the dresser drawer in the shadows and stood there and waited. Did not touch the small meal laid out for them by the clerk. The Dead Ranger, on the other hand, sawed through a steak as he watched his version of dinner theater.

Beyond town, the Haestrum hunted the Mi-Go, shooting its acidic stream of fluids on them and collecting their skulls. The Mi-Go were powerless against the ancient god.

"Those creatures with the giant octopus-like mouths and the crab claws all up and down their backs—they're called Mi-Go. They come here to harvest the hellstones in the area. They have a few other places where they go for it, but this is their best bet. They need the rocks purely for ceremonial reasons, but they will destroy whatever's in their way to get it. The Haestrum on the other hand, he's like a god, and he loves to kill Mi-Go. Has hated them since forever, like they were a race of horse-thieves or something. So all we had to do was get the two together and the problem would fix itself naturally."

"Why me?" she said weakly.

"We've been scouting for it for a long time now. There are signs. Omens, mostly. Calves born without legs, strange sea creatures turning up in lakes, unexplained damage to buildings. Eventually, a missing girl. Haestrum loves possessing young girls. It was one-part luck that I found you. Since you were in one of the counties I work, I was the one sent to wrangle the monster in. I've tussled with him before. Mean SOB."

"Good thing you're tough, though," he added. "I could tell you're tough from the first time I put eyes on you. If you weren't tough, I would have had to force Haestrum out of you, which would have meant cutting out your heart."

She swallowed his words hard. They left a bitter, metallic taste in her mouth. She knew he was telling the truth.

From down in the kitchen, a pan fell.

"Maybe it was the hotelkeeper?" the girl presumed.

"Keep's in the church with everybody else." He finished chewing his steak and put down the plate. "Stay here."

"Don't go! You don't even have a gun."

"Got everything I need. Now stay here."

A silence enveloped the hotel, so that the slaughter outside was muffled and he could clearly hear the augmented sounds of the boards creaking under his every boot step. He walked down the stairway and stretched his body to see around the staircase. He knew he was coming into a blind spot where he could be ambushed. But there was nothing there. He crept down the main hallway towards the kitchen. The dark was as palpable as the quiet. He twisted the knob to the kitchen door. It groaned for all the world to hear, and he cursed himself.

He entered the kitchen. There was a cast iron stove that also served as the heater, a breakfast table, and a wooden counter with vegetables scattered all over it.

On the floor lay a single pan, knocked over. He looked up. The giant creature, which had clawed itself into the ceiling, pounced on him, opening its wide trunk into a giant maw.

His hat was shredded into a thousand pieces as those teeth came on him like a combine. Dozens of long, crab-like arms flittered around him to prevent his retreat, and he knew he was trapped like a fish under the canopy of an octopus. The only way out was through those teeth. That open mouth. He reached for his hellstone but nothing was there. Suddenly, the young woman appeared at his side. She had snuck down with him. *Too bad that'd be the last choice she ever made*, he thought. She pulled out two large hellstones and chunked them into the Mi-Go's open mouth. The stone broke to pieces in its combine-like teeth. The Dead Ranger barely had time to pull her down to the floor before the creature exploded. The blast took out the entire kitchen and most of the hotel, but left them both alive, if not unscathed.

When they finally crawled out from under the remains of the hotel, the din of battle was gone. The predator had followed his prey back across the spirals of space and time. From the church, the singers were finishing a somber rendition of "Go Tell it On the Mountain."

# # # # #

The preacher caught him saddling his horse and straightening out the saddlebags. "I'm sorry for doubting you," he said.

"You're good people. You were only doing what good people should do."

"We're having a revival next week. You should come."

"Thanks, but I'm needed up in Cataweh. There's been a Nyarlathotep sighting."

The preacher did not understand, but asked, "What of the girl?"

She walked around of her own accord, wearing a smile and humming a spiritual. Above her, the sky had turned from black to purple. Rays of light shot out of the east.

The Dead Ranger looked at the girl and said, "She will be returned to her family, no worse for wear, though I'd wager they're anxious to see her again. She's been missing for five days."

"We're indebted to you, Ranger."

"Consider the slate clean if you move your congregation away from the black rocks." He put his hand on the pommel and climbed into the saddle. Then he helped the girl up behind him. "Keep your eyes on your people, preacher, but keep a third eye on the stars." Horse, rider, and girl walked off into the sunrise, bats wheeling and diving above them.

# STAR⊨CROSSED

Bennet Reilly

*. . . One sees that all the astronomers have to do is to discover that stars have sex, and they'll have us sneaking into bookstores, for salacious "pronouncements" and "determinations" upon the latest celestial scandals.*

—Charles Fort, Lo!

 **rouched on a fat, gnarled tree root** grown too large for the soil to contain, Shub-Niggurath idly toyed with a lock of her hair and watched the night sky. There were so many stars . . . despite having personally visited many of them, the limited field of vision that her two eyes provided made Shub-Niggurath feel she would never be able to see them all as she quickly lost track of one as soon as she focused on the next. In her time, she had encountered the true limits of the universe and the many things that crawled and squirmed in the spaces between those stars. Many were of her own creation and even more worshiped her with unending praise and adoration. Nevertheless, as the stars above glittered down at her, Shub-Niggurath realized that she had never felt this small before. Small and infinitely alone.

The creeping sensation of loneliness had been with her for quite some time. Sure, she had company in the Dark Young that sporadically sprung forth from her being, and she loved and cared for them as any mother would. But it had been a long time since she had enjoyed the company of a contemporary. A peer. There existed other Elder Beings like her, but most were aloof and self-absorbed. Not at all the sort of connection she was longing for. Folding her arms about her chest to ward off the chill night air, Shub-Niggurath had to wonder, was a companion really too much to ask for?

Releasing a heavy sigh, Shub-Niggurath stretched out her limbs, then stood and paced to expend some of her nervous energy. She had been on or around this planet for some time, though this spot held no particular significance for her. She merely enjoyed being surrounded by growth and living things. So these woods, huddled around the shore of a deep lake teeming with biotica, were *comfortable* for her. She wanted to be her best for tonight's appointment.

Pacing, Shub-Niggurath reflected on the idyllic conditions set for the night's meeting; the new moon left the woods at their darkest, and the clear sky left nothing to blot out the blanket of stars overhead. The still air left the waters of the nearby lake smooth as glass, perfectly reflecting the starlight and the dark spaces between. She had chosen well. Shub-Niggurath approached a tree hanging over the rocky little beach separating the woods and the waters of the lake, then leaned her human body up against its trunk and tried to force herself to calm down. Nervously she looked up at the sky again, her attention held entirely by distant Aldebaran. She watched it with rapt attention, the star seeming particularly brilliant. It appeared to momentarily flare even brighter, and Shub-Niggurath knew her waiting was nearly at an end.

The lack of wind did not prevent the branches of the trees around her from groaning with movement. The woods and those things that were a part of it knew that they were in the presence of their Dark Mother this night. Her visit had filled them with excitement, making them twitchy and restless. Her approach had been coming for some time, and the closer their matron came the more her young had been drawn to this place. Now, on this night, there were perhaps as many of her tree-like offspring clustered about this lonely copse of woods as there were *actual* trees. Mostly they just stood in place, shifting their weight from hoof to hoof, gurgling happily if Shub-Niggurath deigned to give one an affectionate pat. She didn't mind having her Young clustered about, so long as they didn't distract from her meeting, but she was reminded of just how limited they were. These offspring were more like pets than actual children and would never develop as Shub-

Niggurath wished they could. It was maddening. Similarly, Shub-Niggurath had no doubt that her human priestesses and worshipers were close by, or at least would be soon. They believed it was their work that was responsible for their Goddess's physical manifestation in this time and place. Shub-Niggurath did not choose to disillusion them. With their rituals and ceremonies complete, the cultists were content to observe her and her actions from a distance, hopefully remaining out of sight.

Precisely three lunar months ago, one of their number had been killed here. More properly, she had been sacrificed by her sisterhood as part of the call to their matron Goddess. The sacrificed sister was dead and buried now, her corpse embraced by four feet of damp soil and carrion worms. But it served as a convenient vessel for Shub-Niggurath's purposes. From the decay of her flesh came new growth and fecundity, of fungus, beetles, mold and more. From this stuff of unrestrained growth was Shub-Niggurath's temporary human form built. In appearance, she was modeled after the slain cultist, as the Dark Mother had no particular concern regarding the human aesthetic. Still, her estranged husband sometimes paid attention to that sort of thing, so she was satisfied that her body would be considered by humans to be "attractive."

Weaving her fingers through long, curly locks of auburn hair, Shub-Niggurath wondered if Hastur would be impressed and what form he might take. As Outer Gods, they existed on all planes of reality and could have just as easily held this meeting as sentient nebulae swirling between stars, or obscene writhing masses of protoplasm wriggling on an ocean floor. But just as she had chosen the location of their meeting, Hastur had chosen the form their manifestations would take, and taking the form of humans had seemed . . . a novelty.

Hastur had always possessed a subtle humor. Certainly, this form was not one Shub-Niggurath was accustomed to, and had found it rather awkward at first. She had to take a few minutes to learn the nuances of things like breathing and walking as she stumbled about in the woods. Even now she was not entirely comfortable with having only two eyes to see with or being confined to such a limited spectrum of visible light. She felt blind and deaf, straining from her perch at the edge of the woods to make out the tiny lights of torches being lit among the cliffs on the far side of the lake, straining to hear the distant chanting of the Brothers of the Yellow Sign.

Shortly thereafter, Shub-Niggurath spotted the first of Hastur's heralds descending out of the sky towards her woods.

The lone forerunner was quickly joined by another and another until there was a host of winged creatures swarming through the night sky. As they settled on the thicker trees their combined weight bowed the branches towards the ground. The flock peered their half-wasp, half-vulture faces down from the canopy for a closer look at the Dark Mother. Their shrill animal barking and the excited chattering of their membranous wings announced the imminent arrival of their lord, and so Shub-Niggurath turned her attention back to the lake.

There, despite her diminished senses, Shub-Niggurath spotted the one for whom she'd been waiting. A layer of mist rose from the surface of the water, obscuring the lake, and through that mist strode Hastur. He strode down from the cliffs as though the fog bank were the steps of some palatial estate, a king emerging from his castle to survey the lowly grounds of his territories. Amidst the swirling clouds on the lake, Shub-Niggurath observed a handful of small boats crewed by Hastur's followers, following closely in the wake of their God. Several of the boats carried standards bearing Hastur's mark, the dreadful Yellow Sign. Shub-Niggurath smiled at the memories it conjured within her.

At last, Hastur set foot upon the shore and turned his head up to face Shub-Niggurath. Feigning disinterest, Shub-Niggurath continued to toy with her locks while subtly peering past her concealing bangs at the form of her mate.

Clothed in a tattered yellow cloak and wearing a polished pearl mask over his face, Hastur was resplendent in his guise of the Tatterdemalion King. The cloak could not completely conceal the tall, well built frame of the man who had assumed the King's mantle. When Hastur reached up to pull back his hood and cast aside his pallid mask, Shub-Niggurath ceased her idle fidgeting and watched with undisguised attention.

"Shub-Niggurath," he spoke, choosing his words carefully, "it is . . . good to see you again."

She didn't immediately reply, but offered a warm smile. It was good to see him as well . . . particularly now that his head and face were visible. Doubtless the members of Hastur's cult had chosen this body because of its good looks. Possibly, it was some kind of plan the Brothers had devised with the intent of impressing her, to influence the night's proceedings by bringing her under the sway of Hastur's charms. Pale of skin and blue-eyed, strong features and well groomed except for a hint of shadow across his jaw; these sorts of features shouldn't have meant a thing to Shub-Niggurath. One human was basically indistinguishable from the next, should a Goddess such as herself actually deign to notice one at all.

But nevertheless, Shub-Niggurath couldn't help but stare. Fascinated, she stood and leaned closer with one hand gripping the tree beside her, trying to get a better look at this man in front of her. She beckoned him closer, feeling too shy to speak just yet. Why did he have such an effect upon her? Hastur walked steadily and with a confident smirk up from the shore and into the shelter of the woods to meet her. His eyes roamed over her body as he closed the distance between them. Did she have the same effect on him? Shub-Niggurath again considered what it meant to be beautiful on this world, and whether or not it was a quality that she possessed. Novelty though these bodies were, she had to admit this was much more fun then roiling about as an inky cloud of tentacles.

"Thank you for coming." Shub-Niggurath said softly, now that Hastur was close and his expression relaxed to a neutral calm. She wished that he would continue to advance, reach out and embrace her with his arms. As soon as the notion occurred, she wondered where that impulse had come from. This body she wore, it longed for his familiar touch. Hastur bowed his head respectfully in response, remaining just outside her reach. Shub-Niggurath knew that she would eventually have to get to the matter at hand, but she didn't feel collected enough to do so just yet. She wanted to understand why Hastur's presence was filling her with these alien thoughts and desires. In the mean time, she would just have to make "small talk."

"How have you been?" she asked, keeping her tone casual.

Hastur cocked an eyebrow and smiled slightly, curious. "I've been well." He didn't seem quite sure how best to approach her either, and was undoubtedly feeling out the situation. "I've been spending my time in the Hyades."

Listening only half-heartedly, Shub-Niggurath nodded and encouraged him to continue. "And what have you been up to out there?" she prodded, though she wasn't terribly concerned with his answer. Out of the corner of her eye she could see that the brothers of the Yellow Sign had docked their boats and were creeping their way up from the beach, trying to keep out of sight while getting close enough to overhear their conversation. It didn't bother her *per se*, in fact she was certain that her own worshipers were scuttling between the shadows of the trees and eavesdropping for the same purpose.

That was the entire point of the sacrifice that lead to her current incarnation, after all. Their respective cults had arranged these bodies as vehicles so that they might observe the actions of their Gods, like divining knowledge from astrological movements or the guts of a slaughtered goat. But before the cultists began interpreting any divine missives from Shub-Niggurath's meeting with her husband, there were these unanticipated *emotions* to deal with. The chemicals and impulses clouding the judgment of this human brain made it difficult for Shub-Niggurath to think clearly and that was an issue she would like to deal with privately.

Appearing similarly uncomfortable, Hastur filled the awkward silence as best he could. "I've been keeping busy. Yhtill requires near-constant attention, and I visit Azathoth's court on an irregular basis." Gesturing with his arm to indicate the crouched horde in the trees above them, he added "And as you can see, I still breed and train my *Byakhee*. They are delightful pets, and delicious."

Despite her attempt at emotional control, Shub-Niggurath found that she was smiling again. Their mutual affinity for the lesser creatures of the universe was one of the common interests they shared. When they were younger, the two of them took delight in crossbreeding radically different species, or squeezing Shoggoths into different shapes to see which ones would thrive and which would dissolve back into puddles. Eventually Hastur developed a particular fondness for a creation he dubbed *Byakhee,* and trained them to follow him through the voids of space.

"As a falconer you are without peer," she agreed. He gave her a pleased look at her compliment. It was almost enough to make her forget why they had arranged this meeting. She wanted it to feel like old times again, when the cosmos was young and so were they. She wanted so much for their friendship and marriage and the stars to all be *right* again; to be back in the embrace of her beloved. But with a sobering sigh, Shub-Niggurath reminded herself that there were yet obstacles to overcome. "I think it is time that we re-examined our relationship."

Folding his arms over his chest, Hastur looked on expectantly and waited for Shub-Niggurath to continue. She walked slowly through the clearing, pacing as she composed her thoughts. "I've missed you Hastur. I've missed you terribly. And I want you to come back to stay with me, but—"

" . . . But?" Hastur prodded.

"I'm still angry with you," she finished, casting him a dangerous look. And why shouldn't she be? They had pledged themselves to each other as mates. Through their bond, she would fulfill her ultimate potential. He had promised her this. And then, when the time had come for Hastur to father Shub-Niggurath's children, he had refused!

"You stymied my entire being! My purpose!" Shub-Niggurath snapped. She was, in a literal sense, fertility. It was her nature to grow, multiply, expand, gestate, and produce. To *breed*. But, on her own, she would only ever replicate her own being, budding off minor little abortions of hooves and drooling mouths. Her essence was that of enhancement, to foster the growth of *another*. She was tired of granting her favors to the petty races that clustered about her in worship, begging for her fertility. She wanted to create something worth the effort of birth.

And Hastur could do that for her. Alone among the Great Old Ones that capriciously ruled existence, Hastur shared her passion for creation, albeit in a rather different fashion. He was the Living Muse, the Supreme Note of Art. His understanding of the subtle interplay between existence and decay was marvelous, and he loved the beauty found in madness and ambition. It left Shub-Niggurath a bit in awe, actually. He could see the universe in ways she never would. Long ago, he had seemed the ideal mate. His seed of inspiration would be fostered in the fertility of her womb and grow into something . . . something *glorious*.

In ancient times they had cemented their bond. The two lovers roamed the galaxies at their whim, planets shaking at their passing, even carving their true names into the face of Yuggoth's moon as a symbol of their commitment. When that wasn't enough they danced together in the Court of Azathoth, and the daemon-sultan's soul and messenger carried the news of their marriage to every corner of existence.

But that same temperament that made Hastur attractive had resulted in their present situation. Estranged over seemingly irreconcilable differences and living many light-years apart.

"I do not want you to be angry with me, Sheol." he said, paradoxically using his private pet name for her even though he knew it got on her nerves. Only three beings in existence knew her childhood name of Sheol-Nugganoth, and Shub-Niggurath aimed to keep it that way. If either of the other two had called her that, she would have given them a taste of what the Black Goat could do. But with Hastur it just made her wonder; why was he trying to aggravate her?

"But, you also know why I will not sire children." he continued, his expression a controlled calm.

"Yes, yes . . . your precious *art*." Shub-Niggurath said derisively.

"The King in Yellow *cannot* have a legitimate heir, it would defeat the point of the play. The royal succession must be contested."

With a huff to denote her growing annoyance, Shub-Niggurath shouted back, "Well excuse me if I am not particularly concerned about your damnable little play!"

Though Hastur's features worked to remain neutral, she could tell by the set of his jaw and the intensity of his glare that she had struck a nerve. But he appeared to refuse to allow his anger to get the better of him. That would turn this meeting into one more pointless argument, another link in a chain stretching back millenia. Shub-Niggurath's control was not so complete. Absolutely, she understood. Hastur's art was who he was, and asking him to deny that was exactly like asking her to deny her own fecundity. But damn it, why should his nature trump hers? Why did she have to be the one to sacrifice a part of herself for the sake of their relationship?

"You stubborn, insufferable *gnoph-hegg! Nafl-gnaiih li-hee fm'latgh n'gha!*" Shub-Niggurath cursed, her grasp of human words quickly failing to convey the depths of her anger. She stalked away from him, anger churning within her and radiating out into their surroundings. If he had been trying to upset her, it was working! Shub-Niggurath had always been notoriously prone to mood swings, and this human body amplified that aspect of her personality. Palpable waves of her frustration were felt by the lesser creatures watching them, who were quick to respond.

The waving branch-like limbs of the Dark Young flailed about in anger. Many of the *Byakhee* perched on them were snatched up before the flock could fully scramble up into the sky, and were dragged screeching and gnashing into the wet maws of Shub-Niggurath's brood. The two cults were similarly at each other's throats, stabbing at each other with curved daggers in fits of induced rage. All around them the woods erupted in violent conflict, the faintest reflection of the tension hanging between Shub-Niggurath and Hastur.

Pursing his lips, Hastur gave a complex little three-toned whistle and put an end to the violence just as quickly as it had begun. The sound of his whistle was carried through the woods on a sudden wind, and with it the warring cultists were rendered catatonic, the Young and the *Byakhee* pacified.

"This isn't what I wanted," Hastur said, stepping closer to his upset wife.

"And just what *do* you want?"

"I want us to be together again," he said a little more forcefully, "just as you do."

Shub-Niggurath spun to face him, her face flushed and eyes flashing. "We've said that before. It never gets us anywhere. Neither of us can give up our natures, so we're stuck . . ." Her voice faded. She felt defeated. Now they would argue over which was more important, then they would call a temporary truce, and Hastur would retreat back to Aldebaran to give Shub-Niggurath her space. And she would be alone again, with nothing but her misery for company.

Reaching out a hand and gently placing it on Shub-Niggurath's shoulder, Hastur drew her towards him. She allowed herself to be held with little struggle. Despite their ongoing fight, she could always count on Hastur's touch to comfort her, no matter the situation or what forms they occupied. "Why can't you just give me a baby?" she pleaded, hoping against reason that his answer would be different this time.

"Is that all you truly want? There are other adequate Great Old Ones that you could have courted by now, if you'd wished."

His answer slightly confused her. Wasn't it clear that she specifically wanted *his* child? Yes, that was clear. Which meant Hastur was hinting at something, trying to lead her to a particular conclusion with his mind-games.

"I could have, but they would only want me because of my fertility" she said, noticing that Hastur's disinterest in children put him clearly outside of that category. He wanted something else from her . . . and *ipso facto*, she wanted something else from him, as well. "I want *you*, Hastur. Your company, your attention, your imagination. But why must that mean we can never conceive?"

"Because there is something that I need to know. And you'll just have to trust that it is absolutely vital to me. More than my play or anything else I've ever asked of you before."

"Tell me what it is" she begged. Hastur's eyes caught her own, and she could see a deep regret in them. Regret . . . and hope, too.

"I cannot."

Hastur cradled her head against his shoulder, saying nothing else. Shub-Niggurath had missed this so much. The familiar feelings of intimacy seemed magnified by their corporeal forms. Shub-Niggurath felt her heart beating quicker, her throat clenching in on itself, and an almost magnetic quality drawing her in closer to her former lover. She could never feel this comfortable with any other entity in the entire cosmos, she knew, because she could *trust* him.

He had put the decision to her; her potential as a mother against her fulfillment as a wife. Every other time this question had been asked, she had chosen motherhood. It was the core of her being. She was the Black Goat of the Woods, She with a Thousand Young. And she realized that so far, that had given her very little satisfaction. What was motherhood without a child to nurture? How satisfying would even that be if she had no one to share the pride of parenthood with?

He was stroking her hair now, subtly calming her. Her arms wrapped around Hastur's sides, clutching him tightly. If she agreed to give up on parenthood, she would gain her lover in return. Hastur's entire being was a thing of mystery, and he had asked her to trust him. Trust that he wanted what was best for her and did not wish to hurt her. Could she risk her entire identity on his words alone? And what would be the cost if she didn't?

Shub-Niggurath pressed her face against Hastur's collar, letting the darkness and Hastur's arms envelop and soothe her. Perhaps it was foolish, perhaps her thoughts were influenced by the hormonal dependencies of the bodies they occupied, but she could not give this up again. She hated Hastur for making her choose between him and being true to her own nature. But still, for the first time in eons she found herself choosing him.

Her body softly shook in Hastur's arms, surprising him. Looking down he saw Shub-Niggurath's beautiful face streaked with tears. Concerned, he asked "Are you alright?"

"No, I'm not." she said weakly, her voice cracking. "I'm never going to have the children I want."

Her deep frown split her face, and the sympathetic look on Hastur made her want to cry even more. This body was full of unexpected and inconvenient physiological reactions. She didn't want to spread this pain to Hastur as well. Restraining her sobs, she said "But I'm happy too. Well, I will be happy soon, anyway. We'll finally be together again."

The look of hopefulness returned to her husband's features, and Shub-Niggurath got the impression he was desperate to say something, but could not.

"Please, take me away from here," she said, waving an arm to indicate the woods, and probably the Earth as a whole. "This cradle that I have prepared will only depress me now, reminding me of what I have given up."

"Thank you." Hastur whispered.

"You can thank me by taking me someplace far, far away," she said bitterly. "Procyon, or Thuban perhaps. I don't care really, so long as it is as barren as I am."

"Not just yet. We have much to do here, amidst this 'cradle' you've fashioned from this world." Hastur said.

Shub-Niggurath was quite drained already . . . couldn't he grant her this one mercy and take her someplace they could rest? She at least deserved that much, after what she had just sacrificed. Walking a short distance, eager to find some new setting to share with her husband, Shub-Niggurath glanced at the comatose forms of her cultists scattered about. Their minds had been dissolved by a touch from Hastur's will, but their bodies remained to remind her of the constant worship she received. If she was to be doomed to never bear children because of her choice, then she wanted no distractions. She would have her husband, and he would have her, and nothing else would come between them.

If he insisted on keeping her here on Earth, then she would sweep aside all life just to have the privacy she craved. It would do her good to vent some of the anger she felt, too. No cultist or sorcerer or intrepid investigator would remain to disturb her grief.

"You don't know how much I regretted having to deceive you Sheol, but as I said, it really was necessary. I needed you to show me that when it came down to it, you really did care about us, rather then simply following your urge to procreate. But now that you have—"

"Now that I have, can we at least shed these frail little bodies? I would much rather be something with an excess of teeth right now, and some horns as well."

Hastur walked after her, catching up in a few long strides. With a short laugh he caught her by the hand and turned Shub-Niggurath to face him. "There will be time for that soon enough. But first—"

"Good!" Shub-Niggurath interrupted him, her short temper displaying itself again. "If I cannot create, then perhaps it would please me to destroy instead!"

"I will be happy to father your child." Hastur blurted out, before his wife got carried away with her rant or started to make good on her threats. Needless to say, his announcement did its job and took the breath out of Shub-Niggurath's lungs. A pregnant pause passed as she simply stared at him, disbelieving.

*"WHAT?!"* Shub-Niggurath yelled at length, totally in shock.

Hastur laughed, though Shub-Niggurath did not join in. What sick joke was this? "You mean you lied . . . kept me barren and yourself exiled to a distant star. For forty million years. As what? A test?!"

"And you passed!" he exclaimed joyously.

Shub-Niggurath slapped him across the face, sending Hastur reeling.

When he had recovered, he was still grinning. "I knew that our fundamental natures were at odds with one another. Which is mostly my fault. True Art refuses to compromise, or explain itself."

"That's true." Shub-Niggurath grudgingly agreed, "You're terrible at doing both."

"So I've changed the situation. Now that you've agreed to go without procreation, it has turned our potential offspring from a compromise... into Art itself."

Her brow creased in confusion. Shub-Niggurath could barely follow Hastur's logic. Because she desired him so greatly that she would betray her own being . . . and to make her happy in return he was willing to ruin his greatest work, his lauded play *The King in Yellow* . . . that somehow made their child a greater conceptual perfection than the mere combination of the two Great Old Ones. A sum greater than the whole of its parts. It made her fragile human brain hurt to think about it, but Shub-Niggurath understood.

Their natures were no longer in conflict, but instead working towards a common goal. Shub-Niggurath's face brightened, and she flung herself into Hastur's arms. It had taken them far too long, but the stalemate was broken.

"You know, I think I should perhaps still be angry with you." Shub-Niggurath said, though the smile on her face said otherwise.

"Perhaps." Hastur agreed.

"And I think that sometime you should probably still make it up to me."

"Probably." he agreed again, with a slight incline of his head.

"But right now I'm too happy for that. I would rather take you down to N'kai where it is private and dark and—"

Her words were interrupted by Hastur's lips pressing against her own. These human bodies . . . a novelty indeed! Shub-Niggurath's immediate concerns melted away, replaced by her familiar trust in Hastur. They would make sure everything went as they wished it to be, in time. When their embrace ended Hastur looked into Shub-Niggurath's eyes, trying to find the right words. Finally, he said:

"Y'haa leuh-rhth cf'ayak, Shub-Niggurath."

Blinking away a few more inconvenient tears, Shub-Niggurath smiled and answered back: "Y'leur-rhth cf'ayak syha'h, Hastur."

She stole a quick kiss, and added a soft "Ia!"

# THE COVENANT

Kim Paffenroth

As many readers of Herman Melville's Moby-Dick are aware, a most curious thing happens in Chapter 23 of this novel. A character from Chapter 3, Bulkington, reappears in Chapter 23, where the narrator, Ishmael, makes an impassioned and very eloquent meditation on the meaning of this man and his life. And yet, this man who seems so important and full of meaning then disappears from the narrative and plays no part in the further adventures of the Pequod and her crew. In a novel which many consider one of the greatest ever written, but which is also acknowledged to be full of false starts and dead ends, Chapter 23 has been put down as just another example of poor editing. Until now, the only defense that could be offered by those of us who are Melville's admirers was something along the lines of Horace's observation that "Sometimes even Homer nods."

You can therefore imagine my excitement when I discovered the following manuscript, which appears to be a quite different version of Chapter 23. In it the obscure character Bulkington does not reappear. Instead, we are granted our first glimpse of the mysterious Captain Ahab and tantalized with allusions to much of the action and themes of the rest of novel. Some of the images that are much milder in the final version of Chapter 23 appear here in a darker, more scandalous, more blasphemous setting. It is certainly a chapter that would have substantiated the claim Melville made elsewhere that, "I have written a wicked book, and feel as spotless as the lamb." I offer it here to you in its entirety, without comment or emendation.

# Chapter 23
## The Covenant

HEN ON THAT SHIVERING WINTER'S NIGHT, the *Pequod* thrust her vindictive bows into the cold malicious waves, who should I see standing on the blighted deck but Captain Ahab? Surely many a man before the mast is as tall and gaunt as the figure I saw before me that dread night, defiantly erect and angular as a gallows, and as grim and bleak as the men who ascend those fateful steps. But the one point of his appearance that made it clear I now beheld the captain of the ship was one that I doubt very many men possess. I had heard hushed whispers of this detail since boarding the ship. For it was said that the captain of the *Pequod* strode about the deck on one living leg made of human bone, and a dead one made of the jaw bone of his eternal and implacable foe, the giant sperm whale. The human original of this limb had been taken in furious combat off the coast of Japan, and since then Ahab had hobbled along on a cold, inflexible tool that was both grim reminder and hideous trophy of his indomitable—some would say mad—attacks on these monsters of the deep.

I looked with sympathetic awe and fearfulness upon the man who, so recently landed from a dangerous voyage, could so unrestingly push off again for still another tempestuous term. The land seemed scorching to his one, live foot, while the other perhaps mystically longed for the roll of its original home, drawn inexorably once again toward the briny blast that now harshly but lovingly embraced it and all of the horrifying captain on this wolfish, remorseless night. Wonderfullest things are ever the unmentionable; deep memories yield no epitaphs. Such was Ahab, and such was his leg as he made his way across the storm-swept deck and to his cabin.

I did not then know what dread and dire force it was that bid me follow my new captain below decks, though in the subsequent few lines the reader will discover, as I did that night. Elijah's predictions in port had attuned me to the daemonic on this voyage, and whatever lurked about the captain of this doomed vessel demanded that I investigate further. That night it seemed I could no more refuse the siren call to follow Ahab than I could willfully stop myself from breathing for more than a few moments. And it almost seemed that something fatefully conspired to aid me in my clandestine pursuit, for when the captain entered his cabin, the door was left slightly ajar. Standing outside it, my heart pounding and the blood singing in my ears, I could see within, but at various and nightmarish angles as the ship pitched and yawed and the tiny door swung back and forth, revealing sometimes more, sometimes less of my captain and his nocturnal activities. The first thing he did in his cabin, after lighting several lamps, was to open the window wide onto the storm. The wind whipped about the enclosed space, and Ahab's coat flapped in the gale as he stepped away from the window. The lamps flickered, but shielded in their glass enclosures as they were, the wan flames continued to illuminate the room, however weakly and wretchedly.

The wounded king of this domain crossed his cabin and opened a cabinet, producing a large, thick tome. It was bound in the shiniest, blackest sharkskin I'd ever seen. No shark was that color; heathenish curing of the predator's hide must have turned it that inky, unnatural hue. Even in the dim light, it shimmered brightly with an unearthly iridescence, slightly tinged with blue, as Ahab held it above his head. He then brought it down, murmuring the whole time in what sounded to me like the language of the Romish sect. When the volume was in front of his wizened face, he brought it to his sere lips and kissed it, then laid it on the table before him. He unfastened the black metal lock that held it shut, and slowly turned the pages, still murmuring. The wind from the open window blew the pages about, but Ahab held them down with both hands as he searched for the right place, whatever his intent was this night. When he had found it, he lifted his eyes heavenward and the murmuring rose till I could make out the final syllables, before he slammed the book shut: "In nomine Dagoni!"

He stood there, leaning forward on his fists, pressed down on top of the ancient and malignant book. The gale blowing in the window seemed to increase, taking Ahab's hat off, so that now his grey locks blew about freely in the tempest. In the flickering lamplight, I fancied his hairs were like those of the ancient gorgons—wild and maddened snakes writhing from out of his overheated brain. Ahab's eyes narrowed and he howled back into the storm's fury, "Father Dagon! As a priest of thy Order, thou wilt hear me! Dost thou know me, Father?! For I am thy Son and would have words with thee!"

The wind died, with a suddenness the likes I'd never seen before or since. It vanished, leaving me there more in terror of its uncanny absence than I had been at its awesome power. Ahab remained like a statue at his table, staring out the window into the blackest night that was surely a mirror of his forsaken soul. It was then that I heard a wet, slapping sound, but on account of my limited visibility into the cabin, I could not see its source. The sound was repeated, and now accompanied by a wet gurgling. It was then that I could see two tentacles come in from the side of the room on which was the window. They were a dark green color, dangling long strands of sea grasses and shining moistly in the lamplight. Much more horrible than the tentacles, however, was that they were attached at the shoulders to the frame of a man, and between them was a human head. Seaweed for hair and skin a translucent grey, it looked up at Ahab with enormous black eyes that were as cold and soulless as Ahab's were burning hot with the intensity of his enraged and unholy spirit. The tentacles pulled the creature along the floor of Ahab's cabin till I could see that its lower half was that of an enormous fish, the same color and iridescence as Ahab's eldritch book. The tentacles finally reached Ahab's table and pulled the creature up to sit across from the mad Nantucketer.

The being gave two long blinks with its watery, obsidian eyes. "Aye, Ahab? What wouldst thou, of all people, have with me?"

Ahab stood to his full height. The very spawn of hell appeared to sit across from him, yet he stood there as disdainful as a Stoic philosopher or a Roman emperor before some primitive being, some recalcitrant slave, some truculent child. "I have come to acknowledge thy paternity, Father, by the ancient rites, and ask for my birthright."

I believe the being gave a laugh, but it sounded more like a shark vomiting forth a jelly fish, it was so wet and bilious. "Oh, ye Nantucketers! For nigh on thirty centuries I have lured or aided men to the wide and unforgiving seas. Sometimes I demand much of them, sometimes they demand much of me. But ne'er has any tribe of mortals had the effrontery of ye Nantucketers! The industrious Philistines, the bear-like Norsemen, the greedy Spaniards—all casting their barks onto seas they had no business even thinking to cross! Oh, but ye Nantucketers! No one has thought to put themselves on a nasty spit of sand, a pathetic and vulnerable little besiegement far behind enemy lines, eat my children for every meal of every day of their spiteful, bellicose lives, then put to sea to do war with me, finally even butchering my most beautiful and sublime children, my beloved Leviathans . . . and now dare to call me Father! And mean it!"

Ahab gave a sneer. "I'll grant thee, 'tis been a long and strained relationship, like many a father and son, I'll warrant. But we are thy children. We have forsaken everything to be so. And thou wilt acknowledge us."

"Oddly enough, Ahab, I would be right glad to do so. But forsaken? Thou hardly knowest the meaning of forsaken. Thou hardly knowest the meaning of sacrifice. Ye at least give as good as ye get, most days. In the time since I crawled up into thy miserable little cell here, a thousand beings as good as thou have died screaming and begging for my help. And thou thinkest thou hast suffered?"

Ahab swung the bone leg up onto the table with a loud thud that made me jump. He steadied himself by holding on to the table with both hands, drawing breath through clenched teeth, then continuing in a lower voice. "I care not a whit for them. There be a piece of me down there in thy darkness, and I'll give up all claim on the light if thou wilt help me find out why."

The right tentacle came up to rest on the table, and the being leaned its human head on it. "Oh, Ahab, I feared thou wert after such a mad object. If it were killin' thou wert after, I'd settle thee in my books in no time. But this tricky little bit of *why*—that be something else entirely."

He nodded to the dead leg. "The Father of us all has been dismasting and unmanning us for a hundred hundreds of years, Son. I am one of the Old Ones and I have no idea why *I'm* here, so I can hardly offer thee any help with thy quest, I fear."

Ahab swung the leg back to the deck and again stood to his full height. "Very well. Thou leavest me no choice, Father. What canst thou give me, then?"

The creature smiled, the wide and deep grin of a shark, revealing rows of irregular and razor-sharp teeth, dark and deadly. "Choice, Son? I do not know if we ever have a choice. I am fairly sure I never did. But 'tis good, Son, 'tis right good. 'Tis the mark of a man, when he learns to accept what he can't change. And if not knowledge, Son, I canst still give thee much. Power over every force of Nature. No Mother to ye, Son, will Nature be, but only a stepmother who flees from thy power and wrath."

"Good, Father, 'tis good. And be there naught else?"

"Oh, aye. Power over men's minds. To thy inexorable will they will bend. Like slivers of metal to the most potent loadstone, they will come into line with the course thy soul dictates, the iron rails down which it rolls. Will this be enough for thy task, Ahab?"

"Aye, 'twill do."

"But there must be some offering on thy part, some gift to balance the favor for which thou dost ask."

"Aye, Father Dagon. I know." Ahab clumped to the back corner of his cabin, and returned to the table with a large carpetbag. He hoisted it up onto the table before his deity and opened it. "A fine Father thou art. No pathetic little gifts of foodstuffs. No furtive and horrible murders of infants. Thy Sons always brought before thee their trophies of war, as real men should. Here are some of mine, Father."

The tentacles reached in and pulled out two sperm whales' jawbones. "Oh, Ahab. So much killing already, and thou wantest more?" Those jawbones were returned to the bag, and the being took out two smaller ones. "The poor orca, Ahab? Not enough oil in that poor fish to bother, I would have thought."

"It did attack my kill, a mighty spermaceti, lashed to the side of the ship. 'Twas a hard won prize, and I'd have none of the maraudings of some lesser predator. The hyena dost know to stay away from the lion's kill. Or should."

"Very well, Son. I know of thy needs, and I know of thy prowess in battle. I will find a fit resting place for these relics. Thy offering is acceptable, if sorrowful to me. Now, what dost thou need help in killing?"

Ahab crossed his arms before his aged but powerful chest, across his too-large heart. "The White Whale, the one they call Moby Dick."

The tentacle flopped back onto the table, hitting it with a loud, wet slap. "No! I'll grant thee that to which I have agreed, but I'll have naught to do with killing my own Son! I'll leave thee right now if thou sayest such blasphemy again! A Father help kill a Son! And a God committing the horrible crime, no less! Who e'er heard of such blasphemy?!"

Ahab smiled a humorless, closed-mouth smirk. "Some would say that the White Man's God once did just that."

The being leaned closer to Ahab, and a piece of seaweed by its right eye rose. "What, Ahab, art thou not a white man? No? Some dark, savage wolf in white sheep's clothing? Aye, I suppose thou art such a one. Well, Son, some sweet young bride waiting for thee back in ole Nantucket might say that the Father had the Son lay down His life. Mayhap she'll even raise thy son to believe such nonsense. A few fools, and knaves, and a handful of hardier souls with deeper eyes, such as thy first mate, might believe such. But not thou, Ahab." Those two huge, shiny black orbs turned towards me, and it instantly felt as though the briny wash from under a Lapland iceberg was flowing out from my heart into every vessel and tissue of my body. After one beat it was already in my forehead, and all thoughts seemed to stop and focus on those empty, bottomless, black wells. "And not that greenhorn outside, either."

Ahab turned, and now his fiery eyes were nailed to me as well. "Come in, boy," he commanded quietly but firmly. "I thought someone was about, but suspected Father Dagon intended it as some part of these adoption proceedings."

I took a step forward, opened the door, and entered the cabin with the madman and the monster. The room was icy cold, and the smell was like a Nova Scotia cannery, brimming over with the rich and vital mortality of the deep. "We must have a witness, Ahab, to our covenant," the tentacled one said across its shark teeth.

"Ne'er been on board a whaler, I daresay," Ahab said as he looked me over.

I barely found my voice, and it was a raspy whisper. "No, sir. Merchant ships many times."

Ahab laughed with real mirth, breaking some of the tension of the horror in his cabin, while from across the table there was the sound of another jelly fish being coughed up. "Leave him be, Ahab. He ne'er would have seen the likes of me, even if he'd been before a whaler's mast his whole life. Not all my children are elder sons, Ahab. He will serve his task, I think, for I do need an evangelist, Ahab, and thou wert never the literary sort. This one looks like he could spin a yarn worthy of Dagon and his favorite Son. And thou needst one to escape to tell thy tale."

Ahab's flame-rimmed eyes held me in place. "What is thy name, Son?"

I barely managed to breathe, "Ishmael, sir."

Ahab nodded. "A fine name. Some of the Nantucket surf may yet flow in thy green veins, boy. Some of her soulful sand may yet cling to thy follicles and tear thy mortal flesh." He slid the hellish tome across the table towards me. "Dost thou swear it, Son, to be my acolyte, and the evangelist of our Father Dagon? Put thy hand on the ancient writ of all wandering, cursed Sons, and swear it."

My mouth hung open, but no sound came. My hands stayed limply at my sides.

The thing he called Dagon spoke. "Now is the time when choice is of the essence, Ahab. He must choose this calling. Thou canst not force him."

Ahab took a step towards me, and with a surprising gentleness took my right hand and placed it on the book. The book was slimy and cold; Ahab's hand, like the burning sands of some unknown beach on a lost world. "See, boy? 'Tis but a book. And thy words—so much breath, so much empty vanity, as that Hebrew sage Solomon would remind us. Swear it, and follow me into the eternal infinite."

"Thou must tell him the cost, Ahab."

"Aye, 'tis true, Father. One should always know the price, 'tis what makes one appreciate the bargain all the more." His eyes bore and burned into me. "Harbor, Son, safe harbor, is the price of being Dagon's Son, of being a true Nantucketer."

I nodded. Whether from heart or brain, I know not, but the words came. "I will neither seek nor have any harbor, evermore."

Ahab's hand squeezed mine with something like paternity; it was, at least, like sympathy and appreciation. "Good, Son. Thou knowest that the port is pitiful; in the port is safety, comfort, hearthstone, supper, warm blankets, friends, all that's kind to our mortalities. Glimpses dost thou seem to see of that mortally intolerable truth; that all deep, earnest thinking is but the intrepid effort of the soul to keep the open independence of her sea, while the wildest winds of heaven and earth conspire to cast her on the treacherous, slavish shore?"

"I do see, captain."

"Good, for in landlessness alone resides the highest truth, shoreless, indefinite as God. So 'tis better to perish in that howling infinite, than be ingloriously dashed upon the lee, even if that were safety! Bear thee grimly, demigod! Up from the spray of thy ocean-perishing, straight up, leaps thy apotheosis!"

Ahab turned to his other-worldly guest. "Thou hast what thou needst, Father. We are now thy Sons, thy evangelist and thy eldest, the Sons of thy covenant."

The thing called Dagon took his bag of offerings, turned and slithered back to the open window. He turned back towards us for one moment, as the winds began once again to whirl about him and into the cabin. "Yes, Ahab. And now I can only leave you to your Fate, over which I have no control or knowledge. I would give you my love, but I have none."

"I did once, Father, but have none left, only the barest savor of it that I share with my doomed siblings, like this fellow wraith here."

"I know, Son. 'Tis the way with my children." And with that, my newly adoptive Father turned and slipped from the window into the loveless, infinite sea below.

# THE HINDENBURG MANIFESTO

Lee Clark Zumpe

## Prelude

> At 2 a.m. today when I visited the town, the whole of it was a horrible sight, flaming from end to end. The reflection of the flames could be seen in the clouds of smoke above the mountains from ten miles away. Throughout the night houses were falling until the streets became long heaps of red, impenetrable debris.
>
> Many of the civilian survivors took the long trek from Guernica to Bilbao in antique solid-wheeled Basque farm-carts drawn by oxen. Carts piled high with such household possessions as could be saved from the conflagration clogged the roads all night.

George Steer. The Times. April 27. 1937

THE PATIENT'S NAME WAS MAX DEWART. His hollow cheeks and sunken eyes demonstrated chronic malnourishment. Though the facility's clerical office had made inquiries, little had been ascertained about his life before he had been institutionalized.

"What do you remember from your dreams?" Dr. Sid Tasic, a short, stout man with greasy salt-and-pepper hair plastered to his pasty scalp, slumped forward on a stool at the foot of the bed. "Tell us everything you can."

"Flashes of red, brilliant bright red, the night sky ruptured by crimson light . . . and the earth beneath my feet trembling, again and again, like some angry god was pounding the landscape." The patient fidgeted anxiously, biting at his cuticles until they bled. He perched on the edge of his soiled cot, his knees tight against his chest, rocking back and forth. The screams of persistent nightmares filled the Arkham Sanitarium. "They follow him, don't they? Their uniformed legions, their synchronized squadrons that blot out the stars, they hear and obey. There is such beauty in destruction, such pleasure to be found in ravaging the work of man."

"Who do they follow?" The doctor glanced at another man in the room, a man who worked for the government. Corey Kaswell visited the facility often, transcribed the testimony of its piteous, demented residents. Though he rarely commented on his findings, the doctor understood that he sought a pattern to the phenomenon that plagued asylums all over the country. "Whose name do hear in your dreams?"

"Don't you know? The crawling chaos," the patient said, trying to stifle a maniacal giggle. "Nyarlathotep, of course."

# One

> Those who once stood against the darkness have been ousted, their champions shunned, their wisdom suppressed and their counsel ignored. In their absence, civilization takes no notice as its cities perish, its monuments crumble and its armies, swept up in pointless conflict, fall.

*Erich Christoph von Goerdeler,*
*personal memoirs, 1937*

THE FORMER BÜRGERMEISTER OF Königsberg waited patiently, desperately trying to blend in with the crowd. His paperwork—professionally forged—had apparently raised no concerns among the omnipresent Nazi authorities. So long as no one who knew him noticed him, all would go as planned.

In a few hours, he would be en route to America, leaving behind most of his possessions. He had no reason to believe he would ever be allowed to return . . . . . . and every reason to believe that should he return, he would be thrown into a prison or suffer an even more appalling end.

Every pair of eyes that scrutinized him, every lingering glance and suspicious stare made him squirm. Sweat cascaded down his pallid face in serpentine trails. He glanced nervously at his watch, fixating on the lethargic progress of the secondhand. Time, he mused, had adjusted its pace to torture him. He immediately brushed aside the thought as abject paranoia . . . but if those things he knew to exist beyond the acuity of man could so effortlessly warp space and devour stars, then surely they could influence the measure of time.

For now, he could not dwell on such abstract worries: He had more pressing issues with which to deal. A group of uniformed Gestapo officers swaggered across the room toward the check-in desk.

Still hours until the passengers would begin boarding, the man did his best to conceal his fear.

# Two

Saturday, May 8, 1:49 A.M.

> *Besides the halls and galleries, the theaters of royal estate, there are mysterious passages and sequestered nooks that whisper a thousand secret histories.*

Francis Loring Payne.
The Story of Versailles. 1919

TWO GRIM-FACED MEN SAT FACING EACH OTHER, each perched atop a stool on either side of a makeshift bar stained with liquor, sweat and blood. No words had been exchanged in well over an hour when the howl of an alley cat outside stirred them from silent contemplation.

"He's likely dead. You realize that, don't you?" Wallace Welles, a former New York City beat cop turned night watchman for Manhattan clothiers Brooks Brothers, seized a gin and tonic off the bar without spilling a single drop. He put the glass to his lips, jerked his head back and gulped, wincing like he had just taken a wallop to his gut from the Bulldog of Bergen. Cigarette smoke floated overhead in a hazy, spectral miasma. "He'd have been here by now. He'd have made contact with one of us."

"All we can do is wait," David Oldrock said, though he shared his companion's pessimism. He lowered the pulp magazine that had kept him from dozing all evening. The two seemed an odd pair: Oldrock, a bookish academic with disheveled straw hair and a terminally peaked countenance, wore a bottle-green blazer and slate-colored slacks. Welles' charcoal-colored eyes matched his business-like, square-shouldered, double-breasted, narrow-striped suit with long, baggy trousers. The two had been tapped by their organization to rendezvous with a German named Erich Christoph von Goerdeler in the bowels of Hell's Kitchen. "The *New York Times* said that more than half of the passengers survived. He may yet show up."

"He was probably traveling under an assumed name, maybe even as a stowaway," Welles said, massaging the furrows in his brow. Shadows mocked the unmotivated light radiating from a single bulb in the dank, deserted former speakeasy. Since the end of Prohibition, all the significant late-night action took place in trendy, crowded nightclubs run by gangsters. Basements and backrooms had become the refuge of more noble crusaders—sanctuaries for vigilant and perceptive individuals who sensed an imminent, unnamed threat. "Hell, he may not have even come. We're probably waiting for a ghost."

"It's still early," Oldrock said, glancing at his watch. It was almost 2 a.m. A copy of the previous day's edition of the *Times* had been unceremoniously dismissed, though its banner headline remained painfully legible from the floor— "*Hindenburg* burns in Lakehurst crash." Their informant, von Goerdeler, had stated in an encrypted message that he would be traveling on board the zeppelin, carrying crucial information to corroborate their suspicions about the impending war, about alliances being formed with powerful, unearthly entities. The German had requested the meeting following the recent unexpected death of an American writer—a man known to have had certain prophetic visions. "I don't plan on leaving until just before sunrise. If this von Goerdeler can actually supply all the records he claims to possess, it will change everything."

"And if he's dead . . . and the material has been destroyed; or worse, fallen into less sympathetic hands?" Welles shook his head and stared at his pudgy fingers. "I've spent half my life chasing things—indescribable things—through the sewers of this great, old, terrible city of unnumbered crimes," Welles said, his body slumping over the bar. Only forty-five years old, his posture and his demeanor added twenty years to his appearance. "For what? So some muck-raking journalist could ridicule me for suggesting that there may be more out there than thugs in pinstriped suits?"

An officious investigative reporter with a flair for lurid, tabloid tales had published a piece on Welles' regrettable comments regarding a series of murders eventually attributed to the Grey Man, Albert Hamilton Fish. The story—and the public uproar it generated—ultimately cost him his job as a flatfoot. He had been in a tailspin ever since. "Nothing has changed since then. Even if we manage to come up with unassailable evidence, no one will believe us."

"They don't have to believe us, Wallace," Oldrock said, patting his companion on the shoulder. "It's best that they don't, really. If people really knew what was happening, they wouldn't have time to live, would they? They'd be too busy trying to cope with their fear."

"They should be afraid," Welles quickly said, pummeling the bar with a red fist. "They should fear what has been hidden from them for so long, fear what is coming. Fear is healthy . . . keeps you sharp, cautious, wary. Ignorance has left humanity vulnerable and reckless. That is why the tide is turning, why those with dark designs have been able to easily manipulate the course of events to suit their purpose."

"Right now, Wallace, it's all just speculation and legend." Oldrock, a professor of English literature who had taught at prestigious schools throughout New England, allowed himself to resume thumbing through the pages of a recent issue of *Doc Savage Magazine*. He had already plowed through the feature story, Kenneth Robeson's "The South Pole Terror," and was trying to persuade himself to embark on a short yarn penned by Frederick R. Gibbs called "The Vanishing Barges."

"Those who would communicate the secret doctrines which accurately depict our civilization's genesis and justification do so in codes and riddles and ciphers and symbols. We can't be sure where fact ends and fiction begins."

The group to which Welles and Oldrock belonged had itself been founded on little more than anecdotal tales and the muddled memories of a few elderly citizens claiming to have seen impossible things. Calling themselves Seekers of Forbidden Wisdom, twenty like-minded men had first convened in an abandoned church in Arkham, Mass., on Sept. 29, 1929, to share whispered rumors and implausible accounts. They questioned the widely-accepted version of truth as dictated by preachers, politicians and intellectuals.

"Why do we keep up this charade, Mr. Oldrock?" Welles stood, stretched his legs and tilted his head from side to side until an audible pop ricocheted off the far wall. He forsook the circle of light, prowling the dim shadows that inundated the room. "Have you ever asked yourself that question?"

"We all have, Wallace," Oldrock said.

"For me, it's partly legacy, I suppose," Welles admitted. His grandfather had told him about a distant relative who had devoted his life to battling nameless inexplicable horrors for an avant-garde, orphic fraternity of academicians and literati known only as Sodalitas Invictus.

That organization, however, had ceased to exist near the end of the last century. Whether its surviving members had simultaneously renounced their undertaking or the group had been forcibly disbanded no one could say. Its last known gathering allegedly took place in Versailles in 1889, the year the Eiffel Tower was constructed. All that, though, amounted to nothing more than hearsay and unconfirmed reports. The German promised verifiable documents proving the existence of Sodalitas Invictus. "We fancy ourselves the next legion of soldiers in this honorable campaign, successors of countless generations of nameless guardians and faceless sentinels. Even as history overlooks them, we honor our predecessors, though we know very little about them."

"Historians are always inclined to record the names of those whose wealth or influence or notoriety may benefit them, directly or indirectly," Oldrock said. "Those who actually steer the course of civilization are seldom praised or penalized."

"What about the prophets, Mr. Oldrock?" Welles lingered just outside the glow of the light, darkness fervently veiling his weary eyes. He referred to the unfortunate inmates of Arkham Sanitarium whose deranged and apocalyptic visions seemed to be glimpses of approaching catastrophic events. "What about those whose unsolicited clairvoyance has imparted nightmarish dreams, intuitive revelations and the names of our would-be overlords. How will historians remember them?"

"If they are wrong, historians will not waste so much as a footnote upon them."

"And if those who hear the name 'Nyarlathotep' whispered in their dark dreams are shown to be genuine seers?"

"If what they claim to see comes to pass," Oldrock said, "then, it does not matter how history remembers them. There will be no one left to read the works of historians."

The sudden sound of footsteps in the alley brought an abrupt end to their melancholy discourse.

"The German is dead." Corey Kaswell's words resonated through the room before he emerged from the shadows. Kaswell, now in his late sixties, had helped found the Seekers of Forbidden Wisdom and continued to be its principal facilitator and unifying force, he reported the news with more than a hint of disgust. What he said next, though, took both Welles and Oldrock by surprise. "They killed him. They killed all those people to keep the truth from getting out."

"What are you saying?" Welles shuddered at the implication.

"Someone didn't want us to hear what von Goerdeler had to say," Kaswell said. "It's clear to me who was behind this massacre."

"Then it's over. There's little more we can do," Welles said. His defeatist attitude aggravated Kaswell, who shot him a disapproving glance. "What," he said, sensing Kaswell's dissatisfaction. "Do we go back to our dim little caves and listen to the grave predictions of madmen and speculate about the end of the world? What good does that do?"

"I know someone," Kaswell said, a look of self-satisfaction momentarily displacing his scowl. The only member of the group connected to a government agency, Kaswell served as an agent of the Bureau of Investigation until 1931 when he became involved in a new incarnation of the State Department's Black Chamber, a cryptanalytic organization. Through his profession he had established a network of contacts and stool pigeons. "And I happen to know that at least some fragments of von Goerdeler's manifesto were recovered amidst the wreckage. I'll be driving to Lakehurst in the morning to claim the papers personally." Kaswell leaned against the bar and drew his associates close. "I know this may sound outlandish, but it is imperative that other members of our group remain unaware of this conversation. It is possible that someone among us is not who—or what—they seem to be."

One by one, they shuffled out into the sticky, stifling streets that had seen bountiful bloodshed over the last century—the same streets where the Dead Rabbits and the Roach Guards clashed in bloody battles, where the Gopher Gang reigned from their stronghold inside Mallet Murphy's Battle Row Saloon, where Big Bill Dwyer and Owney Madden forged a bootlegging empire during Prohibition, where a faceless seer now corrupted the minds of his victims with unsettling revelations. Each man felt the city slowly succumbing to an alien influence just as the sickly moon's ghastly radiance pathetically capitulated to the dominion of darkness. Each man sensed the implicit threat of butchered armies, starving children, mass graves and dusty ruins.

Each man heard the name "Nyarlathotep."

# Three

Saturday, May 8, 1:13 P.M.

*There is no doubt that here and then were developed the rude, powerful, terrible "ice-giants" of the legends, out of whose ferocity, courage, vigor, and irresistible energy have been evolved the dominant races of the west of Europe—the land-grasping, conquering, colonizing races . . . They are now taking possession of the globe. Great races are the weeded-out survivors of great sufferings.*

Ignatius Donnelly,
*Ragnarok: The Age of Fire and Gravel.*
1883

KONRAD GEMPP AND ERWIN BONHOEFFER inspected the wreckage scattered across the field. Posing as assessors from Luftschiffbau Zeppelin, builders of the ill-fated *Hindenburg*, the two men searched the debris for any trace of von Goerdeler's dossier. Assigned by the Abwehr, the German intelligence organization, the agents were tall with broad shoulders and slicked-back blonde hair so golden it almost sparkled in the sun. So physically analogous they could have been brothers, their glossy eyes of sapphire blue softened their chiseled features.

"We are late," Gempp said quietly, mindful of the Americans' vigilant surveillance. Before the men had been allowed to examine the crash site, they had been detained for several hours for identity confirmation. "The interrogation may have cost us our objective."

"I don't expect to find anything. Herr Vermehren would not have resorted to this spectacle unless he was certain the documents would be destroyed." Bonhoeffer squatted, prodded a bit of charred flesh with his pen. Ants scattered at the disturbance. "Canaris will not be pleased, nonetheless."

"You assume Vermehren was responsible for this," Gempp said. Vermehren, hand-picked by Wihelm Canaris, had been trying to intercept and apprehend a traitorous German smuggling restricted material to unknown foreign emissaries. "It is possible that this was nothing more than an unfortunate accident. Von Goerdeler may have survived."

"If that is so," Bonhoeffer said, "let us hope our Egyptian colleague is more fortunate than we have been today." He hesitated, staring up into the blue skies. The Abwehr had assigned the agents an expatriated Egyptian mystic as an advisor regarding matters of the occult which affected their assignment. Though he pledged allegiance to Rome and Berlin, he maintained ties with a dissident brotherhood based in Ismailia that sought the ouster of King Farouk. He possessed a disquieting quality and threatening eyes that evoked ancient acts of pagan immorality. "What do you think of him, anyway?"

"He comes with the proper recommendations," Gempp said. "And he professes intimate knowledge of the material thought to be in the documents."

"But, do you *trust* him?"

"I trust no one who does not share our common ancestral pedigree—particularly those who seem to have no verifiable history other than the testimony of Italian officials." Nodding and smiling amiably at the American officials who had grilled them hours earlier, the Nazi spies continued their search. "Speaking of defectors, once we're done here, we have business with our American collaborator. Apparently, he lacks the fortitude to carry out simple assassinations."

"Perhaps our Egyptian friend can help us dispose of the bodies . . ."

# Four

> *Its wards lined cot to cot with seared and broken survivors of the Hindenburg disaster, the Paul Kimball Hospital was a house of agony and horror today.*

*Marguerite Mooers Marshall.*
*New York Evening World*

COREY KASWELL SAT IN AN UNCOMFORTABLE CHAIR at the German's bedside. It had taken hours to locate him in the hospital. Von Goerdeler, like so many others in the ward, had suffered broken bones and extensive burns over most of his body. His clothes had to be cut away from the remnants of his flesh. Bandages covered his face, cloaking his identity. Kaswell knew that only his disfigurement had kept him from being discovered by other government agents who had differing agendas—agents who sought the documents he had been carrying.

The only doctor willing to speak with Kaswell offered little hope.

"He's being kept under opiates," the doctor explained. "Otherwise, the pain would drive him mad."

"What are his chances?"

"Of recovery—none." The doctor appeared aggravated by the momentary distraction. Kaswell had only managed to divert him by showing him his government credentials. "And there's not much hope he'll regain consciousness. I expect that he'll die before the end of the day."

Kaswell had known of von Goerdeler's condition before he arrived. Even though the German could not communicate, every precaution was taken to protect his identity. Kaswell had lied to his most trusted friends. He had filed a report with his Washington, D.C. overseers stating that von Goerdeler had never even been on the *Hindenburg*, that the entire incident had been an intricate ruse to ensnare American spies.

Unlike other members of the Seekers, Kaswell had discerned the network that connected recent events. He had gleaned information about certain Nazi experiments that had inadvertently magnified existing ultrasonic sound beams that had been emanating from an unknown source in the South Pacific. Though technology had not yet caught up with conjecture, he had been told that an advanced ultrasonic beam could theoretically be directed inside a person's skull, allowing them to "hear" a transmission that no other person would be capable of detecting.

That phenomenon, he believed, had resulted in an epidemic of apocalyptic dreams united by one specific word: "Nyarlathotep." For some, the dreams had served as morbid inspiration—a Boston painter's macabre works began depicting chilling monsters; a Miskatonic mathematics student whose sudden genius bordered on insanity; an author from Providence whose stories were populated with a pantheon of nonhuman entities. For others, the dreams revealed unambiguous omens of an imminent conflict.

Many buckled beneath the strain, their sanity sapped. They ended up in places like Arkham Sanitarium.

Von Goerdeler heard the voices, too. Kaswell had already secured the German's dossier from his contact at Lakehurst. Though he had no reason to linger, he waited, counting the hours as they passed. By nightfall, the victims' groans had intensified into a nerve-racking cacophony. The stench of putrefying flesh, of urine and excrement languished in the stagnant air. Even the nurses found Kaswell's resilience inspiring, which brought the German more attention than other victims.

"Family or friend," one of them asked.

"Neither . . . a business associate," Kaswell answered. "We had never met face-to-face." Kaswell paused, gauged her curiosity. She seemed to wordlessly implore an explanation for his thoughtfulness, one that he could not immediately justify. After a moment of reflection, he said, "He's far from his home. I just felt he should have someone here when he dies."

"You're a good man," she said as she administered another dose of painkillers. "Although, I should tell you—he must have had one other acquaintance here. A man visited him earlier this morning, just before you arrived. Odd looking fellow, Arab I think. What country is it where they have those tall red felt hats with the black tassels?" She paused, anticipating a response. When she decided none was forthcoming, she continued. "Well, he was wearing one of those. He said nothing to anyone, asked no one for help. Just walked right up to your associate here, leaned over him and whispered something to him. I didn't have the heart to tell him that he wouldn't be able to hear."

Several hours later, von Goerdeler's eyes grew wide, his limbs shook convulsively and he gasped for breath. In that brief span of time between awakening to agony and surrendering to death, he said four words.

"Dachau . . . Sachsenhausen . . . Buchenwald . . . Nyarlathotep."

# Five

> *His tomb beneath the sands*
> *upon which Giza's greatest guardian stands,*
> *The Faceless God rests still,*
> *the prophecies of old ready to fulfill.*

*Erich Christoph von Goerdeler.*
*personal memoirs. 1937*

WALLACE WELLES PEERED OUT THE WINDOW of his fourth floor apartment. On the corner of West 39th Street and 10th Avenue, a gaunt figure skulked beneath a street lamp. Though Welles could not see his face, he recognized him.

He'd run into him the night before at some nameless jazz bar down near the Hudson River—a seedy joint with plenty of shadows to cover up all the illicit transactions being negotiated by mobsters, crooked cops and those with even less reputable vocations. There, he had met fellow Seekers of Forbidden Wisdom Corey Kaswell and David Oldrock. Kaswell assured them he had taken possession of the complete manifesto. He had already deciphered some of its passages, interpreted some of its meaning. It would take him some time, he said, to fully comprehend its contents.

Oldrock vociferously asserted his frustration at not being invited to assist in the translation and analysis of the manifesto. Kaswell's explanation—mostly based on the inescapable dogma of national security—did little to placate Oldrock, who grew increasingly incensed at the situation. Eventually, the two men retired, leaving Welles alone to spend his most recent paycheck on booze—which he did, until he noticed the stranger.

The stranger—a tall, sinewy foreigner—made no effort to communicate, but did not hide his unsettling interest in Welles. Wearing a traditional black, ankle-length robe and a fez, he navigated the crowded establishment barefooted, attracting considerable attention. Settling into a vacant niche at the back of the bar, the stranger watched Welles' every move, shadowed him, and, when Welles finally took his leave, followed him down the side streets and alleyways, through the black patches of midnight that seldom knew the touch of light.

Welles' mind raced over a dozen mugs' faces as he thought about who he had sent up the river, about whose little brother or criminal accomplice or gang family might be looking to settle an old score. Ultimately, he rejected every plausible known enemy. The stranger kept pace all the while, staying about a half block behind the former New York City cop, biding his time, keeping his identity obscured.

Welles was no tenderfoot, though. He knew the streets, knew the city, knew the game. He took a dozen detours, never straying from heavily-trafficked thoroughfares, avoiding his own neighborhood so as not to reveal information that might cost him his life at some later date. Slowly, he traced a circuitous route and led his stalker back to the river, to the warehouse district, to an abandoned depot once used as a clearinghouse for bootleg alcohol.

Welles ducked into a murky alcove, pulled out his .357 Magnum and waited for the confrontation.

The stranger walked by the recess without altering his pace, without even bothering to glance sideways into the darkness. Welles pounced, springing from the shadows with a grunt that echoed off the warehouse sidings. Tired and out of shape, he practically botched the ambush, almost losing his footing on the slippery ground.

Back on the open street, the stranger had disappeared. Welles searched the shadows, waiting for a counterattack that never materialized. Finally, weary and discouraged, he shrugged off the incident and headed home.

And now, there he was, the stranger, standing on the street corner, skulking like a sewer rat waiting for the day's trash to hit the curb.

Welles slammed a shot of whisky and made a wish that dawn would send the rat scurrying back home.

## Sir

Tuesday, May 11, 5:33 A.M.

> *Friday, February 13, 1903: Categorizing them as heretics, all surviving members of Sodalitas Invictus are butchered in Austria. Also put to death is the last Sentinel, who had been imprisoned in Burg Hochosterwitz, a medieval castle east of the town Sankt Veit an der Glan in Carinthia. The executioners themselves are later slain to ensure the names of those responsible for authorizing the act remain unspecified.*

*Erich Christoph von Goerdeler.*
*personal memoirs. 1937*

COREY KASWELL OPENED HIS EYES, casting off the stubborn residue of a particularly unpleasant dream. Spread before him across his dining room table lay the lingering ruminations of Erich Christoph von Goerdeler, some painstakingly recorded on a typewriter, others scribbled chaotically on wrinkled stationary. Each fragment meant little or nothing by itself; together, though, the pieces combined to form an extraordinary document.

Scrupulously researched and carefully encoded, the patchwork manifesto incorporated esoteric exposition, unexpurgated history, religious treatise and epic verse. Some men claim moments of complete lucidity, fleeting epiphanies which tantalizingly offer an ephemeral glimpse at the naked cosmos. Von Goerdeler had lived for years with such clarity of vision. He had heard the disembodied voices whisper the name "Nyarlathotep," experienced the cataclysmic visions that caused some to be labeled prophets, others lunatics. Somehow, it had not driven him mad.

Kaswell had fallen asleep. He had gone for days without more than a few hours of rest, without adequate meals, without thinking of anything but deciphering the document. The German had used various ciphers as well as several different languages to frustrate those attempting to crack his code. The first page of the manifesto contained an ostensibly inexplicable sequence that Kaswell managed to unravel in little time:

i.2.2    i.22.8 i.94.8 iii.233.5 i.166.1 i.185.6 i.318.1 ii.360.8

i.5.3    i.4.1 i.707.2 ii.186.1 i.349.4 i.555.4 i.648.5 iii.246.6

Much of von Goerdeler's personal memoirs had been written in a simple substitution cipher Kaswell referred to as the Walpurgis Code, and consisted of reflections, predictions and poetic observations such as:

EDPQ PEF FEHQ NUW UEQGFK APFR VWWI

PQ ZPNU NUW TEIN BQX NUW BENUPFI PV XBFS XWWXI

The enigmatic passages pertaining to the history of Sodalitas Invictus, the legacy of forgotten civilizations and the entities that eternally sought dominion over all regions of the universe defied Kaswell's attempts at rendition. Line by line, though, Kaswell had begun to unchain each mystery from the complex labyrinth of language von Goerdeler had used to imprison the truth from all but the most zealous seeker of wisdom.

With each riddle resolved, each revelation realized, Kaswell felt the burden of arcane knowledge saddling his soul. The significance of both religion and science withered beneath the affliction of centuries of intentional deceit. Humanity, he realized, had been blinded and beguiled, maltreated and misled, tyrannized and tortured.

"It seems you've found the Holy Grail." The voice startled Kaswell, and he mechanically reached for his Colt M1911. He lowered the weapon when the man stepped from the shadows of the adjoining room, his own weapon holstered. "Metaphorically speaking of course." Patrick Nelson, another agent of the State Department, skimmed the documents with counterfeit fascination. "A bunch of gibberish from what I can see. I had a peek while you were napping."

"Thanks for dropping by and breaking in."

"Oh, I prefer to think of it as a kindly gesture of friendship." Nelson, tall and wiry with curly red hair and a fair complexion, came from a wealthy Boston family. He had avoided service in the war, had bribed and cheated his way through college, and routinely bought his way into increasingly influential positions in the government. No one liked him, but few had the courage to admonish him. "People are worried about you, Corey. Important people. People who might be interested in your . . . off-duty pursuits."

"It's none of their business," Kaswell said. "None of yours, either."

"Corey, everything is the government's business these days, thanks to Roosevelt and Hoover." Nelson plucked one of Kaswell's notebooks off the table, flipped through the pages of commentary. "Sodalitas Invictus. Sounds familiar. One of those quaint little European spiritualist groups that used to gather for parlor tricks, wasn't it? Thinking of taking up magic in your retirement?"

"I'm hoping to be the next Houdini."

"Charming." Nelson dropped the notes haphazardly, disturbing one of the piles of papers Kaswell had organized. "I came here to warn you about some Germans poking around the *Hindenburg* wreckage, looking for something you said didn't exist. I'm assuming that you'll be filing a follow-up report . . ."

"Of course," Kaswell said, knowing that Nelson would leave him no choice. "Look, Patrick, you haven't been around long enough to know that sometimes you have to safeguard valuable information. It's not that anyone at the bureau would intentionally misuse it. Sometimes people just don't realize the ramifications."

"All I need to know is that you'll get around to doing the right thing." Nelson's attitude surprised Kaswell. "If you can assure me of that, I'll be on my way. You seem to have a lot of work to do."

"You have my word, Patrick."

"Then get busy. And watch out for those German boys," Nelson reminded him. "They're Abwehr, which means they won't be as understanding as I have been."

# Seven

Wednesday, May 12, 4:18 P.M.

> *I do not blame them all for these atrocities they will commit. As their leaders are exploited by the authors of this cosmic tragedy, so too are they duped into blind faith and immoral collusion.*

*Erich Christoph von Goedeler,
personal memoirs. 1937*

"SO YOU LOCATED ONE OF THESE AMATEUR OCCULTISTS, THEN?"

Erwin Bonhoeffer did not bother to mask his disdain. The two Germans met the Egyptian on the observation deck of the Empire State Building overlooking the city. The 102-story art deco skyscraper impressed the Abwehr intelligence agents in particular, its design and execution an engineering marvel that had no rival in Germany or elsewhere. Still, in their eyes its opulence stood as a bitter contrast to the poverty and indignity they felt the world had imposed upon their homeland following the last war. "Have you approached him?"

"I have made him aware of my presence," the Egyptian said, staring at the horizon. Where his gaze focused, storm clouds seemed to gather. "It is unlikely he has the documents you seek."

"Then kill him," Gempp said.

"That would be unwise," the Egyptian said. "He will lead us to the others."

"We are wasting time here. We have sufficient information to know who to target. I don't really care if we ever find von Goedeler's notes, as long as we dispose of the Americans." Gempp turned away from the wind and lit a cigarette. "I have no patience for these little games. Our orders were to work with you, not to let you lead this operation. We have waited long enough for you to provide the information we require."

"Your colleague, Herr Vermehren; he, too, was an impatient man." The Egyptian removed his fez, ran his tan hand over his clean-shaven scalp. Around the crown of his head, cryptic symbols had been written in reddish-brown henna. "His impulsiveness resulted in failure."

"Failure," Gempp said angrily, "is not an option for an Abwehr agent."

"Nonetheless . . ." The Egyptian glared at Gempp, the shadows in his eyes born in some churning black void of ancient history. To look into his face was to look into the face of the pharaohs of old, the lost dynasties of that early empire, the culture that connected the current age of man with forgotten remnants of the Theosophists' fourth root race. "Kill him if you wish. Do so, and the documents will be lost, and your enemies will gain valuable insight into your goals—and glean wisdom which will strengthen their defense."

"We will wait," Bonhoeffer said, swayed by the Egyptian's argument. "But we cannot wait indefinitely. With each passing day, these Seekers of Forbidden Wisdom will harvest new information from von Goerdeler's notes." Though his fellow agent could have been his twin, the two men differed in intellect and in their understanding of their place in history. Gempp saw himself as a dutiful soldier serving a general for the benefit of the Fatherland. Bonhoeffer, though a devoted Nazi and loyal agent, served a higher purpose. He brushed Gempp aside, directed his last few comments to the Egyptian. "We are at a decisive crossroads in our history. Forces have aligned, the auguries favor our aspirations. We simply cannot allow the rebirth of Sodalitas Invictus."

The Egyptian acknowledged his understanding silently, glared at Gempp one last time and disappeared into a crowd of tourists watching the sun's slow descent in the west.

# Eight

> *An atmosphere of mysticism, of superhuman insight, of secrets intact for many centuries appeared to emanate from these heaps of dusty volumes with worm-eaten leaves. And mixed with these ancient tomes were others red and conspicuous, pamphlets of socialistic propaganda, leaflets in all the languages of Europe and periodicals—many periodicals, with revolutionary titles.*

Vicente Blasco Ibáñez.
*Los Cuatro Jinetes del Apocalipsis.*
1916

TWO WEEKS AFTER THE *HINDENBURG* TRAGEDY, a leaflet appeared on newsstands, bulletin boards and storefronts throughout the Atlantic seaboard.

"They're everywhere," Oldrock said, passing the crude publication around to other Seekers of Forbidden Wisdom who had gathered in a conference room at the library. A four-page, saddle-stapled pamphlet with printed card covers bore the unusual title "Schwarzer Stein" and presented a rambling treatise linking recent events in Europe to astrological portents. It spoke of German superiority, their "genius of organization" and of the supposed dawning of an Age of Teutonic Expansion—an epoch that could only begin "when the countless stars are so aligned as to signify their implicit sanction." On the last page, in large, bold capital letters, was the name NYARLATHOTEP. "I've spoken to four Seekers in other states this morning. They report seeing them in Newark, Boston, Arkham and Providence. I've even heard a rumor that they may be as far south as Smithville."

"Smithville, North Carolina?" Mark Moeller, an attorney with ancestral roots connecting him to colonial Dunwich, flipped through the pages scanning the text. "How is that even possible? Someone would have had to have planned this, distributed advance copies and set up a specific date to filter them out to the public."

"That would imply large numbers of followers, like some widespread cult or something." Wallace Welles grimaced. "And if that was the case, I would have heard about it already. You can't keep folks from gabbing about something like that."

"This one came from the circulation desk," Oldrock said. "There's a stack of them over there; or there was, anyway. I asked one of the librarians about them and she didn't know where they came from. She threw them in the garbage."

"This still proves nothing," Welles said, voicing his reservations without even studying the publication. "Anyone can pick up an old copy of *The United Amateur* and find the name."

"We've all spent hours combing tomes in this library trying to find a single reference to Nyarlathotep before 1920." Moeller looked at his associates as he considered the facts before him, analyzed all available information and began forming his own inference. He easily read Welles' cynicism and Oldrock's perplexity. Of the other four members present, army veteran Thomas Dickens and antiques dealer Emory Cain kept their reactions shrouded, their comments unuttered. Two newcomers had little to say, or held their comments out of wariness or respect. Kaswell, occupied with decoding von Goerdeler's manifesto, had been unable to attend. "I think that this is all nothing more than a means to publicize the author's works."

"Maybe," Oldrock said. "Or maybe this was produced by a legitimate group—a group not unlike ours—familiar enough with American literature to use it to their advantage, to publicize their political agenda." Oldrock knew Moeller would not accept the hypothesis, particularly when he had formulated his own. "Besides," he added, trying to discredit Moeller, "the author of whom you speak is dead."

"But he had a circle of admirers . . . people who will probably be praising him for decades to come." Moeller had settled on his line of reasoning and would not veer from it unless further evidence came to light. "That is your 'cult,' Wallace. Nothing more than aficionados of an accomplished storyteller, one who was so adept at suspending his readers' disbelief that fiction becomes as convincing as fact."

"You've always been skeptical," Oldrock said, his gaze falling on both Moeller and Welles. "And your skepticism is welcome here. It keeps this group honest." He paused, summoned up every ounce of composure he possessed to make a compelling case. "But at some point, dismissing everything as mere coincidence becomes irresponsible—even when irrefutable evidence is unobtainable. We have gathered too many testimonials, seen too many people driven to the brink of madness by this phenomenon to continue to dismiss it as unworthy of our attention. When Kaswell brought us together, we all acknowledged our individual conviction that something underlies the histories we have been taught, the religions we have studied and the news we read every day. We concede that science cannot yet illuminate every shadow that haunts this world and that eldritch things beyond our limited perception survive."

"We all bow to your eloquence, Mr. Oldrock," Welles said, slumping forward in his chair in artificial awe. His tone more derisive than usual, he looked to Moeller for a show of support. "To summarize your verbose oration for our newer members: Believe nothing, fear everything."

For a moment, silence smothered the sealed conference room. Oldrock disliked serving as interim group leader in Kaswell's absence because members' conflicting personalities often led to minor skirmishes. Much of the discord could be traced to the disparity in their academic and professional backgrounds.

"Weren't you just telling me a few days ago that fear was a good thing, Wallace?" Oldrock gazed into his friend's eyes and noticed for the first time something different, something aberrant. Fear had finally eroded his nerve. "And all the things you've seen . . . are you telling me now that it was all a mistake? If that's the case, Wallace, why are you even here? You've apparently lost your confidence, or your courage."

Welles swallowed his anger, fought back the urge to lunge over the table and wrap his fingers around Oldrock's throat. Had anyone else slighted him so callously, he would not have been able to control himself. Oldrock had seen through him.

Moreover, Oldrock knew what had put the fear in him. Oldrock knew he had seen the stranger, too.

"The Aryan plot," one of the newcomers said, his voice so soft it sounded like the rustle of lingering autumn leaves swept by a gentle winter breeze.

"What did you say?" Oldrock shifted his gaze, trying to remember the man's name. Though embarrassed he could not recall, he was thankful for the interruption. "I'm sorry . . . what was your name?"

"Alex," the man said, fidgeting with a pencil. The youngest man at the table, he had endemic freckles, rust-colored hair and wore Oxford bags and a red gaucho-style shirt. "Alex Henderson."

"What did you say?"

"The Aryan plot," he repeated. Seeing the confusion in Oldrock's eyes, he explained. "Nyarlathotep . . . it's an anagram for 'the Aryan plot'."

"Jesus," Welles said. "Why the hell didn't anyone notice *that* before?"

In the next moment, the lights in the room flickered and dimmed.

"That's peculiar," Oldrock said, his hand reflexively digging through his pockets for a matchbook. Upon striking a match, he was startled to see Kaswell had joined the group. "Corey . . . what's going on?"

"Follow me," Kaswell commanded without explanation. "Say nothing until I say we are safe."

In the subsequent silence, more than one member considered voicing opposition. All resistance, however, evaporated at the first sound of gunfire in another part of the library.

"What's this all—"

Moeller never finished his question. Kaswell had a knife at his throat when he repeated his instructions.

"Say *nothing*." Kaswell no longer acted as a Seeker of Forbidden Wisdom. He now assumed his role as a United States government agent, protecting American interests. "The Germans are on to us. We've got to get out of here or we're all dead."

The men filed out of the meeting room quickly, quietly, with Kaswell leading them through aisles of bookshelves toward a distant corner of the library. There, they slipped unnoticed through a door marked "Staff Only," along a long corridor with marble flooring and down several flights of stairs into an underground chamber that other members could only assume served as a storage facility.

Kaswell tripped a hidden lever and a bookshelf slid a few feet to one side revealing a hidden passage. He stepped through and stood to the side, ushering each man into the secret passageway. When Moeller, the last in line, stepped through, Kaswell threw another switch and the shelf slid back into place. He double-bolted the doorway, then activated a secondary steel barrier that would make certain they could not be followed.

"That will stop the Germans," Kaswell said. Turning to Moeller, he frowned. "Tip 'em off, did we?"

"What are you talking about? Tip who off?"

"Come on, Moeller, I watched you plant that doubled-up Sturm cigarette near the trigger mechanism in the basement—trying to give your Nazi chums a little clue?" With speed and agility no one expected from the aging Kaswell, he lodged Moeller against the wall with his left forearm and prodded his ribs with a knife. "Too bad they don't trust you with a weapon, Moeller, or we could end this all right here. I'm sure the boys at the bureau will be keen to hear you squeal your secrets, though."

"Sorry, Mr. Kaswell," Moeller said. Kaswell tensed instinctively, anticipating an attack. Instead, Moeller ground his jaws together, jerked his head back against the wall. An audible crack reported the fracture of a false tooth. Its toxic chemical contents spilled directly into the agent's bloodstream, poisoning him.

"Potassium cyanide," Kaswell said, disgust registering on his face. "Coward."

Kaswell watched the German die a slow death, the knife still fast at his belly. When he felt satisfied that he would cause no more trouble, he released his hold and Moeller slumped forward, collapsing onto the floor. Next, Kaswell turned his attention to the group members, all visibly astonished and alarmed by the fast-moving events.

"Which one of you told him?"

"I did," Welles said, promptly acquitting Oldrock of complicity. Since the night of their last meeting, Welles had wrestled with his affiliation with the group—questioned in particular Kaswell's divided loyalties and his refusal to let Oldrock assist in deciphering the manifesto. "It's my fault. I thought you were overreacting. I never knew . . . I never expected any of this."

"Well," Kaswell said, letting the blood drain from his face. "At least we know who was feeding information to the Nazis. He was probably behind the printing of the pamphlets, as well. I see you managed to find a copy. From what I gather, bureau agents are confiscating them now all over the country." Kaswell finally took a moment to study the faces of the attending Seekers. "You should go," he said, addressing the four most recent additions to the organization. "Had I known anything like this would happen, I would have disbanded this group years ago."

"One of them—Mr. Henderson there—provided us with a bit of a revelation just before you arrived." Oldrock smiled, pleased with the new recruit, and explained the anagram Henderson had worked out. "Considering the few details you've told me about the manifesto, I can't accept that it's a mere coincidence."

"Neither can I," Kaswell admitted. "For now, though, until we can sort everything out, I think it would be best if you all distanced yourself from me. Follow this corridor. At its end, you will find a door. Beyond the door is an unused lower platform of the 42nd Street station of the Eighth Avenue Line. You'll be able to make your way up to the street from there."

"You'll be in touch?" Cain, a soft-spoken man with an affinity for Mesopotamian artifacts and magic tricks, seemed crestfallen at Kaswell's proposal that the Seekers temporarily disband. "I don't know about the others, but I'm still willing to participate. I still believe in our cause, with or without proof."

"What about that proof, Mr. Kaswell," Welles said, his inquiry less a challenge than a plea. "Have you found anything in those documents to make all this hocus pocus stuff legitimate?"

"Proof," Kaswell said, "is now something we do not lack." He unruffled himself, scattering his anxieties as best he could. "In the last eight years, Seekers of Forbidden Wisdom has grown from twenty members to more than a hundred, men and women from all walks of life, with all kinds of backgrounds. We all share a common consciousness—we have each experienced an epiphany illuminating an ancient influence governing the evolution of civilization. Until now, our convictions were nothing more than conjecture. Von Goerdeler has provided clues to locating evidence to substantiate our beliefs."

"And Sodalitas Invictus," Welles asked.

"It's there," Kaswell said, "Not a thorough history, but enough that we can piece together the facts. There's even a mention of your relation, Mr. Greenheath. He was one of the last known Sentinels—guardians designated as civilization's sole defenders. You may well have inherited some of his qualities, Wallace."

"Maybe that explains why they've been tailing me," Welles said. He glanced at Oldrock, wordlessly confessing his growing apprehension. "Seems like everywhere I go, there's some guy right on my heels."

"The Egyptian?" Oldrock had seen him, too. "Who is he?"

"If he is what I think he is," Kaswell said, his voice tinged with a hint of despair, "then we have far less time than I would like to believe. I suspect he is an avatar of Nyarlathotep."

Welles asked no further questions and sought no advice. He knew what had to be done.

# Nine

*NEW YORK CITY—A midday shooting rampage took place at the Fifth Avenue library yesterday. Three library patrons were killed along with two police officers.*

*One of the suspects, a German national, was gunned down on the front steps of the library. A second assailant, also believed to be of German or European origin, was captured last night trying to board a merchant vessel bound for England.*

*Authorities have secured the library which will remain closed through Monday as they search for clues in the brutal attack. Federal investigators are calling it a "random and senseless act," but hasten to add that there is no evidence that the men were acting on behalf of the Nazi government headed by Adolf Hitler.*

*Brooklyn Beacon.*
*Saturday. May 15. 1937*

TWO DRUNKS SLOUCHED AGAINST THE WALL outside a disreputable saloon a few blocks from the Hudson River. They traded sob stories, occasionally accosting passersby for spare change. Their combined stench was enough to make a man gag.

When the Egyptian approached, one man rapped the other on the chest, pointing toward the stranger. They eyed the peculiarly dressed foreigner for a few seconds, then disappeared into the saloon.

Wallace Welles paid them in cash for living up to their end of the bargain. They scrambled out the back door along with a few other patrons, sensing the coming showdown.

"Been waiting," Welles said, his Magnum trained on the doorway as the Egyptian stepped in from the street. "Figured you'd catch up with me eventually."

The owner's daughter had been tending bar since just before midnight. A skinny little waif with an old scar that ran from her left earlobe to the corner of her mouth, she stood her ground, too frightened or foolish to flee. Welles sensed her over his left shoulder, knew she was about to say something pointless. Whatever threat she could muster would wilt without the firepower to back it up. "Listen, doll, you might want to clear out for a few minutes. I'll handle this. If your old man asks, tell him Wallace Welles had some private business."

With that, she flitted off into the back room without making a sound.

"We have not met," the Egyptian said, "but I recognize your blood."

"And I recognize that you may look human, but you are something quite different, aren't you?" The Egyptian smiled, and the jackal's smirk made Welles shudder. "Shall I call you Nyarlathotep?"

"You have inherited some of your ancestor's gifts of intuition." The foreigner took a few steps forward, letting the door close behind him. He hesitated, raised an eyebrow. "That name is not my own, and but one of thousands I have been called. This guise is not my own, but one of thousands I have claimed." He studied Welles, searching for corporal details that would connect him to his forebears. "I wonder if you are even familiar with your forerunner's deeds. He performed extraordinary feats over his long lifetime."

"I'm afraid I was never much of a genealogist." Welles nodded toward a nearby chair, but the Egyptian declined the offer. "As for you, seems you have taken quite an interest in me. Mind telling me why?"

"Initially, I was simply following you to determine the whereabouts of certain documents. While I do not personally care who possesses them, my current benefactors are eager to retrieve them."

"That didn't work out very well, did it?"

"The Germans are ambitious, but rarely patient," he admitted. "That will be their undoing I suspect."

"If Nyarlathotep is a name simply ascribed to you by those you torment, who are you? What is your purpose?"

"I am the distillation of humanity's collective consciousness," the Egyptian said. He pondered the question further, searching for the appropriate words. "I am both sides of the coin in every conflict in the history of civilization. I am both intolerance and the vengeance it spawns.

I inspire both tyrant and rebel, instigate both torturer and criminal and arouse the fanaticism of both dictator and insurgent. Religious zealots of every denomination have mistaken my whispers for the advice of their gods." He smiled again, and his eyes grew narrow with mischief. "Isn't it ironic that some days your enemies are friends, and your friends are foes?"

"If you aren't interested in the manifesto, and the Germans are out of the picture, why are you still following me?"

"I wanted to gauge your power. I wanted to see if anything remains that made the Sentinels such worthy adversaries."

"You can see I'm not in the best physical condition," Welles said. "But I have this," he added, glancing at his gun. "And if you're nothing more than flesh and blood, I'd think that would make me a worthy adversary."

"You can't kill me."

"Funny. I hear that a lot right before I plug somebody." A single shot rang out. The Egyptian somehow sidestepped the projectile, leaping forward with a maniacal howl. Welles bolted to one side, grabbed the Egyptian by the collar and slammed his head into the bar. The foreigner's fez tumbled to the floor as he clambered to right himself.

Without hesitation, Welles buried the gun in the soft flesh behind his left ear and pulled the trigger. A geyser of blood and brains erupted, splattering the bar, the floor, the stools and the bottles of liquor lining the back wall.

Then, with half of his melon blown off, Nyarlathotep cocked his head sideways and stared at Welles.

"You can't kill me," he repeated. "I always return."

Hours later, Welles dumped his body in the muddy waters of the Hudson River where it would find company with all the sorry suicides and the crooks who riled the wrong kingpins. The river might swallow his corpse, but Welles suspected it would not contain the entity that governed it.

#  Ten

"LOOK AT US," Kaswell said. "We're so obsessed with this that we have lost hold of our lives. It cost poor Welles his job, his dignity. And I know you've made sacrifices, David." The government agent stared toward the shadowed rafters of the abandoned chapel on East Church Street in Arkham where spiders congregated to worship their own secret gods. Neither Oldrock nor Kaswell had been in Bayfriar's since the inaugural meeting of the Seekers of Forbidden Wisdom back in 1929. "I let it ruin my marriage. I let a perfectly good woman slip away because I couldn't separate myself from this . . . this obsession."

"Any one of us could have turned our backs on it," Oldrock reminded him. In Arkham for a symposium on the occult in literature, Kaswell had contacted him requesting an immediate audience. "We are not pawns of destiny. We pledge ourselves to this crusade of our own free will."

"Crusade or custodianship?" Kaswell had finished his work. He provided Oldrock with a summary of von Goerdeler's manifesto. Perched on the end of a rickety church pew, he thumbed through his notes. The original documents had been turned over to the government along with his translation and his resignation. Though he had successfully deciphered the entire text, he omitted certain passages which he deemed too controversial, too dangerous, considering the growing rift between isolationists and proponents of war. It would take the best cryptographers decades to work out those segments. "How do we face these odds? How do wage war against an enemy that is practically omnipotent?"

"Sodalitas Invictus managed to do it."

"They had their Sentinels and the support of many wealthy patrons."

"Then, perhaps it is time to reevaluate our position," Oldrock said, brushing aside cobwebs as he paced the dusty floor. Narrow bands of sunlight leaked through cracks between the planks that had been used to board up the windows. A breeze swept the sooty steeple and produced a ghostly moan. "If the choice before us is extinction in a global holocaust or survival through alliance with these invincible entities, perhaps it is time we made a pact with the so-called devil."

"Impossible," Kaswell said, his conviction returning. "Von Goerdeler makes clear their intention is nothing less than the annihilation of civilization and the subjugation of humanity."

"Civilization has already spawned one great war that almost brought ruin to this world. It will surely do so again with more advanced technologies. As for subjugation, governments already regulate the disposition of its citizenry: mollifying them in times of peace, provoking them in times of war, beguiling them with little lies and rewarding them with empty promises." Oldrock wavered, wondering if he had said too much. He had never given Kaswell reason to question his dependability, had always been a dedicated colleague. His commitment to Kaswell's principles, though, had diminished. "What did Wallace tell you when you presented him with this evidence."

"He passed this test, David," Kaswell said. "He has affirmed his commitment to reviving Sodalitas Invictus."

"I'm afraid I simply cannot let that happen, Corey." Oldrock sprang several feet through the shadowed chamber, upsetting several pews and generating vast clouds of dust and sediment that had settled on the church floor over its long years of neglect. Kaswell reacted instantly, reeling forward to lessen the impact of Oldrock's initial lunge. The men struggled on the floor, neither gaining an upper hand for several moments.

The sound of a single gunshot was muffled by the church walls so that no Arkham residents took notice.

"How long has it been, David, since you allowed your mind to be twisted?" Kaswell gripped his midsection. The bullet had ripped through his guts and blood surged from the wound. "How long have you been swayed by his voice."

"He speaks to me to, Corey, but not in my dreams. I find his messages hidden, in classical literature, in pulp magazines . . . everywhere I look, I find evidence of his cryptic authorship compelling me to do what must be done to restore order to this world."

"You published the 'Schwarzer Stein' pamphlet," Kaswell said. "You work for them, for the Nazis."

"Not the Nazis," Oldrock said, "but an American organization that sees the logic in their objectives. And because Sodalitas Invictus would not allow us to forge the alliances that will guarantee our survival, we cannot allow its rebirth." Oldrock knelt beside his former mentor, mopped sweat from his forehead. "I'm sorry it had to end this way, Corey. I respect your thirst for wisdom. I only wish we could have agreed on how best to protect humanity."

# Eleven

Saturday, June 26 11:04 P.M.

*NEW YORK CITY—Former New York City police officer Wallace Welles has been credited with solving the murder of government agent Corey Kaswell, whose body was discovered three weeks ago in the ruins of a church in Arkham, Mass. The suspect, David Oldrock, was shot and killed Friday afternoon during an altercation with Welles outside Brooks Brothers in Manhattan.*

*Welles was held for questioning but authorities report no charges will be filed against him.*

*Brooklyn Beacon.*
*Saturday. June 26. 1937*

WELLES, standing before a podium at the far side of the abandoned warehouse, watched as people began to arrive. He had no chairs to offer them, no beverages to help banish the summer heat. He had only his resolve and Kaswell's concise notes regarding the *Hindenburg* manifesto. Two months earlier, the thought of conducting a meeting like this would have sent him straight down the neck of a whisky bottle. Since reading Kaswell's notes, he had renewed his courage and his determination. In addition, he had stopped drinking and smoking. For the first time in years, he felt as if he had a purpose.

Thomas Dickens, Emory Cain and Alex Henderson stood at his side.

"I hadn't expected this many people," Dickens said. "What do you think brought all of them out tonight?"

"They can sense the truth," Welles said. "I'm not the only surviving heir to the legacy of the Sentinels. If I've inherited a fraction of their insight, others may have the same traits. That's why I tapped them first. They will become our first followers, our first legion."

In all, more than 300 people crowded into the shadowy warehouse, willing to hear Welles recount the contents of the *Hindenburg* manifesto, eager to learn the secret history of civilization and ready to sacrifice their lives in their pursuit of the truth.

"We meet tonight," Welles began, "not as Seekers of Forbidden Wisdom. Tonight, we reclaim the cause of our predecessors, reignite the struggle they sustained and resurrect the society of guardians once known as Sodalitas Invictus." Sporadic applause followed, followed by the muffled voices of nervous participants as Welles began his discourse.

With the dawn, Sodalitas Invictus had been reborn.

# IN OUR DARKEST HOUR

Steven Michael Graham

**I'd tell you it was an ordinary day,** but I'm a masked vigilante, and it was three weeks after 9/11, and nothing felt ordinary. Still, I was doing my best to get back into my normal routine. I'd had an idea for Gamma Radar Goggles that could see through walls. I thought if I could get a pair to work, it would help with the recovery efforts down at Ground Zero. Being in the Lab calms me. It takes my mind off the state of the world, how there's always been more villains out there than I can catch. When I stare down into gears or circuits, the curtain pulls away, and I see underneath the chaos of the world, how it's supposed to be . . . and suddenly, I know how it all fits together. That's how I make all of my gadgets. I just go to that orderly place in my mind, and I know how, without knowing how I knew. Some guys fly or burst into flames. I know things.

I was in my lab when I got the message from Doctor Nyx. I wouldn't expect a sorceror to use a cellphone, but it's still creepy when I look up from what I'm doing to find a piece of vellum lying on the table next to me that wasn't there a minute ago. All this one said was,

119 E. 105th Street, on the roof.
10 pm, tonight. I need help.
Yes, it's important.

—Nyx

I landed my airship on the rooftop at 9:58. I stepped out dressed in my battle-suit and loaded for bear. The last time Nyx called, I wound up in a subway tunnel surrounded by huge man-eating cockroaches, so I wasn't taking any chances. I had earplugs, wirecutters, anti-toxins, lock-picks, and plenty of shells for my trusty compressed-air Midnight Multi-Pistol: rubber bullets, door-breakers, thermite shells, and more than a few armor-piercing hollow-points. I didn't have the radar goggles figured out yet, so I was wearing my usual night-vision pair. (Later on, I'd regret not bringing tear gas, but a man only has so many pockets and no way of knowing how things are going to turn out.) There was no sign of Nyx, not that I expected any. Just to be safe, I checked the whole roof, every hiding place, door, and skylight. Nobody. Then he spoke from behind me. "A watched pot never boils, Scarab."

"Nyx, why do we have to play this game every time we meet? Couldn't you just walk into a room like a sane person?"

"Don't talk to me about sanity."

"Why don't we just talk about why we're here?"

Nyx shook his head as he stepped into view. "Not yet. I'm still waiting for someone." He looked at me from under his heavy eyelids and frowned slightly. "I asked the Atlantean to come in from Boston."

"Why?" The Atlantean has always given me the creeps. Something about the fishy way he smells, the way those big glistening eyes of his never seem to blink, the way he listens to everything you say like he's memorizing it. Supposedly, his mother was a mermaid or something, and his father was human. No, I think I have that backwards. I'd figured he'd adventure for a few years, then set off, searching the oceans for the undersea cities where his father or mother or whoever was from, and we'd never see him again. That's usually the way it is with the aquatic heroes, but Lan has hung around, maybe ten years now. I'm not sure why. It's not like he fits in. Then again, none of us really fit in. Nyx knows how I feel about Lan . . . but he doesn't care.

"I called him in because he's a good fighter and a better thinker and we're likely to need both tonight."

"Cold fish have to stick together, I guess. Wouldn't"—I stopped when I heard the wet slapping sound of the Atlantean's feet landing on the roof. One thing I can appreciate about Lan: I know when *he* shows up. We turned to look at him. "Hey, Lan. Nyx told me you were coming."

The Atlantean spread his arms and ducked his head in a bow of greeting that would've looked less ridiculous if he wasn't still squatting like a frog from his last leap. "Midnight Scarab . . . Doctor Nyx . . . a pleasure as always." Then he planted his hands in front of himself and looked up at us, as if standing up straight was something that hadn't occurred to him. Lan's scabby pale skin didn't have any hair except the mess of black strands stuck to his scalp. The expectant look on his long wet face made him look like a gangly teenager. After a few moments of polite awkward silence, I decided to cut to the chase.

"So, Nyx. What's this about?"

Nyx gave me a smile as thin as his mustache. I hate when he does that. "I just thought you'd like to know that an unspeakable evil from the depths of time has been released down the street from here."

"Nyx, please. Enough mystical nonsense. What's been released, where is it, what are we going to do about it?"

Nyx stopped smiling. "I've been hearing rumors that a small black circle, a lens, has been found in the debris at the World Trade Center. Supposedly, it was as big as the palm of one hand, made of heavy glass, and it glowed with black light."

"You mean ultraviolet light?"

"No, this was literally black."

"Nyx, that doesn't make any sense. Black is the absence of light. It—"

He held up his hand. "So it was unlight, or it radiated darkness, or it swallowed light. None of that matters. The point is, I recognize the description." He glanced from my eyes to Lan's and back. "It's called the Lens of Va'ir, or the Eye of Eternal Night. I don't know how it got here, but it's very dangerous."

"Dangerous? How?"

"The Lens is a window into dark places where no light ever shines. There are horrid, unnatural things living in the Dark, waiting to speak to those who gaze into the Abyss."

"Gee, Doctor, you sound like the old men back home in Marshport." Nyx flashed the Atlantean a sudden startled glance. It was gone almost instantly, but I was sure it had been there. Understand, I've seen Doctor Nyx take bullets to the shoulder without looking startled. "Did you just say you were from Marshport, Massachusetts?"

"Yeah . . . my Mom still lives there, but I don't go back much. Even the way Boston Harbor makes my gills itch, I'd rather be there than back in Marshport. Everything's creepy. Even the *water* is creepy. Why do you ask?"

" . . . No reason, Atlantean. It's a small world, that's all. Perhaps I know a few of those 'old men' you mentioned."

"Really, Doc? Which—"

Nyx held up his hand to the Atlantean and flashed me a look. I gave him a tiny nod. "I'm sorry, Lan, I shouldn't have let us get sidetracked, but this matter really is of some urgency, and I didn't leave time for digressions."

"So, Nyx . . . what's so urgent about people talking to monsters with this Lens, anyway?" I said, pushing forward before Lan could think about whatever it was that had Nyx so worried.

"Such things as these don't chat and share gossip. These creatures make bargains with humans. They insinuate themselves into them to enter our world."

"But, Doctor, you said something was released *here*. Correct me if I'm wrong, but I thought Ground Zero is at the other end of town."

"I believe the Lens was brought here, to a building down the street. It's an auction house owned by one Phillip Rensell. There hasn't been an auction there in months, but in the last two weeks they've held nightly meetings." Nyx pulled out a small pamphlet from inside his coat and handed it to Lan, who scanned it quickly and handed it to me. The grainy photo copied on the front fold was of the towers smoking just after the planes hit. They probably lifted it from a magazine. Underneath, a headline read, "Are You Angry? Do You Feel like There's Nothing You Can Do? There IS something you can do!" Inside, the first lines read: "Come Pray with Us! The Apostolic Chapel of St. Michael the Avenger welcomes those crying out for Justice!"

"Nyx, you have got to be kidding me. There're hundreds of religious wackos in this city. What does this have to do with the Lens?"

Nyx turned it over, and tapped a fingertip on the symbol drawn on the back fold. "This sigil was familiar to me." He didn't bother showing it to Lan. He didn't need to.

"Doctor, do you mean the silhouette of the angel with a sword in front of some sort of sunburst?" Lan had spent maybe ten seconds with the pamphlet, and he described the wavy-fringed circle and black shape inside it better than I could have looking at it. I never was very good with inkblots.

"No, Lan, that isn't a sun. That protruding line isn't a sword . . . and it may have wings and legs, but it's not what you would call an angel."

"I don't understand, Doctor. What is it, then?"

"It's the sign of Se'eschaal, the Whispering Dark . . . a demon, or a god, or something worse. It lives in the dark places I spoke of, feeding on fear and anger and death . . ."

"No wonder it likes this place, then," I said.

"Yes. Its cults surface in places and times of turmoil. This symbol is always present, no matter what else is different . . . and more death invariably follows. The Whispering Dark burns through the population like a wildfire through dry forests, decimating entire civilizations, until it runs out of victims and returns to its home to rest from its meal."

"You think that's what's happening here?"

"I think that's happening tonight. My sources say this 'Chapel of St. Michael' has already gathered over a hundred followers in just two weeks—although 'follower' might be too strong a term—and tonight at eleven, their mysterious leader has asked that everyone come, and bring their friends, to see for themselves the 'miracle of St. Michael the Avenger,' proof of their holy power and divine mission."

"Nyx, how is it that you already have spies in a group that's only existed for a few weeks?"

"I didn't say spies, Scarab. These are religious zealots. They love to talk about their new faith. All I had to do was show an interest. They asked if I would come to their Grand Unveiling and see for myself. I said I'd bring some friends."

"You expect them to believe we're just three walk-ins that came for the sermon? If you'd warned me, I could've shown up in street clothes."

"No, I needed you armed. This might get unpleasant quickly. I have some tricks, to keep them from looking too closely . . . but you will have to take off those goggles, and the Atlantean will need to stand up." Lan stood up like a piece of rusty iron being bent straight. Even forcing himself to straighten, he looked slouched. I guess that's from swimming and hopping everywhere, and never running.

The Doctor's 'tricks' included two trench coats, fedoras, thick eyeglasses for Lan, a sprinkling of scented powder, and the usual string of gestures and nonsense words . . . but when we got there, no one gave us a second glance. No one offered to take our coats. We were three more vagrants in a sea of old coats, waiting for the show to start. The place was the sort of old brick building that survives in the low rent districts by being too bad a location to replace with anything newer but just sturdy enough to not condemn, the sort of place where the bricks would be red if you could ever scrub the decades of smog off of them. The old wooden floorboards were warped into shallow bumps and depressions. The walls smelled musty under a thick fresh cover of lemon cleaning spray.

The man who walked onto the stage looked more like a banker than a priest. A single purple sash hung diagonally across his sports-coat. When he spoke up his voice was reedy. "Welcome, brothers and sisters, to this auspicious night for our young Chapel! As some of you know already, I am Brother Phillip, apostle to our esteemed Lord Anton Parris, servant of God's avenging angels! Tonight you will see with your own eyes the miraculous power that the Almighty has given unto Lord Parris, to wreak holy vengeance upon the enemies of our fair land!

"Tonight, we begin the campaign to take back our city, our nation, our *world* from the faithless and profane mongrels who sully it! Tonight, right here, we reclaim the world in God's name! Brothers and sisters, Tonight is the Night! Are you ready??" He thrust his pudgy hands into the air and scattered diehards in the crowd thrust theirs up and began cheering. Brother Phillip dropped his hands and began pacing the stage.

"I can see that some of you are still skeptical. You doubt that one man, even one blessed by God, even one trained in the arts of war by our nation's Armed Forces, even one of such exceptional insight and training, even a man who has devoted his very soul to the cause, could possibly bring such a change in the order of the world. Well, brothers and sisters, it is not one man alone, but all of us, and those millions who will rally to our banner as our mission spreads outward, and not mere men alone but the God Almighty and His tireless angels who stand behind us, who *will* do this, who *will* prevail, who will conquer this fallen city and tread the heathen beneath our feet!"

He kept on rolling, stirring the crowd, but I stopped listening. The three of us began to weave our way to the stairwell door. There were no guards, no locks, and no real problem slipping through it, once Brother Phillip had everyone's attention with his spiel about the towers falling and the victims leaping from windows and how the heathens have it coming to them. With the door closed behind us, the roars from the crowd were muffled, but they was still bigger than last round. He was winning them over.

Lan and I took a minute to scan the fire exit map on the wall. Nyx crouched down and waved his hands slowly over the stairs going up and down from the landing. I'm long past asking him why he does things like that. I never like the answers he gives. He shook his head. "No one's been upstairs all day. What we're looking for must be down in the basement." Maybe he saw some sort of tracks and didn't feel like pointing them out. Maybe he knew what we'd find when we got down to the basement. Maybe he was just guessing. It didn't matter to me which way we searched first. As we crept down the stairs, I pulled out my goggles and slipped them on, brightening the dim light from the one window. I smelled more of Nyx's powder and when I looked back at him, somewhere behind Lan, I almost couldn't see him, even with the goggles. He'd faded halfway into the dark.

The basement was full of the sort of junk you'd expect in an auction house: trunks, tons of furniture, so-so statues and mediocre paintings, boxes of books, racks of old dresses, clocks and knickknacks. There were paths meandering through the clutter, but it took us a while to get anywhere, creeping in the half-dark towards the single light-bulb shining in the far corner.

When I finally peered around a row of empty bookshelves, I saw two men standing guard in front of a steamer trunk. One man was wiry, but tall, with toned muscles. He wore jeans and a sleeveless muscle shirt. The other was a small thin man in a tweed suit, his sandy blond hair carefully combed. Unfortunately, I'd rested my hand on the nearest bookshelf and it rocked slightly on uneven legs.

"Ey! Whatayou doin down here!? The show's upstairs!" The man in jeans said, as soon as he saw me. His long black hair bounced as he strode over. He sneered as he smacked his hands on my chest to push me back. "I said, whatayou—" I could see the realization dawning in his eyes a second or two before he ripped open my coat to confirm what his hands had already told him: I was wearing armor. His sneer blossomed into a full-sized vicious grin. I decided that was a good moment to punch him.

"Uh, W-What Brother Andrew means to say is that this area is off limits to—oh." Brother Andrew's partner was still standing next to the trunk. He went silent again as the fighting started.

Punching Brother Andrew was like swimming through jello. By the time I connected, my fist was barely moving. Getting punched by Brother Andrew was like falling off of the third floor. I heard the wind in my ears before I landed flat. Maybe he had some kind of force field or vapor cushion around him that absorbed energy and stored it for him to use. I had a few seconds (okay, minutes) to think while my vision cleared.

When it did, I'd lost track of Nyx completely and Lan was wrestling Brother Andrew into the nearest wall, both of them snarling like animals, although Andrew was more coherent, almost using real swear words. I don't know what those sounds Lan was making were supposed to be. As I got to my feet, Andrew stretched out a hand towards a junction box and pulled electric current out of it to whip at the Atlantean's back like a rope made of lightning. That's what it looked like, anyway. I know as well as anyone that energy doesn't just hold still like that. He must've been generating some sort of magnetic field that kept the electricity moving in circuits where he wanted it to be, to create the illusion that it was solid. Either way, the electrical burns and flames licking at Lan's coat were real, and he let go of Andrew to throw off the coat. Andrew cracked the whip and Lan screamed and spasmed. I pulled a gun.

That's when the little man in tweed decided to get brave. "Y-y-you're too late to stop us, you know. W-we've already assembled the army, and soon we'll overrun this city, and then the world. You can't think that—"

"Buddy," I said, leveling my Midnight Multi-Pistol at him, "I've heard that speech a dozen times already, and every one of them was more convincing than that."

He held out a hand in front of himself and looked away. It started to rain . . . indoors. In a basement. Just over my head. I nearly burst out laughing. The Great and Powerful Oz had given his partner, the violent moron, the power to hold lightning in his hands, and here this poor fool was, at gunpoint, with the power to make it rain indoors. Except, before I could say anything, I noticed my gloves were melting like wet Kleenex. My battle-suit is the most useful of my gadgets. It's bulletproof, fireproof, and spray-coated to be corrosion-proof. I don't know what that stuff was dissolving my coat, gloves, and hat, but it sure as hell wasn't just normal acid. I started running. The rain followed me, oozing along the ceiling. It wasn't able to keep up with me perfectly, probably because all the junk kept blocking his line of sight and he had to guess where I was. Dressers and armoires and a crate of Zane Grey's took a sizzling and melting that was meant for me. I was making a long, rough arc towards Tweed Man through the maze of clutter when I passed near Brother Andrew, who ran after me. Thank God for violent morons.

As he swept out his 'whip', it touched the raindrops and shorted out in a bright flash. I could hear it, but I was looking the other way. Tweed Man jerked as if the electrical flash had stung him. He lost track of his death shower for a few seconds, and as it stopped moving, Andrew didn't, running straight into it, slipping on the wet floor and screaming as the deadly rain began to immediately eat the skin off his naked arms. I kept running until I could clock the little rainmaker with the handle of my gun.

I peeled off my wet outer layer of clothes and looked around. The "rain" had eaten the black paint off my pistol, leaving gleaming, scored metal, but it still seemed functional. Andrew was bleeding to death in a puddle of acid rainwater, his face and torso a mass of red flesh. Lan was on the floor, but slowly getting up. Some of the sprinkler pipes in the ceiling had been weakened by the acid rain flowing past them and were spraying water. I found Nyx after a few tries, standing near the stairs. The rainmaker was out cold at my feet. The steamer trunk was locked. The lock was just a Swenson double-plate. I was taking those apart before I even went to engineering school.

Inside was nothing except a cloth bag holding a dark glass lens, about as large as a man's palm. Of course, it didn't "radiate darkness" or anything. It was just a hunk of smoked glass, with this tiny glimmer of red light inside it. Curious, I peered closer, trying to find out if it was a reflection, a tiny light-emitting diode, some sort of impurity in the glass . . . and that's when I felt it. It was like the feeling I get when I stare into circuits; except I didn't see the orderly purpose of things. I saw the dark: the darkness between stars, filling the cosmos; the darkness between photons on the subatomic level, seeping into every inch of matter. I saw randomness, chaos, and death, surrounding the islands of pattern and law and life on every side, even above and below.

For a moment, I understood why Doctor Nyx had called it the "Eye of Eternal Night" . . . but he was wrong when he said, "There is a place where light never shines." The place is here. The darkness is right here, underneath the light. That's what I was thinking. Then a hand swept it away, and it shattered into a thousand pieces on a concrete wall. I looked up and saw a scaly creature with glistening eyes and a grin full of pointed teeth. It took me a few seconds to realize I was looking at Lan.

"Are you alright? You looked like the Lens was sucking you in."

"I'm fine. It's . . . was just a fancy paperweight. I don't even know why these two mopes were guarding it."

"Because," Nyx volunteered, "their 'esteemed Lord Parris' wouldn't want anyone else staring into it and making their own bargains."

"Well, now it's nothing but black sand and evil splinters. I guess no one will be staring into it anymore."

"I should hope not. Do you hear that?" Nyx turned to look up the stairs. "They're chanting. Chanting is never good."

Nyx trotted up the stairs first, but by the time he reached the top, me and Lan were right behind him. Gentleman and coward that he is, he let us go through the door first. The sound he had heard was a roomful of people murmuring "the Angel . . . the Angel . . ." over and over. From the matching glazed, rapturous looks on all their faces, I figured Brother Phillip could've pulled out a stuffed parrot and they would've seen an angel. Lord Anton Parris wasn't a parrot, but he sure as hell wasn't an angel, either.

He looked like he had been grafted into the middle of some sort of huge dead gargoyle. His skin was a leprous white, except for black splotches of mold. His head and chest, still florid and living, were embedded between huge, monstrous limbs. He stood eight feet tall on double-jointed legs with clawed feet. His wings were huge undulating flaps of boneless muscle, covered in hide that grew ragged at the edges. What Lan had thought was a sword was actually a long thin tail with a sharp spine at the end. When he saw us, his eyes narrowed to slits, his lips pulled back from broken yellow teeth, and a feral hiss like a jungle cat rose from his throat. He made Brother Andrew look like Mother Theresa.

"Iiinnnfidels!! Destroy them, my child-ren!!", he growled. The entire crowd turned to look where he pointed. Our trench coats were gone. We didn't blend in anymore. Every one of them was holding something sharp: camping hatchets, butcher knives, hacksaws. I guess we missed the handing-out part of the program. Their eyes all narrowed to slits. Their lips all pulled back. That same angry-cat hiss began to rise from every throat in the room. I managed to draw my pistol before they rushed us.

Once again, I totally lost track of Nyx. I was too busy blocking, punching, and shooting. The multi-pistol was loaded with rubber bullets, but at point blank, even rubber can do damage. I wasn't in any position to be nice about it. Every drone that dropped was stepped on by the drones still standing as they rushed in like water. I stood my ground, my back to the wall, tripping them on their fallen comrades. Lan started working his way through the crowd, charging forward with quick low jumps, using his arms to sweep aside or bowl over whoever got in his way, matching every hiss with more guttural wet growls. I lost track of him, too . . . until he bounded onto the stage and cut Brother Phillip down with a single swipe of his claws.

Before the shocked spokesman hit the floor, Lan had turned to grin at the gargoyle thing. Despite being dead flesh, the thing moved like a jaguar, slashing Lan with a quick swipe of his tail. Lan leapt at him, and Parris hit him in mid-air with a single slap that knocked him back into the middle of the crowd. The drones swarmed at Lan and he pulled their legs out from under them. (Block. Pistol whip. Disarm. Punch. Shoot . . .) I was starting to run out of rubber bullets by the time Lan leapt out of the crowd again and raked his claws across Parris's chest. The marks he left were long, but the parts that crossed dead flesh didn't bleed and the parts that crossed living flesh began sealing up immediately. Only the seam where dead and living joined stayed bloody. When Lan tried the other hand, Parris caught it, lifted him into the air, and threw him to the back of the room.

My last rubber bullet knocked a machete out of the hand of a thrall in a red and black sweater-vest. I ducked under a clumsy attempt to behead me with a carpenter's saw and switched clips to armor-piercing bullets. There's a moment in every disaster when it's clear things have gone to hell. Usually, it's when I put in lethal ammo and start swearing. I shoulder-tackled saw-guy to knock him into sweater man, stood on a stack of unconscious bodies to get some height, and aimed my pistol at Anton Parris, at his chest, at the line between white moldy flesh and pink . . . at those little specks of red just now drying to black . . . and fired off three shots before someone hit me in the small of the back with something . . . might've been hedge-clippers. I fell to the floor, rolled onto my back, and looked up at saw-guy, sweater-man, and a teenage kid holding hedge-clippers, all standing over me with second-hand murder in their eyes.

Then something fluttered past their heads, a small black transparent shape, like a bat. It swung around to flap in each of their faces, one after another, and I realized it was one of Nyx's illusions. Shadows don't fly around without the bodies that cast them. I stumbled to my feet, slugged hedge-clipper boy, and glanced around. Nyx wasn't anywhere in sight. Lan was covered to his shoulders in a solid clot of grasping thralls. He looked like he was trying to drag all of them forward with him. A woman with frizzy blonde hair was stepping in behind him and raising a hatchet. I jabbed sweater man in the solar plexus and saw-guy in the throat, raised my pistol, and blew the ax's head off its handle just before she could take Lan's head off.

I started working my way towards Lan, but I was only six cultists in before I heard the crash behind me. I spun around, and that damned tail of his knocked the pistol out of my hand, nearly taking off a finger in the process. I should've known that Parris would take a personal interest in someone who'd managed to hurt him. The three holes in his chest were bleeding but not fast enough to save me, now that he was only seven feet away.

Nyx's bat came fluttering back to flap in his face. I dove for the gun, but the drones were having none of that. One of them kicked the pistol away into the sea of feet. Two other drones grabbed me and dragged me closer to their dead-winged master. The rest stood like a wall of sharpened logs, glaring at me. Lan crashed through that wall from the other side. He was splattered with blood, probably not his, and his breathing was deep and ragged; but he saw the bleeding wounds on Parris' chest and comprehension dawned in his eyes like a nuclear bomb, instant and furious. When Nyx's bat flew left, I twisted free of the right-hand cultist and I bolted left, too, pulling the left-hand cultist along with me. As Parris spun, whipping his tail around to trip me, Lan leapt at his torso. Lan plunged his claws deep into the bullet wounds. I jump-roped over the tail and it cut bright red gashes in the front of Lefty's shins. He let go of me as he went down.

Parris grabbed the back of Lan's head and started to pull, but I'd found that dropped machete and I threw it at the bastard's face. He blocked it with his free hand, but Lan had only needed that one second to find the right layer of tissue with his fingers, flex his powerful leaping muscles, and push himself away, still hooked into Parris's wounds. With a sick, wet snapping sound, he tore dead flesh from living, arm and shoulder and wing pulling loose all in a piece. Blood gushed from the exposed muscles of Anton Parris' remaining humanity, and he screamed bloody murder—literally, as it turned out.

The cultists were already mind-controlled foot-soliders set to massacre, but now they turned on each other. Those who still had weapons began hacking away at whoever they could reach. Those who didn't have weapons charged at the ones who did. Those who were on the ground were trampled, speared, kicked or smothered under dead bodies. I just stood there in the widening pool of blood from Parris's fallen body, trying to understand the pattern, to see how to stop fifty people at once from committing suicide. I couldn't see it. I found my pistol, though. I worked my way over to it. I was no longer any more of a target than anyone else in the room.

I realized the cultists would swarm on anyone who was bleeding and cut him down, so I hid my wounded hand under my other arm. The darkness was there again, in the inhuman screams of men gone mad, in the constant sound of metal biting into flesh, underneath the floor now slick with blood. I picked up my gun and shambled back to the nearest door. By the time I got to the stairwell, there were more of them dead than alive.

I shouldn't have looked back. The center of the room was covered with bodies and puddles of blood running together underneath them. Red, raw meat tentacles were snaking up out of the places where the blood was deepest. They were covered in ridges of scar tissue and streaks of purplish-black, like a deep bruise, or meat that's gone rotten with the blood still inside it. They were at least six feet long, sliding out of blood no more than a few inches deep. Maybe, in that moment, I understood how that could happen, but I didn't want to. I'm a man of science. I'd seen the room downstairs, and it sure as hell didn't have any place to hide a goddamn giant squid. That much flesh has to come from somewhere. It doesn't just form. Nyx wasn't a man of science. He'd given up on rationality long ago. He was there, suddenly, shouting in my ear. "Scarab, listen to me. You have to burn them. Now."

" . . . What? Nyx, there are still a few—"

"Damn it! Burn Them Now!! *Before they start getting back up!!*"

I looked closer. A corpse with no throat was beginning to move. "Oh. Hell. Stand back." I dry-fired the pistol a couple times to clear the barrel while I pulled out thermite shells with my wounded hand. I'm not quite as good shooting right-handed, but it was good enough to hit prone targets. Soon bodies and tentacles all over the room were sizzling . . . especially the gargoyle thing. I made sure of that.

I didn't have enough ammo to cook every body one by one. I needed to gut the place. I spun around and bolted down the stairs to the basement. The cellar floor was covered in several feet of water. The main sprinkler pipe must've given way, saving me the trouble of breaking it.

A well-designed weapon is a thing of beauty. These thermite shells are tipped with a small, carefully packed bit of phosphorus. The impact sets off the phosphorus, which sets off the sugar chlorate, which is hot enough to set off the thermite, which burns hot enough to set off anything. Like say, a soaking wet oak-paneled armoire that looks like the one my aunt used to have. Man, I hated that thing. The maple vanity table lit up nicely, too. I was picking out a few more big targets when I noticed movement in the corner of my eye. I pointed my pistol straight at his face. It was tweed man.

"If I feel so much as a drop of sweat, I'm putting a bullet right into your brain." I said, and for once I really meant it. The rainmaker started to put up his hands, apparently decided that was too threatening, and left them, palms up, at his sides.

"I-I-I'll come peacefully. I'm not m-much of a fighter, rea—"

"Listen. Your friends all slaughtered each other. Your only chance of getting out of this alive is going to that fire door over there, leaving this building, and running like hell. Can you do that, or should I just put you out of your misery now?" He could. I knew Nyx would've said I was a fool for letting him go, but I didn't have time to drag prisoners along and I just wasn't cold enough to burn to death some stuttering math teacher who'd already surrendered.

I lit up a few more targets (a dresser with a bunch of paintings leaning against it and a rocking horse) before I found the mother lode: the oil tank for the heater. This early in the fall, it was either nearly empty or nearly full. I put in earplugs as I went up to the fire-door and cracked it open. A nearly full tank would solve my problem, if I didn't get caught in the explosion. I leaned my back against the door, aimed carefully across the room, and shot the tank. It was full. Oh, it was *full*. The shock-wave knocked me through the door and into the alley wall on the other side. I went limp, hit flat, and managed to walk away with nothing but some big bruises.

Nyx and Lan were already across the street. The traffic was sparse tonight, and what pedestrians there were gave Lan a wide berth. (New Yorkers aren't the sort to panic at the first sign of something weird, but they also aren't naive lambs who'll step too close to a clawed freak covered in blood.) Nyx looked straight into my eyes as I approached them.

"Did you get them all?"

"Every last one, Nyx . . . God help me. The outer walls will hold, but everything inside is cooked."

"Even the small one with sandy blonde hair? That tried to kill you with the Rain of Par'egleth?"

"No, Nyx, dammit, not him, but everyone else . . . I swear."

Nyx nodded. "We saw him running down the alley. I'll find him. I'll make sure he isn't a threat anymore. Later. First, I'll call the Fire Department from that pay-phone, as soon as you two are gone. They should get here in time to contain the blaze, but not to see what was inside. I'm sure the *police* have been notified by now," Nyx glanced up at the windows overlooking the street. Plenty of windows had lights in them, but every one of them had the curtain pulled, at least most of the way. " . . . and thank you, gentlemen. I'll be in touch."

"Yeah, I'll bet you will."

"Uh, Midnight Scarab, could I get a ride with you? Leaping away across town might draw undue attention and I—"

"Yeah, Lan, no problem. Mi aeroship es su aeroship."

"Gracias, Senor Escarabajo. Tu es muy benevelo."

Ok, so Lan's still creepy and annoying to talk to, but that night, he saved my ass. I figured I owed him some face time. After I had my hand looked at ("Yes, Nurse, it is a nasty gash. That's what I get for tinkering with the metal grinders in my workshop so late into the night. Twelve stitches? Oh my! Will it leave a scar?"), I found a better class of rooftop, overlooking the lights of Midtown, and we hung out . . . he's not my new sidekick or anything, but I guess he's not *that* bad . . . for a hyper-intelligent humanoid fish-thing. Anyway, I needed to talk to someone who knew how it was. I needed to look at all the light of mankind, pushing back the darkness around them. I needed to remember that light and forget the darkness.

# BLOOD BAGS
# AND TENTACLES

*D.L. Snell*

yan looked out of the hotel's window over the scorched, crumbling buildings and the wrecked ambulances, cars, and police cruisers, scouting for any sign of Shaun. The city had once been Portland, Oregon. Now it was something else. Smoke rose here and there—from a burning tenement, from a crashed Black Hawk—and smog blurred the skyline. Huge hornet-like silhouettes soared through the haze, and every now and again creatures that resembled plants shuffled between city blocks. And those were just the horrors you could see.

Glass crunched behind Ryan and he whirled, drawing his .45.

"Just me," Quincy said. She held up her hands. "See? No tentacles."

"Sorry." Ryan holstered his gun.

They were on the floor originally designated for conventions and other special events. The room they stood in was a lounge, but everyone called it the Crow's Nest. Many of the walls had been axed apart and spray-painted, the couches and chairs ripped open, their stuffing strewn everywhere. Glass littered the carpet, mainly from shattered windows and broken picture frames. Albeit scorched and cracked, the windows in this part of the Crow's Nest remained whole, even after all the riots and the battles with the creatures that had overrun Earth. This was one reason Ryan's people used it as a lookout: you were safer indoors and behind windows; it was harder for something to eat you.

"What're you doing up here, Quincy?" Ryan asked.

"I like the view." She wore her black coveralls and her combat boots; she had braided her blond mane, one plait behind each ear, which she only did if she planned to go out.

"You're not coming with me," he said, and he turned back to the window. He could see her reflection in it, but barely. Just a ghost of her.

"So you *are* going," she said.

"Yes, but you're not coming with me."

"Can I ask why you want to go after him? He betrayed you."

"He's my brother, Quincy. It doesn't matter what he did."

She chewed her lip, and he continued to scan the horizon, although at this point he wasn't paying attention; he just didn't want to face her. He consulted his wristwatch. Shaun had been gone for one hour. Ryan had set his alarm for an hour and a half, at which time he planned to go after his brother.

"Did he let off his flare yet?" Quincy asked.

"No. And he's had plenty of time to reach the river. The tunnels go straight there. It's like a grid, for Christ's sake."

"That doesn't mean something happened to him. I know he said he'd let one off if he was safe, but you can't always count on your brother."

Ryan sighed, deflating like an empty sack. The Willamette River was grey, distant, and cold. He checked his watch again; the time had barely changed.

"If you could count on him," Quincy continued, "we wouldn't be in this mess."

Ryan bit down and his temples throbbed. Quincy always said the things she shouldn't.

"*Me*," he said.

"What?"

"*Me*—not *we*. It's my mess."

"Ryan—"

He started to push past her, but she caught his arm and forced him to meet her eyes, calm and blue like water. His cheek twitched and he wanted to look away, but couldn't.

"You don't have to do this alone," she said. Much quieter she added, "You don't have to be alone."

Her breast brushed his arm, and his cheeks heated up. He hadn't been this close to her before. She smelled clean, like the herbal shampoo they had scavenged. She smelled like a woman. Her grip softened on his arm and she searched his eyes, searched them too deeply.

He tore away from her and stalked toward the stairs.

"Ryan!" she called, but he was one to never look back.

# # # # #

In his room on the second floor, Ryan packed a backpack with a flashlight, batteries, and extra ammunition. He sheathed a machete and buck knife on his belt. Then he opened the drawer on his nightstand. The courtesy bible was of no use to him. What he needed lay next to it: his silver Peace Dollar, issued in 1926. His grandfather had carried it during his Air Force duty in World War II, and its good luck had helped him split a German train in half at the coupling. Shaun possessed the coin's equally lucky twin, the one their grandmother had held onto with the hope that their grandfather would come back from the war, which he had.

Ryan looked down at Lady Liberty's profile on the front of the dollar. "Go?" he asked her, and he flipped the coin. Heads, yes. Tails, no.

It landed on tails.

Ryan sighed. He tucked the coin into the pocket of his camouflage fatigues. Then he blew out his candles and walked out the door.

The community lived on the second story of the hotel; the first floor had no rooms, just the lobby, restaurant, and indoor pool. Only security occupied the downstairs, armed with shotguns, handguns, and a few M16s from the National Guardsmen that had joined the group. Two sentries armed with M16s were also posted on the sub-floor in the parking garage, under the fluttering wing of lantern light. They saluted Ryan as he came out of the stairwell.

"At ease," he said. He had never served in the military. In fact, before the end of the world he had been a framer with his own work crew. He knew how to lead and that's why everyone saluted him. But they had only adopted that custom after the National Guardsmen had shown up. In some ways, things had been better beforehand.

"I'm going into the tunnels," he told the sentries. "Don't let anyone follow me."

Ben, the big black guy, nodded and blew a bubble in his strawberry bubblegum. But the other guard, Derek Spencer, pushed his glasses up his crooked nose and said, "Sir, you can't go into the tunnels alone. That's against the rules. That's—"

Ryan stepped up so close that Spencer had to lean back. "A little more than one hour ago, my brother Shaun Adams went into those tunnels unescorted. Do you mind telling me how long you've been on shift, Spencer?"

"Exactly three hours, sir, but—"

"My bad," Ben said, chewing his gum. "I let your brother through."

Ryan stepped back from Spencer and adjusted his backpack. "Good," he said. "Because you're doing the same for me."

Ben shrugged, but Spencer pursed his lips and shook his head. "Sorry, sir. Not on my watch. I'll have to come with you."

Ryan said, "I don't have time for this shit." He started off toward the entrance into the tunnels and Spencer jogged after him.

"Wait up, sir!"

The guard walked heavily, his footfalls echoing into the concrete passages of the garage. Like Ryan, he wore fatigues. But his were too big for his stick-figure frame, and he had to constantly hitch up his pants. He looked like a kid in grownup clothes. Practically was.

Spencer dug a flashlight out of his cargo pocket and turned it on. Ryan had his out too. There were no lights beneath the city. Not where they were going.

"People *die* down there," Ryan said, speaking of the tunnels. "You want to die, Spencer?"

"Hey, I've killed one of those floating vampire things before. One of the invisible ones that get all red when they drink your blood? One of those blood bags? I painted the room with that son of a bitch."

Ryan chuffed. "We're in for much worse."

# # # # #

No one knew how the world had ended. The last emergency broadcasts speculated that the creatures had come from outer space, but before that, some cult leader wearing the clerical garb of the Anglican church had sent a video threat to the President of the United States; the cultist claimed to possess a set of ancient tomes, books full of spells and incantations, and he would use these volumes to unleash Hell on Earth. He called his cult the Clergymen of Evil.

Whatever the cause, every country in the world was soon overrun with monsters, things with tentacles and amoeba-like bodies, things with pincers and things with wings, some of them bigger than the Pentagon.

Every government crumbled, every military fell, and the streets soon grew teeth. Up there, something could ambush you from any direction. That's why Ryan's people traveled via the tunnels: attacks could only come from ahead or behind, and only a few aggressors could come at you at once. A bottleneck.

The entrance was in the southern part of the parking garage. Ryan's group would have never known about the underground network if a monster hadn't burst through the garage's concrete wall; it ate three guards before they blew it to a pile of twitching tentacles. Since then, they parked a van in front of the hole to prevent anything else from slithering in.

"Move it," Ryan commanded.

Spencer said, "Yes, sir," and he pulled the vehicle forward until the passenger door lined up with the cavity. Then he and Ryan climbed through the van, into the tunnels. They locked the doors behind them; they both had a key so they could get back.

The darkness in the passageways was thick and musty with the smell of dirt, stone, and old wood. Their flashlights barely penetrated as they ducked under sewer lines, water pipes, and electrical conduits, as they passed through brick-and-mortar archways and walked by opium dens made of old throwaway cuts of oak. Ryan followed Shaun's footsteps in the dust.

In the late nineteenth century, around Portland's lumber boom, criminals known as "crimps" used the tunnels to kidnap able-bodied men from brothels and bars; the crimps sold these men as white slaves to ship captains. After World War II, someone clogged the tunnels with rubble and debris, but the city's Geographical Society later cleared them out. They were dubbed the Shanghai Tunnels, or the Portland Underground. They went all the way to the river.

"So," Spencer said, a little louder than he should have; he was loading a grenade into the M203 launcher affixed under the barrel of the M16. "What's our mission, sir?"

Ryan answered without looking back or slowing down. "*I'm* looking for my brother," he said. "*You're* being a pain in the ass. Now shut up before something hears us."

"Your brother, huh?" Spencer pushed up his glasses and was silent for a moment, but Ryan could hear it coming; he bit down and waited for it. "So is it true he shot you?"

"Didn't I just tell you to—"

"'Cause I heard you two were on a scavenging mission and he shot you because he wanted to take over—Ben told me that's why he left today. Self-exile. But what I want to know is why he didn't finish you off. Why didn't he shoot you in the head when he saw your bulletproof vest?"

Ryan spun around and slammed Spencer against the wall; he had to clench his stomach muscles to keep from yelling, had to breathe shallowly to avoid the stink of the guard's cavities. "Why did you *really* come, Spencer, huh? Because of the rules, or because you wanted to fucking grill me?"

"I—" Spencer began, but he stopped short when something like a small child tittered in the darkness.

Ryan shined his flashlight down the tunnel, revealing more pipes and a brick wall with a window of iron bars. He knew that sound. It never failed to chill his blood.

"Oh shit," Spencer whispered. "It's one of those things, one of those vampire things—a fucking blood bag." He started to shake. The kid must have really thought there was no danger down here. Idiot.

The blood bag chittered again, and Spencer whimpered. Ryan pressed him harder against the wall, glaring, putting a finger to his lips to hush him. Spencer nodded but couldn't stop trembling.

Quietly, Ryan unholstered his .45. He rubbed his silver dollar through his pocket, laid down his backpack, and crept farther into the tunnel.

Although translucent when empty, blood bags rippled like a heat wave; Ryan could see no such disturbance. But that window of iron bars meant a cell hid behind the wall, one of the many jails where crimps had imprisoned their slaves. A small entrance led into the cell. That's where the noise was coming from. Ryan was sure of it.

He sucked up against the wall right before the opening. The snickering had stopped and the tunnels had fallen silent; everything seemed muffled.

Spencer stood frozen by Ryan's backpack. It was better that way. Safer. The kid would probably sneeze at the wrong time and get them both killed.

Ryan held his breath and waited for the blood bag to make another sound. It didn't. So he pivoted into the opening, shining his light, aiming his gun: concrete, space; a pile of old boots moldering in the corner. The cell was empty.

The blood bag tittered, right behind him.

"Watch out!" Spencer cried.

Ryan turned, reeling backward into the cell. His flashlight illuminated a clear jelly-like shape undulating in front of him, small, just a yearling, but big enough to kill. He knew from experience that they were covered in countless tentacular trunks with little suckers at the end, always opening and closing like the mouths of needy infants. Transparent as they were now, the trunks looked more like cilia moving the vampire along. The thing's talons were well defined. They reached out to snag him.

Boom!—Ryan's .45 punched a hole through the creature's stalk. Globs splattered the wall behind it, and the blood bag faltered, wobbled—and then it came forward, cackling. Ryan drew his machete, stumbled over a piece of rubble, almost fell.

The monster's talons shot forward.

He darted between them and hacked through its torso. The two halves plopped to the ground, twitching and pouring out clear entrails, stinking of minerals and burnt ozone so sharp Ryan could taste it. One of its talons reached up and he cut it off. The thing lay still.

"Sir?" Spencer called, his voice high and cracking. "Sir?"

Ryan stepped over the corpse, back into the tunnel. Spencer flinched as if ready to run, but he halted when he realized who had prevailed.

"My bag," Ryan said, wiping his machete on his pant leg.

Spencer picked up the backpack and hurried forward. He was much whiter than usual.

"Thought you'd dealt with these before," Ryan said.

"I... I *have*, it's just—what the hell was it doing underground? It—"

"I don't know," Ryan admitted. "They're usually too big for the tunnels; this one's probably a baby. I have no clue what it was doing, but—look, kid . . ." He sighed and laid a hand on Spencer's shoulder; the guard was still shaking, but not as badly. At least he hadn't run. At least he had *some* metal in him. "If you want to turn back, do it now. It only gets worse."

Spencer stroked his M16. He glanced toward the parking garage and pushed up his glasses. "No, I can keep going—if you want me to."

Ryan squeezed his shoulder and let go. "Just, next time, use that rifle of yours," he said. "Don't just stand there."

Spencer beamed and started to salute. "Yes, sir—"

The back wall of the cell exploded, and a tentacle shot out.

# # # # #

In a blast of dust, the feeler wrapped around Spencer. It was thicker than any anaconda. As it tightened, the guard dropped his flashlight and his M16. His eyes bulged, knocking his glasses off one ear—he vomited blood.

Spattered in the kid's gore, Ryan staggered back. All that dust: he could barely see, could barely breathe. He could still make out the tentacle's flesh, black with orange diamonds, lumpy with human faces that screamed and moaned silently as Spencer's bones ground together.

The kid gurgled something. Something like, "Help me." And then the feeler wrenched him into the cell and disappeared in the cloud.

With his sleeve, Ryan wiped the blood off his face; he spit out the coppery tang, spit out the gritty debris between his teeth, struggling not to vomit. He ran to the chamber and shined his light inside. He almost called Spencer's name, almost shouted it, but he restrained himself.

The kid was gone.

And something was coming back.

He could hear it slithering across the dirt.

Holstering his handgun, Ryan picked up the extra flashlight and the M16. He took one step forward, ready to run, but another tentacle barged in and bowled him over. He dropped everything and landed on his side.

The tentacle hovered over him, highlighted in the fallen light. Like fleshy satellite dishes, two sensors blossomed on either side of its tip. They were ribbed with cartilage, and each had a pore at the center.

*Fucking ears*, Ryan realized. *It's blind.*

Suddenly he had to cough. The dust irritated his throat. He swallowed, tried holding his breath, tried scratching his throat with his tongue.

The tentacle turned its head down the tunnel and pricked its ears. It was so close Ryan could feel its heat. Its faces mouthed curses and pleas. Obviously, the feeler could not see through their eyes. Otherwise he'd be dead.

Finally, Ryan suppressed the cough—just in time for his watch to start beeping; he had set the alarm for an hour and a half.

The big serpentine creature locked in on him, its ears alert. Ryan reached for his gun.

Someone in the tunnel behind them shouted, "Hey!" A bullet pierced the tentacle diagonally through the tip, blowing the brains out of a face on the opposite side, along with ropes of blue fluid. The feeler lunged forward, toward the sniper, but another bullet punched through it, and Ryan rolled out of the way. The beast thumped to the ground, writhed, and then pulled back through its hole, bashing into the walls and knocking down more brick.

The sniper hurried forward. All Ryan could see was an approaching light. He clicked off his watch's alarm and picked up the two flashlights and the M16.

"Ryan!" the sniper called, drawing closer.

"Fucking Ben," he mumbled, and then he coughed into his hand.

"What?" Quincy asked as she stopped next to him, panting.

"I thought I told you not to come," he said, fitting the M16 into an adjustable harness he'd rigged on the side of his backpack; the M203 still had a grenade in it.

Quincy grinned. "You know I'm a rebel." She peered into the cell, through the settling dust. "What the hell was that thing anyway? And where's Spencer? Ben said he followed you."

Ryan put the kid's flashlight in his pocket and stared down the tunnel. "It ate him," he said. "And if you don't shut up, it'll eat you too." With that, he marched off, deeper into the darkness.

# # # # #

Quincy and Ryan traveled in silence, past intersections of the Underground, past heaps of rubble and broken chairs dating back to the late 1800s. He walked fast, but she hounded him.

"Think it's safe to talk now?" she asked.

He didn't say anything. He hoped to set an example.

"Okay," she said, "I get it. You don't have to talk. That way it'll only eat me. But that's really not why you're ignoring me, is it?"

He gritted his teeth, walked a little faster.

"Jesus Christ, would you slow down? Ryan! Why the hell are you going kamikaze for someone who doesn't give a rat's ass about you?"

He bit down as hard as he could, eyes boiling in their sockets. If she had been anyone besides Quincy he would have socked her.

"Go back," he told her.

"No." She grabbed his arm and halted him. "Your brother's *gone*, Ryan. Let him go. Come back to where people care about you."

"No one fucking cares."

She frowned. "I do."

"Quincy . . ." he said, voice quivering.

"What? What is it? I want to know."

He shook his head and stared at the ground. "He's all I have left," he said quietly. "The only thing I have since before the world went to hell."

"You have me," she replied.

Ryan shook his head and finally met her eyes. "You don't understand. He's the only person I know *exactly* who he is. I know him so well that I knew, I *knew* he was up to something that day we went out—he's always tried to beat me—so I wore that fucking vest. And yeah, he shot me, he stabbed me in the back. But he's my brother, Quincy. He's my goddamn brother."

He was trembling by the time he finished, and his eyes burned. Quincy's eyebrows were arched with concern, and she was caressing his arm. Then suddenly she was kissing him. She pressed her breasts and hips against him, soft and warm, and her lips tasted like strawberry gloss. Heat kindled between them, a fire he felt most in his loins. He put his hand on her waist, and their lips parted. She rested her forehead against his, arms draped over his shoulders.

"You could get to know *me*," she said. "You could come back with me."

"My brother . . ." he said, but she took his hand and placed it on her breast—God, it had been a long time since he'd felt a breast. Not since before the end of the world. Not since his wife.

He took a deep breath and nodded, not really thinking anymore, drunk on hormonal champagne. "All right," he said. "Okay."

Quincy smiled and took his hand. Hers was warm and soft and electric. They started toward home, and as they drew parallel with one of the offshoots, something metal glimmered in their beams.

"Wait," Ryan said, tearing away from her. He knew what the metal disc was before he reached it: his brother's Peace Dollar, heads-up in the dirt. He hadn't noticed it before, too intent on ditching Quincy.

He picked it up. Shaun would have never discarded it on purpose. And when Ryan examined the dirt around the coin, he noticed that his brother's footsteps stopped there. Drag marks led down the intersecting passageway. Big ones, as if a tentacle had passed through. No blood trail though: Shaun hadn't been crushed like Spencer.

"What is it?" Quincy asked.

A blood bag answered, tittering as they always did when they spotted prey.

Ryan stood slowly and dropped the coin into his pocket. He told Quincy to run, quietly. Because the tentacle that had snatched his brother was coming back.

The blood bag was calling it.

# # # # #

The beast bolted toward them like a bullet train, bursting through water mains and cracking supports. They hurtled homeward down the tunnel, dodging pipes and piles of rubbish, shooting pistols at their pursuer. They had a head start. But it was faster.

Quincy tripped on an old boot.

Ryan stopped, helped her up.

Then the tentacle grabbed her away from him, and her scream faded into the darkness.

"Quincy!" Ryan called.

The tunnel fell silent and cold.

"Fuck that," he said, and he started yelling and hammering the walls, jogging toward the place he'd found Shaun's coin.

The moment he'd heard the second blood bag, he had known the tentacles used the invisible vampires as alarm systems. The big beasts were attracted to noise, and maybe the blood bags' laughter emitted a frequency they could hear from far away, like a dog whistle.

He came to the intersection and cupped his hands around his mouth. "Hey, you bloodsucking shit! Come and get some!"

Nothing. No titter, no ripple in the air—nothing.

Ryan strode into the new passageway, pulling out his machete and his .45. Blood stippled the ground. More and more as he went.

*Quincy's*, he thought. *Oh shit.* He began to feel sick to his stomach, as if someone had kneed him in the crotch.

The red droplets grew into splatters, and then they veered toward the wall, smeared in a long arch across the brick. At the end of it, Ryan found a mound of guts, bladders, and stomachs, all in a twist of flesh. The stink was salty, coppery, and horrible, and the blood bag's talon was still convulsing. The big tentacle had obviously squashed it as it bulled through. But whose blood had the vampire sucked? His brother's?

Roaring, Ryan put a slug through the vampire's torso and it lay still. Then he ran, booing and jeering as loud as he could, not even sure where he was anymore, weeping and lost in the maze. The tentacle's drag marks turned left, then right, then left again, deeper and deeper until at one of the intersections they disappeared.

Ryan cursed and shot a support beam, shot it again and again until the damn thing exploded into splinters. "You hear that!" he cried, turning around and around, sending his voice down every corridor. "You hear that, you son of a bitch! Come get me—*come get me!*"

Silence. Nothing but his heartbeat in his ears.

He cursed again and sat down hard in the middle of the intersection, shoulders slumped. His legs ached, his back was sore, and his throat felt scratchy as hell. The dust had even sifted under his watch, had stuck there in his sweat. He undid the wristband so he could clean off his skin—and suddenly he had an idea.

# # # # #

He crouched in the corner between two intersecting passages, gripping his buck knife. Lying in the center of the crossroads, his watch started to beep. His eyes flicked from tunnel to tunnel. *Come on*, he thought. *Come get it.*

He speculated that the tentacles could only hear high-frequency sounds, which was why they utilized blood bags as sirens; in general, human sounds registered below that range. Which meant he owed Quincy an apology. He had told her to shut up or she'd get eaten like Spencer, but maybe the guard hadn't died because he was talking— maybe he'd died because he was standing in the same place the blood bag had sounded its alarm.

Two minutes passed.

Nothing.

*Come on, come on.*

The beeping watch shut off automatically.

"Damn it!"

Ryan stood to reset it. Or to stomp it. He didn't know which.

The air shifted behind him. He had no time to move—the tentacle shoved past and threw him to the ground, knocking the wind out of him. He couldn't breathe.

The feeler's ears sprouted and listened for the watch. It moved its head back and forth, directly above the timepiece. Faces writhed in its flesh.

Ryan stood, grimacing at the heavy ache in his stomach, struggling for air. His knife, he still had his knife. So he flung himself onto the creature's back. He stabbed it with his blade, used the hilt as a saddle horn, planted his feet into a couple mouths and used them as stirrups.

The tentacle reared and struck him against the ceiling. The impact flattened his backpack and bruised one of his ribs; a hot splinter of pain pierced his chest, but he held on. Why the force hadn't crushed him, he didn't know. Luck, maybe. A godsend from the coin, the same luck that had helped his grandfather bomb a German train, the very fortune that had brought the pilot home to his wife.

With a jolt that almost knocked him off, the beast pulled itself back down the tunnel. Wind and darkness whipped at Ryan's hair and fatigues. His backpack brushed the joists above him. He squeezed his eyes shut, waiting for the worm to bash him into the roof, smear him across it like it had smeared the blood bag.

It didn't.

But something snagged his backpack and ripped him off the tentacle. He landed hard in the dirt. With his knife still in it, the feeler sucked back up through a hole in a cellar wall. Wincing, coughing, clutching at his ribs, Ryan hobbled after it.

The building upstairs used to be a restaurant. To reach the cellar, the tentacle had smashed a big hole through the mahogany bar and through one of the exterior walls. From outside, the tittering of blood bags filtered through the breach.

Ryan walked in the tentacle's wake, flanked by chairs and tables and hunks of brick that it had shoved aside. The floor was grooved, which meant the beast traveled this path often. He drew his .45, put in a new magazine, and peeked his head through the exterior hole, careful not to tread on the bent-over rebar lest it make noise.

Across the street, protruding from the windows of a two-story building at the end of the block, black tentacles with a pattern of orange diamonds wriggled in the air. Some of them loomed seven stories tall. Fatter tentacles stuck out from holes in the building's front and side wall; they had burrowed into the pavement. To penetrate the tunnels, Ryan deduced. The whole thing looked like a giant squid.

On the roof, the tentacles held countless poles over the street. Hanging from them on ropes, human corpses decayed. Some were bloated and runny and full of maggots. Some were skeletal and sunken in. And then one of them was fresh. Blood bags swarmed around this newer kill, sanguine with its blood, and a few translucent ones picked at the putrefying cadavers with their talons. They laughed like cruel, idiotic children.

A tentacle plucked one of the vampires out of the sky and disappeared with it into a hole in the sidewalk. A new alarm for the underground. *It's fishing*, Ryan concluded, watching the bodies sway. *Jesus Christ.*

He studied the fresh bait, squinting to see between all those quivering red blood bags. He didn't have to stare long before he glimpsed fatigues, shredded now from all those needy mouths. Quincy had been wearing black coveralls. Shaun had been wearing an orange jumpsuit, his idea of a joke. So the body up there must have been Spencer.

Behind the windows that the feelers hadn't burst, black flesh pulsated, smearing the glass with some kind of clear secretion. The tissue looked tender, vulnerable, as if it used the building as a shell. *Like a fucking hermit crab*, Ryan thought. He aimed his .45 at one of these windows. He could shoot it, maybe hurt it. But the blood bags would engulf him.

He needed to find a way into the hermitage. He had a feeling that's where he would find Quincy and Shaun.

To the right of the hole in the bar, bottles of hard alcohol lay tipped-over on the shelves; some lay on the floor. Ryan selected a vodka and took a swig. The burn felt good, but he couldn't drink enough to dull the splinter in his ribs because the booze would also dull his mind. He went to the exit, which faced a different street than the hermitage. He opened the glass door, reared back his arm, and chucked the vodka as far as he could. He shut the door just as the bottle shattered.

Lured away from the shell, the blood bags began to cackle and swoop down around the decoy, accompanied by a tentacle. On the rooftop, a horde of vampires still surrounded Spencer's corpse, but they were focused on suckling.

Ryan scurried outside.

He couldn't run—the monsters would hear. He glanced back but couldn't see them around the corner of the restaurant. Too soon they would realize they had been tricked.

Hunching over, Ryan wove between the cars stalled and wrecked in the street, trying not to step on the pebbles of glass or shards of brake light plastic, avoiding the loose newspapers and the human skeletons. He was rounding a SUV, almost to the sidewalk, when a blood bag tittered nearby. One was coming back.

Ryan pressed up against the vehicle's fender and held still. He clenched his gun and touched his lucky coin through his fatigues.

The blood bag's talon scraped along the hood of the SUV. The creature clucked. Ryan wanted to look up, but any movement—any at all—and he might as well eat his .45.

The blood bag glided over him. He almost pointed his pistol, almost shot, but the vampire ascended to the rooftop, toward the carcasses; it hadn't seen him at all.

After checking that the street was clear, Ryan started toward the hermitage. A tentacle shot out of a window and almost collided with him. It reared back as if it knew he was there, and in the window next to it, embedded in the hermit's slimy black flesh, a giant fish eye focused on him. The hermit chortled so loud that human bones rattled on the pavement.

"Damn," Ryan said.

The tentacle wrapped around him.

# # # # #

He blacked out for a few moments, aware only of the whooshing wind and the pressure around his midsection, the pain in his ribs, aware only that the ground was no longer beneath his feet. For a second, he and his brother were on the Matterhorn at Disneyland, raising their hands and cheering as they zipped up and down and around and around, casting manic grins at each other, the taste of cotton candy still on their lips. On a heart-stopping dip, they both grabbed the lap bar, and Ryan's hand landed on his brother's—they kept them that way for the rest of the ride.

# # # # #

When his vision cleared, Ryan saw that the tentacle had brought him into a room inside the hermit's shell. Black, pulsating flesh covered the walls; he only knew it was a room because of the rectangular shape. Hanging from the ceiling on organic cords, three veiny, transparent-red sacs sloshed with viscid fluid. Ryan didn't recognize the man floating in the first sac. But in the last two Shaun and Quincy drifted like fetuses. They were naked and unconscious.

Clogging the doorway, a huge orifice puttered and sighed, lined with thin feelers and stinking of methane. The feelers coiled around the first sac and picked it like a fruit. The man inside jostled but didn't wake. The tendrils fed him to the oral cavity.

Rumbling and grumbling, the hermit digested him, and Ryan witnessed something he would just as soon die to forget: the man's face surfaced on a nearby tentacle. It pressed at the flesh at first, just an eyeless, mouthless shape like a head pushing against latex, and then the black skin parted to form lips and eyelids. The man's eyes rolled as he screamed in silence.

It didn't make sense. How the hermit could absorb someone like that. Did it feed off them from the inside? Did it digest their flesh?

Done with the first sac, the oral feelers came back for Shaun.

"Hey!" Ryan called. "Shaun—*Shaun!*" He couldn't yell loud enough. The tentacle was compressing his chest. And shouting hurt his ribs.

Growing from the substance on the walls, hundreds of small worms wriggled through the air toward Ryan. They secreted some kind of warm, yellow ooze all over his fatigues. It melted the fabric right off of him without burning or irritating the skin.

"Get away!" He slapped at the worms, and they simply worked around him. His belt dissolved. His machete thunked to the floor. As its straps disintegrated, his backpack started to slip off too. He groped for it, got a handful of gunk, grabbed again. This time he caught the stalk of the M16.

Shaun passed into the hermit's mouth, and the worms blew a bubble around Ryan, a wavering membrane that began to solidify and fill with fluid.

"Shaun!" He aimed the M16 at the orifice and pulled the trigger. One burst, three bullets, and the rifle clicked empty—Spencer, the stupid kid, had forgotten to reload the magazine. Unfortunately, the burst had little effect: the bubble around Ryan quickly healed, and one worm grew down and attached to it, forming a cord so that Ryan was now anchored to the ceiling like Quincy. But the hermit's cheek leaked blue liquid, just like the tentacle had leaked when Quincy had shot in the tunnel. It was *bleeding*.

As he was integrated, absorbed, Shaun's head began to form in the tentacle next to the first man's face.

The feelers reached out for Quincy.

Everything looked red to Ryan as his bubble began to congeal into a sac. Veins grew down from the cord, pulsating and multi-branched. Fluid sloshed at his knees.

He aimed the M16 at the orifice, using the magazine as a grip for the grenade launcher. The worms, strong as pythons, curled around the rifle and tried to yank it out of his hands. He pulled the barrel back down, too high for his target.

"Fuck it," he said, and he discharged Spencer's grenade. The projectile tore through the sac and flew right into the hermit's mouth, deep down into its gullet.

The beast let go of Quincy's pod, looking puzzled—and then it belched. Blue guts exploded into the room.

The tentacle holding Ryan relaxed, and he fell through the bottom of the sac. The whole building quaked, as if it would fall apart, and then everything stilled. Outside and far away, blood bags continued to cackle.

Ryan stood up, breathing shallowly to alleviate the pain in his side. The two silver dollars lay at his feet where they'd fallen out of his pants. He grabbed them and held them tightly, hoping, praying, drawing on the good luck that had until then helped his family. He staggered forward, wiping worm mucus out of his eyes, trying not to slip in the entrails as they squished between his toes, trying not to gag on the smell of cooked guts. He went to the tentacle where his brother's face had begun to emerge from the black, diamond-patterned skin. Shaun was there, staring up at the ceiling, his mouth agape, exposing his teeth and his silver fillings.

Ryan tightened his jaw. "You deserved it," he said, his voice thickening, his body trembling. "You bastard—you shot me and you *deserved* to die." Tears trickled down his cheeks, and he clenched his whole face. "But you didn't—oh God, you didn't . . ." He bowed his head and let the flood die down inside him, let the waters calm. His jaw slowly unknotted. "You deserved better," he said. He shut his brother's eyelids and laid a silver dollar over each one, tails-up. "May you rest in peace."

He bowed his head again, and he listened to the blood bags outside, listened to the building settle as all that black flesh relaxed.

"Ryan?" Quincy said, stirring beneath a pile of gore. God, he had almost forgotten about her. "Ryan!"

He ran over and unburied her, scooped and shoved and heaved aside chunks and steamy innards. Her braids were matted with the hermit's blood, with the clear fluid from the sac. Her whole body glistened. He cradled her head in his lap, and she smiled, soft and sympathetic. "Hey, stranger."

"Hey," he said.

She reached up and wiped tears off his cheek. "My name's Quincy. What's yours?"

"Ryan."

"Well hello, Ryan. So I guess we're not strangers anymore."

He smiled and slicked a few strands of hair away from her face, feeling a pleasant little fire next to the hole his brother had left. "Good," he said, "good. Now come on. I'd like to get to know you a little better."

# BUBBA CTHULHU'S LAST STAND

*Lisa L. Hilton*

rother-Who-Is-Not skulked in the shadows along the walls of the inn. A year ago, he wouldn't have been able to merge with the darkness. A year ago, his hide had been pure white, reflecting light like unbroken snow under the midday sun. A year ago, his horn glistened silver, even in the darkest forest.

A year ago, he hadn't known about the black unicorns.

At the largest table, Sir Tanlith and his two friends discussed their plans. Kilee tilted back her chair and put her feet on the table. "Before we do this, I need a hot chocolate, straight up."

The mage, whose name Brother-Who-Is-Not could never remember, said, "Don't ask for hot chocolate here. That's so girly."

"I *am* a girl, you twit." Kilee smacked the mage on the back of the head.

Brother-Who-Is-Not groaned and stepped forward. The shadows clung to him, trailing like a cloak. "Are you done discussing the plans? Night comes."

Kilee stared at the plans for the Cthulhu mansion. The mage's eyes darted between the flickering fire and the serving wench. Only Sir Tanlith, knight of the Order of the Wingéd Shoe, met his gaze. "It's not too late to change your mind, Brother-Who-Is-Not," Tanlith said.

Brother-Who-Is-Not shook his head, his dark mane sliding along his arched neck. "It was too late a year ago. Are you ready?"

"We're deciding which of these paths to take." Tanlith waved at the map.

Kilee poked the map with her dagger. "This path has the most loot."

Tanlith rolled his eyes. "That's not going to attract the most attention, which is the plan, remember?"

The heroes started arguing. Again. Brother-Who-Is-Not sighed, his breath whickering out through his nostrils. The thought of interrupting the argument crossed his mind, but the distraction the heroes would provide wasn't technically necessary for the success of his plan. Let them argue the night away. It wouldn't matter in the end. He turned and walked away, his hooves clopping on the wooden floor.

The night welcomed him with a breeze that smelled of frost and burning hay. Before the inn door swung shut, he heard Kilee say, "If he goes without us, we won't get any loot."

# # # # #

In the mansion, Scooter Cthulhu waded through the pool, his tentacles flicking beer cans out of the water. They hit the walls with hollow, metallic clatters. He cursed Bubba with an embarrassing skin condition. The curse wouldn't stick to his older brother, but it relieved Scooter's feelings. Bubba had no understanding of the demands of being an evil overlord in a modern society. Neither had their father, which is why he was in the slammer in R'lyeh. Not that he was any worse of a father from prison than he'd been when he'd been around. Pa Cthulhu preferred blood sacrifices to watching his kids at their Little League games. Scooter threw a can particularly hard at that memory.

Ma Cthulhu rose from the hot tub in the corner of the pool room. A curl of rancid-smelling smoke rose from the cigarette that clung to her lower lip. "Scooter, why are you makin' so much noise?"

"Sorry, Ma," Scooter said, pausing mid-fling. "I was just trying to clean up."

"Well, stop it. It's not even midnight yet."

Scooter sagged. Given their lineage, he considered that Bubba didn't really have much of a chance, brains-wise, and Bubba hadn't been able to go to college like Scooter had.

"Uh, excuse me, Great One?" Winston, the Cthulhus' personal secretary, clutched his clipboard like a talisman. "There are some heroes attempting a break-in."

"What's that?" Ma Cthulhu said, her tentacles making wet slapping noises as she crossed the pool room, her bloodshot eyes swiveling. "We haven't had a good break-in since we started with the tours. Yeehaw!" She crawled her way to the door and shouted. "Bubba! Get down here!"

Scooter set down the beer can he had been ready to fling and slithered out of the pool. The complicated plans he had created to protect their mansion scrolled through his mind. He snagged a towel from a chair and wiped the chlorine-laced water from his thick hide. "What have you done so far?" he asked Winston.

"I've called out the ninjas, sir."

"Ninjas? Since when did we have ninjas?" Bubba asked, crawling through the door. "Don't rightly recollect seeing ninjas around the place." Bubba exuded an aura of physical menace that made Scooter cringe, even though it had been several millennia since his older brother had shoved his head in the toilet.

"The ninjas have been on the payroll since the fifteenth of last month," Winston said.

"Never seen 'em." Bubba had brought in a number of beer cans, grasped in his many tentacles, and he tossed one of the empty cans into the pool. Scooter sagged.

Winston tried to smile. "No, sir. They *are* ninjas."

"What?"

"Very stealthy, your average ninja."

Scooter could see Bubba try to work this one out.

"Oh. Yeah. Sure." Bubba took a swig from another can and then smashed it against his forehead.

Scooter's tentacles curled in embarrassment. He said to Winston, "Well, get the bugs ready, just in case. They take a while to warm up."

"They'll never drive us out of this house," Bubba said, slapping Scooter on the back. "I'm not going back to the double-wide. Git to it, Winston." After another swig, Bubba added, "And make sure the video feed to the widescreen works. Haven't had this much fun since those exploding paintballs hit the market."

# # # # #

Brother-Who-Is-Not grabbed a mouthful of leaves from a nearby bush. He chewed the rough leaves, which left a sour taste in his mouth. *Perfect.* That fit his mood.

The mansion was in uproar. Lights flickered off and on. Dogs barked. Shouts, hoots, wails, and swearing filled the night air. The heroes had pulled themselves together after all.

Brother-Who-Is-Not picked his way across the lawn, his light hooves making only soft thumps, drowned out instantly in all the commotion. His black coat absorbed the moonlight. It had taken months of exposure to turn his once-glowing white hide to utterly black. He had seen hate, treachery, vile lusts, horrors that Tanlith's order could never have imagined. "Know your enemy," they'd agreed when he presented his plan. Then they worried he'd feel too much sympathy for the enemy. What Brother-Who-Is-Not had seen made him angry, and it was that anger which finally finished his physical transformation.

Now he could pass for one of the dark unicorns that served the Cthulhus. Reports of their atrocities had come to the Order. Results that included names. His own siblings. And *her*. Brother-Who-Is-Not shuddered at the memory of reading those reports. A unicorn's horn could do horrors to the average human. And for what evil purpose? Tonight, it would end. For them all.

# # # # #

"Winston? Where are the wings? Gotta have wings with a break-in." Bubba lumbered down the hall, weaving a bit. Scooter had found that cheap beer was the best way to keep his brother mellow. Relatively mellow. "Popcorn's about ready. I need my wings!"

"We seem to have lost track of the ninjas, your Dreadship," Winston said, consulting his clipboard.

"Are you *sure* they really exist?"

"Of course. We pay them every week." Winston looked to Scooter for confirmation, but the younger Cthulhu could only wave his tentacles diffidently.

"Huh. Oh well. So where's our batch of heroes?" Bubba plopped down in the large recliner in front of the TV. A tentacle snaked out and grabbed the remote from Scooter's chair.

"They crossed the lawn, but only after a rather vicious slaughter of the pink flamingos."

Scooter interrupted. "What? Killed them?"

"Hacked to pieces, the report says."

Bubba whistled and turned on the TV. "Ooh, Ma's gonna blow a gasket about that. She's been stealin' them things for years. They don't make 'em anymore, ya know?"

"There is a certain element of personal attack in this, er, attack."

Bubba flipped through the channels, searching for the broadcast from the hidden dungeon cameras. "What? Speak American, man."

"What I mean," Winston said, glancing at his clipboard, "is that you should consider that this attack may be part of a larger, er, feud."

At the word "feud," Bubba slapped the wall, his tentacle going through the plaster. "The Great Old Ones! I shoulda guessed. They've had their eye on this place for years. And they probably think I ain't fit to run things, just because I didn't have no book-learnin' education."

"But you did make it through third grade. Twice." After his years of service, Winston could sound like he meant it for a compliment. Scooter made a mental note to give the man a raise.

"Not good enough for 'em. So I haven't sent my mind beyond the galaxy. So what? I know what I'm doin' here."

Scooter snorted and said under his voice, "And that is?"

Bubba heard him and slapped him with a tentacle. "Havin' a barbeque. Have the heroes hit the bugs yet?"

# # # # #

Brother-Who-Is-Not nuzzled open the back door. A vampire sat in a chair tilted against the wall, his feet up on the table.

"Evenin'," the vampire said, raising a glass filled with a dark red liquid.

The coppery smell of blood and pain permeated the air. Brother-Who-Is-Not's legs itched. He'd seen feedings, when mortals gave blood and soul, unable to resist the vampire's psychic force. This one had taken not only what he needed, but collected blood for later, leisurely consumption. It would be so easy to stop him. One quick lunge, the horn straight into the heart.

Brother-Who-Is-Not shuddered against the urge to destroy the vampire. It wouldn't be enough. The anger inside him demanded a bigger target. He had to go to the top. With stiff legs, he walked passed the vampire and deeper into the mansion.

# # # # #

"Well, at least we'll save some money on the exterminators," Scooter muttered. "Cancel the appointment, Winston."

"Very good, your Mightiness. The heroes have reached the next level, and I've sent someone to look for any surviving ninjas."

The damages were adding up. Not only would they have to replace staff, but the mage's fireballs had done terrible things to the paint and woodwork. "Maybe we should move," Scooter said.

"Not a chance, Scootie," Bubba said, using Scooter's least favorite nick-name. "This has been a good neighborhood, and we haven't had any problems for years. I ain't gonna let some do-goodin' morons drive us out of our home. Besides, the trailer park won't let us back after that thing with the rain of frogs. Git to work."

"I still don't understand why they were so cranky about it," Scooter muttered, hauling himself out of his creaking chair. "It's not like it was a tornado."

He had an escape plan, but until the last minute, it was easier to do what Bubba said. There were still bathrooms in the mansion. He rubbed a tentacle that had once gotten stuck in the plumbing during a particularly prolonged swirlie. Given a choice between a band of adventurers and his brother, he knew who he'd rather face in a final battle.

# # # # #

A woman came down the hall towards Brother-Who-Is-Not. Her head tilted, and her nose twitched. Werewolf. Brother-Who-Is-Not moved aside, panicked. Could she smell that he didn't belong? Would she try to touch him? He shied away from her. A magical explosion this low in the mansion might catch the heroes in its blast radius—which was a hazard they'd all waved aside—but it would not take out the Cthulhus. Useless. Brother-Who-Is-Not tried to calm his racing heart.

The werewolf passed him by and went into the kitchen. "You seen any ninjas?" she asked the vampire.

Brother-Who-Is-Not snorted in relief. If the ninjas had already been released and defeated, then the heroes were taking the long way, as Tanlith had suggested. That made his task a little easier, kept the Cthulhus' henchmen out of his way so he could move faster, shortened the time before he rid the world of the corruption of the Cthulhus. His lips curled back from his teeth in a savage grin.

# # # # #

The heroes crowded into the alcove. "Tanlith, your sword is jabbing me in the back," Kilee whispered.

"Well, you're standing on my foot," the knight replied.

The mage made a shushing sound. "They'll hear us."

"They're not going to hear us," Kilee said, still whispering. "Somebody brought a tray of free food into a break room. Everybody's going to be eating."

"Fine, then we should sneak past," Tanlith said, trying to get his foot out from under the thief.

"I say we go in and get some food. I'm hungry." Kilee slid a dagger from its sheath.

"But the food isn't for us," Tanlith said.

"I don't care. They've got brownies. I didn't get my hot chocolate because In-Tune-With-The-Mystic-Forces here thought it was too girly." She elbowed the mage and then advanced into the hallway.

Tanlith drew his sword with a sigh. The mage muttered, "Those brownies had nuts in them. I'm allergic to nuts."

# # # # #

Brother-Who-Is-Not's path took him through the solarium. Or perhaps it should be called a lunarium, since the only light came from the moon overhead. Brother-Who-Is-Not took a few steps in before he noticed the dark shapes under the shade of the fake trees.

A dark unicorn stepped out into the shaft of moonlight. Her dark hide devoured the silvery moonlight and cast a shadow on the tiled floor. Still, he knew her shape, the feel of her presence, despite the dark pollution that twisted through it now. Brother-Who-Is-Not stumbled to a halt. "Rowena?" His voice echoed strangely in the large room. The other shapes shifted, settled. They were asleep.

"It's Raven now," she replied, her voice soft. "I never expected to see you here." Her inflection turned up at the end, making it a question.

"I know. Neither did I." Brother-Who-Is-Not felt bile rising, bringing back the sour taste of the leaves. His Rowena, come to this. "Until I heard you were here. Then I knew I had to come."

Her eyes flashed with pleasure. "You came for me?" She dipped her head, tilting it as she'd once done when he told her she looked beautiful. And she was still beautiful, though caressed by the shadows.

Brother-Who-Is-Not held his head stiff. "Sort of," he said, his old, awkward shyness returning.

She smiled, baring her teeth. Brother-Who-Is-Not stared in shock. Her teeth, once even and sparkling, had been filed to points. *The better to rip your flesh with,* Brother-Who-Is-Not thought, his complex digestive system twisting hard in disgust.

"I'm so glad you've come," she murmured. She lowered her head and looked up at him through her lashes. Her voice sent shivers down his spine. "Your herd mates are all here. It'll be just like old times. Only better." Her tail flicked, suggestive, inviting.

*Whore!* Brother-Who-Is-Not bit down hard, shutting the word in. "I, uh, I have to see the, uh, Cthulhu. Report in." Brother-Who-Is-Not side-stepped.

Raven sidled into his path. "Come back down when you're done." Her horn, the horn that had torn through unprotected humans, inched towards him shyly, as she had done before she had disappeared, before the darkness. They had touched before, a sign of love, a promise of things to come. It could be so again, if he just let go.

Brother-Who-Is-Not pulled away at the last instant. "Um, yes. When I'm done. But I have to hurry. You know how it is."

Raven nodded and let Brother-Who-Is-Not pass. "It's so good to see you," she said as he walked away.

"Likewise," Brother-Who-Is-Not said. He had to hurry. He couldn't give in to temptation. He would not be happy with her, not like that. She was not his Rowena any more. He had given up on his family, his friends, even his name. There was only one thing left to give and only one way to give it.

# # # # #

Bubba lounged in his recliner and chain-fed pieces of popcorn with his tentacles. Scooter stared in horror at the screen. "I've never seen anything like that," he said.

Bubba swallowed another mouthful of popcorn. "You need to get out more, Scootie. This is nowhere near as bad as the Summoning of 1951."

"But the coffee. It's all over the walls. Do you know how hard it is to clean that?"

"Oh, quit being such a whiner. If you want to worry about anything, you better worry that they're getting closer. I'm not lugging Ma's junk to another house, so this next room had better stop 'em."

Scooter wiped his forehead. "It will. This one is guaranteed." Still, he might want to slip away to make sure his escape tunnel's exit was unblocked.

# # # # #

Brother-Who-Is-Not found the service elevator. He pushed the button marked "Penthouse" with his horn.

"Hold up!" A young man in a pizza delivery outfit ran towards the elevator. Brother-Who-Is-Not stuck his head out, stopping the elevator from closing. It buzzed angrily. The delivery boy ran into the elevator, and Brother-Who-Is-Not pulled his head back. The doors slid shut.

"Whew, thanks. You saved me there. These guys get nasty if their food is late." He held up a warming bag of the sort that normally held pizza.

Brother-Who-Is-Not froze. Saved him? No, that's not what he was here for. Well, yes, broadly speaking, the demise of the Cthulhus would save millions from death, torture, and slavery. Brother-Who-Is-Not hadn't really thought about that. He was here to punish, not save.

The dark anger flickered like a candle in a strong breeze. He was so bent on destruction. How was that any better than any of the Cthulhus? Brother-Who-Is-Not looked around wildly, but there was no escape from the elevator. He saw his reflection. The blackness of his hide taunted him. How had he not seen? How had he been so blind? The Order was right after all. He had become one of *them*. Like *her*.

The elevator shuddered to a stop, and the doors slid open. The pizza boy walked into the large living room. "Wings are here," he said, holding out the bag.

"Y'all are far too late," said the larger of two Cthulhus lounging in armchairs watching a large TV. The pizza boy gulped and paled. The large Cthulhu chortled, and a tentacle whipped out and hit the other Cthulhu on the back of the head. "Good one, huh?"

Brother-Who-Is-Not had reached his destination. He stepped into the room, and the elevator door closed behind him, almost catching his tail. All this effort, the heroes risking their lives, and yet, how could he go through with this if his motivations were so impure?

An aging, decrepit Cthulhu, cigarette dangling from her mouth, limped across the living room. "How much?" she croaked.

The pizza boy quoted her the price, and she dug about in a coin purse.

Voices came from the TV screen. The heroes' voices. Brother-Who-Is-Not saw them rooting through a treasure chest.

"You got the last three rings, and it's not like you even wear them." It was What's-His-Name, the mage, petulant.

"How do you know? I might put them on my toes." Kilee's defensive wheedling.

"Maybe we should make her take off her shoes to prove it. Right, Tanlith?"

The knight was too rapt in examining a sparkling sword to pay attention to the mage.

"This is your best trap yet, Scooter," said the larger of the reclining monstrosities.

The smaller one smirked. "Heroes are so predictable, Bubba. You just have to out-think them."

The pizza boy pocketed the money, and the old female Cthulhu opened the top box. The smell of frankincense, myrrh, and crisp snow overpowered the odors of vinegar and ranch dipping sauce.

"Wings?" Brother-Who-Is-Not asked, his voice catching in his throat. A light shone from the box, wavering from the echoes of pain like a mirage in the desert.

"Yeah, angel wings," the pizza boy said, grinning. "I got my first promotion, too. Next week, I get to start hunting the angels we use. Good opportunities for advancement with the Cthulhus, my parents say."

Bubba laughed, a gurgling sound that sent a shudder along Brother-Who-Is-Not's spine. The pizza boy's smile took on a menacing edge. On the TV, Kilee pulled out her knives, and the mage's hands lit up with eldritch fire.

Brother-Who-Is-Not's lips pulled away from his teeth. Angel wings. Vampires. Turning good into bad. Preying on greed and anger. It had to stop. Brother-Who-Is-Not lowered his horn and charged.

# TURF

Rick Moore

hen Michelle Harris heard the front door crash open, she silently prayed a megaphone would announce that this was a police raid. Hearing only gunfire by way of introduction, she knew instead it had to be the act of retaliation her husband Derek had long anticipated. For years Derek had warned their home in Chingford might one day come under attack by one of his rivals. The security gate, the dogs, the armed men patrolling the perimeter wall—these had evidently been no match for the intruders. Three more armed men were posted inside the house at all times—and now the gunfire had ceased, they'd either succeeded in defeating their attackers or were dead. If it was the former, they would have called out by now, would have offered her some assurance that the situation was under control.

Michelle quickly crossed the room and removed a small handgun from beneath Derek's pillow. She clicked off the safety, just like he'd shown her, then got down on the floor and crawled beneath the bed. Aiming the gun at what little of the door she could see, she forced her breathing to slow and waited.

Though she knew it was unlikely, Michelle allowed herself to hope they were only showing what they were capable of; like one dog baring its teeth to another. Maybe she and Nicola would survive this.

Nicola.

Until now, her daughter's safety hadn't even entered her mind. This did not really surprise her. She'd never felt connected to the child as a mother should, the role performed more as a duty than out of maternal instinct. Michelle liked sunbeds and salons, champagne and nightclubs, swimming naked at midnight high on cocaine. She was a Gangster's wife. That was the role she'd been born to play: being a mother just wasn't in her repertoire. But Derek wanted a child, and who was she (a hairdresser giving bad perms when they met twenty three years ago) to ever deny the wants of a man like Derek Harris?

Still, it was terrible, she supposed. Despicable really; valuing her own neck more than her daughter's. Any normal mother would not think twice about sacrificing her life to protect her own flesh and blood: until this moment, Michelle hadn't even remembered she had a daughter.

*If I live through this,* Michelle thought, *and they kill Nicola, I'll have to find a way to deal with that. And that's not going to be easy, Shell. Not going to be easy at all.*

*Mind you, on the plus side, I'd have Derek to myself again. It'd be like it used to be before she was born.*

Michelle had always known she was no saint, that she was vain, greedy and self-obsessed. But she'd never considered herself evil. But when the thought entered her mind, quick to arrive and slow to leave, there was no other explanation. She had found herself hoping they killed Nicola and let her live. Not that they left them both alive, but that the child be killed so she didn't have to compete with the fifteen-year-old for Derek's attention.

*Evil bitch,* Michelle thought. *Sick in the head, you are.*

Michelle wished she could take the thought back. But it was impossible to erase now she'd given life to it.

Footsteps on the stairs.

*You have a gun. Do something. Protect your child.*

Nicola was in her room, doing whatever fifteen-year-old girls did when they got home after school.

*Do something. They're going to kill her.*

Michelle remained where she was.

The footsteps were closer, at the top of the stairs.

"Michelle?" She heard a man call. "Nicola?"

Terry?

It couldn't be.

Michelle told herself she was mistaken.

"You can both come out now," the man called. "It's safe."

It was Terry. Michelle had known him almost as long as she'd known her husband. He'd been Derek's best man at their wedding. And rightly so. Terry wasn't just Derek's right hand man: he was his brother.

Michelle's mind spun out of focus as she tried to make sense of what this might mean. She could find no answers. Terry was supposed to be on holiday with Crystal, his wife. Some island in Greece. That he would have any part in all this just didn't add up. Unless Terry had decided to become the heir-apparent.

The door slowly swung open. She saw a man's brown suede brogues and needed no further evidence. The shoes had been a present to Terry from his niece last Christmas. Michelle had been shopping with her daughter when she picked them out for him.

Bizarrely, a stench rolled into the room, like the day's end stink of Billingsgate fish market. Michelle gagged and had to will the bile away from her throat and back to her stomach.

"Uncle Terry?" Michelle heard Nicola say out in the hallway. "What's going on? Where's Mum?"

"Don't worry, sweetheart," Terry said, the brogues turning away. "Your Uncle Terry's here. You'll be safe now. Go on down to the car, and I'll explain it all when I get there."

Michelle heard her daughter say, "I thought you were in Greece with Aunty Crystal. And how comes you're wearing that balaclava?"

"Go on down to the motor and I'll explain when I get there. And try not to look at the bodies. Do as I ask. Alright love?"

"Okay . . ." Nicola said, sounding uncertain, but a few seconds later Michelle heard her daughter's feet on the stairs.

Michelle aimed the gun at Terry's ankles, so tempted to let the fucker have it. Of course he'd only be injured and then she'd have given away her hiding place. Better to let him take Nicola now, keep quiet, then call Derek and tell him what had happened as soon as they were gone.

Terry's shoes remained in the doorway. Something black fell to the floor, and she realized he'd removed and dropped the balaclava.

Michelle mentally willed him to leave.

Terry turned around and entered the room.

The stink of dead fish intensified so much that her tear ducts opened.

She clapped a hand over her mouth. Watched his feet move across the carpet, over to the wardrobe. She heard the mirrored door sliding open and saw the wheels turn in their runner.

"Shell? You in here?" Terry called. "Shelly? Come on girl, don't mess about. The sooner you show yourself, the sooner we can all go down the pub for a knees-up. A few drinks, a few songs. What do you say? Shell? Ere, remember this one . . ." Terry started to sing then, only something sounded wrong about his voice, as though it were clogged with phlegm and grit. "We will have a fishy on a little dishy . . . Yes we will have a fishy when the boat comes in."

Terry turned away from the wardrobe and slowly walked towards the bed, singing, "Dance to thi Daddy, Dance to thi Mammy . . ."

Michelle prepared to fire, wanting to shoot him in the foot or ankle, but deciding to hold off until she had a shot at his head.

Terry's shoes were just inches from her face. The clotted, guttural voice sang on, "Yes we will have a fishy, on a little dishy . . ." He suddenly squatted low and looked beneath the bed, finishing the ditty face to face,". . .when the boat comes in!"

Something hideous had happened to Terry's face.

"Like my new look, Shell?" he asked.

The compulsion to scream wiped all thought from her mind. But before she could make a sound (or remember the gun in her hand), Terry brought up his sawn-off shotgun and fired it into her face. What remained of Michelle's head slumped to the carpet.

"It has to be said, Shell," Terry said. "I really do like yours. New look that is. It really suits you. Too bad nobody thought to try it out on you before."

# # # # #

Derek Harris was in the middle of a business negotiation. He didn't like doing deals with these Johnny Foreigners (he was a Xenophobe at heart), but London was awash with the fuckers these days, all of them so hungry for success they'd pimp out their own mother for forty quid and a carton of B and H, and Derek knew if you didn't move with the times you got left behind.

Derek looked into the eyes of the man sitting across from him. For all intents and purposes, they were two men sharing a drink in a seedy Soho pub, the clientele mostly prozzies and their would-be punters; the air thick with their cigarette smoke and prologues of meaningless conversation. This was Derek's manor, and that meant every pair of tits with a slit that sold it paid to work his turf. The same went for their pimps. Like Boris here.

"So do we have a deal?" Boris pushed up his glasses; scratched a pimple on his nose.

Boris wanted to open two knocking shops, both of them fronted as businesses that were legit; one a massage parlor, the other a motel.

Derek sipped his cognac and took a puff on his cigar, considering the man's proposal. As specified, Boris hadn't brought along any muscle, arriving at the pub with only a sample of his merchandise in tow. She was seated at the bar, batting her eyelids and playing all coy with Fred and Albert, two of Derek's top henchmen.

"I don't know, Boris," Derek said. "I have to admit, I've some doubts."

Boris asked, "Why doubts?"

"Well for one thing," Derek said. "You told me most of your girls were average looking, and only a few were what qualified as that little bit of something special. Being as the majority of your girls are average, I told you I wanted to see one of the tarts that wasn't all that fit, so I could gauge their marketability."

Boris looked confused. "This girl? This girl I brought like you ask. Average girl."

Was he having a laugh? In Derek's estimation, and he'd estimated more than his share of tarts in his day, the brunette was a total knockout. Teeth a bit manky, bit skinny, like she'd skipped a few meals here or there, but other than that immensely fuckable. And this was Boris's idea of average?

"How many girls you got in all?"

"Fifteen," Boris said. "Three more we smuggle in on Friday, another seven over the next two weeks."

"I have to hand it to you, Boris," Derek said, appraising the girl's plump lips. "You've got an eye when it comes to the ladies."

"You like Vanya? I give."

"Give?"

"We make the deal now, I . . . how you say? Transfer ownership?"

Derek imagined having the girl as his personal slave, his to do with in whatever way he chose. He smiled slowly. He was about to agree, about to extend his hand and make the deal, when his senses suddenly returned. This was his gaff: his manor. Spotty little Herberts like Boris didn't do *Derek Harris* any favors—he was the one who did the favors for them.

"I will take a girl as a deal closer, Boris. But I'll make my selection after I've sampled the rest of your stable. As for this one, I'm going to borrow her for an hour. Off you trot, and send her over on your way out the door."

Derek saw a flash of anger in the man's eyes. Boris was clearly unaccustomed to taking orders. In whatever part of Eastern Europe he hailed from (they were all Russian to Derek, mind you) he had likely been a local crime boss. But here, in London's East End, he carried no clout: just another illegal trying to claw his way out of the rubbish heap and find a foothold of respectability in the criminal underworld. Sensible enough to stow his anger and save it for later (probably for one of his girls, Derek thought), the Russian grinned.

"Thank you, Mr. Harris. Thank you."

And they said the English practiced poor oral hygiene.

Derek sipped his cognac and studied the Sun's crossword. He watched from the corner of his eye as Boris hurried to the bar and said something to Vanya, then headed for the pub's front door. Vanya walked to his booth and sat facing him. She waited patiently, expressionless until Derek at last set down his newspaper and looked at her. Her eyes found his and became lit with excitement. Boris must have told her who he was prior to coming here. Derek intended to fuck her and forget her—even if he really liked the girl and wanted to keep her—that was how it had to be, now. But for the next hour they would share a drink or two and flirt, and he'd let her bask in his power; let her believe she was something special to him.

"Vanya is it?" Derek asked, all hush-hush and never more friendly, trying to decide whether to do her fast and nasty, maybe in the toilets with a few lines of coke, or whether to take her to the flat he kept over his nearby betting shop, so he could get her fully undressed and take his time enjoying her body. The girl nodded, smiling but keeping her mouth closed, self-conscious of her teeth.

"No toothpaste in Russia?" Derek wanted to say, the callousness of his nature rising to the fore, but instead he asked, "Something to drink Vanya?"

Again Vanya nodded. "Thank you,"

Derek looked towards the bar. Catching Fred's eye he raised his glass.

Derek looked at his watch. Almost five. Shit. Michelle would be expecting him home pretty soon. They'd have to dispense with the formalities and get right down to business.

"Like a toot do you, Vanya?"

"Toot?"

"You know—"

Derek's cell phone rang. Fred brought two glasses over and set them on the table, then silently withdrew. Vanya waited. Searching for his phone Derek nodded and gestured towards her glass, "Go on love, drink up,"

Vanya sipped her cognac and Derek at last located the cell phone and answered.

"Derek?"

Derek recognized the voice but couldn't put a face to it. "Who's this?"

"Derek, it's me, Burton."

Bob Burton. One of Derek's friends on the force.

"Can this wait, Bob? Only I've—"

"I'm afraid it can't," Burton said. "I'm at your house, Derek."

"My . . . What are you talking about?"

"I think you'd better come home."

Derek understood.

# # # # #

Approaching the house, Derek saw something he'd never before seen: the security gate stood wide open. From the back window of his Roller, he looked out at the two uniformed policemen, arms behind their backs and standing to attention, acting as a barrier now the gate had been compromised. Fred, who was driving, instinctively tensed up.

"Easy Fred," Derek said. "And for fuck's sake Albert, get your bleeding hand off that shooter. These are friendlies, you pillock."

Albert, a huge hulking flat-nosed thug, did as he was told and said, "Sorry Mr. Harris,"

What Albert lacked in brains (the effect of too many bare knuckle boats in underground parking garages), he more than made up for in loyalty. They'd been together twenty years, and next to his brother Terry, there was nobody in Derek's organization he trusted more than his personal bodyguard.

Fred pulled to a halt and Derek lowered the back window. The officer, recognizing him on sight, nodded and waved them through.

Derek kept the window down and looked out at the carnage. Two of his men were dead on the ground, heads and torsos covered with blankets. Derek saw that his Dobermans, Lulu and Twiggy, were also dead, bodies torn open by blasts from a shotgun. He felt a deep pang of loss. The men were replaceable; the dogs his babies.

They reached the end of the gravel driveway and Fred stopped the Roller behind three parked police cars (another anomaly). Derek got out and walked towards his house. The door had been smashed open, like somebody had gone to work on it with a sledgehammer. The cops out front must have radioed ahead, because Derek found Burton waiting for him in the hallway.

"Del," Burton said, nodding.

"Bob," Derek nodded in return.

There was blood on the cream colored Axminster carpet, the body it had leaked from a few feet away. This was another of his boys (they'd covered the face but nothing else, and Derek recognized the clothes). So far it looked like the home team had taken a hammering.

*Michelle'll go bloody barmy when she sees them stains,* Derek thought dully. His wife's death momentarily forgotten, Derek knelt down and untied his shoelaces.

Burton said, "Derek?"

Derek slipped off his shoes and set them by the door. His slippers were right there, still in their usual place, and Derek pushed his feet into them. There was little could compare to coming home and slipping on an old pair of comfy slippers. Derek could feel the day's tension slipping away from him. Sensing somebody's presence he started to smile, home at last, ready to greet his nearest and dearest, but of course it wasn't either of them. Not Michelle, big fake boobs jiggling as she ran to the doorway to give him a kiss and a cuddle, nor his little angel, waiting at the foot of the stairs for a hug from her Dad. His wife was dead and his daughter missing. Instead all he had was Bob Burton's ugly mug waiting for him in his hallway. And as much as Derek could use one right now, Burton didn't look like the hugging kind.

"Not much of a consolation prize, are you Bob?"

"Not much," Burton agreed.

Derek saw more plainclothes bizzies now; and realized they must have been there all along. One knelt on the stairs digging a bullet out of the wall; two were examining the body of another of his men, dead in the kitchen. There were even rozzers in his living room, out of sight but audible, discussing in muted tones how somebody had died. Thinking it was his wife, Derek was suddenly furious that his home had twice been invaded this night.

"Where is she?"

"Upstairs," Burton said. "In the bedroom."

# # # # #

The mattress and bed frame leaned against the wall, revealing that Michelle had been hiding under the bed when she'd been killed.

Derek stood looking down at his wife's body, at what remained of her head. He felt no remorse. No loss. He couldn't. Not with somebody else standing there. Derek had learned at a young age never to walk out the door without the hard-man's face. Never to show weakness or fear. Wannabes came and wannabes went, but when a real hard-man proved his worth, the day came when the face ceased to be a mask and it wore the man instead of the other way around. After that it was showing emotion that became the task to master. Showing it like you really meant it.

"Any idea who might have done this, Derek?" Burton asked.

Derek shook his head. There were plenty of villains with a grudge against him, but they were small-timers. He couldn't believe a single one of them had somehow grown a set of balls big enough to do this. And the men who did have the stones had nothing to gain from it. Derek hadn't warred with another East End gang in over a decade. London was long ago carved into sections, street by street, road by road. An alliance, however uneasy, was maintained to serve the bottom line: profit. The days of faces, of gangland warfare, had gone out with the swinging sixties. London's bosses kept a united front. They had to, what with all the homegrown wideboys, the Eastern European immigrants, the Yardies, and even the fucking Yakuza, all trying to operate on the sly within their territory. But somebody had the balls— somebody had declared war. The question was, who?

"At least she didn't suffer," Derek said, looking at the bloody mush that had once been his wife's lovely head.

"Actually," Burton said. "There's a pretty strong chance her death wasn't instantaneous."

Hearing this, Derek at last experienced the emotional outpouring he'd needed to release. He spun towards Burton, his hand shooting out, gripping the bent copper by the neck. Unburdening his pent up rage, Derek squeezed tighter, restricting Burton's air supply.

"What?" Derek hissed, spittle spraying the choking man's purpling face.

"She left a clue, Derek . . ." Burton wheezed. "A letter . . ."

"A letter? Are you taking the fucking piss? You're telling me my wife lived long enough to write me a letter?"

"Near—her—hand"

Derek released him, and Burton staggered away, simultaneously coughing and trying to gulp down air.

Derek looked at Michelle's body. Sure enough, there on the carpet by her right hand, written in her own blood, he saw the letter 'T.' Derek didn't want to think of how she'd done it, how in her dying moments she must have reached up to her own ruined face and used it as an inkwell to offer a clue to her attacker's identity.

T?

Derek drew a blank. He needed distance, needed some place quiet where he could sink a couple of cognacs and grieve in solitude. And seeing the T, Derek was reminded of what he needed most of all. He needed his brother, Terry. As soon as he arrived at the club, Derek decided he'd call Terry and tell him what had happened. It might take a few hours for Terry to arrange a flight back to England from Kos, the Greek island where he and his wife were on holiday, but by morning his brother would be by his side.

Then together they would find who'd done this—find them and make them pay.

# # # # #

Sitting at the bar, Derek realized coming to the club had been a bad idea. In two hours his staff would arrive: the manager and bar staff, the bouncers and DJ. It would be an hour again before the doors opened to the punters. People came to the club to forget their troubles, to celebrate life. But there was no life here now. With the lights on, and only Fred and Albert on either side of him for company, the place felt like a huge empty void of nothingness.

Derek finished his cognac. Fred rose and went around the bar to fix them all another drink. To Albert, Derek said, "Go put some music on. Don't want none of that boom, boom racket. They got some slowies CDs behind the DJ booth somewhere. Put one of them on, eh Albert? Anything's gotta be better than this silence."

Albert nodded and set off across the club. Derek reached for his cell, remembered from earlier it wouldn't make the call overseas, and asked Fred to pass him the House phone. The first time he'd tried to contact Terry, there'd been some confusion at the front desk of the hotel they were staying at. The Greek running the front desk said his brother had checked out, and Derek had to repeatedly tell her to put him through to the room of Harris, room 244 Harris, Harris room 244, until she at last said "You want Mrs. Harris?" and did as he asked. The phone rang but nobody had answered. There was an hour's time difference, and Derek decided they had to be out eating dinner, sampling the fresh Mediterranean seafood the island was well-known for (served with the heads on Terry had told him, laughing at Derek's sounds of disgust, calling the day after they first arrived). When the same woman answered and said "Skol Hotel," Derek started to ask for Terry Harris, then thought better of it and said, "Harris, room 244."

The woman said, "One moment, please."

Derek waited. Fred set a fresh drink in front of him.

The phone rang three times, then somebody answered, and he heard Crystal say, "Hello?"

"Crystal. It's Derek."

"Hi Del," Crystal said, slurring, drunk.

"Can you put Terry on? Something's come up, and I need to talk to him."

"He's not here, Derek," Crystal said.

Derek didn't want to tell Crystal about Michelle's murder and Nicola's abduction. His sister-in-law and wife had been close friends, like sisters in many respects, and Derek knew she'd break down when she heard. The last thing he wanted right was exposure to raw emotion.

"Any idea when he might be back?" Derek asked.

"Back?" Crystal sounded confused. "Here? You mean he's coming back? Well he might have told me, Derek. I haven't heard a word from him in three days. Not since he said you needed him to come back to London."

Terry was back in the UK? Had been for three days? Why had he lied to Crystal about Derek needing him back in London? Why had he returned? And if he was back, why hadn't he called Derek to . . .? The 'T' Michelle had written with her blood pushed its way to the front of Derek's mind.

No, it couldn't be Terry. Couldn't be. It made no sense. But something was fishy about Terry's return.

"How did he seem to you, Del? Be honest with me, because I can't deal with him coming back if he's going to act like he did before he left."

Derek decided to let Crystal go on thinking Terry was about to return to Kos, and went along with the lie his brother had told her. "He seemed a little out of sorts . . ." Derek said. "Definitely not his usual self,"

"Well I'd say that's putting it mildly," Crystal said. "I don't know what happened to him out on that scuba dive, but he wasn't acting at all like himself after he came back, and he just got weirder and weirder as time went on. If I didn't know better, I'd think it was some other person entirely."

"When was this, Crystal?"

"The scuba dive? He went out with two locals Monday afternoon. They've got a boat with all the gear just off the beach. Or at least they did have. I wanted to ask them if anything had happened while they were out taking Terry for his dive. But when I went to the beach neither of them were there. Not Tuesday, not yesterday, and not today, neither. You should have seen him, Del. Acting like a right headcase."

"In what way?" Derek asked.

"The boat never came back. I waited until there was nobody left on the beach except me. It was as the sun was setting that I saw him. Terry just came up out of the sea. He was still wearing the wetsuit, but the mask and air tank were gone. When he finally got back to shore, he turned around and stared out at the waves. Refused to say a word when I tried to get him to come back to the room, acting like he didn't even know I was there. I told him, 'sod you then', and came back here to the hotel on me own, thinking he'd make his way back when he got hungry. But I didn't see hide nor hair of him. I couldn't eat, not with him still out there, not with it being night-time now, so after I showered I went back to the beach. He was still standing there, only now he was looking up at the stars. He did that for maybe half an hour, never taking his eyes off them, not even when the water reached his waist. Then he turns around and starts wading in. At last he gets back onto dry land. When I see his face I can hardly believe it's my Terry. He gave me this look that was totally alien, Del. Like nothing I've ever seen before. He grabs me by the shoulders and starts laughing, then he yells in my face 'In his house at R'lyeh dead Cthulhu waits dreaming.' Then he walked off towards the hotel, and by the time I got back there, he said you'd called and needed him to come home and that he'd booked the next flight out. Took his passport and the keys to the rental car, threw some clothes on and left. Didn't even shower. Stunk to high heaven, he did. He—"

Derek hung up.

His wife dead, his daughter abducted (possibly also dead since there had been no ransom note and nothing from Burton saying the kidnappers had called), and now his brother going off his nut and behaving in ways that did Derek's head in just to think about. Terry was here in London. His wife had written the letter 'T' with her own blood.

Could Terry be his wife's killer and daughter's abductor?

On more than a few occasions, Derek had seen his brother's eyes shine with maniacal glee; the inner psychopath let loose as they gave a beating to some wide boy with ideas above his station, or when they tortured and killed Mickey Brown that time after they got word from Burton he was a grass. Sure, Terry had always been a bit of a nutter; a bit psycho. But no more than Derek himself. In Derek and Terry's line of work, having a few loose screws was what qualified you for the job. If not, they'd be just two more in the queue of wannabe villains, at best jumping to another man's tune; at worst, still stuck in the block of council flats they grew up in, cashing giros at the Post Office and wearing hand me downs from Oxfam.

On the bar top in front of him sat a small mirror with four lines of coke laid out on it. Derek had intended to divvy them up with Fred and Albert, but after the call to Crystal, he no longer felt like sharing. Derek rolled up a twenty pound note and spent ten seconds vacuuming.

If what Crystal had told him was the truth, and he had no reason to think she'd lied, then Terry had apparently gone completely bonkers while out scuba diving and had returned spouting some gibberish about dreams and someone called Cathy Lou. A fan of the Alfred Hitchcock film *Psycho*, Derek wondered if Terry might have developed some sort of alter-ego, like Norman whatshisface with his mother, and it was this other identity that had taken control and made Terry kill Michelle and kidnap Nicola.

*What a load of codswallop,* Derek thought.

Terry wasn't involved. No way whatsoever. Derek thought a more plausible solution was that he'd done some dodgy Greek E before going out for the scuba dive, and the way he'd acted afterwards was simply a bad trip that lingered so long he'd headed home to get away from Crystal's yakking while he recuperated. Probably hadn't called because he still felt rough: most likely holed up in his house under a duvet drinking Lucozade and watching DVDs.

*Yeah, that's more like it. Loves his drugs does our Terry. Be just like him to get fucked up on some foreign muck.*

Derek took out his cell phone and dialed Terry's number. After two rings somebody answered.

"Tel?" Derek said. "That you?"

Waiting for a reply, Derek heard a slurping sound, like somebody sucking an abundance of saliva into the back of their mouth.

"Terry?"

The reply, when at last it came, sounded wet, as though whoever was on the other end drooled as he spoke, "Y gnaiif gof'nn hupadgh n'ghft."

For all the weird salivating sounds, and the gobbledygook language, Derek thought he recognized his brother's voice.

*It's the alter ego,* Derek thought. *Fuck me. I was right.*

"Cathy?" Derek ventured. "Cathy Lou?"

He heard it then: a faint cry in the background, a voice that was unmistakably his little Nicola, "Help!"

A fury of words pressed at Derek's lips, but before he could let loose the first profanity, the line went dead.

Derek looked up and saw Fred behind the bar; forehead raised in folds, eyes questioning.

"He's got her, Fred," Derek said, a tremor in his voice, the hard-man face close to cracking.

"Who has?" Fred asked.

"Terry."

"Terry? No . . ." Fred said, and shook his head. "Not Terry."

Derek nodded. Tears were in his eyes. "He has. Gone fucking batty. Killed my Michelle. Stole my little girl."

"It can't be," Fred said, and could think of nothing else. "It can't be."

Over at the DJ booth, Albert finally figured out how to get the CD player to work, and music came over the speakers. It was the Bee Gees, *How Deep Is Your Love*. One of Michelle's favorites. On hearing the Gibbs falsetto, the memory returned of holding her close on the club *Deltel's* dance floor, of opening his eyes and seeing Terry and Crystal also slow dancing, and of his brother giving him a grin and both thumbs up. The Harris brothers, ever united, ever side by side, had made it all the way to the top of the world.

The memory died in his mind, and Derek finally crumbled.

# # # # #

Explosive charges were being set on the security gate's lock when Derek got there. His brother's house was no less a fortress than his own, but a fancy hi-tech lock was no match for Semtex. The explosives experts, two of them, yelled something incomprehensible, then ran back to the vehicles, where the rest of the specialist firearms officers were crouched.

There was a small explosion, not much more than puff of smoke to look at, then the gate slowly swung inwards.

Derek climbed from the backseat of his Roller. Burton saw him and trotted over.

"You are sure about this, Derek?" Burton asked.

Derek's face involuntarily worked itself into a scowl. "What? You think I'd make something like this up?"

A uniformed man dressed in a blue flak jacket and holding a Sig Sauer pistol was crouched along with his squad a few feet away from them. He looked to Burton, awaiting the signal to advance. Burton wearily nodded.

"Advance!" The squad leader yelled. "Advance!"

The team of armed men dashed forwards, disappearing from sight as they passed through the open entrance. Derek watched as the last of them passed through; his mind's eye seeing the SFOs fanning out, using the trees and bushes for cover as they traversed the acre of grounds between the entrance and the house.

Derek raised the boot's lid and reached inside.

"No way, Del," Burton said, seeing what Derek reached for. "This is police business now."

Derek ignored him, closing the lid with one hand and holding the Heckler and Koch MP5 in the other.

The succession of tragedies thrown in his face this night had weakened him like nothing before in his life. But Derek would not stand idly by and let these men do all the work. This was his business—his to deal with. For reasons Derek couldn't comprehend, his brother had lost his mind. His insanity had driven him to murder and abduction. But for all he'd done, he was still Derek's brother; was still the one person he loved more than any other. To stand before him, to see what he'd become, to be the one to end his suffering would not be easy; but Terry had to die tonight. Derek didn't want his brother arrested and sent to some loony bin, and he didn't think Terry (the Terry he'd known anyway) would want it either.

Burton put a hand on Derek's shoulder, "Sorry Derek, but I can't let you—"

Derek slammed the sub-machinegun's butt into Burton's gut. The policeman *oofed*, clutching his stomach as he doubled over.

"Listen to me, you slag," Derek sneered. "This is my manor. I let you pigs operate on my turf. Mine. Not the other way around. And if I say I'm going in, I'm going in. You got that?"

"Got it," Burton wheezed.

"Now you get on that radio," Derek said, "and earn your fucking reddies, Burton, you useless lump of shit. Tell your team I'm right behind them. If one of them gets the killshot, fine. If not, they're to hold him until I get there. Then I want five minutes alone with him."

"They won't like it, Del."

"Do tell me you were smart enough to use people on the payroll for this."

"I didn't have time," Burton complained. "Some of them are on the books. Not all."

"It's not rocket science. Simple arithmetic: add the right numbers and subtract the wrong ones."

Burton looked confused.

Derek sighed. "Tell the ones who'll turn a blind eye, if I bung them a wedge, to hold him, and them that won't to fall back." Barging past the doubled over DCI, Derek said, "Now get out of my fucking way so I can get this over and done with."

Derek advanced towards the open gate. Once inside, it was as he'd imagined, the armed police had spread out and were slowly moving forwards, keeping low to the ground.

Derek had never bowed his head to anyone, and he wasn't about to start now. He fixed his tie, threw his shoulders back, and walked straight up the center of the long gravel driveway, eyes fixed on his brother's front door.

"Movement!" An SFO to Derek's right shouted. "We've got movement!"

Derek saw something small and dark spring forwards, aiming for the man who'd called the alarm. All he saw was its outline, a shape about knee high that took impossibly long hops across the grass then launched itself into the air. The thing collided with the man's throat. Whatever it was must have had teeth sharp as razors. The man's neck opened up, blood arcing high. Attacker and victim fell together to the ground.

Some of the men ignited flares and threw them to the ground. From the shadows more of the hoppers emerged. They had to be attack dogs— some new breed—there was no other explanation for it. Derek saw at least ten, all hopping across the grass towards the members of the armed response team. Bursts of gunfire rang out: the policemen trying to defend themselves as the hoppers advanced. The semis were useless, the men no match in speed or aim for the things attacking them. In seconds every man but Derek had been felled; their anguished cries and pleas for mercy deaf to the ears of the dark things ripping their throats out.

Derek waited, MP5 ready, knowing he had to be next. Over on the grass, the only man still alive wailed his last, and Derek was alone. He saw a streak of movement and fired the MP5. Bullets tore into turf. In the flickering illumination provided by the flare, he saw it: a glistening frog body about the height of a two year old child. Its head was the size and shape of a rugby ball; features identical to those of a piranha, albeit enlarged many times. The creature turned its head, its bulging fish-eyes fixed on him. Its mouth slowly opened, emitting a pressure cooker hiss as it revealed teeth an inch in length—like rows of tiny lethal daggers. Derek raised his weapon, but before he could settle his aim, the creature kicked with its powerful back legs and hopped away, protected by the shield of darkness.

Derek couldn't allow himself to think about what he'd seen. He knew that if he did he might go mad. He had to focus on Nicola. His daughter, the only thing he'd created that was good and decent, was somewhere inside Terry's house. Getting her out of this nightmare place was all that mattered.

Derek saw the frog children (he could not for some reason shake the sense that they were children), hopping away from their slain victims. Hopping, not towards him, nor the house, but in the direction of the only source of visible light.

Derek knew where they were going. Annexed to Terry's house was a low building that housed a heated indoor swimming pool. He and Terry had taken swims there together on many occasions. It was towards this building the creatures hopped. The first to arrive disappeared through an open doorway. Moments later Derek heard a splash. The others followed suit, hopping inside; further splashes audible as they jumped into the pool.

Derek headed after them; the house forgotten, drawn towards the pool as if by some magnetic force. Somehow Derek knew that was where he would find them: both his brother Terry, and his daughter Nicola.

\# \# \# \# \#

Derek entered the building and walked through to the pool. The water, whose color was now the algae-green of a long forgotten fish pond, had dark shapes moving beneath the surface.

He saw Nicola. She lay on her back in front of the Jacuzzi, arms fixed to the concrete floor by a grey-white mass comprised of barnacles and tiny living tentacles. Whatever the stuff was, it held her in place; pinning not only her wrists to the concrete, but also her ankles. Nicola was naked, legs raised and open wide. She screamed—not in fear—but in pain. Derek had walked in just as his daughter was giving birth. The MP5 fell from his hand.

The wet and slimy thing that came out of her was a smaller version of one of the frog children. Free of the womb, it tore through its sack and crawled forwards several inches. Working its back legs, the infant took its first tentative hop. Already the thing was larger, its accelerated growth-rate occurring before his eyes. It hopped again, splash landing in the Jacuzzi with a plop.

Derek staggered backwards, his mind reeling. His feet slid out from under him and he tumbled through the air, landing in the pool on his back. Sinking, he saw shapes in the murk: the Frog Children all around, eyes staring, mouths open wide as they came at him with their teeth. Something swam through the water above them—a man—inky black liquid leaking from his mouth. Derek had time to see the Frog Children suddenly change direction, turning away simultaneously, as though following some unspoken command. Then his head connected with the bottom of the pool, and he was engulfed by blackness.

# # # # #

In the dream, Derek was now Terry, swimming beneath the ocean's surface with the Greek islanders. For a time there were only the fish, and Derek was amazed—just as Terry would have been amazed—by the myriad varieties of life that teemed all around him. Then he saw it rising; a mass of moving blackness. *Looks like oil*, Derek thought, just as Terry would have thought. But how could something with no life or consciousness move straight for him? The dark stuff enveloped him. The Greek scuba divers frantically swam for the surface. Derek lost the mouth piece to the oxygen tank strapped to his back. And the ink, finding its entrance, pushed at his mouth, moving through his throat, until everything that had been outside was now inside; the sea water around him once again clear. And Derek understood what Terry would have understood: something ancient was alive within him. Something from another world. Terry went insane as the Dark One's memories became his own; and in the dream, Derek went insane likewise. Sanity could never permit such complete comprehension of the inhabitants of the city deep beneath the ocean.

In the dream, Derek, like Terry, could only live as a bubble of consciousness—a bubble soon to burst as the Dark One absorbed that little remaining speck of identity.

Derek could see himself now, watching his body perform actions no longer under his control. Derek's body swam towards the shallow end, where his brother Terry waited. Terry stood naked, penis erect, black goop leaking from its tip. At first, Derek though his brother had contracted German measles. But as he swam closer—that is, as his body swam closer—he saw that the mass of red blotches covering Terry's skin were not welts, but cephalopod suction cups.

Terry reached out to help him from the pool, and Derek saw that from the elbows down Terry's arms had undergone additional transformations, flesh and bone replaced by muscular hydrostat. The cylinders of muscle unfurled and Derek watched his hand grab on to it. Using the writhing octopus arm for support, his body climbed the steps at the edge of the pool. Terry's eyes, though the blue Derek had always known, were wide and staring, with no lids above or below. He smiled, revealing the same dagger teeth as the Frog Children.

"You ready for some fun then, bruvva?" Terry asked; his voice clotted and guttural, now a parody of its former Cockney.

"Tel' you old tosser," Derek heard himself say in greeting, though it wasn't him who'd said it, not from back here in this tiny bubble inside his mind. "Been lookin' all over the shop for you, I have. What you got lined up for me then, eh?"

"Got you a lovely little filly, bruv," Terry tried to wink but his eye wouldn't close. "Come and have a butchers."

Derek felt his head nod, though he had not intended it to do so. And then Derek realized his body was disrobing, removing his sodden clothes and walking towards his naked daughter.

*Please don't make me watch this,* Derek begged. *Anything but this.*

*Very well,* a voice said.

*What are you? Derek asked. Why you doin' this?*

*I am the living dream,* came the reply. *A nightmare made flesh. I am the Dark One, the one without form, floating as liquid within liquid, floating into you and becoming you until you become nothing but me. Soon, the stars will be right and He will return to bring the Earth beneath his sway. Before then, many shall know the Dark One. They will meet me from the touch of your tongue and your seed; will meet me wherever liquid flows. I alone will remold the minds and flesh of men and inspire unknown life within the wombs of your women.*

*As for you Derek Harris, I think it's time you buggered off. Don't you? After all, I'm the new Guvnor of this manor. This is my turf now.*

Derek saw blackness closing in and knew there would be no return from it. He straightened his tie, threw his shoulders back, and marched forwards, determined to greet the darkness with a head-butt.

# THE MENAGERIE

### Ben Thomas

he crocodile's vast jaws clamped shut on the chicken in Scarlatti's hand. With a twitch of its head, the beast bolted the meat down its throat, then returned to absolute stillness, a sculpture in scales and teeth. It had nearly torn a piece from the cuff of his chemise this time. Though he performed the task every morning, it never ceased to send a slight shiver down the beast-keeper's spine.

On the other side of the wrought-iron fence, the nobles grinned. They patted the Prince on his fur-clad shoulder, congratulating him on the wonders of his exotic collection. The crocodile grinned as well. Scarlatti fancied that the beast perceived the nobles as its own menagerie.

"Scarlatti," the Prince tilted his head back, so he could gaze down his aquiline nose.

"My lord."

"I've a mission for you."

"But the griffins, my lord—"

"We have no wish to see the griffins today." He glanced at the nobles surrounding him, and they nodded in agreement.

"No, my lord; I mean they must eat."

The Prince frowned, and answered with some annoyance.

"I'll see to it that one of the stable boys feeds them. Such tasks are below you, in any case. Now come forth."

Scarlatti picked up the hem of his gown and made his way to the gate, watching the crocodile all the while. As he locked the gate behind him, the Prince spoke again:

"Let us discuss this in my audience chamber."

"As you wish, my lord."

"Antonioni," he turned to one of the nobles, a fat fellow in a burgundy doublet with enormous puffed sleeves. "Fetch the Book."

"Sire," Antonioni's voice was as reedy as his cheeks were plump. "The words of the Mad Arab are not—"

The Prince placed a palm upon the fat fellow's chest. "Shall we send the cook to market without a list?"

The noble made no answer, though his jaw pumped, masticating the air.

"And we shall not send Scarlatti in search of the beasts without the formulae."

The Prince grinned again, as though pleased with his own logic. The rest of the nobles grinned with him. He lead the way to the castle, and Scarlatti walked at his side. Behind him, he thought he heard Antonioni snickering at his back, but after a moment, he realized the man was whimpering.

# # # # #

Sprawled on his plush throne, the Prince tucked one leg beneath the other, his slippered feet hardly reaching the ground.

"What think you of my menagerie, Scarlatti?" He twirled a finger idly in the air as he spoke.

The keeper stood before the dais, and felt the eyes of a hundred courtiers upon him.

"I have scoured all of Europa, Africa, and Asia, my lord, to procure the most wondrous beasts and birds for you."

"Indeed you have." The Prince might have been speaking solely for his own ears.

He extended his right hand, and an elderly adviser placed a sheet of parchment in his palm. He ran his eyes over its translucent surface, then passed it to Scarlatti.

It was a letter in French, a tongue of which Scarlatti spoke little. He could discern a few phrases by their similarity to Latin and to his native Italian. The letter told of a menagerie; that much was certain. He recognized the name Versailles, which he knew vaguely to be a wealthy holding near Paris. His eye was quickly drawn past these details, however, for at the bottom of the sheet was sketched a creature most unusual. The beast resembled somewhat the jellyfish he had seen dredged from the waters near Portugal, but its body was covered in writhing tentacles, and its form seemed amorphous, as though the artist had been unable to perceive its shape clearly.

Scarlatti raised his eyes to the Prince, who was frowning.

"What is this beast?" he breathed.

The Prince reached for the vellum, and Scarlatti placed it into his hand. The Prince returned it to the adviser, never taking his eyes from Scarlatti. Then the Prince drew a deep breath, and released it.

"It is a shoggoth," said the Prince.

"Is it—Asiatic?"

The Prince rubbed his eyes. "I am a wealthy man, Scarlatti. In these lands I have wealth beyond measure, and my lands and gardens are the envy of every lord who pays me tribute. But there are other princes, other lands. And one of those princes has acquired a shoggoth for his menagerie."

A smile spread across Scarlatti's lips. "And it is your wish that I should procure one."

The prince sat in silence for a moment. When at length he spoke, his voice thundered across the marble columns of his chamber.

"Antonioni! Bring forth the Book!"

A shuffling within the crowd of courtiers signaled the fat fellow's emergence from their midst. In his arms he held a codex bound in a strange, smooth hide. Though he gripped it tightly, he held it away from his body, as though wary of some disease it carried. The Prince did not extend his hand, and Antonioni paused between Scarlatti and the throne. At a gesture from the Prince, he unlocked the codex and opened it to a page marked with silken cloth.

The book was clearly of great age, for its vellum was torn in many places, and it crackled as Antonioni gently flexed its spine. The page was covered with Greek writing in a smooth hand, and Scarlatti found no comfort in the words he could translate. In its center was another beast unlike any in Pliny or Polo; its shape was that of a man, but its hands bore claws like scythes, and its face split vertically, revealing a maw lined with curved teeth.

Antonioni turned the page, and on the next sheet was a thing that was neither plant nor animal, a slender fungus equipped with wings and tentacles. At a nod from the Prince, more pages followed: beasts with ragged wings and tangled appendages, bulging eyes and cavernous throats. They were without number, without restraint, these designs that no Christian mind could have conceived nor Christian God created.

Several summers ago, Scarlatti had traveled to Sicily aboard a fishing boat, and had been shocked at how poorly his stomach and legs had adapted to the vessel's movement. He felt a bit like that now, as though he had trespassed in a land to whose knowledge he had no right. Had he been asked why he felt this, he would have had no words to express his loathing for this Book. Even half-mad Bosch could not have conceived the devils that populated its pages.

"I want them, Scarlatti," said the Prince. "I want as many as you can possibly find."

Scarlatti's tongue cleaved to the roof of his mouth; he ran it across his lips, seeking his voice. "How—how may I find them?"

The Prince smiled, showing his teeth. "Antonioni will help you, of course. He is eager to serve his Prince and his country, and he has spent many months deciphering the formulae and rituals in this Book."

Antonioni's plump face drained of color, and his lower lip trembled.

"He is at your disposal," said the Prince, "as is what gold you deem necessary."

Antonioni closed the codex and locked its latch. On the hide of its cover, Scarlatti thought he glimpsed a navel of the sort possessed by no mere animal, but he knew this could not be true.

The Prince turned to another adviser, signaling that the interview was over. Scarlatti opened his mouth, closed it, and choked out a final question.

"The Book, your lordship; if you please, how did you come by it? What is its name?"

The Prince turned his gaze back to Scarlatti, favoring him, then Antonioni, with an inscrutable stare.

"In the tongue of Araby, it is known as *Al Azif*, the sound of locusts, for it is said that the lunatic who wrote it heard the ceaseless buzzing of insects in his mind. This translation, however, comes to us from Elizabeth's alchemist John Dee, who titled it the *Necronomicon*."

With that, he turned back to his counselors.

Antonioni nodded toward the chamber door, and Scarlatti walked with him past the stares of myriad nobles, through the antechamber where guards closed the doors behind them, and out into the verdant hills of the royal garden. Scarlatti found a spot where he knew peacocks to forage and sat himself on a bench to watch their strutting. Antonioni collapsed next to him, and the two sat in silence for several minutes.

"It is real, then?" Scarlatti said at last.

Antonioni only nodded, for his throat was dry.

"Do you believe we may capture these beasts?"

The other man drew a deep breath, and spoke thus, in tones almost too low to hear: "Other men have done so, in times long past. We shall use not net or spear; no such beasts are these. But with certain words, and with the Sign . . ."

This speech meant little to Scarlatti, but he allowed the fat fellow the indulgence of his rambling.

"Shall I hire sailors, then?" he asked after a time. "Hunters?" He tossed a hand into the air. "Alchemists, like this Dee?"

"None," said Antonioni. "None, I should say, but us and the Book, and they who transport what we capture."

"And where shall we travel?"

"To Araby. To the desert. With luck, we shall arrive with the new moon."

"And what manner of beasts shall I prepare to find there?"

"Whatever sort will answer us."

# # # # #

The Tunisian smelled of fish and fig liquor, and his teeth were each capped in gold. Scarlatti knew this because each time the man smiled, he flashed every one of those gleaming plates. Excessively toothy grins, he had read, were not a hallmark of honesty, but no one else would cross the Aegean in this weather.

His trip on the Tyrrhenian had been a tranquil sleep compared to this. Waves the size of mountains flung the ship amidst crackling tendrils of lightning, and torrents of rain lashed his skin like tiny whips. Antonioni was clinging to the side-rail, offering his unused dinner to the sea. Scarlatti clung to the mast with all his might, and did his best to keep his feet pointing downward.

"Just bit of rain," beamed the Tunisian. He had told them to call him Ferhat, which was almost certainly not his real name. Ferhat was pacing about the deck, impatient and choleric, without a hint of nervousness.

"How much longer to Izmir?" shouted Scarlatti, spitting out mouthfuls of rain.

"Izmir," Ferhat titled his hand, "two, three hour. Then my gold?"

"If we're alive, yes, then the second half of your gold."

Ferhat threw back his head and laughed, a bellow that fought the wind for supremacy. And the sea spat, and tossed spume across the deck; and the wind shrieked, and the rain lashed the men's faces. It was a night that lasted an eon, a hell worthy to receive the lustful souls of Alghieri's verse.

When at last they docked at Izmir, Scarlatti's linen shirt was stained beyond repair. Antonioni plucked at the sleeves of his doublet, trying in vain to sculpt them into proper form. The beast-keeper and the courtier staggered up the dock, and entered a land where their names, and that of their Prince, meant nothing.

With a thin pouch of gold, they bought a few loaves of flat-bread and wheels of the sharp cheese made by the Turks. Asking no directions, they carried the Book east into the desert, following the landmarks it described in riddles. They rested only fitfully, sleeping in tumbled-down inns and farmhouses. When they passed into the desert, far beyond the most meager villages, they slept beneath cliffs in the clefts between boulders.

Each day, they rose with the sun, bundling their coats about them, eager to be off. Neither spoke of the reason for this hurry, but the sagging eyes of both men made it known: their dreams were filled with visions of appalling creatures, writhing and shambling across the heavens as a cat circles a cornered mouse. It was the Book that brought these visions; it was the Book that was leading them to beings akin to the haunters of their dreams. But Scarlatti's honor and Antonioni's fear of the Prince's wrath were yet stronger than their dread of what they sought.

After three weeks of marching, they reached the end of their food.

"A fast will aid us in focusing the spells," said Antonioni.

"Spells are your concern; survival is mine. I cannot tame a beast if I am fainting."

Antonioni smirked, a grin expression without humor. "You will not tame these beasts. They will return with us, or they will not."

"But what of our return?" Scarlatti scraped a few crumbs from the bottom of the sack, and drank deeply from the bag of water.

"It will be quick," Antonioni eased himself onto a rock, and opened the Book. "We need follow no obscure directions on the way back. In any case, only one remains: *When twenty days and two have you walked east from the pointed cliffs, then shall you behold the plateau.* Only a few more days, I'm sure. Now, might I have the water?"

Scarlatti trusted the fat fellow, and his trust was repaid: three nights later, they came to a plateau, a place where the sand had polished the rock to a smoothness like that of glass. No wind blew here, nor did scorpions crawl over the rock, as they often did at night. The stillness was unnerving to Scarlatti, after so many days of trekking through windy dunes. His stomach ached with hunger, and he knew by his companion's gasp that this was the place they sought.

"So, now, the formulae?" he asked.

"Exactly." Antionioni opened the Book, drew a deep breath, held it, and released it with a whistle. His breathing was shallow, and Scarlatti guessed it was more than hunger that agitated the man.

Antonioni read from the page in a tongue that was neither Arabic nor Greek, a phlegmatic mass of grunts and groans that sounded more akin to the sounds of apes than to any language of men. The words resolved into a chant, though its rhythm was none Scarlatti recognized; the meter was consistent, but complex, and aligned to a beat he found inexpressibly disturbing. When Antonioni fell silent at last, they waited.

"What happens now?" Scarlatti whispered.

Antonioni opened his mouth, but clapped it shut. His eyes bulged, and his double chin was trembling. Scarlatti followed the man's gaze, and at first saw nothing. Then, out of the curve of a nearby dune, shapes resolved and solidified. He felt an indescribable shift in his sight, a displacement, in which he perceived movement in odd directions, at angles that made no sense. He had fasted before, but never had that sacrament given him such perceptions. It was a disorienting geometry, and it seemed to incorporate time as well as space, though he had no idea why he thought this.

"Not—shoggoths," he choked.

"Hounds. Hounds of—Tindalos." Antonioni's eyes were rolling; spittle hung from his slack lips. He was about to drop the Book.

Scarlatti summoned what composure he had left. "The formulae! Speak them!"

The Hounds were but moments away now--both in space and time. They were vast blankets of shadow, all teeth and claws that undulated and folded without ceasing.

Antonioni dropped his eyes to the Book, gazing at the page without apparent comprehension. A second passed. Another. "*Faughn aghnaghr!*" he suddenly screamed. "*Agn ftaghah ohgtn'laa!*" And the verse came pouring forth, line upon line of in that meter as alien as the beasts it controlled. But control them it did, for they slowly ceased their undulations and settled upon the polished rock. The unearthly geometry settled in Scarlatti's mind, and a glance an Antionioni confirmed that he too was regaining mastery of himself.

"They are ours, then?" Scarlatti breathed.

"For now."

"How are we to—to bring them with us?"

"Presumably—" Antonioni ran his eyes over the page. "They will come when we call."

Scarlatti's jaw dropped. "So you suggest we return empty-handed?"

"Indeed, no," Antonioni was trembling again. "They must mark us."

Before he could speak another word, Scarlatti felt a fiery pain in his left hand. For an instant that lasted forever, he was trapped in that same distorted geometry, watching, immobile, as one of the hounds raked its claws across his palm, and the other marked Antonioni. When all was still, he opened his fist, flexed his fingers, and stared at the angular glyph burned into his flesh.

"Home, then?" Scarlatti winced.

Antonioni nodded. When he turned for one last glimpse of the hounds, Scarlatti could see nothing but the dunes and the stars. He shivered.

# # # # #

Their return to the castle must have seemed absurd to the nobles: a pair of ragged men, tanned and raw from the desert, bearing no gifts but the gangrenous welts on their palms. But both travelers wore grins in secret, for they knew that the men who mocked them would soon be trembling before the beasts they commanded.

The Prince, who understood something of the ways of magic, allowed the men a night to rest. They were given fresh pheasant and honeyed wine, and they slept on linen sheets for the first night in more than a month. It was a fitful sleep, filled with restless dreams and strange visions.

After breakfast the next morning, the Prince summoned the travelers down to the gardens, where he had gathered his nobles about him.

"In your absence," he said to Scarlatti, "I have had a mighty cage constructed; a net of steel and iron that can hold any beast. I have even had the Cardinal bless it with holy water, that it might burn any beast of spiritual aspect."

The cage was a towering dome, large enough to hold a herd of giraffes. Its mighty beams were crossed not only with bars, but with a grid of iron chain-mail, through which a man could hardly slide his finger. In his mind, Scarlatti sneered at the Prince's plans, but he bowed and offered thanks.

"Now, my travelers," the Prince showed all his teeth, like Ferhat the sailor. "Where is the first of my fantastic beasts?"

"My lord," said Scarlatti, "if you would direct your eyes to the cage."

He and Antonioni strode to the center of the cage, and he locked its gate. Antonioni unlocked the Book; with a voice grown slightly more sure, he read the passage that summoned the hounds. Across space and time, they came, unfolding from nowhere and everywhere, materializing out of every shadow, every corner where eyes had failed to glance. The cage was filled with the magnitude of their gnashing, flailing forms. They filled the cage to bursting, and their claws passed through the iron as if it were air.

For several minutes, all was silent. Even the birds and beasts in the garden beyond, Scarlatti knew, were cowering in the hounds' presence. At last, the Prince clapped his hands furiously, and all the nobles followed suit.

"Truly Daniel in the lions' den!" the Prince exulted. "A feast tonight for my brave travelers, and all the gold they desire for their next journey!"

The nobles cheered, though their faces were pale. A great many ladies had fainted, as had several men. They were eager to be away from the garden, which pleased Scarlatti far more than he had expected it would. Only the Prince remained, watching the unearthly movement of the hounds, without a suspicion that they remained in their cage only at Scarlatti's behest.

There was a banquet that night, but Scarlatti was absent. He had locked himself in his room, poring over the Book. Antonioni, however, was pleased to attend, and he drank himself into an idiocy from which he never again emerged.

# # # # #

Scarlatti made the next journey alone. He had requested permission to better his Greek before he set off, and the Prince had allowed him time.

"You will surely be a better scholar than Antonioni," the Prince had said, snarling the man's name, as one might say *plague*.

Three sleepless months later, Scarlatti was ready to depart. The moon was entering a phase fortuitous to his next objective, and it was with the Prince's most profound blessing that he made for the frozen North. No man-made map told the location of the Plateau of Leng, but he had deduced it precisely, and had memorized the formulae he would need to tame the savage Voormi.

He booked passage on a freighter heading northeast to the tip of Anatolia, and from the merchants on the coast he learned of a seal-hunter who hove farther into the ice than any other living man. The hunter's name was Soren; his very skin seemed forged of ice.

"I will take you as near the pole as I can," said Soren, "but where can a man wish to go at such longitude?"

"Hunting," said Scarlatti, and Soren laughed uneasily. Well-paid sailors asked few questions.

The passage was slow, impeded by towering bergs that sent their ramparts crashing into the frozen sea around the ship. Scarlatti's hands grew frostbitten, his hair encrusted with icicles. The Book, it seemed, could be damaged by no earthly force: each night as he consulted it, shivering in his tiny bunk, Scarlatti felt its warmth in his hands, as though it were a living thing.

At last, the hunter found the ice shelf where he was fond of trapping seals, and he bid Scarlatti farewell.

"You'll freeze in this, you know," he said. "Nothing up here but frost giants."

Scarlatti knew better, but he kept his thoughts to himself.

Darkness covered the frozen earth for twenty hours out of every day. On foot, it took Scarlatti less than a week to reach the Plateau of Leng. The pace he set for himself was thus: walk in the darkness; hide in the light. The sun blinded him when it reflected from the snow, making progress slower in the day. At least, that was the reason he gave himself. Some nights, halfway between shivering wakefulness and the terror of his dreams, he wondered why he hardly tired, and why he felt the cold so distantly.

The Plateau itself was fairly remarkable: an endless sheet of flat ice gave way to a verdant forest that flourished upon craggy grey cliffs. Up from those snow-capped trees thrust a myriad of spiked towers, pale walls resplendent in the moonlight.

Scarlatti had no need to call the Voormi; they were here, thousands of them: furry half-men who skulked and scampered over every inch of the ruins like rats in a bilge tank. They saw him, and he returned their gaze, showing them the sign on his frostbitten hand. Seeing the mark, they leaped and cowered, covering their hairy skulls in submission. He chose a pair to return with him; a male and female, who he doubted would breed in captivity. Still, it was worth a try.

As he turned to leave, Scarlatti caught a glimpse of another figure, one too straight-backed and bulky to be a Voormi. It too was followed by a few of the beasts, but it vanished too quickly for Scarlatti to make out any detail. He made a mental note of the form as best he could, vowing to be wary of it from now on.

For the trip home, he clothed the Voormi in thick sackcloth and told the sailors they were lepers. He paid the men well, and they asked few questions.

# # # # #

"What might *these* be?" asked the Prince.

"Voormi, my lord, from the Plateau of Leng, far north of Anatolia."

"They look like shriveled men," one adviser knotted his bewhiskered brow.

"Indeed they are, or were," replied Scarlatti. "But long ago they bred with monsters, and now they dwell in places man cannot. Of course, they will eat human flesh, so be cautious."

Several nobles shrieked, and hoarse cries of "blasphemy" could be heard from several quarters.

"Blasphemy it certainly is not," remarked Scarlatti. "At least, no more than eating the flesh and drinking the blood of one's own God every seventh day."

He smirked, and the response was far from welcoming.

"Oh yes, I do apologize," he bowed his head, then turned to a group of bishops. "Some of you are proud to cannibalize Him each morning!"

The entire court looked about to riot, but Scarlatti held his place inside the cage. Only the Prince seemed unperturbed.

"Yes, yes; but when do I get my shoggoth?" he asked, waving his hands for silence. The crowd settled into a subdued mutter.

"We'll have it soon, my lord" said Scarlatti, "and we shall have much more."

# # # # #

The shoggoth proved hardly any struggle at all. Coaxing its wheezing bulk up through the mouth of an extinct volcano was more a physical challenge than a necromantic one. It was a bit like the time he had had to force an elephant to cross the Alps, but with a great deal more slime and pseudopods.

Tsathoggua, the squatting toad-god of N'kai, was shouting after him as he scrambled up the obsidian steps. The raging god's syllables translated loosely as "Bring back my pet this instant, or your soul will burn eternally with the agony of a million red-hot irons!"

Scarlatti thought of several witty retorts, but he repressed the urge to shout them. He had already decided to return for Tsathoggua and the rest of N'kai's oily inhabitants once his mastery of the Book's formulae was complete.

It would take time, yes; but youth seemed to be smiling on him more every night. Each time he awoke, throwing wide his window to bathe himself in moonlight, he felt his skin tightening, his hair growing thicker. Even the mark on his palm had healed; it hardly looked like more than an exceedingly strange tattoo.

He pondered how to disguise the shoggoth as he trudged through the jungle; an amorphous beast the size of a house could hardly pass for any ordinary animal. The problem was solved when they had to ford a river, and the shoggoth simply slipped beneath the water and emerged on the other bank. The night they reached a seaside village, Scarlatti booked passage on a lobster-trawler, and the shoggoth swam a fathom beneath its prow.

When the ship docked at Scarlatti's port, the beast heaved its bulk onto the shore, and Scarlatti watched its translucent mass glistening in the golden rays of dawn. He realized he would have to take more precautions among the towns of civilized men. Bidding the shoggoth to wait in a nearby forest, he stole a steed and rode hard to the castle.

"The shoggoth is here, my lord," he exclaimed, collapsing to one knee. "It awaits you in the forest beyond the farms."

"Well, summon it forth!" cried the Prince.

"Of course, my lord, but I wish to be discreet. How shall we bring it through the streets of the city?"

At that moment, a messenger burst through the doors of the Prince's audience chamber, doused in sweat and ash.

"What's this?" the Prince raised an eyebrow.

"Sire," the messenger could hardly catch his breath, "The devil has attacked the city! He lays our houses to waste! He devours our children with his thousand mouths!"

The Prince shot a hard look at Scarlatti, who said, "I told it to wait in the forest."

"And?"

"Presumably it grew bored."

The courtiers were already drifting toward the windows that looked out upon the city, and the Prince rose from his throne. Scarlatti followed, pressing his face to the glass.

Below, in the stark light of midday, the shoggoth was devouring the city. It had extruded a pseudopod that was currently wrapped around the spire of the cathedral, where Scarlatti had once said his confessions weekly. Several other translucent tentacles rose from the amorphous bulk of its body, clutching screaming children, terrified women, and one extraordinarily angry cow. A wide avenue of slime and rubble stretched to the edge of the city and back across the farms, where flames erupted from every mill and shack. At the very edge of his vision, piles of uprooted trees marked the shoggoth's emergence from the forest.

This was the city where he was born, Scarlatti reflected. There was the book-shop he frequented, crushed beneath a portion of the shoggoth's formless body. There was the theater where he'd had a private box, now reduced to smoking heaps of brick. *Well, it shall certainly be less crowded now*, he thought, but he smiled and kept this sentiment to himself while the nobles gasped and shrieked.

# # # # #

Princes, while they make a great show of having their subjects' best interests at heart, are often far more concerned with how the neighboring kingdoms perceive theirs. This was certainly the case with the Prince who commanded Scarlatti. He took out a great many loans, none of which he had any intention of repaying, and he left the task of reconstruction up to his municipal ministers. Meanwhile, he dispatched Scarlatti to continue collecting specimens.

In Macedonia, the beast-keeper caught something called a byakhee, a snarling monster with wings like leather and jaws that tore through rock. It was in that land, amidst hills peppered with shriveled trees, that he once again caught sight of the straight-backed figure he had glimpsed in the North. It was coaxing a byakhee down from a sheer cliff. Scarlatti spoke a guttural word to the byakhee at his command and made haste for the docks.

After six months' journey across India, he came to a village of huts by the sea, where an old man whispered of things that were neither fish nor men. By the light of the full moon, they came crawling up from the reef, flopping across the beach on their scaly webbed feet. Scarlatti promised them the loveliest women in his country, should they be so kind as to return with him. In the end, they were forced to draw straws, and two Deep Ones were allowed to travel with Scarlatti, while hundreds of others returned to the depths.

The jungles of Siam were filled with every manner of biting and stinging insect, and tangled foliage slowed the progress of his native guides. At last, they reached a clearing which caused the porters to shudder and flee; Scarlatti took this as an encouraging sign. Indeed, after a few moments, the hunched forms of the Tcho-Tcho people slinked out of the shadows. Neither man nor beast, they flicked their forked tongues, and scratched at oozing patches on their warty skin.

"I come to offer you a gift," said Scarlatti, mimicking their speech as best he could.

"What gift?" asked a Tcho-Tcho with a face more cracked and withered than the others.

"Entertainment," he answered. "Courtly men and women will parade before you in throngs, and you may laugh at their foolish ways."

"Tempting," hissed the Tcho-Tcho. "And do you wear the mark?"

"I wear many," said Scarlatti, and he doffed his shirt. Jagged red glyphs adorned his arms, his chest, his back. The Tcho-Tchos beheld the many signs, and they stood in awe of this strange man. Several of their number returned with him, clothed in rags; he offered no explanations to the sailors this time, for men who looked into Scarlatti's sallow eyes found that they had no desire to question him, or even to look again.

The Tcho-Tchos enjoyed Europa, and the Prince enjoyed the Tcho-Tchos. He drew more loans against his lands and castle, and he gave Scarlatti free rein to travel where he would. The Book, he was delighted to hear, told of many more strange beasts.

Scarlatti explored beneath the pyramids of Egypt; in the bowels of darkest Africa; across the mountains of Tibet, which scraped the very sky with their frozen peaks. He gathered men with the heads of animals, creatures without faces, things that were somewhat like birds of prey, or insects, or enormous animalcules, but not entirely any of these.

The Prince delighted in all Scarlatti captured. Many of the new creatures ate the ordinary birds and beasts of the menagerie. Some ate the nobles. But Scarlatti hardly noticed, for he was rarely at home; and when he tarried there for a time, he locked himself in his rooms, and would emerge only on the occasion of new orders from the Prince.

And in the depths of some jungle, or on the other side of a treacherous mountain pass, he would almost always catch sight of that shadowy, straight-backed man, of whom Scarlatti always saw a glimpse and no more.

# # # # #

If Scarlatti's hair had not sloughed from his head in the passing years, would have begun to turn grey. His beard ran with streaks of silver.

The Prince, who had long ago become the King, was blessed with ten children, one of whom would be his heir. The holdings he had inherited spread far along the coast, and his vineyards were known for their spectacular Chianti. But far eclipsing all these delights was the King's menagerie, which was known throughout the Mediterranean as the most astonishing collection of beasts ever exhibited.

It was an afternoon in autumn when the King requested Scarlatti's presence in the garden. The beast-keeper was meditating in his room, recording omissions and fabrications in Prinn's *De Vermis Mysteriis*. When the summons came, however, he returned the stone to its cabinet, for age had taught him patience.

The King was waiting for him on the garden path near the enclosure that had once belonged to the crocodiles. It had been converted into a watery dome for the shoggoths, who were dividing frequently, and often had to be released into the sea. They walked among the netted spire that held the byakhee, the aquaria where the Deep Ones swam, the artificial forest where the Tcho-Tchos dwelt.

The garden had become a metropolis unto itself; a prison for the mightiest creatures in existence. All had lived well; many had thrived and even multiplied here.

"I received a strange message this morning," said the King.

Scarlatti raised his eyebrows.

"It was a communication from Ruthenia."

Scarlatti glanced at the rune-covered stone planks encompassed the dhole enclosure. They were irritated, snapping at one another; he made a mental note to offer them another plump cow soon.

"They ask for our help, and the sanctuary of our lands."

"Your pardon, my lord, but what is this to do with me?"

The King was silent for some time. When at last he spoke, his voice was heavy, his eyes downcast.

"They have also assembled a menagerie. This has . . . *displeased* certain powers."

"Powers? Do the Mongols envy them, then?"

The King was about to make an answer, when the earth rumbled, as if a quake had seized the land. The rumbling resolved into a steady pounding, and presently Scarlatti discerned the snorting of horses and the pounding of hooves.

"I have told the guards not to impede them," said the King, as though it were somehow reassuring.

A vast army galloped through the streets of the city, through the gates of the castle, pulling their mounts to a halt in the King's promenade field. Scarlatti could see them clearly from the garden; the spikes on their fur helmets gleamed in the sun. Their horses were stocky beasts whose legs rippled with muscle, and whose thick tails hung nearly to the ground.

In their front ranks was a man Scarlatti would have recognized from leagues away. He sat straight-backed in his saddle, even in his advanced age, but no hair grew upon his head. His eyes were haggard, his skin sallow. If the man opened his hand, Scarlatti knew, he too would bear a mark there.

Several riders dismounted, but no stable boys came forward; there were no stables to house an army, even here. Maids emerged from the larder, carrying pails of water for the men.

The King approached the men who had dismounted, and an escort surrounded him as he strode across the field. Scarlatti walked with him, encircled by muscular guards in lavish uniforms. They, he knew, were what the King maintained in place of an army.

"Welcome, General Suzdal of Ruthenia," the King spread his arms in welcome. "You may take sanctuary here."

"You honor us," said Suzdal, "but I am afraid we can take no such thing, nor can you offer it."

The King took a step back. "I understand that certain powers have awakened against you—"

"No!" snapped Suzdal. It was the first time Scarlatti had heard anyone interrupt the King. "You understand nothing. Your entire land— our whole country—is burned as black as ash, and festers with beasts even Nitchev cannot control."

Nitchev, the straight-backed man, stepped forward. "We ask not for your help, or your sanctuary," he said in a voice like tearing parchment. "We beg you to set your beasts free, before all Europa--and perhaps the world—is destroyed!"

The King shook his head. "And you bring an army to tell us this?"

"We bring an army," said Suzdal, "because it is here that we must make our last stand. Our lands are naught but ash and rubble. Now They are less than half a day behind us, and my men have ridden harder than any army I know."

"Who pursues you?"

"The Other Gods," said Nitchev.

Perhaps something in the Ruthenians' eyes, the vehemence of their speech, turned the King's mind. He signaled Scarlatti, and they conferenced a short way off.

"What shall I do?" asked the King. "Scarlatti, speak true: will freeing our menagerie appease these gods?"

"I know not, my lord."

"Then what are we to do?"

Scarlatti turned over the thought that was forming in his mind. He knew his control over his menagerie was absolute, for even the King had never guessed that it was Scarlatti who had set the shoggoth on the city's populace, and the byakhee and the Deep Ones upon the nobles. All this he knew, and he lately had no fear of death, or of damnation; one was all-but barred from him, and the other was eventually guaranteed. He voiced his thought.

"We might turn the beasts to our own service, my lord."

The old King went pale for a moment, but slowly a grin spread across his face. It was a grin not entirely bereft of madness.

"Can this be done?" he asked.

"It can be attempted."

"Attempt it."

# # # # #

The King and the general conferenced together, planning the placement of the army and the guards, and the closing of the city gates. Both men knew, however, that their forces would be useless against the arriving powers.

Scarlatti and Nitchev also conferred, sealed in Scarlatti's chambers with a pile of texts older than mankind. They found few definite answers, so their plans were drawn in their own minds.

"Did you ever manage to capture a shantak?" asked Scarlatti.

"Beasts of the dream-world are exceedingly flightly," Nitchev answered, "and I'm not entirely sure they can be imprisoned on this plane at all."

"As I thought," Scarlatti mused.

The sun passed overhead and twilight spread across the fields. In the gardens, the beasts stirred, sending howls and shrieks of unearthly quality to the grey sky. In the distance, thunder rumbled again. But this time, it resolved itself not into the galloping of horses, but the stomping of appendages of incalculable size. Splashing sounds, like the crashing of mighty waves, accompanied these titan footsteps.

Freezing winds from the stars whipped through the city, carrying fungous winged things with them. The lords of Yuggoth had arrived, and they sounded the horns of battle: high-pitched hooting sounds that vibrated to no rhythm of this world.

Scarlatti looked up. Far beyond his window, shadows the size of mountains crested the horizon. Night was falling, and the earth shook with the rage of the Other Gods.

Nitchev was already out the door, scrambling down into the garden. Scarlatti followed, his aged legs bucking as he hurtled through then halls of the castle, out onto the promenade field, down the path. He shouted three syllables, words in a language that died before the first man was born, and the door to every cage flew open. He spoke again, Nitchev now underlaying his words with commands of his own; the beasts tore forth from their prisons and gathered on the field. Here were the secret inhabitants of the city, as many in number as the villagers who labored outside the gates, whispering secrets of what lay within. Here were the primordial devils that populated the nightmares of all men. They would now do battle with their masters.

The Ruthenian cavalry had assembled on the lawn, but it made no charge, though the general was at its head. Every eye was turned to Scarlatti and Nitchev.

Both men raised their arms, and the byakhees, the hundreds of them who had bred and lived in captivity, took flight, like a cloud of leathery locusts that screamed in the night air.

From the southern coast marched Dagon, standing head and shoulders taller than the castle, loping across the farms on scaly legs that dripped with bilge and seaweed. His mouth was the mouth of a snarling fish from the deepest sea, and it snarled with fury, but the byakhees flew at him without ceasing, tearing into his armored flesh with claws and mouths like daggers. He flung his webbed hands about, batting their air, but they were quick creatures, and they swarmed around him like gnats.

Great Cthulhu followed, dwarfing Dagon utterly; a mountain of gelatinous green, with wings that spread high over his broad back and blotted out the stars. The tentacles covering his face struck like whips, snatching windmills from the fields, tearing towers from the roofs of churches. A single stride brought him across the farms; two carried him into the city. He left burning piles of brick and wood in every footprint. Shoggoths clustered around his feet, and he crushed them flat in an instant, then sparing one swipe of his clawed hand to smash the cathedral, which exploded in a shower of bricks and windows that fell like stained-glass missiles from the sky. The byakhees assaulted his head, to little effect; great Cthulhu was a walking citadel, a tower of globular flesh that reached to the moon, and the byakhees were as gnats that swarmed around him.

En masse, the other gods charged: Nyarlathotep, the crawling chaos, moved far too quickly for the eye to track, but the Hounds of Tindalos were at his throat, shredding the perfect skin of the immortal Pharoah in a thousand dimensions. Yog-Sothoth burst forth from his shining globes, his infinite tentacles writhing ceaselessly as he descended upon the city like a pestilent cloud, flinging houses into the air, tearing up roads and raining their bricks upon any structure still standing.

And in return, Scarlatti and Nitchev sent forth their legions. The dholes, crawling upon and within ground of all textures to seek the feet of the gods; the Tcho-Tchos and Voormi, who unleashed unholy spells that made the air crackle and the ground churn; the Deep Ones, who shambled into battle, where they snapped and tore with vicious hunger at the flesh of their adversaries.

Mere minutes had passed, and already the gods had filled the city with impenetrable clouds of smoke and dust, with madmen who ran naked through the streets, rending their flesh in terror.

Scarlatti caught sight of the King, who had gathered his guards around him. He and the generals were fleeing for the castle, casting horrified looks behind them. Scarlatti turned to Nitchev, who was crouched behind a fallen guard tower.

"This was a fool plan!" he shouted over the deafening clamor.

"Had I told you, would you have listened?" Nitchev yelled.

Scarlatti threw back his head and laughed, his voice rising above the roar of great Cthulhu, the howling of Yog-Sothoth, the thunder of the feet of a dozen immortal gods.

"What need have I for a menagerie?" he howled, that all might hear. He made a sign to Nitchev, who nodded. They began to chant, in synchrony with one another, but in a rhythm unnerving to the ear. Calling on all his strength, Scarlatti bellowed the guttural words that all the creatures of the menagerie might hear.

The byakhees turned to listen, and their attack became a demure gathering about the head of great Cthulhu. The shoggoths clambered down from Yog-Sothoth's tentacles and squatted obediently on the scorched ground. Dholes and Tcho-Tchos, Deep Ones and Voormi, all cocked their heads, then ceased in their assault.

The gods took notice. They stopped their swatting and their stomping, their flapping and their writhing. They gazed at the ruination around them, and at the parade of strange beasts who now sat before them like obedient dogs. One by one, the gods turned and departed the way they came, flattening the rubble of the city with every earth-shaking footstep. Behind them came their pets, lurching and writhing on their way, obedient once again to their primordial masters.

But great Cthulhu spun on his heel, and with a mighty swipe of his hand he smashed the castle to dust. When the dust had cleared, and no structure of man stood from the forest to the sea, Cthulhu sighed deeply, and took himself away to his sunken city of R'lyeh.

# # # # #

Dawn broke, and hardly a rat stirred in all the city, or in the farms beyond. Everywhere were columns of flame and smoke, vast heaps of shattered brick and glass, steaming craters that dripped translucent slime.

Scarlatti and Nitchev sat with their backs against the fallen guard tower and stared out across the endless ruins.

"What will you do now?" Scarlatti asked.

Nitchev was silent for some time, and when at least he spoke, his voice was breathy and hoarse.

"I will return to Ruthenia, to my village, and die in peace. I am old, and I deserve some rest before I am delivered to—to them. And you?"

A grin spread slowly across Scarlatti's face. "I still have the Book," he said.

"You're mad!" Nitchev gasped.

"Yes," said Scarlatti, "I suppose that shall help."

# THE PATRIOT

John Goodrich

"Contact!"

My brawny mechanic muscles my propeller around, and it finally catches on the fourth rotation. Clouds of smoke rise from my sputtering engine. He steps back from the whirring propeller of my SPAD VII and scurries, surprisingly quick for a man of his bulk, to remove the chocks from my wheels. I can barely contain my nervous excitement. I am about to fly my first combat mission; the date is 12 July, 1917. We four are on patrol looking for Boche; Lieutenant DePout, Sous Lieutenant Alibert, and myself, with Capitaine Lefeure himself as the flight leader.

The engines roar as we race them, and on the Capitaine's signal, our formation moves towards the end of the airfield. We lift more or less simultaneously, clearing the trees at the end of the field, and climb into the sky over France. We soar for some time, continuing to gain altitude. Once the uncertainty of take-off is over, my nervousness turns into a pleasant sort of sloth. Flying is a pleasure, despite the hundred things I have to remember in order to keep my fragile SPAD in the air and flying in formation. On the ground, the air is hot and still, but up in the sky, it rushes by, making the flight pleasantly cool. The green fields of France stretch below me, verdant despite the war. I cannot imagine a more pleasant day, or a better way to fight for my country.

Ahead is the great scar of churned-up Earth that marks the trenches. I can see fast-evaporating puffs of smoke that mark artillery emplacements, so far below that they look like balls of cotton. Surely nothing so far away can possibly affect me, safe in my plane, five thousand feet above the endless slaughter on the ground. I've done my time as a member of the infantry—more than any man should have to. I remind myself that I am not a tourist, and I look around as I was taught in flight school; I see no black specks, but only peaceful, empty clouds like those from a Monet painting.

After nearly thirty minutes of pleasant flight, Capitaine Lefeure dips his wings, indicating that he has seen Boche aircraft. I search the sky, but do not see anything until the Albatrosses are among us, and the flight scatters like children let out of school, each going our own way chaotically, and by some miracle we do not smash into each other.

The fight is an abrupt and terrifying whirlwind of planes and open sky. I twist and turn, listening to my ailerons protest. I cannot count the black Albatrosses, but their color and bird-like wing-extensions distinguish them from our brown SPADs. Working myself around to a position behind where one black plane should be, and I see nothing but open sky. The fight is behind me, and I kick the rudder pedals and wrench the stick around.

Bullets hammer into my plane; an Albatross is coming down on me from above my right fore wing, tiny flames spitting from its guns. In spite of everything I have been taught, I freeze like a rabbit confronted by a poisonous snake as I hear the bullets tearing into the fabric of my plane. A shadow passes over me, and a plane—Captaine Lefeure's— flies through the rapidly-narrowing space between me and the onrushing Albatross. The moment's relief I feel gives way to horror as his engine blooms flame, and he passes so close to me that I choke on the smoke and heat from his burning craft. The Albatross zooms past us, but all I can do is watch as Capitaine Lefeure, Fernand, I remember his name is, leaps from his aircraft, choosing a quick death by impact rather the prolonged agony of burning. In seconds, he is little but a tumbling speck quickly lost against the brown scar that is No Man's Land.

His death jars me from my unresponsive dream-state, and I am filled with the desire for bloody revenge against the black butcher who murdered my Capitaine. Kicking the rudder pedals as hard as I can, and nearly standing my plane on a wingtip, I whip my SPAD around and drop in behind the murderous Albatross. He twists and turns as I cling to his tail; he cannot get rid of me, and yet I cannot get a good shot at him. I wait for my opportunity, rather than waste bullets on air, and it comes when he pauses to look behind him. Just as he sees me, my bullets slam into his fuselage, and the murderer slumps down in his cockpit, his black plane winging over to dive for the ground.

I have done it! My first victory!

My exultation at this bloody deed is cut short by the *spack spack spack* of bullets hammering at the fragile wooden frame of my machine. I wasn't watching my tail! Convulsively, I wrench my plane around, and with a heart-stopping *crack*, my right, lower wing snaps off, and my plane begins to follow my erstwhile opponent's in a terrifying, spinning dive for the ground.

I have no time to worry if my opponent is still on my tail or not, I am too busy fighting to stop my plane's disastrous descent that will certainly kill me. The stick tries to wrench itself out of my hands, and I pull on it as hard as I dare, knowing that I could snap off the remaining wings if I'm too violent. Somehow, I manage to stop the whirling dive once, less than two thousand feet above the ground, only to resume it. I again wrestle desperately with my plane, which seems determined to meet the ground with as much force as possible, and I curse gravity, wind, aerodynamics, and my instructors as the ground spins wildly and looms in my vision, inescapable.

# # # # #

"Sorry, there. I didn't see that you were still alive."

I open my eyes and see an overwhelming dark, punctuated only by the occasional flash of artillery. The reek of death is all around me. I must be in No Man's Land, pinioned somewhere between friendly trenches and the Germans.

My leg is an agonizing ball of fire. I look down, and even without the intermittent light of exploding shells, I can see the white gleam of bone jutting from my shin amidst a fast-growing black stain that I know is my blood. I wonder how I managed to drag myself from my plane, which I cannot see in the darkness. I am cold, although I remember that it is July.

I try to slip my belt off, but my fingers are too clumsy and too weak to pull the belt from under me, and more pain grinds my torso when I try to lift myself.

"Help," I say, but I am desperately weak, and the word is immediately absorbed into the torn and bloody mud.

"Is anyone there?" I have a vague recollection of being woken by words, and look around. I am unimaginably alone in the midst of the greatest of all wars.

A dark shape in the lesser darkness of the ground shifts near me, and I can see that his head is tilted sideways in curiosity. He is bareheaded, and I cannot tell if he is German or not, although I seem to recall him speaking French.

"My belt," I gasp. "Help me make a tourniquet for my leg."

He is strong, and I clench my teeth against many pains scattered throughout my body as he rolls me to one side and pulls my belt from under me.

"Now what?" His speech is odd, he must be some sort of provincial, or perhaps British.

"Fasten it around my leg, as tightly as possible, to stop the blood."

It is torture, as sure as any a Medieval man suffered, but it will keep me from bleeding to death. His strong hands are none too gentle as the belt becomes a throbbing noose just above my knee, and what little strength I have left goes into throat-shredding screams of agony, and then oblivion claims me.

# # # # #

I awaken, I do not know how much later, a waning quarter moon is up—it must be past midnight. I can distinguish only the few things that are close to me, but the thick, choking reek of opened graves assailing my nostrils tells me that I am still in No Man's Land. The occasional shelling continues, the stuttering light revealing that I am in a wasteland of corpses. Sticking up out of the mud are hands, legs, heads, coats, helmets, rifles, arms, and other, less identifiable parts; some of them are whole, many of them have been torn asunder, and where the exposed flesh is not coated with mud it has been blackened from days of exposure to the sun. They surround me as far as I can see in the wan moonlight; my hands are resting on them, and surely I am lying on them. These must be the remains of some poor infantry platoon sent over the top, now left to rot, forgotten amidst the mud and stench. My leg is on fire, but the agony is not what it was. I risk a glance at my leg—it is a barely-visible dark shadow, caked with dried blood and mud. I won't be walking anywhere, and I won't make much progress by crawling, either. I won't

216

know until the sun comes up which direction the French lines are, and which way are the German. If I choose wrongly, a sniper will get me. If I choose correctly, there's still a good chance a frightened and inexperienced sentry will think I'm German.

I try to crawl into a shell hole, because I don't want to be exposed when the sun comes up, but there is no strength in me. I am weaker than I remember feeling when I nearly died of mumps as a child. The simple act of lifting my arms is an effort, and even attempting to drag my heavily inert body triggers a grinding pain in my chest that leaves me gasping. I giggle, then begin to laugh at the mordant irony. I had transferred out of the infantry just to avoid a death like this, lying helpless in the loathsome, sucking mud of No Man's Land. What foolishness, what a stupid, useless waste of time to learn how to fly an aircraft just to end up back in the mud, weak and dying.

In the abrupt flash of a shell burst, I see a crouching silhouette that hasn't been there before. My mouth is dry, and when I try to call out to him, all I can manage is a weak croak. If he hears me, he makes no indication. He is somewhat closer in the next flash, bent down to examine something. In the next burst of light I see he has picked something up– an arm! He is a robber, one of those horrible people you hear stories about that live out in No Man's Land, stripping the dead of their possessions. I flounder briefly, but just the attempt to sit up sets my heart pounding. I have no weapon; there is no way I can stop this defiler of corpses.

The next flash of artillery burns an image forever onto my brain. The shape has picked up a severed human arm and brought it to his mouth. Horror and revulsion send a hot shock through me, and I find my voice.

"*Cannibal!*" I scream, outrage lending me strength, and I again flail around to find a gun. The muzzle of a rifle comes to my hand, but I am too weak to free it from the mud. Nothing else comes to hand, and I am too weak to drag myself away. I cannot kill this horror, cannot catch him and break his spine in my hands even if I were able to reach him. A sense of my own weakened helplessness overwhelms me, and he shuffles over to me with a curious slouching movement.

It is only when he is close to me that a shell flashes brightly enough to confirm that I am in some sort of Hieronymus Bosch nightmare. Something is wrong with the cannibal's face, as if it were more wolfish than human, with powerful, prognathous jaws so greatly exaggerated as to suggest a muzzle. He is caked in mud, as is everyone, and I am unable to tell if he is even wearing clothes. In one claw-like hand, he carries a forearm, and I can see where he has taken bites from it. He shuffles towards me, and I desperately scrabble for something—anything—with which to defend myself. My hands encounter other, colder hands, open mouths, boots, coats, and mud, but nothing with which to fend this monster off.

It squats down to pluck the eyes from a helpless, dead face. I close my own eyes, but the sound, like that of someone enjoying a juicy olive, repulses me even as it reminds me how hungry I am. It swallows loudly.

"Not a cannibal," it says in curious but perfectly understandable French. "In Arabia, the word for us is *ghula*, and that satisfies me well enough."

The words and civilized accent are at utterly at odds with the hideous, distorted appearance. Somehow this thing should drool when it speaks, and slur his words in a vile fashion that lets me know he is purely evil. How much of a monster can this creature be if it can speak French? And yet, for his inhuman and vile diet, he had saved my life by tightening my tourniquet.

War makes all men mad. I am lying on a bed of unknown corpses, staring at the infinitely distant and uncaring stars. Soon I will join the dead men, unless I am found by a night patrol or a rescue party. I watched my Capitaine step from his plane and plummet to his death rather than burn, and the madness of this war rolls on like an unstoppable juggernaut, crushing and mangling the lives of all in its path. Is it any wonder that someone has turned to cannibalism? The only thing this war has in plenty is dead victims, and somehow, it doesn't surprise me that something—someone—has learned or been driven to take advantage of that. Certainly the rats and the lice live better than kings, with all the food they could possibly want, enduring only the occasional enmity of the living soldiers who resent them only briefly.

"Tell me you are not Boche," I say desperately.

"I am loyal to France, if that is what you are worried about," he replies.

I turn my head away, only to hear him shuffling towards me. I am helpless. My heart thunders desperately; he will kill me to preserve his secret, and I can do nothing about it. I grasp the rifle muzzle I had found before, but there is no give, the mud's grip is too sure.

I look back to see his dark shape standing over me, just far enough away that I cannot touch him, and he can't touch me. He is holding something out, and it takes me a moment to realize that it is a canteen. Staring at it, I can feel how dry my mouth is. I don't dare scoop water out of the stagnant pools in the large craters; the water in No Man's Land is scummed over with a layer of trapped poison gas. But what is it that this . . . person has in store for me? Is it poisoned?

If he wants fresh meat, he can easily overcome me. I would lose a wrestling match with a six-year-old in my current state, but he might not know that. I have no gun, no knife, and no means of defending myself. But my mind comes back to the fact that he applied the tourniquet to my leg. Why preserve my life only to poison me now?

I grasp the canteen, my hands shaking with weakness. It is full and heavy, and I almost drop it, but I am so parched that I drain it completely. I feel some energy return to me, but also a renewed insistence of the throbbing pain in my leg.

"Thank you," I say, lowering the canteen, gasping for breath. I pray that he does not offer me food. With my thirst slaked, I am hungry enough that I might accept.

"I am Gaspard, by the way," he says, crouching on his haunches like a bush man.

"Michel," I respond automatically.

"How came you here, Michel?" he asks. "Your uniform is not like theirs." He uses a sweeping gesture to indicate the legion of bodies that surrounds us, half-swallowed in the mud.

"My airplane crashed," I say, and wonder what I am doing. I am talking with a ghoul, an eater of corpses. Something that will see me as food as soon as I am dead, and perhaps is only waiting for a moment of obvious weakness to pounce on and devour me. And yet, the fundamental human need for companionship makes me desperate. I do not want to be alone, more than that, I don't want to die alone, even if I am speaking with one who will feast on me after I am gone.

"Air-plane?" He is testing out the unfamiliar word. "What is an air-plane?"

"A heavier-than-air craft with wings that flies."

"You're mocking me." Gaspard's voice is offended.

"I swear it's true," I insist, amazed that I care what this corpse-eater thinks of my conversation. But talk—any sort of communication—is better than sitting and waiting for a rescue that may never come. "You must be very isolated."

"True enough," Gaspard replies, and looks away. I regret striking the nerve, because he does not elaborate. The silence is interrupted only by the bursting of a distant shell.

"Must you feast on soldiers, like a rat?" The question bursts out of me, the only thing I can think of. Somehow, I imagine he could be some sort of vastly overgrown rat. The rats in the trenches are so enormous that I would not have believed it without seeing them. "Is there nothing else that you can eat?"

"Our earliest stories are told of Sumer and Babylon, where city-states rose and made war on each other, and we feasted on the dead." Gaspard says it in a dreamy and reverent voice that no longer sounds offended. "Other lands have been greater sources of provender for short periods of time, but few countries have ever been so truly generous or so consistent as my beloved France."

The 'we' sends a wave of horripilation across my skin. There is more than one of him—and they have stories that go back as far as recorded history? A *ghula*, he called himself, a ghoul. One of my fellow history students, one with a more morbid bent than myself, had once related a repellant story of a race of underground creatures that lived among the catacombs and sewers of Paris, degenerate remnants of people who fled there during the Terror, living and breeding in the reeking dark, coming up only to steal the unloved and unwanted for their unhallowed feasts. I had dismissed it as a gothic fairytale. Did sanity permit a race of creatures that dwelt below France, gnawing away at her dead?

"You aren't just waiting for me to die, are you?" I ask.

A long, daemonically howling cachinnation that might be a laugh erupts from him, and it chills me to the bone.

"Young men seem so eager to fight and to die for whatever cause, and yet you come over all squeamish if it turns out that you might get eaten," he says when he regains his breath. His eyes glow weirdly in the stuttering light of the bombardment.

"Why does it bother you? To know that after you are dead, one of us will creep up on you and chew your flesh and suck the marrow from your bones? You'll be dead, and so far as we can tell, you won't feel it. How can anything that happens to your unfeeling corpse be worse than dying? If you ask me, it's the killing that's the real crime." Those uncanny eyes fix on me.

"Wouldn't you rather have lived a full life with a wife to make love to, and then some fat children to coo over? Wouldn't it be better to spend cool autumn afternoons at a café sipping coffee, rather than lying at the bottom of a crater, covered in mud, waiting to die? Don't you deserve friends to love and argue with, books to read, wine to drink, and a fire to warm your bones when you get old? Some warm and happy memories to comfort you before that final black oblivion sucks you down, down, down into nothing? Are your lying leaders and their war-profiteering friends worth sacrificing all that for?"

These things I have thought myself; I remember similar sentiments as I waited to go over the top with the 146th at Verdun, while politicians whose incompetence had started it, the generals whose indifference prolonged it, and the profiteers who gained from it, risked nothing. No one who had ever been at the front lines could refer to the massacre of thousands as "the usual wastage" or talk about the loss of half a million men as "quite acceptable." General Sir Douglas Haig had been talking about enough men to fill the city of Lille twice, and he had done so from the quiet drawing-room of some appropriated chateau, I am certain. What makes my life worth so much less than Pétain's, de Castelnau's, Joffre's, or Nivelle's? At least I have never sent a thousand, ten thousand, or a million men into a blind, pointless slaughter. Before I had arrived at the front, I would have said that his was a right war, that defending French soil from the Germans was worth my life. Watching the war as it was conducted had thoroughly eradicated that noble fiction.

"At least it's better for us; it won't be a complete waste," Gaspard says. I should be horrified by his monstrous indifference, but I ask myself if he is any more atrocious or ghastly than the old men who had lead us into this war. "What's this one about, anyway?"

"Curbing rampant German imperialism," I say automatically, feeling the need to explain in more concrete terms. "They invaded France."

"What will happen after they've been expelled?" he asks. "Will you destroy all the Germans? Murder their children, burn their homes, kill their women, taking some home to be your slaves, or maybe a war bride, to make sure that they never invade again?"

"We don't enslave people anymore." I am about to say something about slavery being uncivilized, but I don't want to hear that horrible howl of a laugh again. As it is, he snorts his cynical indifference.

"We'll stop Germany, and then. . ." I trail off. What will we do then? "Then the world will be safe." I know how hollow the words sound.

"I dare say so, with so many men dead," he says with casual misanthropy. "And you will trust the same butchers who have turned France into an enormous garden of corpses to create and govern a lasting peace when all is done?"

"What do you know of war?"

"A great deal." He is unruffled by my outburst. "I do consider myself a patriot, Michel. France has long been kind to us, and where you tell your history by the wars you fight, we tell it by the times of plenty. Caesar's forces were unlike anything anyone above or below had ever seen, and they left mounds of corpses wherever they went. After they conquered old Gaul, there was good fighting over who exactly got to be the Emperor of the Gauls, and Roman executions were always enough to keep us in provender without having to hunt it for ourselves. Imagine thirty, eighty, or a hundred sides of beef left hanging by the roadside. We were mad for choice; the Romans were our best friends for hundreds of years. It was a lovely time, I am told. And when Rome began to crumble, there were barbarian invasions; the Rhenan Franks, the Burgonds, Visigoths and Salic Franks, all laying waste to the countryside, all leaving us meat."

He looks up at the stars, and then down at the darkness of the lines.

"We remember Atilla as a great friend to us and ours." His tone is reverent. "He killed anyone he could catch, leaving them in great heaps, and we gorged ourselves until we couldn't even crawl. Some time later, Clovis unified himself a kingdom, mostly by killing anyone who resisted him, and for two centuries his successors followed in his footsteps. Those were days of easy plenty, and then Charlemagne got it into his head to have a bigger kingdom than anyone else, and we dined regularly on Bretonian and Aquitanian.

"At the same time, there was always something happening with the Emirates near the Pyrenees, and we used to say 'if you're still hungry, go South.' After the internal struggles settled down somewhat, the Vikings invaded from the sea and the Hungarians attacked in the East. Again, we were spoilt for choice. Charlemagne's grandchildren and later descendants never really got along, and they fought each other to claim this or that bit of empire, always leaving fresh provender lying in the fields. The Capetians were no different, and we gnawed the bones of many a Norman duke, thanks to their lust for power.

"We glutted ourselves on Albigensian heretics. The War of Lord and Vassal provided us with nearly a century of fine dining, although we could never tell who was on whose side. A bounty of Plantagenets and Capetians ended up dead on the ground, with no one but us to look after them. It was difficult to go from a century of such plentitude to nearly as long of relative peace, but we adjusted. We moved into the great cities, and began to worm our way into graveyards and catacombs, living on such scraps as we could scrounge.

"We were saved from that ignoble state by the British, bless their ambitious hearts. For more than a hundred years, we stuffed ourselves on the best the British had to offer. And once they were finally driven out, the South began to be interesting again, with another extended conflict with Hispania. When that was done, the French started fighting themselves as the Wars of Religion started up, which we found wonderfully filling. But nothing that good could possibly last, and what followed was the longest famine we have ever experienced. Nearly two hundred years, and not a single war on France's soil. And while the good times don't go on forever, and neither do the bad ones. The Prussians and the Austrians invaded, and we gorged again. But these were merely appetizers for what was to come.

"The Revolution was a glorious time for us." He sighs like an old woman remembering her younger, wilder days. "The food was so rich, so plentiful, and so very tender. I remember a group of us passing around scraps of royalty, because it was too important not to share. Later, when the Terror was in full swing, some of us were bold enough to walk openly among the surface dwellers. Few noticed, and I discovered then that people above really aren't that different from us below.

"After that, there was the little Corsican, who did little for us until he was driven back into France. Still, we get a great laugh out of all those monuments he put up to himself, since all he managed to accomplish was to feed ghouls in other lands. His grandiose Arch of Triumph should be called 'The Feast of Foreign Ghouls.'

"We were afraid that there would be another two hundred year dearth after that, but the Prussian invasion whet our appetites for this great and glorious feast." His sweeping gesture includes all the corpse-filled darkness. "Truly, it is more than we deserve."

I have no answer. I am tired, my spirit drained, and sick to my soul of Gaspard's horribly twisted version of history. I stare up at the black, uncaring sky, filled with a million infinitely remote pinpoints of light. No matter what happens, no matter the course of human history, it won't matter at all to the brilliant, eternally distant stars. I can feel myself drifting towards that final blackness, like a final rest from which there is no waking. I, too, will feed the ghouls as I lay in No Man's Land. I think of my mother and my sister, who will weep for me. It is hard to keep my eyes open, although something nags at me.

"Gaspard," I whisper, but there is no answer.

"Gaspard," I repeat.

"Yes," he finally replies.

"Promise me you will make sure I am dead before you eat."

A hand with thick claws instead of nails comes down on my shoulder, and I look up into the disturbingly wolfish face. "I promise," he says. Although I can sense some dark and still-unfathomed amusement behind his eyes, I believe him, and am in some small way comforted.

"Thank you." I can feel consciousness slipping away from me. I fight it; I don't want to die, I don't want Gaspard to crack my bones and suck their marrow. I think of things that please me; of not lying in this field of death and stench, but of family, and the simple, homey comforts that I miss. I miss the clean feel of getting into a freshly-made bed, the cool touch of a hardwood floor in the morning, the thousand variated greens of a forest, the careless laugh of children, and the company of family. But these longed-for pleasures slip away, and as I close my eyes for the last time, my thoughts are not of my mother, but of the lovely Francine, who I seduced before I went off to war. Her skin was wonderfully soft and warm, her breasts ripe and full, her lips always in a knowing smile.

# # # # #

I wake again, and I am under a white ceiling. The reek of death and decay has been replaced with the sharp stench of ether, and gangrenous rot. Around me are numerous white-sheeted beds, filled with the shapes of the wounded. Somewhere near me, someone is coughing so hard that I cannot see how he will live through it, and everywhere I hear the moans of the dying. It takes a moment for the reality of my survival to sink in, and my head swims with the memories of No Man's Land. Did I imagine the entire grotesque encounter with the inhuman Gaspard? No, it was far too vivid to have been anything but reality. I shudder at the memories.

A nun, seeing that I am awake, appears at my bedside.

"You are lucky to be alive." Her matter-of-fact tone carries over the calls of the dying and the coughing which I know will not end while the damned soul lives. "We weren't sure you would survive the amputation."

Shock runs through me as I look down at my . . . foot. I stare incredulously. I would swear that I am wiggling my toes, but there is nothing below the sheets past my knee. I whip the sheets off, sure that it's some sort of cruel joke, and am confronted with the heavily-bandaged stump of my right knee. My foot is gone.

"They say that you may think you have a leg for some days," the sister says soothingly, a hand on my shoulder gently urging me to lie down again. "You may even forget that you have lost it and try to stand up. These things are normal, and will fade in time."

I am mutilated, a cripple, but all I can think is that I am saved, saved from that hell of No Man's Land, saved from becoming a living sacrifice presented by my country's generals and politicians to the ghouls' colossal feast. I weep with relief. The nun pats my shoulder in a comforting way, and it occurs to me that she thinks I am weeping for my lost leg. I do not correct her. I will not be devoured. I will go home, where there are no corpse-eaters, and when I die, my body will lie undisturbed, my bones ungnawed.

I am so weak that even weeping exhausts me. The sister fluffs my pillow and sets it behind my head, and despite the cries and moans of the unfortunate souls around me, oblivion comes quickly.

In the dark I am jarred awake. The pain that woke me strikes again, even worse than before. I scrabble with the bed dressing, and where the pain strikes I find nothing but stained sheets. It is my leg–my missing leg. When I realize what I am feeling, an inarticulate shriek tears itself from my throat. Two nuns hurry up to my bedside, even as another wave of agony, so like and yet unlike being stabbed with a knife, runs up my right leg.

"*My leg*," I scream in desperate agony at their blandly calm, disbelieving faces. "*I can feel that son of a bitch Gaspard eating my leg!*"

# THE SHADOW OVER LAS VEGAS

John Claude Smith

# 1

*I had the fear . . .*

We were somewhere around Barstow on the edge of the desert when the drugs began to wear off, dissipating in dark, hallucinatory clouds, amorphous and alive. I turned to my attorney, whose face had begun to melt into a writhing mass of tentacles and said, "You look a bit fishy; maybe you should let me drive."

He shook his head—no—and grumbled something about feeling "gibbous," strange word, that one. I suspect it was definition # 2 in *Webster's Dictionary* that most suited his condition: "More than half but less than fully illuminated . . ." as in, not completely wasted—but we could rectify that problem. He chattered something more about needing "drugs, give me more drugs," arms waving around like pterodactyl wings, his ponderous girth making the car shake or . . . could it be that we were pushing ninety in a vehicle not accustomed to such velocity? I popped a couple of shub-nigguraths (black beauties shaped liked scrotums) into his beak-like maw and he immediately transformed into something almost human again, bloated around the gills, but nevertheless unremarkable to those of the Vegas grind—and that was where we were headed: Las Vegas.

There were no innocents in Las Vegas, hence, no reason to pussyfoot around that stained label. The innocence in Las Vegas disappeared upon birth, buried under lights of neon and assisted by one-armed bandits draining money, integrity, hope, and life itself, all for a silver dollar or three, or ten, or . . .

I took a couple of the shub-nigguraths as well, a bitter, chalky, furry flush down my esophagus—it tasted like goat semen (don't ask; *don't ask!*). I was in need of something to curb these weird vibrations, but I knew immediately I would regret it.

With a rush like an avalanche of night, unknown constellations dripped from the midday sky, streaking the hot blue horizon with black slashes like scars that bled onto the grey asphalt beyond the Big Black Tsathoggua—our vehicle nicknamed for some such hirsute frog, so said my attorney ("it's bloated in the same way"), laughing, amused by his bizarre brain. We had rented the vehicle from a used car dealership in Los Angeles a few hours back, putting it on the card—our open-ended expense account: unlimited credit in the hands of such foolhardy tourists as us—sponsored by the editors of *Miskatonic Today*, some cheap exploitation rag into the likes of alien abductions, never-was celebrities, obscure cults, and endless Elvis and/or Jesus sightings in out of the way, rarely-trod-by-human places—mostly in the southern states of the US of A—and/or staring back from used diapers or the sweaty wife beaters worn by some illegal immigrant looking to avoid the publicity—but look what *God* has blessed him with. I was sure, much to their chagrin, that the kind folks at *MT* would regret the free ride they were giving me, hence, us, but I was also sure that the work was going to get done in due time, because that's the price you pay for professional gonzo journalism. Anyway, there's no sense in doing anything unless one does it right and we were well on our way to doing it right.

At least, that's what my attorney kept mumbling over Cthulhu Crushes and mescal, poolside at the Beverly Hills Hotel this morning, something about the stars being right, almost right—right for what? It was probably the alcohol talking, or perhaps he hadn't had enough alcohol yet.

The hour was young, we had time.

I was feeling a bit amphibious—in need of something to drink, to keep me in touch with my own humanity, not that I was in any way related to the Great Old Ones that my attorney incessantly rambled on about and so unashamedly called family—interstellar sea-faring folks, he said (whatever *that* was supposed to mean), and laughed again; strange—an excuse he used to explain his sometimes *green* appearance. I could never blame the drugs; they only enhanced the overall tint. My attorney was singing in some God-awful timbres no human should ever have to fathom; my nerves were doing jumping jacks, the paranoiac adrenaline rush kept me ducking the unseen, the unknown . . .

Our vibrations had amped into overdrive as I screamed for him to pull over; I could not take it any more. The shub-nigguraths were a nasty drug for the desert and would be worse yet if they lingered into Las Vegas . . .

I stepped out of Big Black Tsathoggua and wandered to the back. "Pop the trunk," I said, and my attorney obeyed posthaste. I catalogued the vast cosmos within, dark stars and darker suns, nectar from Neptune, aether from Aldeberan, acid-crystals from R'lyeh, fungi from Yuggoth, a whole fleet full of nebulous drugs and drink to be ingested during our working vacation, the only way a reasonable person could be expected to make it through something as insidious as the Marilyn Monroe Weekend of Memories spectacle, our reason for this expedition to the far side of sanity.

It was going to be a long, long weekend.

# 2

My Attorney had called in to the Starlight Circus on our behalf (NASA, in need of funding, had dropped the government and taken up with Vegas to mount a more viable form of income), the event of which my reportage was deemed worthy being the 21st Century Fox/NASA sponsored Marilyn Monroe Weekend of Memories commemoration of the fiftieth year of her death, a perverse celebration littered with every conceivable Marilyn Monroe imitator this side of Jupiter (it seemed), culminating in a contest to pick the very best Marilyn Monroe . . . to carry on with a movie contract and manufactured career, and to promote whatever NASA needed them to promote. Whores for the universe, prostitutes in league with Republicans, Satanists, and whatever other demented legions would flock to this horrid place this weekend.

I always used a phony name when checking in during my writing ventures; my infamy was legendary, at least in my own mind. But I did not always have a say in the name, especially if my attorney got hold of the reservations. I looked at the piece of paper on which he had scribbled my nom-de-plume and cringed at his perverse humor.

"Sir," said the fiftyish female hotel employee in charge of checking in the wasted souls, looking bored, but I was made squirmy by the bubbles rising to the ceiling as she harrumphed impatiently.

"John . . . Wayne," I said, hiding my face in shame. I wondered how many others were checking in under the names of dead movie stars, self-destructive rock 'n' roll musicians, or assassinated presidents. My attorney laughed, slapped me on the back, and said, "C'mon, Duke, we can deal with this later."

I looked at him and could swear bubbles were floating from his mouth as well. The ceiling was looking crowded. I watched bubbles battle bubbles in a popfest of grisly proportions. There was effervescent death everywhere.

I knew I should not have followed the shub-nigguraths with the yigs: if Las Vegas is no town for shub-niggurraths, it was definitely no place for the psycho-madness of yigs. But they were the only ones handy when I reached into my pocket—and this, mere minutes after I had inspected the plethora of ingestible, mind-altering drugs in the trunk; idiot! I was feeling like a rat in a cheeseless labyrinth, lost and confused. What was I doing here? What was the *true* purpose of this venture? Would that demented fuck LeGrasse show up any time soon with answers, or would I just keep riding this one like an endless wave?

After finding that we *would* have to deal with it later—our room was not ready—we wandered to the hotel bar, past hairy fish-like beasts and star-faced denizens drunkenly swimming about. I worried about my Acapulco shirt—would the colors run? Would I run? Was there any hope? How long would it take for the yigs to run their insidious course? I'd only taken two, but two amidst the constant ingestion of drugs over the last twenty-four hours must have been two too many.

I began to do the breaststroke across the bar, much to the annoyance of the fish-eyed denizens in attendance, when my attorney turned to me and said, "I advise you to head to the room now, before you get yourself killed," and tossed me a green key that felt like the weight of the world—and me no Atlas. I dragged the key on the ground as I slinked out of the bar and made way to the elevator. One of what I expected would be the deluge of Marilyns was stepping out of the elevator, her dress showing much cleavage, and I sniffed her there, wondering if that is where they had hidden the Zapruder Tape—or possibly the lone gunman—and she said, "Oh, Mr. President, wait until Jackie and the kids go to bed." I pulled back, having almost been stabbed by her nipples: nipples that pushed out of the fabric with impressions more akin to Mickey and Minnie Mouse. I closed my eyes and yelled, "Disney have mercy! Take these freakish things away from me!"

When I opened them again, I was on the bed in the room, a pillow case stuffed in my shorts, mustard spirals decorating my nipples like exploding solar systems—no famous mice here, only condiments—and my attorney sawing wood in the same dissonant timbres as his singing.

"Wake up!" I said, kicking at him. "We have a job to do and . . . your snoring is the most horrible thing I've heard since your singing."

He smiled and pulled a harpoon gun from under the bed. "Don't make me use this. There are plenty of scavengers hanging out at the window and I know they'd enjoy a little tender meat."

Tender my ass! I was solid as SpongeBob SquarePants. Squishy even. I laughed, my mind skipping about, and wandered toward the balcony . . . where I saw them, these things crawling all over the window, eyeless, mottled flesh, flapping useless wings.

"I need a drink," I said, turning from the aberration, knowing I needed more than a drink. But God would never show his face here.

At least not the human incarnation of God . . .

It would all come down to me.

# 3

The main event, a cavalcade of Marilyns stomping across the stage, each one made to pout and prance and eventually end up above a grate that shot hot air into their nether regions, lifting their dresses to panty revealing height, much to the delight of the ogling eyes of those in the audience, as well as the so-called judges, a collection of bottom-tier celebrities, no names and nameless, forgettable sorts who gained fame hosting this or that game show, acting on this or that demoralizing "reality" show—really, nothing real there, try these drugs, they will show you things to make your pubes straighten—essentially filling space in the ever obese celebrity fifteen minutes of fame warehouse, was hosted by Mr. Warhol, who understood the value of nothing and so made nothing his goal. Talent, who needs talent? We've got faces and bodies and desperation on display and wouldn't you like to be a star? And what if they saw what I saw on these drugs, star-bodied creatures, fish-eyed with twinkling intent and who knows what purpose? Observing this chow line to Hell, Nietzsche's edict made concrete, the abyss not only looking back but laughing at us—humans—for the folly of our deteriorating existence, I felt the fear escalate; or was that disgust? I mean, could we not expend a little compassion in this commemoration, instead of making it an extended sales pitch to 21st Century Fox and NASA, "Here, here's your new star, she's Marilyn incarnate. Eat her soul as well. Make her a star, or send her to one . . ."

Pathetic I say, but my take on it would be more succinct: place a bed on the stage and make all of the Marilyns strike a death pose, clothing optional (except for the Marilyn I saw with the Disney-inspired anomalies).

What was I doing here? People watching again, that was always the point of it all anyway, watching the natives stumble like drunken giraffes, flirtations bandied like bad sitcoms (a paradox if ever there was one: the mere format zeroed in on the lowest common denominator) and worse yet, watching the ugly make connections that should short out the electricity in every neon sign in Vegas if their copulating culminated in procreation but no, procreation was not their goal and so, if any sperm won the battle and invaded the egg, I was sure a morning after pill or a clothes hanger three months later would scrape the evidence away.

People were my business. That and drugs. Business was plentiful in this obscene parade of demoralized wannabe stars. Stars, like what the yigs always made me see.

My attorney seemed particularly giddy this evening. As we awaited the event's commencement, we grabbed a table with "Reserved for Josh Brande" posted on it (Brande's claim to fame: former game show host, hidden video victim caught with his pants down in a most unflattering situation, culminating in a CD release of sappy love songs, his feeble warbling seeming more appealing to weasels than humans...) and scribbled our names on it instead, blacking out Brande's name, only to be accosted by Brande and causing a scene in having him escorted away for impersonating himself: "That's the man, the imposter: Brande is in Hawaii, we have his itinerary here"—waving my notepad about as if any information within would verify anything passing from my lips—"and the police have been looking for him ever since."

My attorney, giggling now: "And be sure he gets the full treatment, anal probes and gloved fist inspection, that's where he keeps his stolen Screen Actors Guild card!"

Brande looked befuddled but it's probably the best (only) real publicity he (or his imposter?) has had in years.

Our vibrations were shaky, impatient . . .

"Stop this charade and get to the point!" I yelled, toward the stage, where some preliminary entertainment, as in not really entertaining but filling space, had dragged on for way too long. My attorney handed me a couple of flat green pills that looked like miniature pyramids and said, "Take these. You'll really like these."

So, the time had come. I was not about to turn him down, but now it was my time to make a move as well. I may have seemed oblivious, but I was not dim beyond the duty at hand; I had been debriefed about events in motion, I just did not think it would really come down to me— where was LeGrasse?

I stopped a long-legged waitress in full gallop with a "Whoa, darlin'," and set the table for our defense: in defense of the human race.

"We need two Grande triple shot espressos, double whip, jigger of soy with a pinch of almond and caramel and adrenochrome, and snap to it!" It was a ridiculously unrealistic concoction, but the waitress only giggled and snapped gum, able to walk and chew with a modicum of efficiency.

My attorney grew gruff. "You know how I get around that stuff. It makes me gassy and my brain hurts and . . . I want to be in control tonight." But he was already losing it, I could tell. His resistance was already crumbling. The Starlight Circus' version of Starbucks was geared toward the space crowd, aliens and astro-wannabes of every sort. Starbuckaroos: cosmic coffee for space jockeys, grim grounds that left a black hole in one's soul. I'm sure this would make him see the truth.

It would make him see the True Great Old Ones.

But I could use some help in my simmering battle, not sure how this was going to pan out and why did the FBI even think I could pull this off?

LeGrasse, my FBI connection, was supposed to run things, but since he was nowhere to be found, it was all up to me, and I only wanted to watch and ingest more drugs, as I had always done. Of course, the FBI's insistence that they could get me any drug imaginable, without recourse, was incentive enough for my cooperation. But still . . . where was that fool?

Our waitress slinked up and set our drinks down. I paid her and patted her ass, "For luck," I said. I was going to need it.

My attorney and I stared into each other's eyes, searching for something, making a deal, unspoken but understood. We both knew where we stood: with our asses planted firmly in these too-hard chairs as the cavalcade of Marilyns began to prance over the grate, and the hot breath of lust blew warmly onto their straining thighs, moistening their objectives.

After a slight diversion, entranced by the morbid exhibition, I returned my gaze to my attorney's. He had never broken his. He spoke.

"I will not drink any of this. I cannot drink any of this tonight—"

"Why tonight, my friend? What's so special about tonight?"

As if playing it off, he said, "Nothing special, I'm just . . ." but words escaped him. He drooled as the drink, one he had never tasted before, awaited his slithering tongue's approval. I had to find a way to break his will, to make him drink, to make him see the truth.

To save the human race.

"I'll make you a deal. I'll take these pyramid-shaped pills—"

"Nyarlathoteps," he said.

Nyarlathoteps. Sounded vaguely Egyptian to me; my perceptions were still sharp.

"I'll take these Nyarlathoteps as long as you drink some of that delicious, mind-altering, hallucinatory liquid magic."

He shivered as if a chill ran through him. His drool was collecting in his massive belly, dripping further, a waterfall of desire.

As he continued to quiver, his will being broken by the smells and promise of tastes within the cardboard cup, I tried to play it off as if nothing more was in motion, turning to see the most hideous sight imaginable on the stage.

"Shades of J. Edgar Hoover, LeGrasse, what are you doing up there?" But it was obvious what he was doing. LeGrasse, my FBI connection, was wearing a dress and doing his best Marilyn impression, stumbling over stilettos and mortifying myself and all within reasonable viewing distance as the grate blew up his skirt and the stuffing in his white panties (not an FBI registered gun for sure) throbbed with a life of its own.

The groan that passed through the casino was of an eldritch resonance rarely heard.

LeGrasse winked and cooed, "Hollywood is a place where they'll pay you a thousand dollars for a kiss and fifty cents for your soul," puckered, and blew me a kiss, on the house. I ducked, not wanting this sorry fool's wayward affections to corrupt my flesh or focus: I knew his soul was already girdle-squeezed and shrinking with every wobbling stiletto step.

I turned back to my attorney, knowing full well that threats without follow-up were worthless. I raised the two Nyarlathoteps to my lips and popped them into my mouth.

My attorney took this as his cue to give in.

"Shit!" he growled, taking the cup and tossing the whole thing down his throat. He smiled and leered and attempted to grab mine as well, but I needed the caffeinated potion in order to counteract all the drugs that came before and direct the hallucination in progress.

We were linked as one, my mind and his, mine in the driver's seat. His, trembling in the backseat, wishing it were in the trunk.

In our eyes the ceiling opened up, and a universe of stars seemed to align themselves in ways I could never imagine.

"The stars are right, the stars are right," screamed my attorney.

"Not quite," I said, smiling as satellites within the star systems neared us.

"What? What is that?" My attorney scooted under the table. Around us, people grumbled at our antics, not understanding the magnitude of what was unfolding within our vision.

The True Great Old Ones ambled into view. My attorney let out a sound drenched in such fear as to demote all previous definitions of the word to obsolescence.

It stumbled from the right side of the sky, the drunken master of dulcet blandness: Dean Martin. From the left, the hideous cyclopean essence of the ebony one: Sammy Davis Jr.

My attorney whimpered with such abandon as to lose all hold on his masquerade, dissolving into a diseased, writhing mound of chum, a squiggly conglomeration of fish heads and tentacles and fins, flaking scales, aged green sea-algae, and serpentine madness.

From dead center, the ultimate in crooning egotism, the Lord of Las Vegas, the Grand Meatball . . . the dread that is—

"Sinatra!" cried my attorney, falling under His spell. "Sinatra!"

As my attorney thrashed about, whiplash tentacles decapitating enough Marilyns to make this more a Jane Mansfield memorial, the audience scattered, miffed.

All that was left was to let it play out. As the concert went on—the celestial serenade—my attorney began to melt, captivated, even though the spell they cast was the one thing that could deter his quest for world domination.

The stench attained a pungent magnitude that assaulted my nostrils. The percolating eddies of his essence reverted back to their primal form, the first boiling seeds of life that swam in the seas. I doffed my hat in remembrance.

"You gotta clean that up, buddy," said one of the casino bosses, dressed in a space suit and looking quite orbital, staring bug-eyed at me through his helmet.

"Do you know what I just did? I just saved humanity from an eternity of slavery at the hands of the Lovecraftian version of The Great Old Ones—"

"Yeah, yeah, well, we're trying to put on a show right now and if you're not going to at least sit down, I gotta ask you to leave. I mean, there's a stage full of headless Marilyn Monroes about to do a chorus line and . . ."

His rambling fell on deaf ears. I should have known better. I was drafted into the role of savior, and what does it get me? Ignorance from the very beings I was meant to save; annoyance from those who I had just rescued from the infinite drudgery of sub-human existence, cowering at the fins of the slobbering Great Old Ones.

I felt myself shudder at the bad choices I had made.

I wanted nothing more to do with this pitiful race.

I looked to the floor and my dead friend—yes, he was my friend, even if his intentions seemed nefarious, even if he probably would have eaten me at some point, he was a better friend than any of these castoffs and dilettantes salivating over the obscene display on the stage to my left. On stage right, the grumbling persisted.

I grabbed a menu and the marker we had used earlier as I stared at the still singing True Great Old Ones—corrupt, deceptive bastards, all— and began to float toward the stage in the skies.

Passing by Sinatra, he winked as did Dean Martin and Sammy Davis Jr. (a momentary flux of blindness that shadowed the whole menagerie in the blackest gulf imaginable). I gave them the single finger salute, the same one I felt inclined to flip toward the confused mob below me, growing smaller as I surged toward the stratosphere, and as insignificant as insects—I wanted to crush them all.

Floating onward, I popped a few more shub-niggaruths, a few yigs, took a drink from the Milky Way, and decided anywhere but this ignorant galaxy was fine by me.

"I hear there are great drugs in the great beyond," I said.

"That's true, but rumor has it that it will cost you your humanity," Sinatra said.

"Humanity," I laughed. "A cheap price for a good high."

He curled his brow as if a comet where streaking through it. I held up my hand-scribbled sign, and he laughed, almost as if he understood.

I looked at it and smiled. This choice could be no worse than the one I had foolishly made on Earth.

I was a Man on the Move—rising higher, deeper into the stygian vista, referring to definition #2a. in *Webster's Dictionary*: "dark and gloomy"—just sick enough to be confident, crazed . . . *driven* . . .

"Yog-Sothoth or Bust."

# LOCKED ROOM

C. J. Henderson

**J**ohn Raymond Legrasse, a former inspector of police for the city of New Orleans, sat behind the desk of Dr. Anton Zarnak, his fingers moving a small steel ball back and forth across its well-kept surface. It was the work of four fingers only. The thumb could not be convinced to join the rhythm, and his other hand was firmly at work supporting its owner's head. Chin in palm, fingers moving his moustache about, masking the occasional yawn, his hands had found work for themselves and were quite busy, unlike the rest of him—save his eyes. John Legrasse's eyes were keenly at work.

They moved about within their sockets, taking in each and every item in the room one by one. They studied what they found from a distance, analyzing each piece, inspecting it, wondering if it might be a clue that could lead him to the next level. They moved from shelves to table tops, to corners filled to overflowing with stacks of books and other objects all crammed in one atop another. Indeed, there was so much clutter one scarcely knew where to begin.

Behind the former inspector, for instance, hung a mask which had arrested his attention for quite some time. It was a leering thing, a gaudy horror painted in scarlet, black and gold. Its three eyes glared upward, stylized flames pouring from its fanged mouth and flared nostrils. Legrasse remembered it from his previous visit. Zarnak had called it the visage of Yama.

Yes, well, he thought, his mind grim, chiding. Now, *that* fact's a help.

*Is it?*

Legrasse wondered for a moment, what if it was? Pushing his way past his sarcasm, he allowed himself to physically turn and stare at the mask. As he did he forced his mind to jump back, to remember all it had absorbed the last time it was in that room . . .

*Is it?*

Once more unlearning everything he had ever known.

It might be a clue, he knew. Anything within the room might be a help if what he suspected was true. In many ways Zarnak's office was a trash heap, a never-ending, always changing collection of the weird and strange objects of the universe. Legrasse had to force himself to remember that anything around him might also be some Pandora's box of poisonous trouble.

He stared at the things on the desk before him, the closed wooden chest adorned with a checkerboard pattern created from variously colored inlaid woods, the small stone figure of some South American deity, the copper bell with the double clappers, the small oval mirror in the silver frame, even the steel ball his fingers had been maneuvering—

*Any piece of it,* he reminded himself, *could be death beyond reason if handled the wrong way. After all I've seen these past few years it would be fairly stupid to pack it in now from just barging into something.*

It was true. For some time now the former inspector had been handed one lesson after another by the universe proving that there were, indeed, things not dreamt of in primitive philosophies. He had even begun hearing voices. He had never done such a thing before.

*Are you me,* he wondered at the words he heard in his head for the thousandth time. *Some subtle, deeper part of me? Are you?*

*Yes,* he thought, they had to be merely other parts of his brain posing questions to him; he was simply learning to think. Still, it was unsettling. Unnerving.

*Are you?*

Before his interior conversation could continue, a muffled knocking outside of Zarnak's office caught Legrasse's ear. In a moment the office door opened, and two men came forward. The one in the lead was a tall man, lean and rangy. A Hindu, he wore a pair of formless, baggy cotton pants topped by a well-worn sweater of red and blue. A spotless white turban wrapped with careful precision crowned him, if anything emphasizing his keen dark eyes. Though a completely deferential man on the surface, anyone who actually knew what made people tick could easily see he was a confident and dangerous individual. A fool would miss the obviousness of him, but then the world was filled with fools.

The second man, the one behind the Hindu, did not look like a fool. Or someone who missed the obvious.

"Hey, you Legrasse? Howdy—welcome to New York."

He was, like Legrasse, a big man. Balding, he wore his hair on the inside, crowning his shaved and polished dome with a black derby. It was a well known hat throughout much of the metropolitan area as one you did not want to see turning down your street. No matter what street you lived on.

"Lieutenant Mark Thorner, correct, sir?"

"Yeah, that's me." The man in the bowler eyed Legrasse with curiosity. As it had been explained to him, Legrasse had arrived to confer with Zarnak only to find the doctor not at home. This had been explained to the lieutenant whom the Hindu had then asked to come to the doctor's office at 13 China Alley as quickly as possible. That had been eighteen minutes earlier. That meant Legrasse had been on the scene for nearly a half-hour unsupervised. Thorner did not disclose his displeasure with that as he asked Zarnak's man servant;

"Ram Singh, so, tell me you didn't get us here for the reason I think?"

"I am sorry, lieutenant," answered the rangy man, "but I have no one else to whom I can turn. The master of this house, Anton Zarnak, has disappeared."

"That's a mighty powerful word to be throwin' around, Singh," said Thorner. His tone was even, one filled with both questions and implications. "You want to narrow down exactly what 'disappeared' means in this instance?"

"He *disappeared*," answered Zarnak's manservant. "He was there and then he was gone. Is this not plain enough?"

"Not really," said Legrasse. "And I'd think you'd know that. What do you mean—did you turn around and he was gone? Did he just fade away before your eyes, has he merely been missing for a day or two? Did he go out for milk and not come back . . ."

The Hindu raised his hand in apology. Nodding further, showing he realized his mistake, Ram Singh showed detective Thorner to a chair and then explained himself.

"Earlier today," he said, staring at Legrasse, "Dr. Anton Zarnak walked into his office. This office. He called to me as I passed, and he asked me to shut and lock the door."

He's not staring at me, realized Legrasse, his eyes suddenly looking down, senses reeling—

"He had work to do, and he did not want to be disturbed until dinner time. It is a quite common request, and is usually quite helpful to all parties concerned. Much can be accomplished when one's superior is not about."

He's looking at the last place he saw Zarnak.

"So, if I get this," Thorner injected, holding his hands open roughly a half foot above his knees as if to encapsulate the moment, "Anton was sitting behind the desk, you locked the door; you opened it roughly six hours later and he was gone."

"It is all I know," responded the servant.

"Don't worry about it," answered the lieutenant. "Why don't you kick around in the kitchen and find some meat you can throw at some heat, or whatever, for our guest here and me, and we'll keep you posted if we find anything."

After Ram Singh left, Thorner settled himself in one of the large chairs on the visitor's side of Zarnak's desk as Legrasse asked him;

"You don't want to question the man servant further?"

"No need right now," came the lieutenant's reply. "I've been in on plenty of the weirdness that's passed by the windows of this dump. Believe me, if we can't trust Ram Singh, we are about as out of luck as two cops can get."

"Then where should we start?"

"Why don't you tell me what brought you here so conveniently on the day the doc disappeared."

Legrasse's thick eyebrows went up for a moment, then settled back into place. As bristling a question as Thorner's was, as a policeman Legrasse knew he was perfectly right in asking it. Unfortunately, the answer was of no help to them. The lieutenant had been hoping that the very reason which had brought the inspector northward might be a lead, but it was not to be. Legrasse had only come to return a number of rare books he had borrowed from the doctor, and to borrow some more.

"Sorry to disappoint," answered the Southerner, his accent thick with sarcasm.

"Let's not start this out with you bein' a wise guy, okay," snapped back Thorner, his own accent equally obvious. "You coulda been here to confer on somethin' that might have given us a lead is all."

"I'll tell you why we're snapping at each other," responded Legrasse. Getting up out of his chair, he pointed around the room, saying, "it's because we both know we're out of our league here. You, lieutenant, do you actually know any magic?"

Thorner pushed his derby toward the back of his head with a single finger.

"Me, naw," he answered. "Me and the doc were kind of a team ... New York's only recognized ghost grabbers."

"Recognized, you say?" The envy in Legrasse's voice was obvious.

"Well, sorta. The city, they know what the doc does, got it? Before Zarnak, Doc Guicet ran things here. He disappeared, too, and Zarnak replaced him. I've always been the, ah, 'unofficial' liaison between the mayor's office and the chief of police and, ummm, what would you call it? The world beyond?"

"You say this Guicet predates Zarnak at this post? And he disappeared as well? Was that ever solved?"

"No," answered Thorner sourly. "And I'd hate to have to break in another replacement, so why don't we work on what happened to Zarnak, okay?"

Legrasse felt his confidence in Thorner's abilities instantly increase. The man was tough, as all New Yorkers were held to be, but it was a professional armor, a weapon he used to battle the world of evil against which it was his duty to stand watch.

"Have you seen much?"

Thorner let the question hang in the air like an annoying insect. The buzz of it tore through his memories; his earlier days with Guicet had been nothing—ghosts, walking dead, witch women—veritable carnival acts. Then Guicet had disappeared and Zarnak had come to town. Before very long the lieutenant found himself with his service revolver in hand, surrounded by scores of torture-mutilated bodies, facing down a fire demon capable of ravaging dimensions.

"Yeah," he said finally. "I've seen my share."

"I have as well," asserted Legrasse, not bragging, simply trying to give his ally cause to trust him. "Knowing how these types of evil never seem to wait, maybe we should start acting like police men."

"My captain keeps tellin' me to try it for a change. Hey, why not?"

Finished with testing each other, the two lawmen turned to the job of determining how the doctor had vanished from his locked office. Looking over Zarnak's desk, they first went through all his open papers. Every letter and piece of note scrap on its surface was scrutinized by them both as they searched for some clue as to what the doctor had been doing when he disappeared. Every box and chest and container was opened—some more carefully that others. Books were thumbed through to see if anything had been hidden within, or even to see if the topic of the book itself might make it a subject for their further interest.

Long before the pair had finished, it became obvious to them that most everything they looked over might be the springboard to finding one such as Anton Zarnak. Ram Singh brought them a meal of greens in gravy with sliced abalone, peppers stuffed with shrimp meat and chopped nuts, spare ribs, broccoli heads in oyster sauce, as well as bowls of rice and shark fin soup. As they picked over the remains, Thorner complained;

"This is gettin' us nowhere."

"Maybe not," answered Legrasse. "I agree that no single object points us more strongly in any one direction than any other. But, what about combinations of them? I mean, perhaps this piece of correspondence prompted him to gather that note pad and this book of spells ..."

"Ohhhh, I get it," said the lieutenant. Pushing his derby back on his head, he scratched his forehead absently, thinking over all they had just reviewed. Nothing came to mind.

For the next two hours the lawmen struggled to find a connection between the things on the doctor's desk—a letter asking for help and a reference book pertaining to the subject within the letter, a note about some sort of research and an indication that the day he disappeared he had been engaged in such, et cetera. The pair tried mightily, but to no avail. As their third hour of reading and researching began, they heard a noise outside of the office that sounded as if someone had come to the door. After a few moments, Ram Singh entered the office.

"Pardon me, sirs," he said apologetically, "but a gentlemen has come to the door saying that he is aware of Dr. Zarnak's disappearance, and that he wishes to help recover him."

Legrasse and Thorner eyed one another. Each could tell the other was curious, but cautious. Finally, Thorner said, "Hell, we ain't gettin' anywhere on our own . . .'"

Legrasse nodded in agreement. Ram Singh bowed slightly and left for the front door. When he returned he ushered a thin, oddly shaped man with a sallow, leathery complexion into the office. The man's white-grey hair had been combed sometime earlier in the day, but seemed to have suffered the effects of both the weather and the city's bustle. He wore a long jacket, not inappropriate for the climate, but shabby and patched in an odd fashion. The man's shoes, though expensive, were badly scuffed. His manicured hands were filthy, as if he had been digging in the mud.

All these facts and more the police officers noted instantly, almost absently. Consciously, they studied his face, looking for clues as to who he might be and what he might be about. Handing the man's business card to the lieutenant, whose chair was closest to the door, Ram Singh backed out of the office slowly, announcing as he departed;

"Mr. Archibald Melgranir."

The name meant nothing to either of the lawmen. When offered a seat, Mr. Melgranir declared that he would rather stand. Taking no exception to his reply, Legrasse merely said;

"Very well, sir, as you like. I must admit I find your arrival now most fortuitous. If I can cut right to the heart of the matter—what can you tell us about Dr. Zarnak's disappearance?"

"He is missing. He must be found."

Off to the side of Melgranir, Thorner rolled his eyes, plastering an expression on his face for Legrasse to see, one warning that the lieutenant felt something was not right with their guest. The former inspector made a slight nod in Thorner's direction, one indicating agreement.

"Yes," answered Legrasse straight-faced. "We're trying to find him. Can you tell us anything about his disappearance?"

"He hides," replied Melgranir. "He has run to some hole and pulled the world in on top of himself. He hides. But he must be found."

The lawmen listened to the odd man's voice with a dreadful fascination. It was high, too highly pitched for the body from which it emitted. Also, it came in a disturbing monotone, one that made the backs of both men's necks itch.

"Yeah," barked Thorner. "We know he's hidin'. Like the inspector here said, we're trying to find him. But you're not helpin' us any. Savvy?"

"You will reveal his hiding place."

"I don't think you understand," Legrasse pushed Zarnak's office chair back, giving himself room to maneuver. Still seated, but ready to move, he said, "we don't know where he is. We ourselves are looking for him as well. That's why I ask you again, *sir*, can you tell us anything about how or why he disappeared?"

"Where is Zarnak?"

"He's out waitin' for the Sunday edition of the funny papers," growled Thorner. His hand sliding underneath his jacket, he added, "He's a big fan of The Yellow Kid, don't ya know? He's gotta read it as soon as it hits the streets. What about you? You read the funny papers? 'Cause, you know, you look like you *escaped* from the funny papers."

"You defy the questioner . . ."

Melgranir began to shake then, not so much of his own volition, but as if he were in the grasp of some unseen force.

"You can not do so . . ."

Thorner pushed his chair back with a powerful exertion of both feet, putting an extra yard between himself and the vibrating man, bounding out of the chair as it came to a stop.

"You must *not* defy the questioner . . ."

Legrasse stood, the action shoving the desk chair back into a precariously stacked pile of papers. As he did, his eyes fixed on Melgranir's face. On one of his cheeks as well as his forehead, white spots appeared. They were frantic, wiggling things which, second by second began to grow, or more correctly, to elongate.

"You *must not resist* . . ."

As the shrill voice chattered, the lawmen watched as the spots pushed forward, showing themselves to be some sort of wiry, non-human lengths actually forcing their way outward through Melgranir's skin.

"My God!"

Legrasse went white as he realized what was happening. Not recognizing anything in the phenomenon, but having been witnessed enough similar events, Thorner leveled his service revolver, which he had already pulled, at Melgranir's head.

"Give it up, you snot, or your brains are wallpaper!"

"Shoot!" demanded Legrasse. "Do it—shoot! Shoot *now!*"

Thorner needed no coaxing. His trigger finger squeezed effortlessly twice, sending two .45 rounds through the vibrating man's head. Melgranir's skull burst, red and grey matter flecked with bone fragments flying everywhere throughout the office. His body did not fall, however. Nor did it take so much as a backward step from the attack. Instead, much to the shock of the lawmen, the headless body's arms tore at the buttons of its long coat. As Legrasse pulled out his own revolver, the automatic hands jerked the jacket back over Melgranir's shoulders to reveal his naked torso.

Here, as on his face, the same white lengths were seen to be protruding from the body's sallow skin. As the lawmen watched, the pencil-thick things continued to push their way out of their host until Legrasse shouted;

"Dear Lord, they're dholes! Or bholes, whatever they're called . . ."

And then, the former inspector stopped talking and began to fire his weapon. Following suit, Thorner joined in, blasting away at the unmoving target before him. As Ram Singh stuck his head into the office, responding to the sudden increase in noise, Legrasse bellowed over the ringing vibrations set off by the gunfire.

"Fire! We need to *burn* this thing!"

Ram Singh retreated without question as Thorner grabbed up his chair and smashed it over what remained of Melgranir. The body splattered at the blow, blood splashing the lieutenant, bone fragments dancing across the floor, and more than a dozen worm-like creatures dropping everywhere about. Legrasse picked up a particularly heavy-looking jade statue from the shelves next to him and brought it down with all his might on one of the worms. Its body burst, releasing a sizzling purple ichor which instantly sank into the woodwork below, despite its multiple layers of varnish.

Thorner, a quite sizable man, leapt upward and came down on one of the horrid, wriggling things. As both worms died, they released a monstrous whining into the air which shocked the policemen's eardrums even more severely than their own gunfire. As they reeled from the impact of the noise, staggering to find another target apiece, Ram Singh returned.

Without waiting for permission or instructions, the Hindu splashed the human remains and the surrounding worms with the contents of several bottles. He went to strike a match, but the lieutenant was ahead of him, having his lighter ready, igniting it and throwing it into the slopping mess in the middle of the office floor. Instantly flames sparked and again the hideous whine filled the air, forcing all three men to hold their ears. Ram Singh retreated to the hall; Thorner fell to his knees, holding his head, screaming; Legrasse toppled sideways into the shelves from which he had taken the jade statue. His face hit one of the wooden panels badly, splitting open his upper lip and sending a cascade of blood spurting from both his nostrils.

In moments the horrible shrieks of the worms abated. Ram Singh returned to the office with a tub of soapy water which he dumped on the small but raging fire in the center of the office. The maneuver resulted in a thick, unpleasant smell and an offensive cloud of gray/green smoke, but it extinguished the fire before it could spread any further.

Checking the debris, the lawmen found Melgranir to be completely demolished. From what they could tell, none of the worms had escaped their attention. Picking his lighter up out of the smoldering mess on the floor, Thorner asked;

"So what the hell's a bhole, and why'd we need to set the damn place on fire to get rid of them?"

Legrasse dropped his old service revolver on the desk and himself into the desk's chair. As the lieutenant cleaned off his lighter, polishing it against the sleeve of his jacket, the former inspector gasped for a clean breath of air, then answered.

"Dholes, bholes, I can't remember the exact name, but they're terrible creatures. They can grow as large as a dozen whales lined up end to end. I believe I mentioned that I've been studying at Anton's direction. I read about them some months ago."

"What else ya know about 'em?"

"I know that if they'd started to grow, that they would have overwhelmed us in no time. Good work, cutting off their host brain like that. Nice shooting."

"Couldn't hardly miss at that range," answered Thorner modestly. As he carefully reloaded his revolver, he added, "but what'dya think it's all got to do with the doc?"

"These things, I believe, serve some God or some such thing named Shub-Niggurath. It's been worshipped here on Earth for thousands of years, and supposedly on other planets as well."

Ram Singh came in at that moment with a chair from some other room and a bucket. Handing the chair to the lieutenant, the Hindu indicated that he would clean away the remains of their struggle. The lawmen nodded, Legrasse asking;

"By the way, just what was it you used to start the fire?"

"A combination of brandy and kerosene. The kerosene I keep for it is most excellent for removing stains. The brandy, that is most excellent for keeping Dr. Zarnak amused. As you might have put together from the bubbles in the water I brought in, I was doing the household laundry when I first heard your gunfire."

Thorner smiled. Reaching inside his jacket, he replaced his .45 and pulled out a thick cigar. Igniting it with his freshly cleaned lighter, he reached down and grabbed up the top of Melgranir's skull.

"Normally," he said, "I never smoke here in the office. But," he exhaled a large cloud, sighing as he did so, "in light of recent events, I find myself not givin' much of a damn for what's 'normal.'"

"Understood," replied Legrasse with a weary nod. "And the skull?"

"Hey," responded the lieutenant, "the place is messy enough. I need some place to dump the ashes."

"Yes," answered Legrasse absently. "And I think I know of something else we need."

# # # # #

The African woman who entered the office was no stranger to any of the men. She had been summoned at Legrasse's suggestion. The one time he had actually battled those elder forces from beyond with Zarnak, she had been there. Indeed, she had been the deciding factor in their battle. A familiar assistant to Zarnak in his work over the years, she was well known to Ram Singh and Thorner as well.

"Madame Sarna La Raniella," the lieutenant said with an obvious note in his voice. "The most beautiful hoodoo in all of New York City."

"You are looking well, lieutenant." Thorner revolved his head in an exaggerated fashion, making a delighted lalala sound deep in his throat.

"Ahhhhhhh," he said, a playful tone is his voice. "It sounds so nice when she says it."

"The lady is married," reminded Legrasse.

"Ask me if I care."

Madame La Raniella's dark eyes narrowed as she used them to tell the lieutenant that play time was over.

"We are to be searching for the good doctor, no?" she said in her normal throaty whisper. "Before you tell me all de wonderful things I already know about my deathless beauty, maybe you should be telling me what be happenin' here before it happen again, and all dat beauty becomes not so deathless."

Instantly the tone in the room shifted, the layers of societal protection ripped away. The veil of pleasantries pierced, the two policemen told Madame La Raniella everything that had transpired, from the moment of Zarnak instructing Ram Singh to lock his office door up until the decision was made to call her.

"After that, Ram Singh told us to go out to the kitchen. He had prepared a dessert for us, and it got us out of his way. By the time we came back from stuffin' ourselves he had the office fixed up."

The woman looked about quietly, her eyes taking in all beyond her veil. She could see the stained and scorched section of floor, took note of the missing office chair, could smell Legrasse's blood on the shelf, the gag of crimson aroma mixed with the dark poison of worm flesh and nightmare—

"*Mon deux*," Madame La Raniella gasped. Having obtained a comprehensive enough picture of the events, she cut her senses off from the room with a sharpness that made her body quiver noticeably. "Anton, you . . . what have you done now?"

"You got some insight to somethin', Sarna?"

"The worms," she whispered. "I know dese things. Blind and old and bigger t'an pride, swallow up de whole world they could. You pennied de eyes of an entire nest. Lucky damn white men get all de world's good fortune."

"Luck is something you make," answered Legrasse.

"Den you better start whipping up a very big batch, New Orleans," she told the former inspector, "because you playin' with fire so hot it ain't got no name."

Quickly, La Raniella explained that the creatures known as both the dhole and the bhole were indeed destroyers of worlds in the service of Shub-Niggurath, but that they were also indebted to other races as well.

"From what little I know," she told them, "t'ey are used by many of de powers beyond de shade for t'eir various purposes."

"So really," said Thorner, "you're telling us all we did was stop some out of town muscle—some mugs sent in to find the doc. It doesn't tell us where he is, or who's after him, or why . . ."

"Then we must find out."

As the men watched, La Raniella pulled forth a small, but heavy stone dish and an opaque bottle from her bag. Pouring a thick, shimmering green syrup into the dish, she struck a match and lit the center of the resulting puddle. As it bubbled up into a thin, mostly blue flame, she pulled back the light veil of her hat, then set aside the pillbox affair and closed her eyes.

"What kind of mood you out to set, Sarna?"

With a careful motion, the woman pulled her shawl more tightly about her shoulders. The colorfully embroidered black silk gripped her tightly, ridging her flesh as every wrinkle dug into her arm. Waving her hand over the dish, she extinguished the growing flame, replacing it with a smoldering billow of exotically scented smoke. As its bluish tendrils curled toward the ceiling, La Raniella whispered;

"I'm spinnin' a web of memory. You boys, you sit still now, why don't you. De smoke, she goin' to move about the room, back in time until it find ol' Zarnak's trail. Den we gonna see somethin'. Den we know."

Legrasse and Thorner sat quietly, both watching the witch woman as she worked, eyes still shut tight, her body swaying, hands above her head, her supple fingers all moving, each to a different rhythm, all stirring the blue smoke, dragging it this way and that, animating it until finally it animated itself.

"Look," hissed Legrasse. Thorner's eyes followed the former inspector's stabbing finger, watching as the blue layers of haze compressed back into wisps, all of them reaching down toward Zarnak's desk. As the tendril crawled across the littered surface, the lieutenant let out a low whistle, answering;

"Yeah, there's somethin' you don't see every day."

Madame La Raniella let out a low sound as the bluish haze congealed on the desk, binding itself around the steel ball. A hum sounded in response, coming, as best the lawmen could tell, from the smoke itself.

"Oh, Zarnak boy, what have you done." As Thorner and Legrasse stared, La Raniella pointed at the steel ball. Her throat dry, voice shaky, she told them, "that's where he be."

"What?" Legrasse's confusion boiled his short temper. "What's that's supposed to mean?"

"T'ere," the woman pointed to the ball once more. Touching it with her finger, she rolled it across the desk toward the lawman, "In t'ere. Dat's where he is."

Legrasse began to fume, but Thorner held up a cautionary hand. The lieutenant understood the Southerner's instinctive distrust, but he also knew the witch woman far better than his temporary partner did. Turning to Madame La Raniella, he asked;

"What'dya mean, Sarna? He's all shrunk up and buried in that thing?" His tone softer than normal, his question was a plea for understanding.

Knowing what was at stake as well as the lieutenant, she soften, saying, "You both understand t'at t'is world is not t'e only world. You both know t'e elder beasts, know t'ey have t'eir own realms. Zarnak, he in one, and it," she paused, picking up the steel ball once more, "is inside here."

"Do you know what he's doin' in there," asked Thorner. "How we can get him out?"

"He can come out whenever he wants," La Raniella answered. "Unless he forgot how. He not dead. If he was, my smoke could not find him."

"Madame," interrupted Legrasse, his face far away and thoughtful, "if it were up to you, if it were your decision as to what we do next ... what would you do?"

"I would get in t'ere and find him, before it was too late."

"'Too late'?" Thorner repeated the words with more than a little alarm. "What'dya mean, 'too late?' When's it gonna be too late?"

"T'he longer you wait, t'ey sooner t'at time comes."

The two lawmen looked at each other, then at La Raniella. The officers knew the woman was speaking nothing but the truth. When they asked how one could reach Zarnak, she told them she could show them both the ways in and back out again. Though they said nothing, their faces told the witch woman they would both be going.

"It will take some time—t'ere are ... elements I must have to send you on your way."

"That's good," said Thorner, a sly look crossing his face. "Gives me time to make a phone call."

"Hummmph?" Legrasse gave the lieutenant a puzzled look, then asked, "who would you be calling now?"

"They say," he answered, heading across the room to the corner where Zarnak kept his telephone, "that before any long voyage you should look into gettin' some insurance." As he set to dialing the phone's heavy metal disk, he added;

"Well, I got some of the best insurance in the world in mind."

# # # # #

Ram Singh escorted the two policemen into the large side room where Madame La Raniella was setting out the last of her preparations. When he offered them chairs, the officers nodded gratefully, staggered as they were by their loads. Thorner came in from Zarnak's office, rubbing his hands together.

"Okay, boys," he asked, his visage beaming like a child's at Christmas, "what were ya able to liberate?"

"We did the best we could, sir," answered the junior of the two patrolmen. He held out the box he had brought for inspection. Coming in behind Thorner, the printing on the side of the small crate was not lost on Legrasse.

"Police property," he asked. "Evidence room property, no less. What are you playing at, lieutenant?"

"I'm playin' at bringin' Zarnak back out here where the rest of us are in one piece," answered Thorner indignantly. "We're talkin' about goin' to another world. Another *goddamned* world. You ever faced the kinda nightmares live in the kinds of places she's gonna send us?"

"Yes, actually," answered the former inspector, "I have."

"And you feel like takin' on that kinda shit with just your service pistol?" The Southerner's face went dark, but he did not reply. His tone only slightly sarcastic, Thorner said, "Yeah, that's what I thought." The lieutenant wrenched open the box in his hands and then pulled forth an oddly shaped rifle. Handing it to Legrasse, he said;

"Here, wrap yer mitts around this."

The lawman accepted the weapon, turning it over in his hands. For the most part it seemed a normal enough self-loader, save for the oddly wide-mouthed extension which had been fitted to its muzzle. As Legrasse stared, one of the patrolmen explained;

"It's French, sir, RSC Modèle 1917. It's a gas-operated. Takes 8mm shells—five to a magazine. It's already loaded with blanks."

"Blanks?" Legrasse stared absently, not understanding. The patrolman explained;

"Yes, sir. The blank propels the grenade." Quickly the younger man pulled an awkward-looking device out of a bag. Holding it up he finished, "Brit 36, some call 'em a Mills. Don't know why. Just know you load one, aim, shoot, and make sure you don't hit anything close by."

"Why not? Is the force of the explosion that powerful?"

"No, sir. It's not that. Too many people think grenades are bombs. They're not. They're shrapnel weapons. The explosive inside is minimal—just enough to blow the metal casing apart and drive the pieces into the enemy. That and whatever else is packed inside. Wire, nails, whatever."

Thorner slung a different weapon over his own shoulder, telling his men, "Good haul, guys." Then, turning to Legrasse, he added;

# C. J. HENDERSON

"Look, we did a raid on a guy who's connected all the way to Albany. He's gonna get off scott free. And if he buys the right judge, he's even gonna get his property back. Well, myself, I don't give the stink from the station house crapper about this mook's rights. If it was up to me, he'd get it all back used."

Legrasse admired the grenade rifle for a moment longer, then said quietly, "New York is certainly an exuberant town."

"You can bet mammy's grits on that one, brother." Smiling, the lieutenant turned to Madame La Raniella and asked, "Okay, what's it take to send us off to NeverNeverLand?"

"Excuse me, lieutenant," interrupted one of the patrolmen, "but me and Petey, ah ... we was hopin' to volunteer for some extra duty."

Thorner stopped for a moment, his mouth unable to work. His immediate thought was that more hands were certainly welcome. Then he thought again. Remembering others who had frozen when confronted with the impossible kinds of things he had seen at Zarnak's side, seeing again officers torn apart by rampaging hellthings simply because their inability to understand what they were seeing dulled their senses, he said;

"This ain't no picnic, we're headed for, you know."

"We know that," answered the other patrolman. The shorter of the two street coppers, Petey pulled himself up to his full height and said, "but you promised me, you know you did—you said whenever Zarnak and you were heading into something that was going to be bad, you'd take me along."

Thorner scowled. He had made such a promise. And officer Peter Norton was as tough as they came. As the lieutenant struggled, Legrasse said;

"You had your first time seeing these elder monsters, and so did I. Men died all about me in a crazy swamp that bled with fire. It took the guns of a Navy ship to finally knock down what we were up against, and it killed three hundred people just in the falling back to Earth." Silence hung in the room for a moment, then the taller patrolman asked;

"Is that all true, sir?" When Legrasse assured the younger man it was, the officer shoved his partner, shouting, "Christ, this sounds even better than you said, Petey." The patrolman turned to Thorner then and saluted, saying;

"Patrolman Ernest Malloy reporting for duty, sir."

254

The lieutenant put his hand to his face and rubbed, both to show his extreme displeasure with his officers at putting him in such a situation, and also to hide the beaming smile of pride he could not contain. In control once more, he threw both his hands in the air and hollered;

"Okay, okay, everyone has the right to pick the way they die if they want to. You laughin' boys bring enough armament for everyone?" When the two smiled sheepishly, Thorner pursed his lips, then shouted once more.

"All right, fine. But I'm tellin' you dingle heads, this ain't gonna be like nothin' you've ever even dreamed about before. You savvy?" When the men nodded, he added;

"Well, you heard what I told you I seen. If you think you can handle somethin' like that, or worse, let's do this."

As the four lawmen checked their weapons, Madame La Raniella instructed them to move themselves and anything they wished to take with them inside a triangle she had laid out on the floor in the side room. After Ram Singh had both moved the few restraining pieces of furniture and rolled up the rug, the triangle had been quickly painted on the floor with a thin yellow liquid which gave off the scent of both peaches and pepper oil. Within the center of the triangle was a circle painted with the same yellow liquid. The shape was roughly a foot in diameter, and in the center of it was the steel ball from Zarnak's desk. The witch woman cautioned the men to not step inside of the circle, and to not step outside the triangle.

"Just no step on t'e yellow, and you'll be a live fellow."

Once they were all safely inside the correct perimeters, the witch woman began to lay down a circle of powder around the triangle. As she worked carefully to position the purplish grains just so, Legrasse questioned what was in a large box the patrolmen had brought into the triangle with them.

"A bit of indigestion for these new friends we're to be makin'," answered Petey.

Legrasse was about to enquire further, but La Raniella snapped, "Quiet. You listen careful now. In a moment, I'm going to tell you to close your eyes. You do it. After t'at, I light more the powder in the outer circle. As soon as I do, you gonna feel yourselves slippin' away. When the powder she all burned, you no more be here. As soon as you gone, I'll start to lay down another circle. When I light it, you gonna start fadin' back to t'is realm, t'is place. You gonna fade slow, and you gonna come back slow. You understand?"

"How long will we have in this other place?" asked Legrasse.

"Maybe one half hour."

"A half an hour? That's all," said Thorner. "You think that'll be long enough to check this whole place out?"

"Really," answered La Raniella. "You don't find him t'at amount of time—I don't t'ink you goin' find him at all." Several of the lawmen started to fidget, but the witch woman snapped her fingers and said;

"Shut your eyes—I'm lightin' t'e powder. I'll be chanting t'e whole time. You no more hear my voice, open your eyes."

The four officers closed their eyes. In the darkness they could hear the crackling sizzle of the burning powder, the clear, scintillating voice of the witch woman, her hair scraping her shoulders, the soft rush of air as she took each new breath. They stood past the time they all developed itches, and they all stood past the time their eyelids screamed to open. Then, it began.

As their nostrils filled with the scent of the burning powder, they felt themselves becoming light headed, light all over. And then it hit them, all at practically the same split second. They were not growing lighter, but thinner, flatter. And then, as their stomachs churned, they realized the truth—they were becoming transparent.

They could feel the building smoke against their legs, their chests, touching them, moving through them. And then they felt it, heard it all in the same moment, the shrieking flight of their own world rushing away from them. With a silencing gurgle, they could feel the change through their nerve endings. It had worked. They were somewhere else.

Legrasse opened his eyes first. As he did he fell over, unable to stand. Before he could warn the others he could feel them toppling all about him. They had opened their eyes in a world of colored spheres.

"Where in all creation are we?"

"Malloy," answered Thorner, working hard to adjust his senses, "that's not a question worth worryin' about."

Light did not emanate in their new universe from either any kind of central natural point like the sun, or from any kind of mechanical devices. Instead it seemed that everything in the new dimension simply glowed— or nearly anything. The ground beneath the lawmen did not emit any illumination, nor did any come from the sky, outside of that coming from those spheres floating high above.

The spheres were of all sizes and all colors. They each shone with a different intensity, and all of them seemed to follow different natural rules. Some were as solid as rock, others floated in the air. Some moved slowly, some rapidly. Some floated higher and higher until they disappeared, others vanished by sinking into the ground. It was also possible for the heavy ones to float away and those lighter than feathers to fall down to the surface of their world and slide out of sight.

"Humpin' weird—eh, Ernie?"

"Don't worry about the landscape," snapped Thorner. "Let's get done what we came to do." The two patrolmen nodded sheepishly, working hard to get their nerves back under control. Looking for something stronger than his will power, Petey pulled a bottle from inside his jacket. Taking a liberal slug, he offered it to Thorner, asking;

"Care for a nip, sir? Good for what scares ya."

And then, before the lieutenant could answer, they heard it. A hideous baying came to them through the air, through the ground, vibrating everything in the swirling world. Bubbles blew apart, some falling from the sky to split on the ground like rotten melons, other shattering as if made of concrete. Hundreds exploded into shimmering dust, much of that falling sideways and drifting away. Fingers tightened around their weapons. Sweat soaked collars which suddenly felt too tight.

"What the hell was that," asked Petey, his legs forgetting how to move forward.

"Just some new plaything, come to make friends."

Legrasse's voice was so calm, his words given so matter-of-factly, the patrolmen wondered if he might not be serious. Nudging them both into motion once more with the barrel of his weapon, Thorner whispered;

"Just some of that droll Southern humor you've heard so much about."

"I never heard nuthin' about Southern humor . . ."

"Well, now you have. So shut up already and keep your eyes open."

"For what, lieutenant?"

Yeah, thought Thorner, for what? What do I tell these poor mooks to do now?

*Pray*

The lieutenant frowned at the bothersome voice from the back of his head. He had tried prayer when dealing with such things. It did not seem to have much effect. Halting the party for a moment, the lieutenant told his men;

"Now listen up, you two. You knew what you were gettin' into. I warned ya, and you let me know what big damn tough guys you were. All right, you're here. Get yourselves together, or mark my words, there's gonna be some holes in the duty roster."

"Gentlemen," interrupted Legrasse, "time is short and we've none to spare except for being blunt." The horrible baying came again, the air turning sticky as if the breath propelling the noise were as large as the wind. Pulling open the knot in his tie, Legrasse went on.

"Feel the ground under you. It's solid. It's real. You can breathe the air. You're good men, I'm certain. If you weren't, your lieutenant would have sent you packing. All I'm going to tell you is to clear your minds and simply be ready to follow orders. Whatever either of us tells you, trust us. Do it, exactly as we say, and you might survive this."

The patrolmen muttered appropriate responses. The men were not surly, merely frightened, and working desperately to get past their fear. As the hideous howling sounded again, feeling as if its source was unbearably close, Petey stammered;

"S-Sounds like the c-captain, before he's had his coffee."

"You mean," answered Ernie, "before he's poured four fingers of Scotch in it."

All the men laughed. None of them gave out with anything like a hearty noise—they chuckled at best—but it was enough to unfreeze legs and shove hearts down out of throats. All four moved through the bizarre landscape once more, Legrasse and Thorner shoving aside the thinning spheres with their gun barrels, Petey struggling with the wooden box, Ernie walking backwards, watching behind them. The four covered nearly another forty yards, and then the howling sounded once more.

It was a shatteringly loud sound, a thing made of equal parts pain and nightmare. It was a warning and a plea, a murderous volume splashing its way over their bodies, infecting their nerves and clawing at their skin. None of the men spoke. There was no need. Each man knew the horror had found them.

As they watched, an awkward, almost crab-like paw pushed its way through a large mass of multi-colored spheres. The shapes exploded at the touch, revealing a terrifying sight. A bulbous snout, red and hard, masking a jaw possessed of multiple layers of needling teeth and fangs moved forward, attached to a creature roughly the size of a rhinoceros. A bluish pus dripped from the creature's sides, splattering and burning the ground wherever it landed. The thing was long of frame, like a racing hound, but it was thickly solid, and seemed to be covered with an armored shell. Black and yellow gases leaked out of the corners of its mouth as it regarded the men standing before it.

*Sum dee tri hernil, Sum dee tri hernil . . .*

The horror regarded the quartet before it for a long moment, then finally spoke.

"None of you are Zarnak."

As the two patrolmen became animated at the mention of the doctor's name, Thorner cautioned them to silence. Slowly tightening his finger on his weapon's trigger, Legrasse answered;

"That's right. We're not."

"You will reveal his hiding place."

"We don't know where he is," said the former inspector. "We want him as well, though."

"You *can not* have him! He is mine. His blood is mine to spill. His soul mine to drink, to dance upon. You will answer me—where is Zarnak?"

"Catch on, gruesome," hollered Ernie with a voice a half note from cracking, "we wouldn't tell ya even if we *did* know!"

"You must *not* defy the questioner . . ."

Thorner waved his forefinger back and forth in front of the monstrosity's face, telling it;

"You know, I've got the same answer for you I gave the last guy who said that ..."

And then, before the lieutenant could continue, Legrasse tightened his trigger finger and launched the grenade in his weapon into the side of the slavering creature before them. The men leaped for cover as the projectile exploded, burying burning metal in the monster's hide. As the creature screamed, Legrasse fumbled to pull a second grenade from his pocket. The former inspector was successful, but at the last second one of the device's edges caught on a thread from his jacket and was jerked out of his grasp.

"Damn!"

As Legrasse dropped to his knees to retrieve the grenade, Ernie and Thorner stepped forward both firing their weapons. German submachine guns from the Great War, they were capable of firing four hundred rounds a minute. The policeman slammed the creature with lead, screaming as they did so, throwing their voices at the thing along with their bullets.

"Look out!"

Legrasse screamed to be heard over the thunderous firing. As the two policemen caught on to his intent and cleared out of his path, the lawman fired his second grenade. The dull-colored egg flew directly into one of the beast's eyes and exploded, sending shrapnel deep within the monster's head. Immediately the creature howled once more, arcs of a boiling purple slop jutting from the burned and ragged crack which had appeared in its face.

*Sum dee tri hernil, Sum dee tri hernil . . .*

Having exhausted his clip first, Thorner was in the process of replacing his spent magazine with a new one when Ernie's ran out. With no new force being thrown against it, the creature shook off the effects of the damage it had taken in an instant. Its eyes fixing on Ernie, smelling his fear as he realized he could not reload before the monstrosity could take him, the beast slammed one mighty clawed leg forward, hissing;

"You *defy* the questioner. You hide the Zarnak. You attack the unstoppable ..."

His new clip in place, Thorner threw himself forward shouting;

"And you—you *fucking* talk too goddamned much!"

Ramming his weapon against the thing's skull he pulled his trigger and let fly with some seventy rounds before the horror could react.

*Sum dee tri hernil, Sum dee tri hernil . . .*

When it did, though, it flung one of its stout legs outward, smashing it into the lieutenant's weapon. The Bergman MP 18/1, one of the sturdiest armaments of one of the greatest weapon's manufacturer's of all time crumpled like a leaf in December. Thorner felt his wrist break upon the impact a split second before the force of the monster's attack truly reached him. On contact with the thing's appendage, the lieutenant was knocked off his feet, thrown head over heels so far back into the circling spheres that none of the others could see him.

"Eat shit, you bastard!"

As Legrasse and Ernie threw themselves to the ground, Petey flung forward three jamtins, hand grenades also from the Great War. Two of the shredders landed under the creature, the third on his back. Instantly the air was filled with shrapnel. Petey took a large hit in the abdomen which spun him around, then knocked him from his feet, his bottle smashing open, the end of it grinding into his chest. Legrasse and Ernie felt metal tearing into their backs as well.

*Sum dee tri hernil, Sum dee tri hernil . . .*

Sitting up, Petey stared down at the blood oozing out around the twisted pieces of steel wedged in his abdomen. As he looked about, he saw that Thorner was still nowhere in sight, and that his partner and the Southerner were down. Reaching down into his box, he struggled to pull a heavy shape out of it, giggling as he did so. His mind gone, snapped like the slightest twig, he heaved a black sphere free from the confines of the wooden box, thick wads of cotton sticking to its rough surface.

"You want defiance, ya big slab'a beef," he asked with a laugh, staggering forward under the weight he carried. "I'll give ya some— Brooklyn style."

As the creature shook off the trifling pains which the lawmen's last attack had inflicted, officer Peter Norton broke into a run, despite the forty pounds of hollowed-out artillery shell in his arms. The old ball, left over from the Civil War, had been filled with nitroglycerine and fitted with a highly sensitive percussion cap. Called "land torpedoes," such infernal devices had been used to destroy all manner of heavy machines during the Great War. Moving at a run, his eyes wild, drool dribbling from his chin, Norton hurled himself at the creature, using his body as the final force to set off his bomb.

The resulting explosion shredded the patrolman. Much to the surprise of those surviving him, the creature actually fell over from the attack, great gushing showers of its animating fluids arcing high into the sky. Pulling himself to his feet as quickly as he could, Legrasse fitted a third Mills into his Modèle 1917 and fired, blasting the horrid thing while it was down. Ernie followed suit, attacking once more with his Bergman, lashing the beast with non-stop fire while Legrasse fit another grenade into his weapon.

But then, before he could fire, the terrible beast reared up on its hind legs and then brought his forepaws down against the ground. The resultant shock waves knocked both lawmen off their feet, sending their weapons flying off into the spheres. Shaking its vicious head, clacking its rows of teeth together, grinding them, the creature screamed;

"You puny maggots thought to hurt me? *Me?*"

"Seemed . . . like a good idea . . . at the time," Legrasse sputtered, gasping for breath. Clawing the ground, trying to regain his feet, he looked in every direction for his weapon as the monster only yards away from him bellowed;

"Ridiculous, insignificant spec of nothing. You actually thought you could challenge the undying? You really thought to harm one such as me? You shall pay for your defiance."

"Oh, I don't think so."

All heads turned, staring up into the sky at the floating form of Dr. Anton Zarnak.

A demonic delight passed over the horror's face. Its good eye glistening, it laughed low in its throat.

"Now I have you," it snarled, its hideous claws tearing the ground, shattering spheres.

"Well then," answered Zarnak as he slowly descended from the sky, "if you have me you don't need them." Ignoring the beast, the doctor turned to Legrasse, pointing behind himself as he did so.

"Thorner lies in that direction," he said. "Take this young man and head back to the circle." Legrasse's mouth opened to protest, but Zarnak snapped, "Do as you're told."

As the Southerner and the patrolman helped each other hobble away, the doctor's feet touched the ground. As the monstrosity continued to chuckle, preparing to charge, he told it;

"Do not excite yourself, Tind'losi. There is no triumph for you here. You shall be dead in moments." The great beast laughed all the harder, its stamping feet shaking the ground.

"I have owned you since I saw you spying on me through what you call time. I have chased you to this 'now,' and I shall end our contest here. There is nothing such as you can do to stop me. Your soul is *mine!*"

The creature stepped forward, arrogant in its power. It had good reason. Never had a hound of Tindalos failed to destroy a prey once it had taken to its trail. The creature's were susceptible to certain magicks and rituals, of course, but Zarnak had been given no time to make such preparations. No matter how many tricks the doctor might possess, the beast knew it was now only a matter of time. Howling once more, it snapped;

"You have not drawn my essence, you have not spoken the words, you have not shown me darkness . . . without these, you are just another pile of meat."

As the creature's breath poured over Zarnak, he raised a hand to stifle a yawn. Then, moving to the side so that he faced the horror's good eye, he said;

"Ah, but I have been speaking the words since you came together with my fellows here. And as for drawing your essence, Mr. Norton died when first he hit the ground. I animated him, gave him life long enough to do that which I could see in his mind. No, the words are spoken, and your blood is spilt. And . . . as for darkness . . ."

Zarnak stabbed forward suddenly, grinding the broken end of Petey's bottle into the monster's good eye. Correctly anticipating the curve of the enraged monstrosity's attack, the doctor threw himself sideways, avoiding the thing's devastating charge. Running as fast as he could, the doctor disappeared through the spheres in the direction he had previously sent the others. Spotting the three after only a moment, he saw that they had reached Madame La Raniella's circle. Dashing for it, he screamed;

"Where are you, beast?!"

The Tindalos hound, hearing Zarnak's taunt, threw itself blindly forward through the spheres, desperate to catch the doctor. As he threw himself inside the triangle he could see within the circle on the ground, Zarnak observed the rate at which it was burning, put his ear to the wind, and then sighed with relief. Turning to the others, he instructed them;

"The beast is coming. Do not panic. Do not move. We want it to come—" Thorner made to speak, but Zarnak cut him off, shouting, *"Trust me!"*

Putting a finger to his lips, the doctor cautioned the others to be silent as the monster knocked aside the last of the spheres between itself and them. As it nosed the ground, Zarnak studied the rate of burn once more, allowing the blinded thing to wander about, searching for them. Legrasse and the others watched as the seconds ticked by, and then suddenly, Zarnak shouted;

"Now!"

At the sound of Zarnak's voice the beast wheeled about and then leaped. At the same time, the doctor plucked the steel ball from the center of the smaller circle and threw it with all his might at the beast's forehead.

La Raniella's voice broke through the silence—
Steel smashed into bleeding flesh—
The powder burned down—
The spheres vanished—
And the world exploded.

# # # # #

The three lawmen blinked, and suddenly they were back inside the walls of 13 China Alley. Though wounded, and somewhat mentally fractured, they were alive. Later Zarnak would explain how he had erred and allowed the Tindalos hound to see him as he spied on the ancient past through a crystal, how he had timed when the beast would reach their current century to the day, and had ensured that Legrasse would arrive on that day. Later he would give them explanations. For the moment, however, the ability to breathe, to know they would go on breathing, that was enough.

Thorner pounded on the floor, laughing, whooping with joy over still being alive. To the lieutenant, surviving yet another mad adventure with Zarnak was the greatest comedy in the world. When the doctor pointed to the steel ball, steaming in the center of the circle, letting them all know that because of them and their delaying tactics he had been able to trap the creature within its curves, Thorner only laughed all the harder.

Picking up the metal sphere, Legrasse turned it over in his fingers. As he stared at it, Zarnak thanked Madame La Raniella as well as Thorner and officer Malloy, then turned to Legrasse to apologize;

"Sorry to have used you so, but I had to do something quickly. I timed the thing's arrival to the day you were to come to New York, then removed myself from where it had seen me. There was no time for anything else."

"Why did you go where you did," asked the Southerner. "Why not just face the thing here?"

"I chose that dimension because spheres bother Tind'losi, curves trap them. I knew if you could find your way to me that you would be able to distract the thing long enough for me to ensnare it."

As the others stared at the steel ball Legrasse continued to move through his fingers like a stage magician's prop, Zarnak assured them the hound was imprisoned there forever. Then, as he apologized again for bringing them all into his struggle, Legrasse put up his other hand to cut the doctor off, telling him;

"It doesn't matter. Not really. Once you get a taste of this, you know, you either go mad, like poor Norton, or you just spend your days waiting for the next run-in. Used up, spit out, wasted away, dead in some lonely place. It's the inevitable checklist of this occupation."

"Jeez," said Thorner. "Lighten up there, Johnny." As Legrasse turned to face him, the lieutenant said;

"Hey, we're cops, okay? What the hell's the difference between gettin' it tryin' to stop some two bit schnook from heistin' a payroll, or tryin' to stop some runaway god from destroyin' the world?"

"Saving the world is more important?"

All heads turned toward Malloy. Silence reigned for a long moment, then Legrasse nodded, saying;

"Yes—I guess that would be the difference."

The mood lightened then, and Zarnak instructed the policemen to sit so he could attend to their wounds. Madame La Raniella was provided with a sum equal to her highest fee and thanked profusely. Ram Singh was sent to the kitchen to prepare the largest feast 13 China Alley had ever seen.

While the Hindu busied himself, Zarnak set to work with hot water, blades and bandages, removing shrapnel from his rescuers' bodies. Malloy started drinking before the doctor made his first incision and continued throughout the night. Thorner smoked a pipeful of an unknown substance Zarnak had offered him and found himself feeling good enough to sing while the doctor treated his wounds. And all the while Legrasse sat waiting his turn, bleeding, wondering if it were even possible to save the world from the kinds of nightmares he had seen.

Then, he looked down at the monster in his hand.

And smiled.

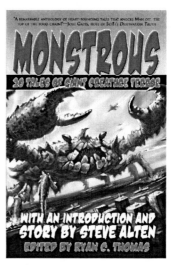

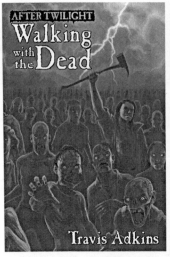

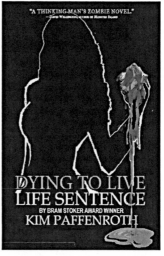

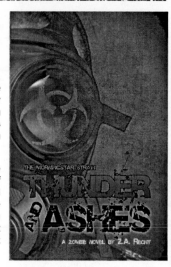

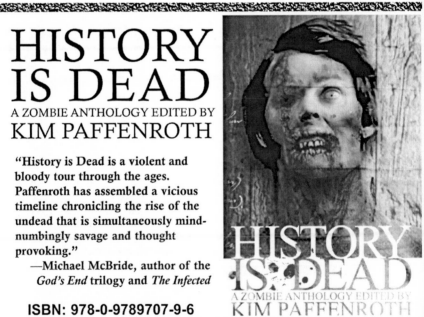

# THE UNDEAD
## ZOMBIE ANTHOLOGY

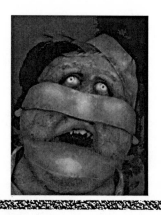

ISBN: 978-0-9765559-4-0

"Dark, disturbing and hilarious."
—Dave Dreher, *Creature-Corner.com*

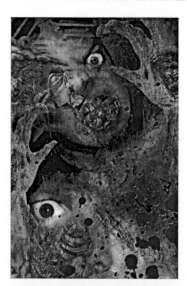

# THE UNDEAD
### VOLUME 2
## SKIN AND BONES

ISBN: 978-0-9789707-4-1

"Permuted did us all a favor with the first volume of *The Undead*. Now they're back with *The Undead: Skin and Bones*, and gore hounds everywhere can belly up to the corpse canoe for a second helping. Great stories, great illustrations... *Skin and Bones* is fantastic!"
—Joe McKinney, author of *Dead City*

## The Undead / volume three
# FLESH FEAST

ISBN: 978-0-9789707-5-8

"Fantastic stories! The zombies are fresh... well, er, they're actually moldy, festering wrecks... but these stories are great takes on the zombie genre. You're gonna like *The Undead: Flesh Feast*... just make sure you have a toothpick handy."
—Joe McKinney, author of *Dead City*

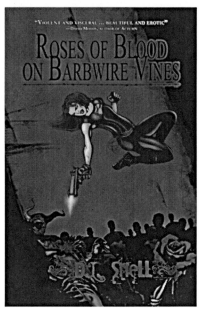

Lightning Source UK Ltd.
Milton Keynes UK
UKOW04f1054021214

242518UK00001B/180/P